THE DIG STREET FESTIVAL

THE DIG STREET FESTIVAL

Chris Walsh

2021
Louise Walters Books

The Dig Street Festival
by Chris Walsh

A catalogue card for this book is available from the British Library.

Produced and published in 2021
by Louise Walters Books

ISBN 9781999630591
eISBN 9781916112308

Typeset in PTSerif 10.5pt / 14.1pt by Blot Publishing

Printed and bound by Clays Ltd, Elcograf S.p.A

louisewaltersbooks.co.uk

info@louisewaltersbooks.co.uk

Louise Walters Books
PO Box 755
Banbury
OX16 6PJ

For Layla, Elliott, Sanna, and Meia.

CONTENTS

SEPTEMBER 2006

SUNDAY

1

THE OMEN

That afternoon, pregnant clouds marched over Leytonstow. We three slackened our walking pace and regarded them, lined up across the broken horizon. It felt like an omen, but I didn't tell Glyn, or Gabby for that matter, pretty sure the former would accuse me of believing my brain was intrinsically linked to the weather. I didn't see why it shouldn't be.

Bathed in moving shadows and a palpable drop in pressure, the normal commercial drone of Dig Street was traded for an expectant air. Pigeons huddled on high ledges. Tower blocks cut the moving sky like great inverted dreadnoughts. At ground level, checkout staff stopped scanning baked beans and peered skywards from smudged shop windows. The normally endemic blare of car and truck horns became muffled and less frequent, and the pavement stank of late-summer's locked heat. Vision appeared to blur, and it was as if the senses had been infected by a species of cosmic déjà vu. Either that, or someone had spiked the water supply.

So thought I.

Then the wind got up, whipping discarded parking fines and pizza fliers around our ears, and the rain came down, sending shoppers scurrying. Not us: Gabriel Longfeather danced in the bus lane catching fat drops on the tip of his tongue while a worried-looking Glyn Hopkins studied the dense horizon, presumably for buses. I stood fast, consciously examining the meteorological changes afoot, and taking deep

3

lungfuls of perfumed air – not so much what they cook up in Paris (they make it on industrial estates but will have us think it's hand-drawn by virgins from the sexual organs of rare flowers) – no, these olfactory experiences were more along the lines of urban fox, council-cut grass, and the trodden dog-ends of a litter-collecting community service gang.

There was a rumble of thunder and the rain intensified. We three cut into a little park and sat on a bench at the foot of a sheltering tree – not strictly advisable in a thunderstorm, but dry enough to be worth pushing our luck. Loaded drops slapped the broad leaves of summer's end, and I thought how magnificent it all was.

'Why are you smiling, John?' grinned Gabriel Longfeather, looking up from inspecting the bench's sexual graffiti.

'Oh Gabby, I just love rain!' I said.

'Because it makes plants grow, man?'

'Yes, Gab. And because it makes me feel like the world was created just for me.'

Glyn gave me a worried look.

Gabby piped up again, 'Look, a man called David has left his phone number here in case anyone sitting on the bench wants to have...' and at this point Gabby peered at the writing and spelled the word out, '...b-e-m sex! Isn't that kind?'

'Ahem,' coughed Glyn.

'Yes, it's considerate,' I sighed, irritated that he was ignoring the dramatic weather, but, for what it was worth, glad David's u resembled an e.

Wearing a bashful smile, Gabby asked, 'What is it?'

Glyn nervously fastened another button on his green work cardigan. Not wishing to explain the premise of David's pledge, I again turned my attention to the weather. Rivulets of seeds and twigs ran down a gully, past the bench, and into a storm drain. There was a flash of lightning. 'Isn't this wonderful?!' I yelled. 'Can't you feel the world's tension evaporating?'

'One, two, three, four...' counted Gabby, on his fingers. Then the rumble of thunder. 'Wow, four thousand volts, man!'

'I don't think the number of seconds elapsed indicates the number of volts, Gabby,' said Glyn. 'The lightning flash might have been approximately four miles from here, but I could be quite wrong.'

'Don't worry about the numbers,' I snapped, peeved my companions were simply missing the guttural beauty of it all.

'Four miles?' said Gabby. 'Is that in space?'

Glyn and I swapped a glance, then Glyn spoke. 'Listening to the direction, Gabby, and if it *is* four miles, which, as I said, might be quite incorrect, I'd say the storm is more likely to be currently over Stoke Newington, or somewhere within that general locale.'

'But Glyn, man,' said Gabby, 'it comes from space, doesn't it?'

'No.'

'Isn't it incredible!' I shouted, to break up such clayish mediocrity. 'The rain is utterly democratic. It rains on rich and poor alike, black and white...'

'And yellow, man!'

'Gab, by saying black and white I mean it rains on *all* races.'

'I'm just saying, what about Chinese people? Or Red Indians?'

'*Native Americans*, Gabby,' corrected Glyn.

'LOOK!' I yelled, then paused to take several deep breaths. 'Look at that storm drain. See how it swallows the water. It's beautiful. The rain reminds us that we're living within a fabulous ecosystem. Down here we're touched by interactions we can hardly imagine in tremendous towering clouds, and we've engineered underground caverns to handle tons and tons of gushing water. It's stupendous.'

'Oh my God!' screamed Gabby. 'It doesn't say *bem*, it says *bum*!'

Glyn wore a look of horror, and I saw in a split second that this was not so much to do with the offering poor Gabby had uncovered; more that his little friend might be on the dangerous verge of being entirely corrupted by knowledge beyond his natural sweet spot. Ashen, Gabby went on, 'But that's... that's where... that's not for... WHAT DOES IT MEAN?'

'JESUS CHRIST, GABBY!' I shouted. 'Why don't you ring David up to find out?!'

Gabby looked at me. 'What, you mean *ask* him?'

'YES!' I said. 'Why don't you tell him to meet you here in this park RIGHT NOW and get him to explain all of it to you face to face, or even better, cheek to cheek.'

'Ooh, I'm not sure!' said Gabby.

Just then, a man with matted out-of-control hair passed the bench where we sat. He was soaking wet, jabbering away, violently pecking at thin air – a local madman, one of several commonly seen wandering alone the streets of Leytonstow; released from a facility for the purpose of exercise, or entirely on-the-loose, I wasn't sure. As we watched, he paused, picked up a wet cigarette butt, tucked it into a breast pocket and continued on his way, chatting incomprehensibly. Then he stopped again and became even more animated; apparently now locked in hot debate with an invisible man, gesticulating with hands held aloft, shaking his fleshless fists at the desert-camouflage of dripping tree trunks. He appeared not to have noticed we three sat on the bench.

'I wish we could help him,' whispered Gabby.

'Yes, I do too, Gab,' I said. 'But other than taking him home I'm not sure what we could do. Plus, he's probably the property of Leytonstow social services.'

Gabby tittered. 'What, you mean they own him?'

'Don't laugh too soon, Gab,' I said, 'they pretty much own you too.'

'Me?'

'Who pays for you to live, Gabby?' I asked.

'What a daft question, John!' laughed Gabby. 'I do! I get money from the cashpoint!'

'Who puts the money in the bank?'

'Beryl.'

'*Beryl*?'

'Yeah, man, from the Jobcentre. I go and see her once a week, then she presses a button on her computer, and the money just appears! She's so kind!'

I sighed. 'Gab, where does Beryl get the money from?'

'I just told you, her computer!'

I must have looked suicidal, because Glyn took up the reins. 'Gabby,' he said. 'I think what John is saying is that you are supported by the state just like that man over there, if indeed that is the case.'

'Which state, man?'

'The British taxpayer,' said Glyn, baring his over-large front teeth.

Gabby smiled, and I could see that he was just beginning to suspect we were having him on. This angered me considerably, and I said through gritted teeth, 'A person who works and pays tax, Gab.' I was about to say something else when I glanced at the madman and saw that he was staring at us. Once observed, he smiled and waved.

We waved back.

He walked off.

As if to beg their help, I looked in turn at the heavy sky, the plane tree, and the water slipping past our feet. All of us jabbering away in an unknown East London park in a thunderstorm. With dread, with a despair I could neither adequately describe nor dispel, it struck me that perhaps Gabby, Glyn, and I, were also part of Leytonstow's furniture.

It stopped raining.

2

AN HEROIC AGE

Gabby tugged at my sleeve as we continued our march up Dig Street, bound for Leytonstow's premier ice skating venue, with the aim of pursuing our hobby: recreating Scott of the Antarctic's ill-fated 1912 push for the South Pole. It had been Gabby's idea. I couldn't speak for Glyn – I hardly understood him at all – but after initial serious doubts I began to enjoy our visits. People did some pretty odd things, after all; we weren't alone. And it was good exercise.

'But John, it's not fair! Oh please, man! I want to be Captain Scott this time!'

'Gabby!' I snapped. 'It's just not the way things are.'

'Perhaps we could *all* be Scott?' suggested Glyn, with a shrug.

'Christ alive, Glyn!' I said. 'Three Scotts? We're not playing at being surrealists, we're trying to get to the South Pole!'

'John,' said Glyn, softly, 'the very act of recreating a polar journey at an ice rink is a bit...' and at this point he gave a nervous cough, '...surreal.'

'How about,' said Gabby, 'you be Captain Scott, but pretend *I'm* Captain Scott!'

I ignored them, and made a stiff show of studying our surroundings. Locals knew the main junctions of the old thoroughfare by landmarks; for the most part tumbledown Victorian pubs called things like The Butcher's Arms or The Edgar Evans; the kind that in London's more affluent areas have long been developed into fashionable gastro-eateries, but here remained old men's boozers with crusted carpets and façade-dominating banners inviting punters to come and watch widescreen sporting events. At intervals Dig Street was criss-crossed by pockmarked railway bridges carrying mile-long freight trains across Victorian rooftops. Old Japanese cars with no MOTs, tax, or insurance, slouched past in clouds of blue smoke. Minicabs jostled for disappointing fares outside Leytonstow Tube Station. Bloodied men shouldered pink and white carcasses from refrigerated vans into open-fronted butchers' shops. Training shoes tied together by their laces hung on telephone wires. The odd dirty-looking bird twittered.

Performing a dog-mess slalom, I recalled the rekindling of my interest in Captain Robert Falcon Scott CVO RN, the second man ever to reach the South Pole. The three of us had been window shopping at a local charity shop when Gabby had pointed at a grainy photo on the cover of an old book, and asked who it was.

'*Scott of the Antarctic*,' I'd said. 'That's his famous diary.'

'Why's he got those funny clothes on?'

'Antarctica can be very cold,' said Glyn, more or less authoritatively.

'He does look silly!' chuckled Gabby. 'What's he doing?'

'Marching to the South Pole,' said Glyn, mournfully.

Gabby said, 'Why? Did he leave something there, by accident?'

I'd bought the book and devoured it that evening: a ringside seat to a slow decline (the spoiler being a matter of national pride). Then, chasing another fix of frozen failure, I'd read biographies of Scott, of his polar companions, their writings, then the biographies and writings of other explorers – Franklin, Nansen, Peary, Shackleton – and so a hobby was born. At work I daydreamed about single-handedly clambering out of crevasses. I wondered if I could stomach pemmican. If the going got tough would I peg out, or die like a man? Scott became my pop star. The other explorers weren't bad, but he was Paul McCartney to their Davy Jones.

It didn't snow much in East London. As mentioned, it had been Gabby's bright idea to march on the pole at the ice rink. What was it to *have a hobby*? I'd always had one or two bubbling away; they roved like involuntary tics. As we continued our trek up Dig Street, I asked my companions, 'Do kids still have hobbies?'

'No,' said Glyn, without hesitation.

'Are you sure?' I asked.

'You can't call the Internet a hobby,' said Glyn.

'What makes an activity a hobby, then?'

'It has to be harmless,' said Glyn, 'and not liable to blow us all to kingdom come.'

'Oh, cheer up, Glyn!'

'Sorry, John, I'll try,' said Glyn. Then he added, 'Perhaps we should go to the pub instead?'

'I thought we were going to the ice rink?'

'If we must,' he sighed.

'Only if I can be Captain Scott, man!' yelled Gabby.

He couldn't.

3

MY OWN PRIVATE ANTARCTICO

I stood on the ice waiting for them to negotiate the sarcastic teenage girl handing out skates. Glyn, nearly as tall as me, but stooped like Richard III, going-on-very-out-of-shape, balding, with wispy blond hair, his gentle features set in a permanent oxymoronic mixture of world-weary righteousness and apologetic shyness. Gabby, still in his twenties, five-foot-three and pale as the underbelly of a penguin; smiling openheartedly at the sniggering girl handing him ladies' skates, and apparently weighed down by nothing in this world except his interesting and very long black heavy metal hairdo. I waved at them as they squeezed into their footwear.

Now there was nothing else for it but to busy ourselves. 'Right, Gabby!' I said. 'Are the supplies lashed to the sledge?'

'Aw, man! I want to be Captain Scott!'

'Gab,' I said, attempting to ape the gravity of the great man himself, 'I'm Scott, OK?'

But it was no good; Gabby was already making just-born-fawn efforts to reach the rink edge, his impressive barnet quivering like a black blancmange.

'Jesus!' I shouted after him. 'How are we ever going to make it to the pole if we can't work as a team?'

There was a polite cough to my left. 'We're only pretending, John,' said Glyn.

'Glyn, I know!'

11

Having also reached the safety of this Antarctica's edge, Glyn and I watched Gabby wrestle with his skates. He was desperate, I knew, to flounce off to the café for a slice of cake. This was old ground: I suspected the lure of cake was the real reason he'd conjured up a row over who'd be Scott, just as a quitting smoker will pick any old argument for an excuse to give up giving up.

'Glyn, I *know* we're not *actually* going to the pole,' I said, bending down to offer Gabby a hand. 'But we're having fun, *aren't we*?'

'I can see how it might be fun,' said Glyn.

'You don't have to come with us, you know.'

Glyn said, 'I'm not sure what else I'd do.'

I continued to pick at Gabby's tangled finnesko. A group of teenagers were pulling on skates nearby.

'Heavy metal is gay, innit!' said a boy in a bright red ski-jacket, presumably referring to Gabby's death metal dunga-rees. The rest of them giggled and fingered cigarettes tucked behind ears.

Glyn skulked atop his skates, looking worried.

'What about stamp collecting?' I said, still working on Gabby's double triple granny knot.

'Pardon?' said Glyn, blushing to the very roots of his thin-ning blond hair.

'*Stamp collecting*,' I said. 'You could collect stamps instead of coming here with us, if you liked. It's really interesting. You can get a good sense of a nation's identity by simply stu-dying the stamps issued.'

'I'll consider it, John,' said Glyn, casting anxious glances at the teenagers.

Leaving the laces, I stood and addressed my audience. 'Listen,' I said, 'I've got a great plan! Why don't we start a stamp collecting club!'

Other than looking horrified, the teenagers evidently did

not know what to make of my suggestion. Indeed, it was clear I'd just calved a sizeable iceberg from a glacier named Street Cred.

I wasn't entirely sure why I'd made the suggestion.

'Are you a paedophile?' asked one of the teens.

'What is a *stamp*, anyhow?' I heard a girl ask a friend, who shrugged.

I told them I was happy to explain, warming to the prospect of delighting them with tales of our first interconnectedness; but spitting, shouting, and offering me two-fingered salutes, the group broke hurriedly out upon the ice. I was pretty sure stamps had been issued in the past depicting Agincourt.

I winked at Glyn, who managed a blushing smile, then returned to Gabby and loosened one more knot. He ripped off the remaining skate, made a fair stab at denting the floor with it, and ran off to the café. I watched him go, and wondered. When I'd read to him the last desperate entries from Captain Scott's diary, Gabby had actually laughed, then asked me why Scott and his colleagues hadn't simply packed up the tent and walked to the nearest McDonalds.

'Come on,' I said to Glyn. 'Let's take a break.'

4

IN WHICH JOHN SUGGESTS THE WORLD MIGHT NEED RE-EXPLORING

We sat in the café, each with a slice of Victoria sponge, as popular in Scott's day as ours, I presumed.

'Come on then, Glyn,' I said. 'What would you suggest we do on a Sunday?'

Glyn shrugged and bared his front teeth.

'What are you interested in?' I asked.

He blushed. 'Women... perhaps?'

'Yeah, man, let's get some women!' shouted Gabby, spraying me with wet crumbs.

'Gabby,' I said, 'what would you do once you'd *got* them?'

Gabby grinned awkwardly, and fixed me with his baby-blues.

'*Exactly*,' I said. 'Anyway, that's not so much a hobby as a basic urge.'

'Pretending to make an attempt on the South Pole at an ice rink...' Glyn said, then looked at me sheepishly.

'What, Glyn?' I asked.

'It's a worryingly strange hobby, John.'

'We're not bothering anyone, are we?'

'I fear on your part it might be a precursor to severe mental illness,' said Glyn.

'*On my part*?'

Glyn nodded and looked sad.

'Bloody hell, Glyn,' I said.

'An appreciation for history and its re-enactment is fine,'

said Glyn, 'as long as you don't start thinking it's real. You're not Scott of the Antarctic. You're not even John Torrington of Leytonstow. You're just John Torrington.'

'Thanks for clearing that up,' I said.

'Sorry,' said Glyn.

I sipped my coffee, and attempted to look out upon a vast expanse of white nothingness. I was used to Glyn telling me I was one march away from insanity. But he was right, it was weird, and possibly worrisome.

'We live in an entirely explored world,' I said, 'but still have the urge to explore; it's programmed into our DNA.'

'We've entirely lived past our usefulness,' said Glyn, enigmatically.

I was about to ask him how we'd ever been useful, but then a hot idea struck me. 'Maybe we could *re-explore* the world,' I said, 'to see if they missed anything the first time around?'

Glyn stared at me.

'Yes!' I said. 'It's a long time since Leytonstow was first explored, and it's probably changed quite a bit. We might gain something by exploring it afresh, *consciously*.'

Glyn continued to stare. If eyes could sigh, his did. 'But John... there was *absolutely nothing* here when humans first arrived. Just trees.'

'And squirrels, man,' said Gabby.

'So there's an awful lot to re-explore, Glyn,' I said.

'But people *live* here,' said Glyn. 'They *know* it. They've updated what they know about it as things have developed.'

'But do they *consciously* know where they are?' I asked. I could tell he thought I was talking absolute nonsense. Was it such a bad idea? It was true I'd felt rather backed into a corner, in general. Things had a last-ditch flavour.

'What about the bottom of the sea, man?' suggested Gabby, now sucking at a banana milkshake.

'They can leave the bottom of the sea alone, as far as I'm

concerned,' I said. 'It's a little dull. Beautiful no doubt, and diverse, and important, but dull.'

'What makes the land less dull?' asked Glyn.

'Us,' I said.

'What, *we three*?'

'Humans, I mean. We're what makes the land interesting.'

'And animals?' asked Glyn.

'No, just humans,' I said. 'Effectively, the human brain is the only interesting thing there is in the world and, as far as we know currently, the universe. Everything else, including animals, plants, the moon, the planets, stars, and even the most beautiful nebulae, are on autopilot. They might as well not exist.'

'That's quite a negative view of things,' said Glyn, which outraged me, as part of me had only said it because I thought he'd wholeheartedly agree.

'Fish definitely don't think the bottom of the sea is boring,' said Gabby.

I didn't think this deserved a response.

'Fish aren't able to hold opinions,' said Glyn.

'Dolphins do!' said Gabby.

'Dolphins aren't fish,' said Glyn, 'and they don't really hold opinions either, not in the human sense, anyhow.'

'Not fish?!' shouted Gabby.

And so the conversation carried on down this cul-de-sac. I let them twitter like baby birds, getting mildly irritated, and thinking my own thoughts. Yes, the world did need re-exploring. Something needed to be done. Where were we? And what did we really know about it? Somewhere along the way, we'd got lost. Take where we lived; I never heard even the smallest reference to our largely deprived area of East London in the media. As far as the world was concerned, nothing happened in Leytonstow; something I knew for a fact was quite false. Though barely ten miles from Piccadilly

Circus, our locale was wild. Beasts lurked here: they could be spotted on match days; pissed up silverbacks with dead eyes. I would hide in cafés and watch them pass, amazed that apes were free to roam a public highway.

They've forgotten, I would think, shivering behind smeared glass. *They've forgotten what we are!*

But what were we, and what did I mean? I was as confused as myself. Sitting there in the café, among old folks in coats, I would tie myself up in knots of fizzy conjecture; that we, human beings, were a singularity of group sentience, defining all, naming all, obsessively organising everything our senses could perceive but making the lot up as we went along; a self-regulating tribe of auto-zookeepers in a permanent prison riot of free will, an entirely unprecedented mutation in the blind paradise of history.

Such thoughts would pass, and I'd sit there sipping coffee, feeling sad and foolish, wanting to run out into the street to apologise to anyone who would listen.

But ideas would again strike; that I couldn't be sure whether the behaviour I witnessed in the men was a conscious protest against terrifying glimpses of a meaningless universe, or an unconscious manifestation of that very meaninglessness.

Again, expired and confused, I'd cringe at such crummy attempts to decode humanity, and see the passing strangers as human beings once more. Human beings who probably worked dull and brutal jobs and wanted to let off a bit of steam at the weekend, and why the hell not?

Oh world, sorry for being so heavy, I would think, and the old folks in the café would shrink from me, lifetimes of experience telling them I was odd.

I was snapped back to the present by a question from Gabby. 'Glyn, how do you *know* dolphins don't live in houses really deep under the sea?'

'Because flippers don't have thumbs,' said Glyn.

5

GLYN MAKES AN
UNFORTUNATE PURCHASE

Having dispatched the cake and postponed a final push on the pole, we handed our skates back to the smirking girl and made our way home, popping first into Mahmood's Hypermart – actually just a corner shop, and a smallish one at that.

'It's the boys,' smiled handsome Mr Mahmood as we filed in. 'Been having fun, have we?'

Mahmood's ribbings, however light and obviously well meant, always needled me. I resented being referred to as a *boy*, being thirty-eight-and-a-half. Gabby (twenty-six) didn't carry such misgivings, presenting Mr Mahmood with a lovely grin, and Glyn (thirty-two) loitered at the magazine rack pretending unsuccessfully not to steal anxious glances at the top shelf.

'We've been ice skating,' I announced in as statesman-like a manner as one can report that activity.

'I see,' said Mahmood, taking half-moon reading glasses from his face and returning an equally weighty expression.

'And looking for the South Pole!' said Gabby, fingering bags of dolly mixtures handily arranged at his height.

'Did you find it?' asked Mahmood, winking at me.

'Did we find it, John?' Gabby asked.

Mahmood leaned upon his worn counter awaiting my reply.

'We were looking for it *figuratively*,' I said.

'I see!' laughed Mahmood. 'Well, if you find it, *figuratively*, please be sure to tell me!'

'We will, won't we, John?' smiled Gabby.

I felt so daft I couldn't reply. The slightest inspection of my activities by this grown-up individual had caused my inner landscape to crumble. I could have cried. When it came to explaining my motivations to anybody but the very young, the very idiotic, or both, I lost confidence.

I watched Mahmood, a knowing but good-natured-enough smile playing about his lips, and reflected with a sigh upon my youth, when things had been different. The world had been young and aching to be accounted for, delineated, explained, and maybe even improved. Vaulting the searing pain of shyness, I'd tried my luck, obsessively attempting to decode everything for the benefit of all, everywhere; in pubs, supermarkets, churches, parks, lifts, graveyards, and on fairground rides. On beaches and behind hedges. On building sites and up trees.

To my great surprise, it became perfectly apparent that no one had wanted to know – hard to believe they could live in the universe, the world, and not desire to investigate, pick it apart. With heavy heart, I'd realised we had no taste at all for examining what lay beneath our very fingers.

Time had passed, and my puppyish charm (any I'd possessed) had ebbed away. More and more, my efforts to get my corner of the world to examine itself garnered the expression Mr Mahmood currently wore – a tilting of the head, a narrowing of the eyes – a barely concealed and firm judgement that I was "not quite right".

What had I done? The only thing I could – I'd given up. I'd withdrawn to save my victims the trouble. I'd taken to keeping my mouth shut. I'd retired, entered a premature dotage. I'd taken to sitting in half-derelict cafés. I'd watched the world occur, and let my eyes do the talking.

Just then, with a grunt, Glyn placed several magazines of a certain genre upon Mahmood's counter, and my embarrassment was complete.

'What have we here?' said Mr Mahmood, licking a thumb in preparation to examine the artefacts in the most unhurried fashion; a little unfair, I thought, seeing as they were stock he himself had ordered and carefully fanned out on the top shelf for shoppers like Glyn.

I stared at Glyn, and he at me.

'This is a good one, no?' enthused Mahmood, holding up a magazine and winking.

'Yes, it's nice,' said Glyn.

Mahmood found this funny. I felt as if I might suffer a panic attack.

'John!' hissed Gabby, tugging at my sleeve as I tried nonchalantly to examine a shelf of canned vegetables. 'John, Glyn's got *those* magazines again!'

'Gab, I have eyes!' I snapped.

6

A MORE THOROUGH EXAMINATION
OF MY COMPANIONS

A little way along Dig Street we passed Alfred Hitchcock's birthplace, marked by a blue plaque. Normally I would have pointed this out, and would have taken the opportunity to wax lyrical about his films, but today I couldn't bring myself to get into it.

Gabby took up the reins. 'I still think it's a weird place to be born!'

'I don't think it was a petrol station at the time of Hitchcock's birth,' said Glyn.

Glyn was man-hauling a not-quite-opaque black plastic bag holding magazine-shaped items. Ever since leaving Mahmood's Hypermart Gabby had been closely questioning Glyn about the contents, and dropping large hints that he might borrow them at a time convenient to Glyn; that is, in Gabby's mind, the very second we got home. Glyn was too polite to refuse outright, and wore an expression of deepest resentment for which from time to time he would mutter an apology.

God knows why, but I came to Glyn's aid. 'Gabby, Glyn wouldn't have bought them if he didn't plan to... you know!'

'Aw man, I wish I could buy some!'

'Why don't you, then?' asked Glyn.

Gabby didn't answer, but instead blushed and grinned.

It might not come as a shock to learn Gabby and Glyn were virgins. Neither had been kissed. Indeed, much to our incomprehension, we'd never met a single woman (or man) who'd shown the slightest flicker. I didn't do much better; occasionally able to seduce drunken women in dark Friday night pubs. The result of our joint experience, or lack of it, was that we seldom discussed sex. Instead, for Glyn and me at least, the whole idea hung over us like an erotic miasma; taunting and shaming, spraying us with maddening musk and laughing in our faces.

The love of Gabby's life was a scrap between his mam and music. This mam, who lived somewhere up north, would often call him on the communal phone in the hall of Clements Markham House, where we lived, to ask whether he was eating, sleeping, enjoying regular bowel movements, and having any success in looking for a job. Gabby was usually able to offer her relief on at least one of these counts.

Gabby's mam was his mam, but music was his mistress. Despite living on Jobseeker's Allowance, Gabby had somehow been able to cobble together perhaps the loudest stereo system in the northern hemisphere. Mr Kapoor, our kindly landlord, had had to repoint the walls adjoining Gabby's bedsit three times in as many years. It was not known whether Gabby's immediate neighbours – Glyn and I lived in bedsits on the ground and first floors respectively; Gabby, luckily, on the third and top – were deaf through age or abuse, but deaf they were, and this enabled Gabby to play his favourite heavy metal tracks at somewhere near Krakatoan levels all day and a reasonable portion of the night.

Glyn was altogether more mysterious. If one could sum Glyn up it would be to say that he was righteous, miserable, and apologetic in equal measure. I'd never met someone less willing or able to make an impact upon the world, or more sensitive to any ripples he did inadvertently make. Living, for Glyn, was an exercise in invisibility, and should his cloak slip, sincere apology was in order. What made him tick? It was hard to say. Buying his weekly grot mags was the most adventurous of his actions by far, entirely at odds with everything else he did, and born, I gathered, of sheer desperation. He wasn't short of brains, and his tastes were, as they say, catholic. Although vague concerning his youth, I'd never got the impression that Glyn was, like me, a dimmer version of a brighter former self, or that his reticence was the product of bad experience, or rejection – that kind of commonplace post-traumatic stress disorder you see in those over thirty who've lived unlucky lives of ever-decreasing hope. No, his personality appeared innate and fully-formed; *a priori,* as the philosophers call it.

But I could only take so much of *our Glyn.* It's fair to say that he drove me bonkers with his constant apologetic grunting, depressing views, and utter underachievement. But the old saying, I'm afraid, was never more apt: *it takes one to know one.* Whereas Gabby, as mentioned, lived off the taxpayers' purse, Glyn and I both had the honour of working as trolley-collectors, floor moppers, and general cleaners at Leytonstow's premier (and only) DIY superstore, Amundsen Enterprises.

7

THE EDGAR EVANS

A creature of habit, Gabby happily jiggled coins in his pockets. Aware that popping into a pub for a pint or two was something Captain Scott and his men simply couldn't have done however much they had desired to, we nonetheless – pointlessly, Glyn said we were tipping our hats to the indisputable reality that we *were* in London, not Antarctica – decided to visit The Edgar Evans.

Once inside Gabby made a break for the jukebox, and began to stuff it with twenty-pence pieces. In no time the strains of "Stairway to Heaven" were affecting a species of spring clean for the cobweb-covered ceiling. For Gabby, twenty-pences were immeasurably preferable to pound coins: they promised a neat transaction; one song each. I'd long since given up asking why he didn't insert a pound coin and enjoy five consecutive plays. There seemed to be something about the repeated act of *insertion-song* which very much pleased Gabby. It was perhaps the nearest he got to copulation.

I waited at the deserted bar, and Glyn queued up behind me. The furthest corners of The Edgar Evans were populated by shadowy old men in ones and twos, nursing afternoon pints of light ale. Smoke silently curled from their tables, giving their waxen faces a look of the recently deceased. I wondered at how many lifetimes were here, represented and mute.

As we waited, the most biddable of the old boys – a skeletal vision of fifty years before, complete with nicotine-stained duck's arse and once-blue suede shoes – rose from his table and began to serenade a slopping pint to Gabby's music. The other old men watched him. A huge smeared mirror behind the bar provided him with a partner.

There were a whole host of reasons the old men came to The Edgar Evans. In my youth I'd have tried to list all of them, *to* them. One very good reason came strutting in from the kitchen.

'It's our favourite intrepid Antarctic explorers!'

Lois, the barmaid: a fully-conscious pastiche of fifties erotica, with a modern gothic twist: hourglass figure, milk skin, red lips, long black hair and high ruler-straight fringe. She was terrifying, an alien among us, and half the reason Glyn queued behind me at the empty bar, the other being his complete inability to claim first place, or even a draw.

Lois (twenty-eight) was one of the increasing numbers of young middle-class people drawn to Leytonstow, rating it for its (relatively) cheap lodgings and proximity to the party opportunities of Central London. Such cosmopolitan young-sters were exotic creatures. Lois had the easy manner of one passing through: for now, roughing it like a real East Ender suited her sense of retro chic. Such people could play at being an outsider, but for some of us it was a full-time job.

Lois had a degree in the History of Art from Exeter University. Her parents lived in Berkshire. She went skiing every winter, and knew the word *Schadenfreude*. I was in love with her. I wasn't alone.

One night I'd told her all about my interest in polar exploration. She'd listened intently while filling and refilling my glass, until I'd become so sloshed that I'd climbed upon the bar and regaled the whole pub with a paraphrased conglomeration of all the books upon polar exploration I'd ever read. Thinking it was a stand-up show, the old fellows had laughed heartily as I'd related how Sir John Franklin had been reduced to eating his boots, and how Captain Scott had eschewed huskies and ski for ponies and man-hauling because the former just hadn't been cricket. Upon reflection, perhaps this was where Gabby had learned to find extreme privation funny.

Just then, Glyn coughed, presumably wanting his pint. A little irritated that he couldn't or wouldn't ask for it himself, I said, 'Two pints of bitter and a lager-top, please.'

Lois was quite the most efficient being in a ten-mile radius. Later in the evening, when the old men reminisced, she would listen and provide sensitive relevant responses, while expertly ensuring their glasses were refuelled the very second they ran dry. It was a pleasure to watch her at work; nice to see a young person who afforded the ancient with emotional lives, albeit with a commercial motive.

She was managed (only nominally; Lois was a self-starter in every respect) by Barry the Publican, a fat mottle-faced man of later years, whose chief hobbies were chain-smoking from the shadows, painful coughing, and eyeing suspiciously the short journey cash undertook from hand to till.

I'd once heard two old duffers discussing the last time they could recollect Barry cracking a smile. One, who had gone to school with him, swore blind that the last grin he could remember which wasn't wry, sarcastic, or prompted by observing misfortune, was in 1954 when the Priest had produced a silver coin from Barry's ear.

The other disagreed, claiming to remember Barry relating an extremely funny Englishman, Irishman and Scotsman joke in the mid-seventies. Unfortunately, he couldn't remember how it had gone, but it turned out he did know a revamped version about an Englishman, a Nigerian and a Pakistani. I'd gone to the loo at this point so as not to hear it.

I sipped my pint, drinking-in the pub, and reflected that it was an odd situation; *it* being the United Kingdom.

It seemed to me that with the passing of the twentieth century and the freeing of Nelson Mandela, we'd decided, officially, that intolerance had conveniently evaporated.

It hadn't.

Leytonstow, like the rest of the United Kingdom, was awash with every form of bigotry and small-mindedness one could imagine. And London, much celebrated as a melting pot of racial happiness, was quite simply nothing of the kind. Instead, a rigid ghetto system existed along socio-economic lines. I'd observed at least four groups of white London "natives", and had elucidated my sociological theses to Glyn many times. He'd appeared disinterested; thus my observations remained utterly unbenchmarked, like the rest of my ideas.

1. Ruddy-cheeked right-wingers with old wealth who didn't give a toss about anyone, and who would find the idea of living cheek-by-jowl with ethnic minorities and/or the poor frankly laughable. Although the most distasteful group, they were also the most sincere and the least hypocritical. This lot wore double-barrelled surnames like erect phalluses and were in charge of the rest of us. I was convinced they'd simply wipe us out were it not for the fact that they needed warm bodies to buy stuff from their companies, and do the dirty jobs. Their kids pretended to be the most liberal beings ever to grace the planet, but were, in essence, gaslighting fascists.

2. Politically-correct clean-faced middle-class liberal professionals who sent their kids backpacking to exotic corners of the world, gave to charity, were extremely concerned about the plight of the less fortunate, read the left-wing press, but again would find the idea of actually living among ethnic minorities and/or the poor, or sending their kids to school with them, *pretty challenging*. The Clergy also belonged to this group, the most po-faced and hypocritical of the lot.

27

3. The urban working classes, a complex grouping, as some were still poor, and some enjoyed new wealth:
   i New wealth enabled the latter to live in bookless houses in soulless new developments, away from the grinding poverty held like blood-memory within their bone marrow. They still weren't happy, weren't sure why, and this unhappiness manifested itself in highly vulgar self-righteous consumption, and a tendency to espouse off-the-shelf right-wing political views.
   ii The still-poor, forced to live among foreigners and their poor peers; this subgroup complained bitterly that immigrants were taking their jobs, their women, and their Britishness. Group 1, and to a certain extent Group 2, kept this lot from overthrowing them by allowing them to believe that if only they could join subgroup 3(i) all of their problems would be solved.
4. The fourth group consisted of Glyn, who, I'd discovered, was quite uncategorisable (Gabby and I being from up north).

I supped my pint and cringed. Who was I to group (and even allot subgroups to) anyone? Didn't this make me as prejudiced as the next man? I glanced at my next man, Glyn, also sipping his pint of ale, and (I gathered from his worried expression) wondering whether Lois and the old men had cottoned on to the contents of his nearly-opaque black plastic bag.

The trouble was, our minds were hard-wired to find patterns in anything, and to lock onto them like meaning-seeking missiles. Not only would we hungrily identify patterns, we would immediately adopt them, fatten them up, farm them, breed and multiply them. It was our genius. The heavyweights of western thought had all been wondrous pattern farmers, ploughing up furrows of meaning with giant red tractors, and planting killer seeds.

The problem was, the human race just didn't stand being grouped. It was pointless to band us together. For a start, we didn't get on with one another.

True, I mused, before the modern era we'd all *looked* the same, wore the same clothes; we'd been ranked, we'd doffed our caps, we'd known *our station*, or at least we'd acted as if we did. Then, it had seemed sensible to group us, and very intuitive. It brought to my mind that Chekhov story where the civil servant accidentally sneezes upon a General's head at the theatre, and is thereafter so panicked about his cross-rank discourtesy that he harries himself to death searching for opportunities to apologise. In my mind's eye, that poor fellow looked like Glyn.

Nowadays, those in power, and, more importantly those in business, knew humanity didn't stand grouping, and it was therefore unfashionable – but that was all. We still grouped people anyway, because we could not help ourselves. The only development was that we'd discovered people bought more stuff and were less likely to revolt if they were empowered to think they were unique, and important – *your thoughts matter*, they said. This was a pleasing new pattern, but those in the know still grouped the vast majority of us as a seething mass of plebs. Many of us were only too happy to play the part.

'A penny for them?' said Lois.

I started, and blushed. 'I was just thinking about patterns.'

'Patterns? What do you mean?'

'You know, patterns,' I said, wondering what she would say if I expanded.

'I don't believe you,' she said, and took my empty glass. 'Go on; tell me what you were thinking about.'

I suspected she was humouring me. Perhaps she wanted me to again mount the bar and download my mind to the pub. I watched her pull me another, glancing at me, smiling, daring me. It got my blood up.

'You know you want to,' she said.

Evidently to Glyn's great surprise, as he suffered a coughing fit, I told all. She listened patiently, as did the now-seated dancer with the duck's arse. Gabby continued to ply the jukebox; what he played was somehow sympathetic, although I wasn't sure why: "Wuthering Heights" by Kate Bush, "Big Girls Don't Cry" by Frankie Valli and The Four Seasons, and "The Drugs Don't Work" by The Verve.

Spent, I handed the baton to my audience, and waited.

'What a load of old bollocks!' cackled Duck's Arse. 'I've never heard such fackin rubbish in my entire life!'

Glyn shifted the nearly-opaque black plastic bag further beneath his stool.

'I think it's fascinating,' said Lois, her eyes shining.

'Bollocks!' repeated Duck's Arse. 'It's obvious to me, mate, you got too much fackin time on your 'ands, simple as that. When I was your age, it was work, union, kids and sports; I didn't 'ave time to think up ridiculous things. You wanna busy yourself, my son!'

I found his assertion a little far-fetched, but didn't say so. His rocker's hairdo spoke of a quite different past than the one claimed. The web of purple blood vessels covering his face backed it up.

'I *am* quite busy,' I said in my defence. 'But the fact is, however busy I am, I'm unable to stop *thinking*. I do it from the moment I open my eyes in the morning to the moment I fall asleep at night.'

'Tell your doctor,' said Duck's Arse. ''e'll give yer summink for that.'

'I think it's admirable,' said Lois. 'And original.'

Luckily, she was too young to realise I didn't have an original bone in my body.

'I wish you'd tell us your thoughts more often, John,' she said.

Had I genuinely piqued her interest? The trouble was, having laid out my thesis like a towel on a sunbed, now *I* didn't necessarily agree with me. This was the first time in years I'd attempted to describe the universe to anyone but Glyn and Gabby. Why had I come out of retirement?

I knew why, but it was hardly worth the trouble. I had as much chance as Glyn, as Gabby, as Duck's Arse, or Barry for that matter.

I was aware that whatever I'd said, however I'd pontificated, whatever efforts I'd made to create the impression that I was implacable and wise as the bedrock to which the pub was anchored, it had all been aimed at trying to engineer even the slightest possibility that Lois might allow me to kiss her.

It was as simple as that.

Surely Lois knew it! My world view had been nothing more than the most complex chat-up line in history. I might as well have cut it all out, and simply said, 'Lois, please let me eat you.'

'John, I think you're talking sense,' said Lois.

'Bollocks,' said Duck's Arse again and, as if I'd driven him to drink, thrust his glass at Lois. Perhaps I had.

'Your theories *are* very interesting, John, but if you don't mind me saying, the problem with you,' Lois continued softly, 'is that you're clearly *upset* about something. You're not *centred*. There's something troubling you, and it makes you think that everything you said is true. It *is* true, John, for you, but it's all negative. If I found you a happy person, I bet they would say something just as profound, just as truthful, but completely different, and totally positive.'

I wasn't sure what to say, apart from the fact that this upbeat world view would be no more than a new combination keyed into the same impossible padlock. I didn't say that. I observed she was now scanning the pub for happy candidates. Slim pickings.

'Gabby!' shouted Lois. 'Come over here, will you?'

Gabby, who'd been headbanging to "Paranoid" by Black Sabbath, looked lovingly at the jukebox as if to say *I'll miss you*, and clopped over to us in his disproportionately large white heavy metal basketball boots.

'Have a seat, Gabby,' said Lois, pouring him another lager-top. Our eyes met, and for the briefest moment I fancied I had a chance.

'Should Gabby have another lager-top?' asked Glyn.

'In the circumstances, yes,' I said.

'Gabby,' said Lois, a twinkle in her eye, 'tell us what you think of the world.'

'This one?' asked Gabby, pointing at the worn floor-boards.

Duck's Arse laughed, and crossed his arms in anticipation.

'Yes, tell us something about *this* world,' said Lois.

Gabby turned red, and began making odd little sounds.

'He's not happy either,' I said to Lois. It was an attempt at a joke, again with a final aim of kissing her red lips.

'He is,' she said. 'It's stage fright. Go on Gabby, you can do it!'

'John,' hissed Gabby, in full earshot of all, 'why does she want me to talk about the world?'

'Bill!' shouted Duck's Arse into the shadows. 'Come and 'ave a gander!'

Bill duly shuffled up and took a pew. 'What's the fuss?'

'This lad's gonna tell us what he thinks about the world,' said Duck's Arse.

'Is he now?' chuckled Bill.

All eyes on Gabby.

'Do you like the world, Gab?' I said, to give him an opener.

'I think the world is lovely, man,' said Gabby. 'I like the way its centre is made of pickle.'

'*Nickel*,' I said.

32

'No, I said *pickle*,' said Gabby.

'It's just a detail,' smiled Lois. 'Carry on, Gabby.'

'OK, man,' said Gabby. 'My mam says that when people are being nasty, it's because they aren't happy, and they haven't had enough hugs. That's why I like hugs, man! John, we like to hug, don't we?'

All eyes on me now, the old men suffering paroxysms of laughter.

'We do occasionally hug,' I confirmed.

Gabby rose and embraced me. I patted his head, and Lois winked.

Glyn nudged the nearly-opaque black plastic bag further still under his chair.

'What else, Gabby?' asked Lois.

Gabby smiled and sat back down, now enjoying himself. The jukebox played "Don't Fear the Reaper" by the Blue Öyster Cult.

'I love touring America, and playing sold-out arenas with my band,' he continued. 'I also like visiting Beryl at the Job-centre. She's lovely! She asks me how I am, presses a button on her computer, and money goes into my account. It's really kind! I always send her a Christmas card. She even sends a Christmas card to my mam. Beryl hugs me too. I think that if only we could get everyone in Leytonstow to hug each other more, people would be much happier. Maybe the Council could pay them to do it, man!'

'Thanks, Gabby,' said Lois.

Gabby grinned, threw back his hair, and skipped back to the jukebox.

'God, I 'aven't laughed this much in fackin ages!' said Duck's Arse.

'I get your point,' I said to Lois.

'See?' said Lois. 'What Gabby said is just as heartfelt, but entirely positive.'

33

"e's a fackin simpleton, Lo,' said Bill.

'Doesn't matter,' said Lois, taking the opportunity to pull Bill another pint. 'Everyone has a truth. If you're happy inside, that truth is happy, and if you're sad, that truth is sad. Why don't you work on making your own truth happier, John?'

I tried not to think too hard about how Lois could assist.

'What about you, Glyn?' asked Lois. 'What are you hiding in that bag?'

'Nothing!' spluttered Glyn.

'Something naughty?'

'No!'

'Sorry, Glyn,' laughed Lois. 'I'm only teasing you.'

'Thank you, Lois,' he burbled.

'Got some blue, 'ave yer, son?' winked Duck's Arse. 'You see, in my day, it was much sexier and not so bloody gyno-whatsit.'

Poor Glyn; he was an easy target, a full moon of defence-lessness.

'So, Glyn,' said Lois, 'what do you think of the world?'

Glyn paused, then looked at the floor.

'Come on, Glyn,' said Lois. 'You're among friends here.'

Glyn opened his mouth. 'Sometimes Mozart visits me in the dead of night.'

We waited for him to smile, but it didn't come. He watched us mournfully.

'His music?' asked Lois.

'No,' said Glyn, 'the man.' It would have been a well-executed joke had Glyn been joking. Then he said, 'Not just Mozart. I woke up the other night and Nietzsche was by my window. I asked him if he was all right. He turned to me, stroked his moustache, and slowly shook his head.'

'What about 'itler?' asked Bill, nudging Duck's Arse. ''ave you 'ad a visit from Adolf?'

'Yes,' said Glyn. 'He and Eva Braun came once. Hitler told

me he was quite sure his actions had been justified. Eva didn't look so sure. Goebbels once visited me with Wagner.'

The atmosphere around the bar had changed. Duck's Arse and Bill muttered things like *You never can tell*, and *It's the quiet ones you gotta watch*, and shuffled back to their table shaking their heads. Lois said she had to change a barrel.

Thus it transpired that poor Glyn had single-handedly turned things a bit weird.

'Come on, let's go,' I said, finishing my pint.

Quietly sobbing, Glyn took his nearly-opaque black plastic bag. We gathered up a protesting Gabby, and left The Edgar Evans to "The Wonder of You" by Elvis Presley.

8

CLEMENTS MARKHAM HOUSE

We lived in a rambling villa, once home to an upper-middle-class family and their staff, once situated a sensible distance from Edwardian London, now the inner-city residence of some thirteen single men, the majority being, apart from Gabby, Glyn, and me, over sixty.

Mr Kapoor, our landlord, had not made upkeep his number one priority, and so Clements Markham House had seen better days. Sapling-sized weeds sprouted through rusted cracks in its iron gutters. Streaks of black moss criss-crossed the crumbling render. The window frames were rotted, and jammed either open or shut (mine the former; cruel in winter but for the best come summer). Malfunctioning cisterns overflowed from ugly plastic pipes protruding into thin air at all angles, which gave the place the look of a giant water feature. The drains were shattered and prone to backing up, in which event the overgrown paths either side of the building became stinking lagoons of brown trouts, discoloured toilet paper, and other nameless items.

We arrived to find a scaffolding lorry parked outside. Two muscular blokes were lugging poles up the front path and around one side of the house, while another pair played heavy duty catch with steel fittings. I asked the bloke throwing down fittings from the lorry what was going on.

'Ain't got a fackin scooby,' he snapped, not pausing. 'They pay me to put up scaff, not plan the fackin works.'

'Right,' I said. 'Where's the scaffolding going up?'

'Statue of Liberty, mate!'

'He's not a very nice man, is he?' whispered Gabby, tugging at my sleeve.

'He's a little brusque,' I said.

'You fackin want some?' said the man.

'Do we, man?' Gabby asked me.

'Pack it in, Stu,' said the guy catching the fittings.

We stood near the bins, waiting for the men carrying the poles to complete their current circuit.

'The outside wall of my room has a hole,' announced Gabby, to no one in particular.

'A hole?' I asked.

'Yeah, man, I was playing Nirvana the other day, and I suddenly noticed that a big bit of my wall was missing! They must be here to fix it!'

'*How* big a bit?' I asked.

'About the size of a mirror, man!'

'What size mirror?'

'About this big, man!' said Gabby, and described with his arms a "mirror" about four feet square.

'Jesus, Gab, didn't that worry you?' I asked. 'How did you know the ceiling wasn't about to fall in?'

'It wouldn't have been a ceiling anymore then, would it? It would have been a floor!' said Gabby. But then he looked worried. 'Do ceilings fall down?'

'What a bizarre question, Gab,' I said. 'Of course they do, if they're not supported by walls.'

'Or windows,' added Glyn, helpfully.

'I never thought of it like that before,' said Gabby.

'You thought ceilings were self-supporting?' I asked.

'I just thought they were up there, and that was it!' said Gabby. 'And anyway, Glyn, don't be silly, windows are for seeing through!'

37

I checked out of this ridiculous conversation, and let Glyn clarify the dual role of glazing and window frames, which he did with much aplomb. It stood to reason that the scaffolding was going up to fix Gabby's hole. It wasn't the first time that Mr Kapoor had been grudgingly forced to repoint Gabby's walls, although I was pretty sure previously there'd been no mirror-sized holes.

The path clear, we filed under the once-grand portico, pushed open the myrtle-green front door and shuffled over mountains of letters offering credit to the uncreditworthy at outrageous rates of interest. Repeatedly I'd had to prevent Gabby from taking up such offers; he was potentially a valued customer for the loan sharks, being as dim-witted as he was kind-hearted. On more than one occasion he'd put forward my name and address as willing guarantor for large deals struck at cut-price shops in the arcade. Over the years I'd found myself in hock to all sorts of unsavoury characters, most just as dense as Gabby, but usually somewhat larger, and less given to kind acts.

Such visits had become so problematic that I now gave Gabby £10 per week *pocket money* on the express condition that he was absolutely not to tell shopkeepers that John Torrington of Flat Seven, Clements Markham House, would honour credit for CDs, hats he'd never wear, Pot Noodles, or any items pertaining to the heavy metal subculture. Gabby took my money in the same appreciative yet entirely uncomprehending manner he drew from the public purse. Most of what I gave him went on the jukebox in The Edgar Evans: credit for music, and not likely to result in a visit from the heavies. It was well worth the tenner.

Glyn coughed, awkwardly shook our hands, and scurried off to his ground floor bedsit, the nearly-opaque black bag swinging as he went. Although Glyn kept the majority of his purchases, a select few would work their way up Clements

Markham House each week. Gabby, being at the top, had a stack in the corner of his room. Only he didn't utilise them in the conventional sense (indeed he seemed entirely uninterested in their contents) but recycled them as templates for his own rock magazine, *Metal Mallet*. He glued A4 printer paper over the pages and illustrated them with made-up interviews with his favourite hard rock acts, pieces of local metal interest, and oddly, the prices of stamps from various outlets in the local area, which were – and this was remarkable, he claimed – all the same. It could be said that Gabby used the magazines purely for their staples.

Gabby lifted the handset of the communal phone in the hallway, pumped in some coins, and commenced telling his mam all about his day.

I climbed one flight of creaking stairs to bedsit seven. It was on the first floor facing the rear. Mr Kapoor called it a *studio*, but I imagined that it might have served the family who first christened Clements Markham House as a walk-in cupboard. Measuring about ten feet square, it had a child's size pull down bed which, once withdrawn, left little room for manoeuvre; a small rotting sash window (which was, as mentioned, stuck half-open); a dangerously dilapidated one-bar heater on the wall with a long pull cord which was black with decades of sweaty hands; a tiny discoloured sink with taps that spat and banged; a plug-in single plate electric hob; a beat-up record player; a scaled up kettle; and a smelly toaster.

In the top right-hand corner of the room was the negative imprint of a flight of stairs. Under the little sash window stood a desk made from an offcut of worktop I'd harvested from a skip, propped up with legs cut from the trunk of a large hat stand I'd found in the room (which together with the pull down bed and the heater were the only three items on the bedsit's inventory). My little desk had just enough room for a sheet of foolscap, an elbow and a glass of wine. The window commanded a view of the desperately overgrown back garden, past which lurked the dark axe-wound of a railway line, past which again ran the wide windowless back wall of Leytonstow Jobcentre.

Infused with the stink of lovemaking foxes, our garden was perhaps as rarely visited by human feet as the moon; the back door having long been boarded up to deter burglars, a disorderly union of whom generally formed on Erebus Road each night as if to mirror the ratty queue outside the Jobcentre by day; a kind of shift work in itself. Rather than cultivate this postage stamp of land, the occupants of Clements Markham House utilised it as a communal landfill and giant ashtray. Anything which could be squeezed through the windows was, from discarded reefers to disgusting fridge freezers. The Council wheelie bins sat pristine and unused on the hardtop at the front. Mr Kapoor said these were a *credit* to his tenants.

Evenings I would sit at my little desk trying to record my thoughts amid a tickertape parade of moss and moisture-loving insects; shouting, clumping boots, passing freight trains, and thudding heavy metal from Gabby's room two floors above mine. As the moon rose, old men warbled tuneless duets with raped cats, or conducted arguments through thin walls, or "entertained" sad hookers, or cried. Only the small hours brought silence, an urban silence, a whirr, a static default of night traffic, sometimes comforting, more often the harbinger of terrible loneliness. I climbed into bed, and hoped Gabby's ceiling really was self-supporting.

MONDAY

9

AMUNDSEN ENTERPRISES

My alarm clock bleated mournfully at 4.45 a.m., perhaps apologising for what it heralded: another week of mopping and trolley collecting at Amundsen Enterprises. I took a "shower" by filling my sink with tepid water and performing various gymnastic manoeuvres – this doubled as a morning workout, infinitely cheaper than joining a gym. Washed and dressed, I went down a floor and knocked for Glyn. He opened his door and peered sadly from the gloom.

'Heidegger last night,' he said.

'Is he much fun?'

'Not really.'

'Can't you ask Mozart to come more often?'

'He's too busy trying to finish his *Requiem*.'

Glyn stood there, presumably expecting me to answer. In truth, I wasn't sure what to say. He locked up and we left Clements Markham House for a clear-skied morning, leaving Gabby and the old duffers to sleep until well after noon. I felt bright. This was the best part of the day, when my mind most fizzed with possibilities. The eastern horizon was tinged with promise, and seemed to suggest that the world was ours – that anything might be achieved – that really difficult things were worth starting, and that our efforts might reap worthwhile results. I walked down Erebus Road with a spring in my step. We had the world to ourselves.

'Isn't it a gorgeous morning, Glyn?'

'It's acceptable.'

'Acceptable? It's lovely.'

Taciturn at the best of times, it was even harder to get a rise from Glyn Hopkins on Monday mornings. In counterpoint to my spring, Glyn lolloped along, dejected.

'Come on, Glyn!' I cajoled. 'Things could be worse!'

'Gabby was playing Metallica last night,' sighed Glyn.

'At least it was one of their better songs,' I said, aware I was clutching at straws. Unusually confrontational, Glyn stared at me until I admitted there was nothing positive about having to listen to dangerously loud metal at one o'clock in the morning.

'Our job is really dull,' added Glyn.

'Yes, it is,' I agreed. 'But, again, things could be worse; we could be employed *only* to mop, or *only* to collect trollies. As it stands we have some variety, and variety, as they say, is the spice of life.'

'Life is variously depressing,' said Glyn.

We were due to start at six, whereupon we would mop every aisle in the superstore before a bearded fellow who never spoke, Brendan, went over our handiwork with a sit-on buffer. While Brendan buffed, Glyn and I spent half an hour clearing the car park of trollies, before breakfasting in the store cafeteria and reporting for our daytime duties at eight.

Glyn, Brendan, and I, were managed by a wily old man named Dave Lofthouse, never seen without an unlit roll-up dangling from his lips or a severely-folded tabloid newspaper tucked under his arm. Dave was the only person qualified to drive Amundsen Enterprises' forklift truck, a task he performed with much skill – indeed, the walls of his little office next to the garden furniture section were proudly covered with framed forklift truck qualifications. He'd once told me that he had the letters FORKdip after his name, and had clipped me around the ear when I'd laughed.

Tradesmen got in at eight, and the store opened to the general public at eight thirty. Senior management would arrive at some point in the morning.

This was Senior Management:

AMUNDSEN ENTERPRISES FRANCHISE OWNER – DOUGLAS DAUPHINOISE (64)
An old soak who rarely arrived before ten thirty, disappearing again for the links early afternoon. Expert at hiding, and adding no value whatsoever. Pleasant nonetheless.

OPERATIONS DIRECTOR – ALAN POVEY (58)
An anxious individual. One hundred per cent sure that Amundsen Enterprises was entirely under his control, and every nut and bolt *accounted fer in me noggin*. One of the foremost health and safety experts in the world, in his opinion. Never wrong. Yorkshireman.

OPERATIONS MANAGER – ERIC BEARDMORE (45)
A bully, notable for his girth, unhealthy appearance, and disgusting habit of spitting in the faces of junior transgressors (as long as Alan Povey not around). Rumoured to be the real brains behind the Leytonstow franchise of Amundsen Enterprises. Apparently, everyone but Alan Povey (and probably Glyn) knew that Beardmore *had his fingers in the till*.

Glyn and I threaded our way through a sea of shopping trollies and flatbed handcarts in the otherwise deserted car park, and were greeted by Stock Manager Dave Lofthouse enjoying a fag out the fire escape.

'Mornin, yer little cants,' he said. 'What time you call this?'

I reminded Dave that we didn't start until six, and that it was currently five to.

'Don't be fackin smart,' he said. He drew the tabloid from his armpit, shook it, and pushed a headline about cuts to the National Health Service under our noses.

'Look at this!' he said, prodding a photograph of a sad-looking nurse. 'The fackin country's goin to 'ell! Now, if I was the fackin P.M. I'd sort it out! I'd make all the fackin foreigners work, for a start!'

It was Dave's belief that the country had been going to pot ever since such vessels were invented. He was an aggressive little old man. I half-suspected he actually lived at Amundsen Enterprises, as it didn't matter how early you turned up, you'd be greeted by Lofthouse jabbing at headlines, half-moon reading glasses perched on the end of a long thin nose, his much-guarded forklift truck keys dangling from a chain attached to his perfectly pressed utility trousers.

I watched him scanning for more instances of the nation going to the dogs. Dave was seventy-five, and fond of telling anyone who would listen that retirement was not an option. Oddly enough, given this, he was Margaret Thatcher's biggest fan, and, supported by his trusty red-top, liked to opine that in relation to any given current affairs problem, 'Our Maggie would 'ave sorted 'em out!'

Dave Lofthouse was also a busybody, and made it his business to know *everything* there was to know about the store and those working within it. Without him it was easy to suppose Amundsen Enterprises' very walls might crumble, and, one imagined, vice versa.

'Now get to work, you little cants.'

10

THE FINE ARTS OF MOPPING
AND RE-EXPLORING

Mopping is art. It is no coincidence that various movie makers have chosen to depict the lonely hero using a mop as a stand-in dance partner. Mopping, if effective, is very much a dance, and, like dancing, the effect can be one of style or awkwardness, as well as great emotion. It is also fabulous exercise. On more than one occasion, mopping away, I'd imagined the activity could be popularised into a leisure craze with multiple personal and ecological benefits, but Glyn had pointed out that due to mopping's blue-collar associations it was unlikely to catch on. Reluctantly I'd had to agree. Glyn had added that people were very touchy about their roots; particularly so those who were apt to purchase lifestyles, engaged as they were in a vicious circle of topping up an empty cup with more emptiness.

Like any art, there is more to mopping than one might suppose:

1. A strong shaft is essential to cope with the forces of wet mop and heavy scrubbing combined.
2. The mop itself must be full and well-distributed enough to ensure the metal mount does not scratch the floor.
3. The mop has to be just wet enough to do the job. Too dry and it won't remove dirt, too wet and it won't dry in time for buffing – this really pissed Dave Lofthouse off.

4. The squeezing mechanism within the bucket must be man enough to provide a good strong grip.
5. The right amount of detergent must be added to the water – too little and it won't clean, too much and a visible residue is left upon the mopped floor – this also angered Lofthouse.
6. One must work backwards so as not to step over what has already been mopped. The path to renew the water has to be left until the very end.
7. It took many hundreds of hours of dedicated practise to become one with the mop. Glyn, in particular, was a Zen Mop Master.

Glyn and I were required to work in harmony, so we'd both arrive at the entrance at seven thirty, the whole store mopped and clean. It's fallacious to imagine that menial jobs don't require brains. They do, as well as grit, determination, and patience.

As we mopped, the sun would work its way up the full-height windows at the front of the store, setting the wet aisles aflame. At such times, my mop swinging hypnotically to and fro below me, the world took on a beguiling simplicity. In these instances I found living extremely bearable. I often wondered whether I could found a mopping retreat.

Today, Glyn and I were dead on time, meeting at the front of the store at seven thirty on the dot. Perfectly in sync, Brendan shot past on his sit-on buffer as we were stowing our buckets and mops. 'Morning, Brendan!' I shouted after him. No reply. I wondered at what moment Brendan had elected to hold his tongue. I didn't even know what his voice sounded like. It was strange. It was either that he'd said all he had to say, had nothing *to* say, or had given up *trying* to say what he had to say. Perhaps it was all of these. Perhaps he'd had a go at picking apart the universe and had, like me, come a cropper.

I asked Glyn what he thought about Brendan's silence. Glyn coughed, and picked at some gum on the sole of one of his shoes. I asked him why he was also choosing to be silent. He shrugged. Irritated, I reminded him that the story of the world, and the story of humanity in particular, was only half-complete, and that consequently there was plenty more to say and do. He opened his mouth as if to speak, then seemed to think better of it. Then I asked whether he'd enjoyed the magazines of a certain genre last night, and he started to choke. I slapped him very hard on the back. We went into the car park to begin the second part of our morning routine.

The car park was a mess of trollies and litter. The back of it was lined by a row of sycamore trees whose leaves wore a layer of dark grime. They separated Amundsen Enterprises from another light industrial plot. One corner of the car park guarded the burned-out remains of a stolen motorcycle. Another was abutted by the gable end of a lonely row of terraced houses, a strange domestic island in a long-since demolished zone: the chance result of Operation Sea Lion, or perhaps a token time-capsule granted at the whim of a 1950s development company? I didn't know. Glyn didn't either. I'd asked his opinion several times – perhaps I'd expected him to go away and read up on it – but he still didn't know. I wondered who did. Dave possibly, although he wouldn't volunteer the information: there'd be a price, most likely a good half hour of pseudopolitical rantings and violent newspaper proddings, or just a good old-fashioned clip around the ear.

The sun was gaining altitude, and cast a sickly warmth. Rush hour was in full swing: Whitehorse Road nose to bumper with modest family cars, vans, and the odd articulated lorry forced down roads designed for horse and carriage. Every now and then a police car would weave its way loudly through the traffic, and I wondered what kinds of crimes were occurring at seven thirty on a Monday morning. Perhaps there were some get-up-and-go criminals. More likely a bad car crash. I shivered imagining it – more than the searing pain of injury, the sheer surprise at the way sensible space is suddenly concertinaed; dewy air mixed with petrol fumes, dense smoke gatecrashing familiarity, disarranging the senses. The noise. The social outrage of holding up strangers, the shock, the panic, the powerful desire to shout I WANT MY MUM…!

Moved by my unexpected imaginings, I turned to tell Glyn, but he was already towards the back of the car park, busily stuffing litter into a black bag. I was in a Romantic mood. Bent, with the morning sun upon his back, the row of dirty sycamores behind him, and the pale bricks of the lonely end-terrace, Glyn looked like an unremarkable but dignified figure at the edge of a Dutch Master. Even the chance patterns of abandoned trollies seemed to take on new meaning. I inspected the angles and attitudes between every object: the sun, the trees, the gable end, the honking traffic, and Glyn. What did it mean?

Then it struck me. I was re-exploring the world. Just as I'd said I would at the ice rink. Oh joy! Yes, I'd seen the grounds of Amundsen Enterprises as if for the first time. My re-examination had included form, emotion, historical context, the cataclysmic experience of one and the imperceptibly changing landscape of all.

'I don't fackin pay you to stand around doin fack all!'

I turned to see Dave approaching rapidly, waving his newspaper in the air like a football rattle. Panicked, I grabbed a trolley and began frantically to mate it with another.

'Fackin lazy bastard!' shouted Dave in his old man's rasp. 'The fackin mob'll be 'ere soon! Get them fackin trollies together!'

'OK, Dave, sorry,' I said. 'I was just admiring the view.'

He stopped and looked around. 'What fackin view?'

'This one,' I said weakly, and made a wide gesture at Glyn, the remaining litter, the dirt-encrusted sycamore trees, the trollies, the houses, and the stinking traffic.

'Are you fackin pissed?'

I shook my head.

Dave stiffly approached, and inspected my orbit with his long nose. Then he stuffed the red-top into a back pocket, told me again in no uncertain terms to get on with the job, lit up his rollie, and walked, muttering, back to the store. I cast about me again, and noted that the view had lost some of its prior charm. Perhaps I had been momentarily drunk after all. With heavy heart, I joined Glyn.

11

THE BEARDMORE PARADOX

As Glyn and I corralled trollies, a dangerous-looking black SUV pulled silently into the car park. My heart quickened, and Glyn began to fight for air. There was something terrifying about this vehicle, not least the fact that it contained Eric Beardmore, a complete and utter bastard. I slapped Glyn hard, and he thanked me sincerely.

The SUV parked up in the most sought after disabled parking bay. Its powerful engine hummed. The tinted windows gave no hint of the occupant, but I knew from bitter experience that Amundsen Enterprises' Operations Manager would be inspecting Glyn and me and enjoying our unsettled body language, and possibly even the violence I'd had to mete out to Glyn to get him breathing again. If my hobby was pretending to be Captain Scott at the ice rink, Beardmore's was Intimidating People. He affected a fearlessness which terrorised his victims far more than threat of violence ever could; although, if required, Beardmore, it was rumoured, was not afraid to speak with his fists too.

Dave Lofthouse had a weakness for gossip. As such I knew all about Beardmore's other hobby: pilfering left, right and centre from Amundsen Enterprises. It was a perfect set-up; Douglas Dauphinoise, the franchisee, was too incapacitated by drink and senility to know or care what Beardmore was up to. Alan Povey, the Operations Director, was much too convinced of his own omnipotence ever to suspect anything dishonest might be going on under his nose. In one of his more reflective moods, Dave had told me that Beardmore's primary modus operandi was to ever-so-slightly damage Amundsen Enterprise goods and sell these on as "shop-soiled" tax-deductible items for his own gain. Dave had also told me that head office was prepared to turn a blind eye to such misdeeds because Beardmore gave a cut to key individuals. In turn, Dave said, Beardmore laundered the proceeds at local establishments including an actual launderette.

Another method, said Dave, was by straightforward thievery. It was true that Amundsen Enterprises suffered from a staggering rate of theft – *you couldn't ship it out any faster*, said Dave – but again, it was rumoured that key figures in the local constabulary were also in Beardmore's employ. Added to this, the store boasted a single security guard, one Benny Kuyembeh, whose generous proportions virtually prevented him from walking, never mind chasing, after thieves. *You couldn't make it up*, Dave had said. My expression must have betrayed some doubt, so Dave had led me to where Beardmore allegedly stowed his booty while it awaited sale: *the fackin Knock-Orf Department*, as Dave had described it. I'd been taken to a door at the back of the garden furniture aisle, behind which lay a mini-hangar packed with every type of slightly-dented object imaginable: chipped marble fire surrounds, drills missing chucks, incomplete sets of wrenches, pots of mystery paint, ladders missing the less essential rungs, garden chairs with three legs, and so on. These goings-on needled me, and I'd oft considered how I might upset Beardmore's rotten applecart.

There were a few blockers here, unfortunately. For one, I was extremely intimidated by Beardmore, which was in line with his general philosophy concerning junior employees. Secondly, I was somewhat unsophisticated (despite my philosophical gymnastics), and other than climbing a step-ladder by the tills and shouting BEARDMORE'S CORRUPT! I just couldn't think how to do it. Discussing the problem at home, Gabby had suggested that I report Beardmore to the IRS, the FBI, or even the CIA. I'd pointed out to Gabby that this probably wouldn't produce the desired results, those being American institutions. Some questioning later it transpired that Gabby had assumed the United States of America was an English county, somewhere off Cornwall. Although I did know that the USA was several thousand miles across the Atlantic, I couldn't think of any equivalent British institutions either, having also watched too much American telly as a kid. We did consider writing to the Prime Minister.

Beardmore's engine cut and a heavy door opened. Strains of Gilbert O'Sullivan poured out of the interior. I thought Beardmore's taste for 1970s melodic pop might be a cover, to throw suspicious minds off track. It did seem a little incongruous with the man himself, who now lumbered out; a giant haystack with a thatch of salt and pepper hair, a hulking red face and eyes which barely opened but took in everything. He puffed on a cigar.

'Ahem!' coughed Glyn.

Beardmore stared at us.

Then Glyn said, 'Sorry for coughing, Mr Beardmore!'

He stared at us some more.

Glyn began to choke, and said, as best he could, 'Sorry for... choking... Mr Beardmore!'

I wondered whether I should simply engage Beardmore in polite conversation. It was Monday morning after all. Surely even Stalin hadn't been averse to passing the time of day sometimes, just by way of easing himself into the killing week.

I slapped Glyn on the back, then opened my mouth, but nothing came out.

'What?' asked Beardmore.

'Did you have a nice weekend?' I said, a little too loudly.

Beardmore grinned and his snake eyes glinted. His teeth looked like slices of brown bread. I was almost going to make the sorry mistake of apologising for asking after his weekend when Glyn, now sufficiently recovered, but evidently not recovered enough to know to keep his mouth shut, did it for me.

'John is sorry he asked you about your weekend, Mr Beardmore!'

Beardmore chuckled, not in a nice way, and waddled towards us.

'Why is you sorry?' asked Beardmore.

'He's sorry because...' said Glyn.

Beardmore and I waited.

'You *know* why he's sorry!' cried Glyn.

'Do I?' smiled Beardmore, lighting up a new cigar, and blowing the proceeds into Glyn's face.

Glyn once again began to gulp for air. 'Because... he's scared!'

Beardmore was loving this. I thought hard about how I might rescue Glyn from calamity, but couldn't for the life of me think what I could do, or say. I knew what was coming, because I'd seen it and had been the recipient before, as had Glyn. It was now just a matter of whom it would be. Glyn shot me searching looks, asking me with his sad eyes to become the recipient. I honestly tried to, but was frozen. I was filled with guilt. Beardmore still grinned, seemingly at one with the universe.

'Why is he scared?' asked Beardmore.

Glyn said, 'Because you might... *you know*!'

'Might what?' said Beardmore, smoke seeping from tufted nostrils. Then he began to hawk.

'Because you might spit in his face!' cried poor Glyn.

A split second later Beardmore launched an enormous globule of yellow-black goo squarely into Glyn's face.

'Oh God Almighty!' shouted Glyn, clawing the stuff away with his hands.

'My weekend was fine, thank you, Torrington,' said Beardmore, before shuffling off towards the entrance of Amundsen Enterprises, inside, and up green metal stairs to his suspended office, his lair.

Poor Glyn wept. I offered him the sleeve of my cardigan, but he fell to the ground and wailed. Traffic still shunted along Whitehorse Road.

'Are you OK, Glyn?' I asked.

'No,' he sobbed.

'I'm sorry it was you,' I said. Then added, 'You're my hero.'

'I'm not, John,' he said, composing himself. He then stood, wiped more gunk from his face, and recommenced pushing a trolley-train towards the customer pick up point.

Thus we had been reintroduced to *The Beardmore Paradox*, where both shutting your trap, and talking, would hasten the same ghastly outcome.

The lonely row of houses looked down at us wearing the same brickish expression they had for one hundred years.

12

A RUN-IN WITH DAVE LOFTHOUSE

Dave was in the cafeteria walking Tracy through the day's headlines, whether she liked it or not. Tracy's defining characteristic was tutting; she did it all day long, so it was difficult to tell whether she was happy or not. She stood there, spatula in hand, tutting as Dave talked. The cafeteria was filled with tired-looking operatives drinking coffee from single-use cups, and nibbling at anaemic-looking breakfasts. Perhaps lured from overseas by the cosmopolitan opportunities of London, these were men and women from all over the world who had none-theless somehow ended up in Leytonstow, and at Amundsen Enterprises. They looked thoroughly disappointed.

Brendan's messy head of hair appeared and disappeared between the aisles of the shop floor as he flew to and fro on his machine buffing up our handiwork. I thought Dave would stop haranguing Tracy for a few moments to enable her to serve us breakfast, but I was wrong.

'Fack me!' said Dave, prodding his red-top with a calloused finger. 'It's the fackin Polacks what done it. The lot of 'em, put-ting our boys arter business!' Dave knew well that his audience consisted of more than a few Poles, and he repeatedly cast an eye over the breakfasting workers. They ignored him. I offered sympathetic looks, but they ignored me too.

Dave's phone rang, and this break in his tirade enabled Tracy to put out our breakfasts. She didn't ask us what we wanted. To make any specific request would be akin to asking for a glass of Pinot Grigio in a Wild West saloon. Tutting, she plonked deflated sausages, dried-up eggs, and burned chips upon two cracked plates and threw them into a multistorey microwave. While the microwave fulfilled its purpose, she poured two colourless coffees into Styrofoam cups. Dave ended his call, and opined further upon the economic decline of Britain. The microwave pinged. Tracy withdrew the food and pushed it our way. The sausages, briefly inflated by the heat, sighed.

'Thanks, Tracy,' I said.

'Sit down and eat the fackin thing,' spat Dave.

I disobeyed him for a fraction of a second too long–evidenced by Dave, who neatly placed his newspaper upon the counter, showed me two remaining teeth, folded his spindly arms, and waited for the sport. With a grunt Glyn took up his breakfast and began to move off, but I grabbed the sleeve of his work cardigan. Dave laughed bitterly.

I felt something explode. '*Dave,*' I said, hardly sensible of what I was doing. 'Glyn and I were up at four forty-five. We were here by five to six, that is, right on time. At six we carefully mopped the entire store. At seven thirty we started clearing the car park. The result is that we have achieved *exactly* what our remit demands, and what's more, we have done it with minimum fuss and, dare I say it, with some amount of pride.'

'You wanna fackin round of applause?'

We had the attention of the whole cafeteria. Silence, save Tracy's habitual tuts. I studied Dave's lined and implacable face. He was smirking. My heart sank as I realised it was simply a matter of battles fought, and years survived. Dave was a life-hardened old stickleback. I was a fresh minnow.

'All I'm saying, Dave,' I said, with less conviction, 'is that we've tried our best and worked hard this morning, so a little politeness wouldn't go amiss.'

With surprising speed, Dave boxed my ears. I collapsed with the shock, and found myself lying on my back looking up at him.

'Know about fackin 'ard work do yer?' he asked.

'Come on, John,' said Glyn.

I attempted to struggle to my feet, but Dave made a deft swipe and I was back on the deck.

'Pack it in, Dave,' said Tracy, absent-mindedly.

'It's nothin personal, my son,' said Dave, leaning over me, 'but you will never ever tell me what to do. Do you understand?'

I kicked out at his leg, but missed. Dave took this opportunity to stamp upon one of my shins with his hobnail boots. I yelled with pain and appealed to Glyn for help. He was nibbling a chip and wearing a singularly worried expression.

''ave you 'ad enough?' smiled Dave. 'Because I ain't got time to do this all day. 'ave you got the fackin message, Torrington?'

I thought about my options. I didn't have any.

'Yes,' I said.

'Up you get then, you little cant.'

I did as he said; my legs on fire and my pride sorely dented.

'Right,' said Dave, resuming his stool, 'take your breakfast, and eat the fackin thing.'

'Gimme your plate,' sighed Tracy.

I gritted my teeth and gave it to her, all the while watching Dave for more sudden movements, but he was once more engrossed in his newspaper. Tracy rearranged my breakfast and handed it back with a tut. Dave chuckled and shook his head, and I hobbled over to join Glyn.

'Are you OK, John?' asked Glyn.

'No!' I hissed. 'I've just been beaten up by a seventy-five-year-old!'

But Glyn was not to be drawn into conversation on this score. The world was a lonesome place.

One of the women from the tills came in and engaged Tracy in conversation. There was no preamble. 'She's got a lump, have you noticed?' said the newcomer. 'It goes from *here* to *here*,' she drew a sizeable circle on the side of her own head.

'I thought she just liked hats,' said Tracy, tutting and making a cup of coffee for the woman – real coffee I noticed, not the watery rubbish Glyn and I had been doled.

I chewed upon the disappointing sausage and looked around the cafeteria for ladies with hats, or large lumps on the side of their heads. There were a couple of borderline cases, but none worth a special trip to the cafeteria to gossip about. My leg hurt where Dave had stamped on it. Why wasn't Tracy relating this to the woman?

'She has to wear her hair on the side, or if she does sport, she wears a big headband,' said the woman. 'The doctor said just leave it, it might go down, but, well it *hasn't* gone down.'

'What is it, then?' said Tracy.

'They don't know. One doctor said, "I've never seen one like that before". They won't operate on it because they're not sure what it is.'

'Has she always had it?' asked Tracy.

'No, it came up a couple of years ago, when Wayne left,' said the woman. 'She thinks it's linked.'

'Do *they* think it's linked?'

'They don't know.'

It struck me that *they* or *them* was a very frequently used coverall for an elusive group of people who apparently knew things the rest of us didn't. Somebody out there knew exactly what the lump was, its cause, and its cure, but it looked like the poor woman with the lump hadn't encountered *them* yet. It was very intuitive and comforting to suppose such beings existed, somewhere out there, sure-footed experts keeping the world safe for the imperfect remainder. But I knew that we were perfectly alone.

13

ALAN POVEY AND THE TAIL-LIFT

The car park was filling with white vans: early birds with paint-spattered trousers collecting the raw materials to ply day trades. I went into the store and found Operations Director and Second-in-Command Alan Povey lecturing a bunch of bored builders' mates on the contents of their flatbed hand carts. Not a single one, so it appeared, had picked the correct ingredients for the job at hand.

Povey was early today, but usually arrived a little after nine. It was unwise to question him on any subject, never mind his tardiness. But gossip-monger Dave had, over the years, found out what made Povey tick. His findings made complete sense and no sense at all. Alan Povey was usually late because he *walked* to work. Not so strange, but unusual when one considered Povey lived well outside of London. In fact, it took him two hours each way to make the journey on foot. Added to this, according to Dave, were the two hours or more he allotted each morning to checking his home was secure and not in danger of catching fire or flooding while he was out. This, Dave reported, consisted of checking all plug sockets were switched off, disconnecting the washing machine, shutting off the stopcock under the sink, and using a special key to shut off the mains water supply in the street. Povey then turned his attention to the windows. The only way, said Dave, for Povey to check they were secure to his satisfaction, was to open each, then shut and lock them, then unlock, open, and shut/lock/unlock/open each again as many times as it took to make lingering feelings of doubt fade away. Finally, said Dave, the front door would be locked, but Povey would walk to the end of his garden path with a growing sensation that he'd forgotten something. He would then return to his front door, unlock it, and painstakingly check everything again. The whole cycle might be repeated several times until Povey felt confident enough to begin the walk to work. Why did he not drive, or get the bus? Simple: it was unsafe. Not only was it unsafe, Povey didn't believe the training bus drivers were given was robust enough. Nor did he consider that the dangers pertaining to the alleged presence of tiny amounts of asbestos in the airbag systems in modern vehicles had been properly ruled out. Dave said the wear and tear upon Povey's property from all the constant checking and rechecking was terrible. He was the best glazing and locksmith customer in the area, almost single-handedly keeping several small businesses afloat.

Dave's inquisitiveness had even led him to visit the local pub, where he discovered that Povey's neighbours considered him stupendously eccentric – the flapping windows each morning giving the impression that he was trying to make the house take to the air. Povey, said Dave, was also engaged in a war of attrition with the local utilities; particularly The Waterboard, who were definitively fed up with his constant tampering with the stopcock in the street. Of course, said Dave, with Povey they didn't know who they were messing with, being, in his own words, the foremost health and safety expert in the UK. There was nothing about keeping safe he didn't know. If he didn't know it, so he said, *it couldn't hut yer*.

Locked in an impregnable fortress of his own inflexibility, Povey thus demanded that everyone else suffered accordingly. He hadn't, said Dave, paid his Council Tax for three years because he didn't think the trousers worn by his local

61

bin men were up to the job. This was one of a whole host of ongoing legal disputes. Amazingly, Povey's knowledge of health and safety law was so extensive that he'd been able to cajole several magistrates into ordering multiple inquiries; into trousers, into the thickness of street sweepers' steel toe-capped boots, into the ability of ambulance drivers to keep control of their vehicles during aquaplaning, and into the consistency of pigeon deterrent in relation to the potential poisoning of groundwater, to name but a few.

I watched Povey lecturing the smirking young labourers by the loading bay. He wasn't stupid, and in any case a basic awareness of health and safety was essential to get through life unscathed. But I suspected that, for him, even allowing a hairline crack to appear in his grip on safe reality would be to risk invalidating a life's work; the ghastly realisation that decades of acute inconvenience had been quite needless.

Severely annoying eccentricities aside, Povey could be pleasant enough. He was even capable of "humour", albeit health and safety related – a specialist genre – indeed his jokes were in truth factual. He didn't have a sense of humour in the traditional sense – this would have required a basic enjoyment of spontaneity – but in one of his more relaxed moods (which for a *normal* person might've been panic) he was capable of giving a wonky grin and asking, "Eh, lad, what's the difference between a wrench and a spanner?"

The answer was, "A wrench has adjustable jaws with teeth. A spanner has set sizes and either an open end or a ring grip."

The accepted etiquette was to laugh. I actually found such jokes quite funny, but only because I appreciated the surreal, and sympathised with poor Povey's neurodiversity.

Lastly, Dave had told me it was folklore in the village that having suffered a back injury in the mid-eighties, Povey had been laid up for three weeks mainlining pain killers on doctor's orders. It was said that during those weeks Povey's house had remained unlocked, the bin men had been able to go about their work without being the recipients of health and safety contravention stickers, and loud reggae music had poured day and night from his open bedroom windows. There'd even been rumours of a house party.

Povey, clad top to toe in Day-glo health and safety work-wear, complete with safety goggles and a hard hat bearing his name, addressed a middle-aged gaffer directing young men loading materials onto the back of a truck. 'Are yewer men familiar wi' Control of Substances 'azardous to 'ealth Regulations 2002?'

'What's that you say?' asked The Gaffer pleasantly.

'I said, are yewer men familiar with the Control of Substances 'azardous to 'ealth Regulations 2002?'

The Gaffer, a big Irishman with a round friendly face and thick red stubble, sucked on a cigarette, and smiled at Povey who continually glanced at the cigarette and seemed to be applying every ounce of his willpower not to scream "FIRE!" The trade area of the store led to the car park via a large roller door, and The Gaffer was standing perfectly astride the boundary – arguably smoking outside, but also suspiciously *in*.

'Now then, I would say *yes*, they've studied the regulations, is that OK?' said The Gaffer, still wearing his smile.

'Of course it's OK, it's ruddy essential!' cried Povey.

'That's just grand, then,' said The Gaffer.

'And I tek it that on-site they're usin safety goggles to British Standard EN 166 2B5?' enquired Povey.

'That they are, is that OK?'

'It's bloody vital!' he blew.

'LADS! IT'S VITAL!' cried The Gaffer to his men humping bags of cement onto the flatbed truck. They saluted their boss and laughed. The Gaffer gave Povey a wink.

'If you're mixin that stuff, I tek it you'll be utilising face masks to EN149 Class FFP1S?'

'Every time, my friend, is that OK?' said The Gaffer.

I wondered why he appended every sentence with *is that OK*? It was so very polite, yet his eyes twinkled with mischief. It certainly wound Povey up – perhaps the ultimate design.

'One of yewer men is wearin training shoes!' pointed Povey, and marched over to the lorry. 'He can't use a ruddy tail-lift in training shoes!'

The Gaffer followed Povey nonchalantly and addressed the operative in question. 'Sean, why are you wearing trainers, now?'

Sean dumped his bag of cement and lumbered up. He was easily a foot taller than Povey, and significantly wider. 'I went for a run before work,' said Sean. 'My doctor told me so.'

'Getting fit so he is!' smiled The Gaffer. 'Good lad!'

'But 'e can't operate tail-lift with incorrect footweyer!' shouted Povey. 'RIGHT, SHUT OPERATION DOWN!' Povey sprinted over to the controls for the roller door and pressed a red button. The door began to lower, presumably the first act of entirely shutting down Amundsen Enterprises in the event of a serious health and safety contravention. One of Sean's mates, an equally indestructible-looking young man, wordlessly positioned himself under the door, braced, and intercepted its descent. The motor made a sickly whirring sound, gave a puff of smoke, and died. Meanwhile Sean-in-Trainers began to overwork the tail-lift, jerking it up and down, perilously close to his feet. This was too much for Povey, who hit the deck and assumed what looked like his own brace – presumably the correct protocol should the procedure of shutting the operation down encounter an unexpected problem.

The pleasant-faced gaffer stood hands-on-hips wearing a kindly smile. 'Right lads, that's enough now, is that OK?' Evidently it was, and they resumed loading up the truck. 'Are you OK, Alan?' asked The Gaffer, helping Povey up.

'No, I am bloody not!' he snapped. 'The 'ealth and safety executive'll 'ave a full repowert on their desk tomorrow morning! They'll ruddy well put *you* out of business!'

'Now, it looks like we've had a little misunderstanding, is that OK?' said The Gaffer.

'You've entirely misunderstood the importance of safe wokin practices!' bleated Povey.

'I see,' said The Gaffer. 'It looks like we've got a little problem on our hands, so we have.'

'Yewer too bloody right you 'ave!' cried Povey.

'I'm just wondering...' said The Gaffer, stroking his bristled chin, '...did you not spot Sean's trainers when your store sold me the cement?'

Povey's mouth fell open. He stared at the wily gaffer.

'Because unless I'm mistaken, Amundsen Enterprises has a duty of care, so it does,' winked The Gaffer. 'Is that OK?'

The Gaffer's question was immediately followed by a bellow of pain. Sean's trainered foot was pinned to the floor by the truck's tail-lift.

'It's jammed!' shouted the lad who'd broken the roller door and was now beating the tail-lift's control panel with his fists.

Povey grinned from ear to ear and began frantically digging around in the pockets of his Teflon health and safety dungarees. The Gaffer ran over to the truck, retrieved a jack from the cab, positioned it beneath the truck's chassis and began furiously pumping. Sean screamed. The other lads took a cigarette break. Next, Povey ran up to the still-writhing Sean and slapped a large red sticker upon his breast. Then he stuck one on the tail-lift, the pumping gaffer, and every lad in turn. Finally, he wandered over to me and pinned one upon my shoulder. I tore it off and examined it: "In contravention of Health and Safety at Work Act 1974".

Sean was at last freed, and fell to the floor. The Gaffer

sighed, lit up another cigarette, and bent over his injured workmate. 'Are you OK, lad?'

'These trainers cost me eighty quid!' cried Sean.

Povey, jubilant and erect, addressed The Gaffer. 'Right, yew are in contravention of the 'ealth and Safety at Wok Act 1974! I'll need to see all the relevant documentation relatin to the use of the tail-lift. The manufacturer's 'andbook, includin the Declaration of Conformity, records of maintenance wok and any repairs, includin the weight test certificate, a record of the past two years' thorough examinations, records of any staff trainin, risk assessments, and any other documentation including yewer Safe System of Wok.'

'Don't worry so, lad,' said The Gaffer, stroking Sean's hair. 'We'll buy you another pair we will, is that OK?'

'Me mammy'll kill me!' cried Sean.

'No, she won't so, I'll have a word with her, is that OK?'

One of the lads tittered and nudged a mate.

Then they humped the last of the bags of cement onto the truck, the tail-lift was stowed, and The Gaffer and the lads clambered into the crew cab.

'Don't forget the documentation!' shouted Povey.

'I'll put 'em in the post, so I will,' smiled The Gaffer, and they drove off in a cloud of smoke, wearing their red stickers. Povey watched them go, turned to me, and slapped another sticker upon my chest. 'You see if I don't ruddy well shut 'em down!' he yelled, then marched off to the customer toilets.

A minute or two later I softly opened the door to the gents. Sobbing came from a cubicle.

'Alan, are you all right?' I asked. It stopped abruptly. I wasn't sure what else to say, and left.

14

BENNY KUYEMBEH

On the way to relate the tail-lift disaster to Glyn, I bumped into Benny Kuyembeh, Amundsen Enterprises' lone security guard.

'John! How are you?' he asked.

Although there wasn't much competition, Benny was the nicest guy in the store. He was built like an extra-wide bowling pin, and never got a hard time from Beardmore due to that gentleman's avowed policy of employing a security operative who was entirely ineffective in his paid capacity. But Benny was fairly brimming with other skills. Relaxation was near the top of the list: he spent many an hour patrolling the garden furniture section, which included a super strength hammock *for the larger Londoner*. Benny was their best advocate, and they flew out of the door, whether by honest purchase or other routes. When not stress-testing furniture, Benny would slowly waddle about the store perpetually tucking and retucking in his beige security guard's shirt, conversing pleasantly with customers and staff alike, listening and counselling, laughing, sympathising, exploring problems, and imparting extremely sound, albeit born-again-religious, advice. Indeed, he had his *regulars*, customers who only visited Amundsen Enterprises to chat. To dip into his easy manner was like taking a mini-break somewhere rather pleasant. Unofficially, Benny was the store chaplain.

Originally from Sierra Leone, Benny and his family had sought refuge in the UK in the early nineties. He didn't like to recall his experiences of the war in much detail, but would occasionally lean on a pallet of nails, grow misty-eyed, and describe the perfect tropical beaches of his youth. He was most given to this on drizzly winter days. Benny said that despite the civil war, the overriding approach to life in Sierra Leone was one of peace, tolerance, and love. To this extent, Benny was a true son of his homeland. To meet him was to get an immediate impression of someone at peace with himself. Part of this, apart from his laid-back nature, and the horrors he'd witnessed and come to terms with, was the fact that he enjoyed an intimate relationship with God. Benny was utterly convinced he was able to converse with someone who *really* knew what was going on. Fully aware that for any one individual, perception *is* reality, I wasn't about to challenge or deride it, understanding clearly that if Benny said he wholeheartedly believed he *knew* God, and given that we could only ever perceive the world through our five senses, then it was fact, *his* fact, undeniable, a truism, just as it was Povey's that if he didn't disconnect his washing machine each morning his whole house, nay the whole village, would be washed away in a biblical flood. There was no point whatsoever arguing with either man.

Benny thrived on good conversation. He was expert at listening, and gently shepherding one towards greater self-insight. He achieved it without humiliation, without power play. Thus we each took a coffee and I related the morning's events – Glyn's disgusting experiences at the hands of Beardmore, my Romantic rediscovery of the car park, being beaten up by Dave, and Povey's disastrous run-in with the wily gaffer. Benny listened with slow shirt-tucking motions, and gasps in all the right places.

'Quite a morning,' he chuckled.

'What do you think?' I asked.

'What do *I* think?' he smiled. 'First, tell me, what *you* think?'

'I wish we were *nicer* to one another,' I said.

'Why aren't we nice to one another?'

I had a think about this while Benny adjusted his wardrobe. It seemed to me there were some key reasons we weren't always nice:

1. Some hadn't been nurtured as children, had no precedent for love, and didn't understand how to give or receive it.
2. Chronic lack of money and the fear of losing jobs and homes stressed people out.
3. Sexual frustration drove people crazy.
4. Some harboured unexamined past hurts, and unwittingly brought them into every interaction.
5. Inner-city living was not conducive to the healthy human animal.
6. Crushing loneliness.
7. A diet of processed food meant many were constantly on the verge of scurvy.
8. Some were wired up wrong – they found pleasure and affirmation in cruelty.
9. The human being had a dark side, always had, and always would.
10. God was dead, and religion was no longer an opium. Opiates were.
11. The people responsible for media content were not wise, but driven by greed, and short-term self-aggrandisement.
12. It suited the rich for the poor to be busy surviving.
13. It was unbearable knowing you would one day die, making it difficult to commit to anything wholeheartedly, including being nice.
14. We were programmed to explore and seek out new worlds, but there weren't any left unless you had a trillion dollars to look around space, which was beautiful, but largely empty. My views on the bottom of the sea are already noted.

'I see you're doing some serious thinking, John!' laughed Benny. I blushed. Benny threw his empty cup into a nearby bin. 'Let's change the question; what can *you* do about the way you feel?'

I thought about my morning, and yesterday's conversation with Glyn and Gabby at the ice rink, and came up with three ideas which, unlike my reasons for not being nice to others, I explained to Benny:

1. Enable people to re-explore their surroundings, and see them consciously, as if for the first time.
2. End all corruption, forgive those engaged in it, and give them a second chance at being good.
3. Encourage people to smile at each other more, accept and value each other as unique human beings all on the same team.

Benny listened to me, then bellowed with laughter. I must have looked hurt. 'Sorry, John!' he laughed. 'It's just that you might need to lower your expectations.'

'Why?' I demanded. 'I am here upon this earth for, what, seventy years, perhaps a bit more if I'm lucky, and I've already wasted thirty-eight of them! Why can't I make it happen?'

I became aware that I was experiencing a delayed emotional reaction to the morning's beating at the hands (well, feet) of Dave. I could tell by Benny's expression that he, of course, perceived this.

'Look, John,' he said. 'It's great to have ambitions, but if they're not achievable I'm afraid you'll set yourself up for further disappointment.'

I sulked.

'John,' he said, heavily engaged in tucking once more. 'You honestly think you can end all corruption, make the entire population of London a bit nicer to each other, while convincing them to take time out to re-explore a very familiar environment?'

'Possibly,' I ventured.

'Why, John? Where will it get *you*?'

The South Pole. 'I'll start small,' I said, 'in Leytonstow.'

Benny looked at me, presumably waiting for me to climb down. 'Look, don't get me wrong, John,' he said, arching his back to tuck in the rear portion of his shirt, which only served to make the front pop out. 'It's a noble idea, but you need to ask yourself, "Why do I want to do this?"'

I thought about what to say. I'd always found it difficult to pin down my own motivations. They varied wildly depending on what time of the day it was, the weather, my mood.

'I want to assist humankind to develop to the next level,' I said. I was just as surprised as Benny.

'The next level!' said Benny.

'Yes, to up our game, and break through our self-imposed limitations,' I said. I don't think I'd ever talked like this before.

Benny started to belly-laugh and his shirt immediately unfurled from his trousers like a billowing sail. 'I'm sorry, John! It's just that I've never come across anyone with the same ambitions before,' he said. 'You're quite unique, John! Isn't that great?'

I sighed.

'OK,' said Benny. 'Why don't you just try it for a while, and see what happens?'

I tried to read his handsome face. I got the distinct feeling he was humouring me.

'You think I'll fail, don't you?'

'You want me to challenge you?' he said. 'OK, my man, I'm betting you can't stamp out corruption, can't make Londoners a bit nicer, and can't get them into re-exploring their neighbourhoods!'

71

'You think it's a really silly idea,' I said.

'No, John! I've heard worse ideas!'

'You think I'm daft.'

'No, of course not!' he said, but I could tell he did think that, really. His encouragement was akin to one of Glyn's non-committal coughs. 'Do you know what I think?' said Benny, his eyes gleaming.

I shook my head and gulped.

'I think you want to fail. I think you want to show the world once and for all that you are worthless, good for nothing.'

'Why would I do that?' I asked, petulantly.

'That's what I'm asking you, John. Why indeed?'

I said nothing. I didn't need to.

'I'm sorry, John,' he said.

'I don't know what to do with the rest of my life,' I said.

'There are plenty of alternatives to planning to fundamentally change humanity!'

I thought of Brendan, the buffer, and realised that he represented what I feared about my future: a silent and invisible man.

'I don't want to be like Brendan,' I said.

'Brendan?'

'You know, Brendan. He never speaks, just appears, buffs, and leaves.'

'What do you know about Brendan?' asked Benny.

'Nothing really,' I said. 'He just looks so... lonely, and I don't want to end up like that. I want to *do something* while I still have time.'

'You know nothing at all about Brendan, but you think he's a lost cause? Why?'

Benny was right, of course. The only thing I knew about Brendan was that he turned up at Amundsen Enterprises each morning to buff the floors. Then he disappeared. 'But he never speaks,' I said.

'It's because he's usually hungover from partying all night,' said Benny.

'Really?'

'Yes. He plays lead guitar in a rock band. Dave says they used to be quite well-known. He has three jobs. He buffs the floors here, works in a garden centre in Woodford during the day, and plays in the band at night. He's got three gorgeous kids and a beautiful wife – an ex-groupie! I think he doesn't say much because he's tired, and he's a bit shy too.'

'That's amazing,' I said, crestfallen and embarrassed.

'What does it tell you, John?'

'That I shouldn't assume anything?'

'Yes, that's true. But it also tells you there are plenty of things to do with your life which are easier and more satisfying than attempting to completely change the world.'

'But why haven't I already got...?' I asked, thinking aloud, realising immediately how childish it sounded, and stopping myself. I was thinking about the beautiful wife in particular. Moppers didn't tend to have groupies. I could have cried.

'Because you're a bit of a perfectionist I'm afraid, John. You're keeping yourself back for something incredible and undefined. But you're getting older and starting to panic. You see, the problem with perfectionists is they're afraid to start out on an imperfect path, but all paths on this earth are imperfect, my friend.' Benny became serious. 'You need to realise something, John.'

'What?' I asked, the hairs on the back of my neck standing up.

'You are already living in paradise.'

'Am I?'

'Yes. You just don't know it. You can't see it. Everything you need is at your fingertips.'

I looked at my fingers. My nails needed cutting.

'But that's what I'm trying to do,' I said. 'I want people to

73

realise they're alive. I want them to run through the streets, celebrating their amazingly unlikely existence!'

'John, what I'm saying is that you don't need to try to alter what is already paradise. The fact is, you are free. You are unlikely to be beaten up as you walk the streets, and you can sleep in your bed knowing you won't be awoken by a desperate young man with a gun.'

I suddenly remembered I was talking to a man from a war-torn nation, displaced for the sake of his family. I gasped at my own selfishness and insensitivity. I began to apologise, but Benny waved it away with a grin. 'Never mind me,' he laughed. 'I have all the satisfaction I need.'

I sensed The Almighty was about to make a cameo appearance.

'If I were you, John, I'd look at *yourself* before trying to sort the world out. Ask yourself, what is *He* telling me? What does *He* want me to do?'

In a roundabout way, this was exactly what Lois had said in The Edgar Evans. For a second I thought of her, and my heart melted. Then I looked at Benny, and wondered whether he had asked this question of The Almighty, and whether the answer had been, "Patrol the gardening section of Amundsen Enterprises and have the occasional lie down".

'OK, I'll ask *Him*,' I said, prepared to try anything.

'Good man!'

'Shall I ask Him now?'

'Any time you want, John, any time. Shall we?' Benny gestured at the sun loungers and we each took the weight off.

'Benny, I have a question.'

'Anything, my friend.'

'If you suspected someone of tax evasion, who would you tell?'

'I didn't expect you to ask that!'

'But who would you?'

'You would tell Her Majesty's Revenue and Customs.'

'Thanks.'

'Anything else?'

'No, that's fine.'

'You do make me laugh, John.'

'I'm glad,' I said, and closed my eyes.

'Let yourself drift,' said Benny.

I was in a snow drift at the end of the world.

15

THE FIREPLACE FELONS

I awoke to see Alan Povey desperately trying to drag Benny from his sun lounger – that seemed to be Povey's aim; in fact he couldn't move him an inch.

'Benny! Benny! Come on, move yer arse, there's bloody thieves!'

Benny opened his eyes, leisurely swung his legs over the side of the creaking lounger, and stretched. Then he lumbered to a standing position and began to tuck in his shirt. Povey jumped up and down, jabbing his fingers at the tills. 'They're mekin off with the ruddy lot of them! Go an' stop 'em, Benny! Somebody call the bloody po-lice!'

I peered in the direction of Povey's frantic air-prodding and saw three young men happily dragging marble fire surrounds through the checkouts towards the exit, laughing as they went, presumably at the ridiculously brazen nature of their morning's shopping trip. They wore brightly coloured shell suits and could not have been more conspicuous. It was Day-glo robbery. Bemused staff and customers alike stood silently watching them. A baby cried – apart from Povey it seemed the only concerned party.

'STOP!' shouted Benny, authoritatively, and commenced waddling in the direction of the crime, adjusting his waistband as he went. He looked like a walrus humping itself towards the sea. Povey assisted by pushing Benny's rear end. I followed them, wondering what on earth Benny could do.

The young thieves paused for a breather, and laughed as they clocked Benny's glacial progress across the shop floor. Even some of the checkout staff were laughing, and in doing so flirting with danger: Povey missed nothing – they might find themselves reassigned to toilet duty by the end of the week, the store's equivalent to being posted to the Eastern Front.

Benny was making progress now, and the young men resumed dragging their booty out of the store. The automatic exit doors swished shut behind them, and normal activity resumed – a low hum of chatter again sprung up, and checkouts chirruped once more with transactions. It amazed me – it was as if this act of thievery had been so brash that those witnessing it had failed to process the information properly. Either that, or it was further evidence that the anonymity of city life led to community breakdown; those present had not contributed to the making of the goods being stolen, nor did they stand to lose out directly as a result of the theft, so they'd just let the thieves get on with it – an amusing sideshow, nothing more.

Benny at last made the exit, followed by Povey, me, and a few inquisitive customers. There was a collective intake of breath; Glyn was *wrestling* on the floor with one of the young men! Benny leaned upon a bin to catch his breath, tuck his shirt in, and mop his face with a large white handkerchief. Fruitlessly, Povey continued to push Benny, threatening him with all kinds of unrealistic consequences. A handful of nosy customers looked on as poor Glyn rolled around on the floor with a young thief who was clad in a turquoise shell suit. The other two felons smoked cigarettes and yelled encouragement.

'Come on, Glyn!' I shouted, aware I should have been running to his aid. But the scene was too interesting to ruin by becoming a part of it. The sun shone happily down upon us all. I was minded of a summer fete.

'Where the 'ell's Beardmore?!' shouted Povey, shooting glances at the windows of Beardmore's first floor office. The nicotine-stained blinds were drawn.

A dirty white van reversed at speed across the car park. It screeched to a halt inches from Glyn and his foe, whereupon the thieves not involved in the scrum flung open the back doors and began to stow the marble fire surrounds, while the van revved like a rally car.

'They're not 'andlin the bloody things correctly!' cried Povey, gripping one of Benny's tree trunk upper arms. Why he should be concerned about the back health of the thieves wasn't clear: I half expected him to begin doling out lifting advice. Finally, tearfully (and very politely), Glyn, previously rolling around on the tarmac, acknowledged his opponent's supremacy. The thieves clambered into the van – I did notice one of them held the small of his back – and with doors flapping the vehicle lurched forward, but stalled, giving Povey a chance to slap a red sticker on its bumper, a significant victory. After furious rocking attempts to restart, the thieves wheelspun their way across the car park, very nearly colliding with a blue Rolls Royce just turning in, before tearing away down Whitehorse Road.

The Rolls Royce glided coronation-like across the car park and parked askew in the second most sought after disabled parking bay (Beardmore's dangerous-looking SUV still occupied the first). The door opened and out stepped Douglas Dauphinoise, the turnip-headed franchisee, blinking in the sunlight, and wearing only one patent leather shoe.

'What appears to be the kerfuffle, gentlemen?' he said to a woman standing next to him.

A police van turned into the car park and pulled up leisurely.

'About ruddy time, too!' said Povey.

Beardmore shuffled out of the store, a cigar clamped between his tuberous lips. 'Fack's going on?' he asked evenly.

'Where you bin, Eric?' whinged Povey. 'We've 'ad all 'ell brek loose!'

'I'll sort it,' said Beardmore.

I walked over to Glyn and helped him up.

'Don't say I'm your hero,' Glyn said. 'They came out, laughed at me, and the one in blue decided to attack me, for a laugh. I tried to run away, but he tripped me up.'

'It was more turquoise,' I pointed out. Some customers came over to inspect Glyn. One of them was heavily pregnant.

'What you 'avin?' asked another woman of the pregnant customer.

'I'm having a boy.' She blushed, her accent Eastern European.

'What you gonna call it?' asked the woman's husband.

'I think something English,' she said, and further reddened.

'Like George?' said the woman.

The girl laughed. 'I've already got George! My husband!'

'George the Second then!' suggested the woman, winking at her husband.

'How about Rodney?' said the man.

The girl looked confused and asked him to repeat.

'All right, Trigger then!' said the man.

The girl's face dropped.

'Uncle Albert!' laughed the woman.

To scandalise the cruel pair, I gave Glyn a loving cuddle, which he tolerated.

'Pair o' fackin benders,' said the woman. The couple walked back into the store.

'How about "John"?' I said, smiling at the girl.

'No, that's boring!' she said, and also returned to her shopping.

Glyn regarded me. 'You're interesting, sociologically,' he said.

We watched Beardmore chatting to the policeman; a

young man who looked like he was in fancy dress. Beardmore was clearly buttering him up, and the young man's demeanour became one of ever-increasing self-importance as the discussion progressed. Povey, having slapped red stickers upon all present, now stood upbraiding Benny by the automatic doors.

'You need to lose weight, fer wun!' shouted Povey. 'You can 'ardly walk, man!'

'Are you setting me up for constructive dismissal, Alan?' asked Benny genially, still leaning on the bin. To be honest I could see Povey's point.

Povey stopped wagging his finger, and looked worried. I surmised that the word *constructive* had set his health and safety alarm bells ringing. 'No,' he said, 'but surely it's not too much to ask for someone paid to chase after criminals to be at least able to walk at a decent clip?'

'Have you considered,' asked Benny, with grave expression, 'the health and safety implications of requiring me to walk quickly?'

Povey opened his mouth and shut it. He then dug into his pocket, and slapped yet another sticker upon Benny's ample breast.

'You're shutting me down?' asked Benny.

'You're too bloody right I am shuttin you down!' shouted Povey. 'From now on yewer confined to the ruddy gardening section!'

Povey flounced back into the store. Benny winked at me.

Meanwhile, the policeman was now practically crying with pride as Beardmore continued massaging his delicate young ego. His chest was puffed out, his cheeks rosy, his eyes sparkling. Finally, he stood to attention, saluted Beardmore, clambered into his police van as if mounting a Spitfire in the Battle of Britain, and drove off, turning the opposite way down Whitehorse Road, I noted, to the fireplace felons.

Beardmore waddled back into the store and up the green metal stairs to his lair.

Douglas sat upon the bonnet of the Rolls Royce, peering around as if trying to figure out where he was. Povey reappeared holding a single black shoe, which he then fitted to Douglas's shoeless foot, muttering about steel toe caps. Lastly, he stuck a red sticker on Douglas's own shoe, some sort of ballroom dancing slipper. Douglas expressed thanks, and Povey returned inside.

'Hello, Douglas,' I said.

'Is today a bank holiday, Gareth?' he asked.

I told him it wasn't.

'And why is that, young man?'

'Because today is not deemed to be a bank holiday,' I said.

'What a wicked sense of humour you have, Gareth!' said Douglas.

'John,' I said.

'What a naughty and wicked sense of humour you have, John! Tell me, do you like puppies?'

I told Douglas I was allergic to dogs, and he looked disappointed. I made to leave, dusted Glyn off, and left Douglas supervising the car park. His Rolls Royce made me think of The Queen.

You would tell Her Majesty's Revenue and Customs, John.

16

THE LETTER AND THE PARK

It was nigh on lunchtime. I hid for a while in the toilets to think. Common to all places of employment, as far as the staff were concerned the toilets at Amundsen Enterprises were very much dual purpose. Today every cubicle was engaged with hiders and thinkers, and in the micro-society of the toilets there was a tacit understanding that if you kept quiet there was no harm done. I sat and regarded the graffiti gouged into my cubicle door. Much weighed on me. I thought over Benny's sound advice – to lower my sights – and reflected, with regret, how *all or nothing* I was. I thought about perfection. Someone in the next stall farted, and quickly apologised. So keen were we all to stay hidden, no one so much as tittered. What did I want? I wanted to tame chaos. I wanted somehow to sidestep losing the game of life by doing something really daring and dangerous. I would, I reflected, have been one of the doomed idiots who thundered into the valley of the shadow of death. I wanted to throw the die. Maybe I wanted to die.

I had an idea. I would write Beardmore a letter. I would detail his crimes in black and white (or blue; I only had a blue biro), and inform him that he could expect the day of judgement to be close at hand.

I stood, left my resting colleagues, and marched outside. Glyn, collecting trollies under the hazy early autumn sun, watched open-mouthed as I swiftly walked across the car park and up Whitehorse Road. I stopped at a newsagent and bought some writing paper – the only paper available had love heart emblems in the corners, but no matter. All set, I walked a little further to a small park which had once been William Morris's garden. I found a bench which looked out upon a kidney-shaped lake, upon which were ducks and Canada geese. They watched me.

'I have no bread,' I told them. Still they looked on with hope in their beady eyes. 'We can't just hope for change,' I said. A duck quacked. 'Quite,' I said. 'It's about being brave. I can't stand by, you know. I have to act.' One of the ducks, a brown hen, hopped out of the pond, and stood before me. 'They say bread is bad for ducks,' I said. The hen quacked. 'So why do you ask for it, then?' She said nothing. Yes, we were always hoping for things to improve. They seldom did.

I put pen to paper. This is what I wrote:

> *John Torrington*
> *Flat 7*
> *Clements Markham House*
> *Leytonstow*

Dear Eric

I know all about your corruption; how you do it, and where the money goes. I know about your "friends" in high places. But I know where you don't have friends, because they don't have any friends – Her Majesty's Revenue and Customs. If you don't stop it RIGHT NOW I will report you as a tax evader. They will crawl all over you, and you will go to jail.

> *Kind Regards*
> *John Torrington*

I folded the letter in half, placed it on the bench next to me, the ducks and geese still looking on. "Bread?" asked their faces. 'What do you lot eat, anyway, in the wild?' I asked. No one said anything. These fowl were as mute as Glyn. 'Say something,' I said. One quacked. Another up-ended.

I bade the ducks and Canada geese farewell and walked, legs like jelly, back to the superstore. Once again Glyn watched open-mouthed as I crossed the car park, holding a folded piece of paper. There was no time to lose. I walked inside, climbed the green metal stairs to Beardmore's lair, and slipped the letter beneath his door.

17

MY INTERVIEW WITH BEARDMORE

Twenty seconds later, the door at the top of the green metal stairs was wrenched open. Beardmore appeared in all his dismajesty, scanning the shop floor for one of his moppers-cum-trolley-pushers.

'TORRINGTON!' he bellowed, clutching the letter. 'WHAT THE FACK IS THIS?'

I walked out from behind a pillar – into the spotlight, as it were. 'Do you want to talk about it out here, or in private?' I asked, amazed at my cool.

I don't think he'd expected me to say this. He stood, blinking. Clouds of cigar smoke seeped out of his lair, silhouetting him against the tusk-yellow light of a sickly fluorescent tube. He looked like an extra-terrestrial standing at the doorway of a very retro spacecraft.

Customers and staff were soon wondering what was going on.

'What's going on?' demanded an old man waiting to pay for five bags of self-levelling floor screed.

Beardmore and I locked eyes.

'I want my sweeties!' shouted a toddler, breaking the silence. Polite laughter rippled up and down the checkouts.

'In 'ere,' grunted Beardmore, retreating into his cave. I swallowed hard and mounted the green metal steps. Here it was, the showdown at the DIY Corral.

Beardmore slammed the door behind us, and dropped into his faux-leather chair which emitted a rasping fart. He picked up a fresh cigar with fat fingers and stuck it in his filthy gob. I drank him in, flooded with powerful impressions. Here was a man at the zenith of his size, if not looks. As Beardmore searched his ash-strewn desk for a lighter, I fancied I could hear his brain ticking slowly behind the thick forehead plate. Hatred of the world leeched from his skin. Bitterness bubbled in his throat and his nose was blocked by black flowers. He must have weighed twice as much as me, this middle-aged, middle-spread, salt-and-pepper fiend of a middle-manager. As a youth he couldn't possibly have imagined he'd had the genetic code, or habits, to become this dark tower of pitiless manhood. I pictured a little old mother somewhere, hooked up to oxygen, puffing Superkings and spitting in an urn. I became aware I was re-exploring Beardmore, just as I had the car park.

My subject took a pull from the cigar, and took up my letter from the desk. He read and exhaled an Etna-like plume, then dropped the letter and stared at the peeling wall. I wondered whether he'd suffered a stroke.

'What the merry fack is that?' he asked.

'In what sense?' I asked.

'*In what fackin sense,*' he chuckled, balancing the cigar on the edge of an overflowing ashtray. 'Oh, you fackin well crack me up you do, Torrington, oh yes, good and fackin proper!'

He rubbed his pockmarked face, and let out a long sigh. *He's depressed*, I thought.

'You know, it's funny,' said Beardmore. 'I thought you'd be no fackin trouble, you and your weirdo mate. And 'ere we are. I only took you on coz I fort you was a simpleton. And cheap!'

'*Were* a simpleton,' I corrected.

'THAT'S WHAT I SAID, YOU FACKIN 'OMO!' yelled Beardmore.

'No, you said, "I thought you *was* a simpleton", there's a subtle difference, but it doesn't matter. Forget I said it.'

Beardmore rose from his chair. 'Are you being fackin funny?'

'Maybe, a bit,' I said, backing away.

'Just fackin remember, you little knob-jockey, I'm the brains of this outfit. Without me Douglas would be pushing up fackin daisies by now, which is what you'll be if you don't fackin watch it!'

'I am quite serious,' I said. 'Either you stop stealing from Amundsen Enterprises, or I tip off Mr Taxman. Oh, and you absolutely need to stop spitting at people too. It's disgusting!'

'It's good, eh?' he grinned.

'It's horrible! I can't believe what you did to Glyn this morning; it was the most disgusting thing I've ever witnessed.'

He commenced hawking. The problem with Beardmore's awful habit was that it was unspeakably vile, and therefore quite effective as a weapon. I felt myself under his spell. But there was nothing for it – I also began to hawk with great big reverberating sniffs. Beardmore stopped. 'What the fack you doin?' he asked.

'Preparing a pre-emptive strike,' I said.

''ave you lost your fackin marbles, Torrington?'

'Maybe I have...' I said quietly. I was amazed to see that Beardmore looked worried. I tried to build upon it. 'Eric,' I said, 'I am quite serious about telling everything to the taxman. You know that if you get investigated, you'll be put away.'

He said nothing. I tried hawking again, and he lunged at me. Luckily Beardmore was as out of shape as Benny, and as soon as he'd tried to punch me, he flumped down exhausted in the faux-leather chair, which again emitted a rip-roaring fart.

'I'll fackin kill ya!' he wheezed.

I've no idea where the idea came from, but I said, 'If you kill me, the tax people will know even sooner. I've written it all down, and given it to a friend. I've told my friend that if something happens to me, or I disappear, they must post the letter immediately to Her Majesty's Revenue and Customs.'

'Is it that fackin gaylord who works with ya?'

'Glyn? No, it's not him. But the same goes for Glyn – if anything happens to him, the letter gets posted.'

'Then it's fackin Benny!'

'Nope. Benny is also protected on the same basis.' I was on fire!

'You ain't got no more friends,' said Beardmore, 'and I fackin well know where you live. You can expect a visit from a good friend of mine. I'll call him right now.' Beardmore picked up the phone and began to dial. I tried the old hawking trick, but it seemed Beardmore had regained his composure. I'd put Gabby and the old men in terrible danger.

'Come on,' I said, 'you don't have to do that.'

He stopped dialling. 'Give me one fackin good reason why not.'

'I made up the thing about the letter being with a friend,' I said. 'It's just you and me.'

'Are you fackin sure?'

'Dead sure,' I said, wondering at my choice of words.

'Coz it only takes one call, and my associate will go and burn the place to the fackin ground, along with the fackin muppets inside. You get my drift?'

'I do,' I said. I found myself wondering what heavy metal track Gabby would play as flames licked around his tiny ankles, this being his likely response to an emergency – "Fight Fire with Fire" by Metallica?

'So?' asked Beardmore. We eyed each other. I still *had him* – he was still fearful that I would tell the taxman, good friend to nobody. I needed more time to think.

'I'm afraid I have no choice but to tender my resignation,' I said.

Beardmore nearly choked. 'What?' he said. 'Who do you think you are, the fackin PM? I can replace you with the click of a fackin finger! You're a warm body mate, nothin more! Tender your fackin... resignation!'

'I'm glad you find my role funny,' I said. 'I happen to think Glyn and I play an integral part in maintaining the smooth running of Amundsen Enterprises – just the opposite of you!'

'Which fackin loony bin 'ave you escaped from, yew little cant?'

'I'm perfectly sane, and you know it,' I said, 'in fact I believe I'm the sanest person working in this store.'

'I'LL POST YOUR P45 DOWN THE FACKIN SHITTER!' shouted Beardmore, 'AND WHILE YOU'RE AT IT, TAKE YOUR LITTLE BUMCHUM WIV YA!!'

'You're referring to Glyn?'

'You're fackin right I am!'

'God have mercy on you, Eric,' I said, and made to leave. I thought it was a great touch.

Then I turned back to him (like they do in movies) and said, 'By the way, Eric, you and I have something in common.'

'What the fack would I 'ave in common with a little cant like you?'

'We both like Gilbert O'Sullivan,' I said, and with that I was gone, leaving Beardmore mouth-agape, presumably reliving more melodic days before it all went tits up; re-exploring the past as I planned to re-explore the entire world, starting with Leytonstow.

18

I Break the News to Glyn

I ran into the car park and found Glyn mating trollies. He gave me a mournful nod. 'Glyn!' I said breathlessly. 'I've done it!' He looked me up and down, but said nothing. I said, 'I've got Beardmore under my spell!' He continued to stare. 'Come on, Glyn!' I said. 'Don't you want to know what it is?'

'It doesn't pay to pry,' he said. 'Besides, I'm scared of Beardmore, and don't really want to hear anything about him.'

'But this is good, Glyn! I wrote him a letter!' Glyn rested both palms on his thighs and began to retch. 'Don't worry, Glyn!' I said.

'It's – raaagh! – involuntary.'

Amid Glyn's automated retching I told him what I'd done – how I'd amazed myself in challenging Beardmore, and affected a fearlessness I'd hitherto not possessed; how I'd threatened Beardmore with Her Majesty's Revenue and Customs; how Beardmore had said he'd kill me, Glyn, and everyone at Clements Markham House; how I'd quit my job to buy thinking time, and finally how Glyn himself was, with immediate effect, fired.

Glyn stood bolt upright and stared at me.

'You got me the sack?' he said.

'Yes; sorry, Glyn.'

'I'm utterly unemployable,' said Glyn. 'How will I pay the rent? How will I buy food?'

'You're a good worker, Glyn!' I said.

'I'm not,' he said. 'I'm strange. People don't like me. I was lucky to get this job.'

'Oh, Glyn!' I cried. 'You underestimate yourself! You're a lovely worker. Anyway, look at Gabby. He gets along just fine.'

'I'm no sponger,' said Glyn. 'I believe that able-bodied people have a moral duty to work for a living.'

'Look, Glyn,' I said, 'you're missing the point! Don't you see what this means?'

'It means I will die, slowly, of hunger and depression. And while I know only too well that no one would care, and that I mean nothing to the world, nonetheless as an individual I'm not sure I'm yet ready to undergo what will in any case undoubtedly be my eventual manner of exit.'

'God, you're a cheery soul!' I said.

'I'm not,' said Glyn.

'Glyn, this is only one part of the story!' I said. 'It's started, don't you see? Beardmore is only one small cul-de-sac off the great path we're destined to take!'

'It would be understating things to say I remain unconvinced,' said Glyn.

'Glyn, remember what I said at the ice rink? Let's do it! Let's start re-exploring the world! Let's do it right now, this very minute!'

'To what end?' asked Glyn.

'To a million ends!' I said. 'And to exactly the opposite end you just forecasted!'

'You're saying that if we re-explore the world we won't die?'

'Yes. No. Oh Glyn, stop thinking about death! Let's live while we're alive!'

'Let's go to the Jobcentre,' said Glyn.

'Glyn, where we're going, we won't need Jobcentres!'

19

AN ATTEMPT TO FIND OUT THE NUMBER FOR DIRECTORY ENQUIRIES

We hit Dig Street. I say hit – Glyn slouched behind me like a Quasimodo lacking charisma.

Groups of gangly schoolgirls let out for their lunchtime chicken boxes stared, probing for sport. Slick young men in souped-up old cabriolets tooted their horns, whipped their fingers, and laughed at our cardigans and general demeanour. Pale crop-headed children sporting outsize Leytonstow Rovers football shirts nudged fag-drooping mothers who slackened skinny pram-pushing to regard us with bagged eyes.

'John,' said Glyn, puffing behind me.

'What?'

'I feel bad for everyone.'

'Bad?'

'Yes.'

'Bad in what way?' I asked.

'I feel sorry for them,' said Glyn.

'Why, Glyn?'

'They all look so happy and alive,' he said, then added, 'and they will all die.'

I stopped walking and leaned upon a red pillar box, being careful not to touch its guano-layered lid. 'Let me ask you this,' I said. Glyn stopped too, and bared his teeth. I continued. 'Are we a singular or collective consciousness?' I wasn't sure what I wanted to say, or where I was going with it.

'You and I?' Glyn asked.

'No,' I said, thinking further. 'Everyone. That bus driver. Those girls outside Chicken Hamlet. Are we all cosmically linked?'

'We're biologically linked,' said Glyn. 'The words "cosmically linked" mean nothing. It's like saying "Polar bears read the *Encyclopaedia Britannica*". The words can be said, but they mean nothing, because...'

'...polar bears don't read the *Encyclopaedia Britannica*,' I finished. He didn't like it. I could tell.

The group of girls passed us, and one flicked a chip. It struck Glyn on his forehead, before falling to the pavement; they laughed, and walked on down Dig Street.

I thought about accosting the girl, but reasoned that she'd flicked the chip to impress her friends. Yes, she needed to flick that chip, to ward off the anxiety dogging her – an unease based, whether she knew it or not, upon the knowledge she would one day die. Glyn was right. I quickly related it to him.

'You're suffering psychosis,' said Glyn.

My mind was whirring. The *Encyclopaedia Britannica*. Did it, or any other source of information, contain anything about young ladies flicking deep fried potato shards at ex-moppers, in this grid reference, or any for that matter? No, it most certainly didn't. Yet this occurrence was entirely possible – indeed had just happened – but the event was already lost to the past. Breathlessly, I told Glyn about our discovery, and added that if we only had a sketch pad, we could accurately portray the grease stain on Glyn's forehead, the spent chip on the floor, and thus begin to catalogue a myriad of unrecorded events to preserve for posterity every facet of the messy dynamism of humanity.

Glyn stared at me, wiped his forehead (in doing so possibly removing important historical evidence) and walked on down Dig Street.

'Glyn!' I said. 'What about the chip?'

'Compiling an alternative *Encyclopaedia Britannica* is an interesting enough idea,' said Glyn over his shoulder, 'but it won't pay our rent. We need to go to the Jobcentre.'

I followed him down Dig Street, trying not to lose my temper. 'Glyn!' I yelled.

But Glyn, wise old annoying Glyn, ignored me and kept lolloping along. I followed him and kept my gob shut for a bit, and this is how we went, until we came to a crossroads, and Glyn stopped in his tracks.

'Oh, God,' said Glyn.

'What?' I asked, casting around for the source of his anxiety. My eyes fell upon the deep purple façade of a sauna called Dark Secrets. As with all poor areas, in Leytonstow sexual services outlets were as commonplace as shoe shops, with no attempt made to hide them from view – just another part of the underlying permanent disquiet of inner-city life. 'Is it Dark Secrets?' I asked.

Glyn nodded. 'I want to visit,' he said. 'Badly.'

'Really?'

'Yes,' said Glyn. Then he added, unexpectedly, 'It's my civic duty.'

I wasn't sure what to say. For some reason, Beardmore popped into my mind. My thoughts since leaving Amundsen Enterprises had come full circle. I had a job to do. 'Listen,' I said. 'I'm going to call Her Majesty's Revenue and Customs, and to hell with the consequences!'

'The best consequence we can hope for is grievous bodily harm,' said Glyn, his tongue lolling, still gazing at the knocking shop.

I located a nearby payphone and pumped in some silver. I peeled chewing gum from the earpiece of the receiver, and dialled the operator. Nothing.

'What's the operator's number?' I asked Glyn.

'I don't think they have operators anymore.'

'Really? When did that happen?'

Glyn shrugged and coughed.

'Who do I call, then?'

'Whom.'

'Jesus, Glyn! You know what I mean!'

'I don't know.'

This was quite frustrating. I didn't know the number for Her Majesty's Revenue and Customs and I didn't know a number to call to find out the number to call. I left Glyn at the payphone and walked into a pound shop next to Dark Secrets.

I addressed a young cashier with piercings and make-up thick as an ice cap. 'I wonder if you could help me? If I want to call a number, but don't know the number, who do I call to find that number out?'

'What the fack you arksing me for?'

I smiled. 'Because I don't know, and I thought someone else might know.'

'Facks 'e want?' asked an older lady on the next checkout.

'Fack knows,' said the teenager.

'I did explain it quite clearly,' I said.

'Fink 'e's takin the piss,' said the young lady.

'Is 'e takin the fackin piss?' said the older woman.

'Are you takin the fackin piss?' asked the youngster.

'No, I'm not. I merely wanted to know...'

'Oi, Dobbo!' yelled the older lady.

Now I was being approached by a large young man affecting a gangsta rapper limp.

'Fack is it?' drawled this Dobbo.

''ave a fackin word,' said the older woman, jerking her thumb at me.

''e's takin the fackin piss,' said the young lady.

'Really, I'm not,' I said to Dobbo. 'I was planning to use the payphone outside, but I didn't know how to find out the correct number, so I thought I'd simply pop into the nearest shop and ask someone if they knew. It's nothing more than that.'

'Think it's a fackin phone shop?' asked Dobbo.

'No, I know it's not a phone shop,' I said. 'I asked a simple question, which should be relatively easy if you know the answer, but if you don't, then I'll be on my way.'

'Think we're fackin simple?' asked Dobbo, blocking my exit.

'No, of course not,' I lied.

'You a fackin copper?' asked Dobbo.

'No!' I said. 'But would it matter if I was?'

''e's a fackin copper,' said the older woman.

'Or a fackin batty boy,' added the teenager.

'God almighty!' I yelled. 'Can't I ask a simple question without being insulted?'

''e's clenchin 'is fist, Dobbo,' observed the older woman.

I looked down and indeed my fist was clenched. I unclenched it.

'You want some, do ya?' asked Dobbo. He grabbed my wrist, twisted it painfully, and dragged me towards the exit while the ladies said I was overwhelmingly gay. I was delivered to the street with a kick. Then I was on the deck.

'Look at that man!' said a passing kid.

'Cam on, Brandon!' shouted the boy's mother.

'But why's 'e layin on the floor?'

''e's a fackin piss 'ead,' said the mother, and they were gone.

Where was Glyn? I brushed myself off and walked to the payphone. Then, I was amazed to see Glyn Hopkins leaving Dark Secrets, clutching a scrap of paper. 'Here's the number,' he said.

'Glyn, what were you doing in there?'

'They're very helpful.'

96

I took the piece of paper and dialled the number.

'Which number, please?' asked the voice.

'Her Majesty's Revenue and Customs, fraud division, please.'

'Putting you through.' *Click.* It rang for a while, then someone picked it up. 'Hello, Majesty Fireworks, Leytonstow?'

'What?'

'Majesty Fireworks, Leytonstow, how can I help you?'

'I asked for fraud division,' I said.

'Well, you got Majesty Fireworks!'

'Do you know the number for Her Majesty's Revenue and Customs, fraud division?'

The line went dead. I pumped more silver in and dialled directory enquiries once more.

'Which number please?'

'Listen, last time I asked you for Her Majesty's Revenue and Customs, fraud division, and you put me through to–'

'Putting you through.' *Click.*

Someone answered. 'Hello, Majesty Fireworks, Leytonstow?'

'It's you again!' I said.

'You're not having much luck, are you, mate?' *Click.*

I stared at Glyn in disbelief. Then I dialled directory enquiries a third time.

'Which number please?'

'DO NOT PUT ME THROUGH TO MAJESTY FIREWORKS!'

'Putting you through.' *Click.*

'Hello, Majesty Fireworks, Leytonstow?'

'THIS IS A NIGHTMARE!' I shouted.

She laughed, and put the phone down.

I turned to Glyn, seething. I was ready to destroy the world, even the moon if needs be.

'Let me try,' said Glyn. 'You need to make them use their brains.'

Glyn dialled up directory enquiries. I pressed my head against his and listened in.

'Which number please?'

'I'd like to report a fraud.'

'Putting you through.' *Click.*

We listened again to the ring tone, then someone answered. 'Hello, Majesty Fireworks, Leytonstow?'

Glyn replaced the receiver in its holder. 'It didn't work,' he said.

20

THE BAND AND AN INVITATION

When Glyn and I turned into Erebus Road I was glad to see the familiar worn shape of Clements Markham House. I would go to my bedsit, have a lie down, and think. Benny was right. I needed to lower my expectations, accept the world, and limit my objectives. Perhaps I'd take up the guitar.

'What now?' asked Glyn.

'I'm going to have a lie down,' I said.

'I mean what now, in terms of work?'

Before I could answer I spotted a letter addressed to me on the dog shit-saturated welcome mat. It looked like a *nice letter*, from a person; not something I was used to. Glyn made a break for his ground floor lair, and I opened the letter as I walked up the stairs:

Dear John
I really enjoyed hearing what you had to say about patterns and the world yesterday. It made me laugh, but I also found it interesting. So, I wondered whether you'd like to come to a little soirée I'm holding at my place? I think my friends would like you. It's tonight – hope that's not too short notice. Look forward to seeing you, about seven thirty!
6 Bramble Cottages, Church Road, Leytonstow Village
Love,
Lois xx

Right there, on the stair, something dropped into my heart, and – to be fair – my loins. Something I'd hardly dared acknowledge: Lois. The pain! My legs turned to jelly, and I had to cling onto the bannisters for fear of passing out. She wanted *me* to go to her party! I somehow got to my room and put the key in the door. Once inside I pulled down my bed, and threw myself upon it like a middle-aged male Scarlett O'Hara.

Just then, the whole of Clements Markham House began to shake with deafening heavy metal, which did rather kill the love-boat mood. I'd completely forgotten: Monday was *band practice day*. As if Gabby's love of thrash metal wasn't bad enough, he also dabbled in musicianship with two friends, Marcus and Barney, young men of a similar disposition whom he'd met at Leytonstow Jobcentre on one of his trips there to get free money from Beryl.

I should have encouraged them, but it irritated me how seriously Gabby and his friends took *the band*. Of course, it wasn't lost upon me that this irritation was partially born of the fact that we weren't all that dissimilar – they emulated rock gods just as I did Scott of the Antarctic. For this reason alone, I should have been more tolerant. But for me, Scott was just a hobby, and I knew it. For Gabby, Marcus and Barney, on the other hand, *the band*, an entity with no financial (or musical) value whatsoever, represented a deeply serious, and imaginary, multi-million-dollar enterprise.

I sighed. The lads were simply having fun. I was an old bore. By way of penance I decided to pay them a visit. As I climbed the stairs to the top floor the waves of sound coming from Gabby's room became ever less tolerable. It was no use knocking; the door itself was hanging on for dear life. I opened it carefully. The effect was akin to explosive decompression at 35,000 feet. Gabby and his boys were headbanging in sync with such commitment and energy that it almost looked as if they were going for a circuit-training world record. Hard as it was to think, I realised they weren't actually playing their instruments, or singing – the drums were vacant, a guitar and electric bass leaned upon one of the remaining intact walls, the microphone stood unmanned on its stand in the centre of the room. Gabby waved at me, went to his stereo, and turned the volume down.

'John!' he yelled, jet black hair hanging down his face. 'You're just in time, man!'

'For what?'

'To hear us play!'

Marcus, a lanky lad of eighteen with boiling acne and frizzy hair in the manner of Art Garfunkel, stepped forward. 'But we still need to think of a name, Gab!'

'What's wrong with what I suggested?' said Barney, a small round fellow with a mouth which looked like it would break into a smile, but never did.

'Jesus Army and the Herods?' laughed Marcus. 'It's shit!'

'It's not,' said Barney, clearly crestfallen.

I sighed and waited for the next instalment of predictable idiocy. Their Monday band practices were always the same. First, they wound themselves up into a phantasmagoria of excitement by headbanging to earth-shatteringly loud metal. Secondly, they argued about what the band would be called. Next, Marcus and Barney tuned up their guitars for half an hour while Gabby pretended to adjust his drum kit, and got over how little they'd liked his own band-name ideas. Lastly, they attempted to play something for a few minutes, before getting bored, packing up, and heading to The Edgar Evans to tell Lois and the old men that they'd been signed to a famous label and were planning a world tour.

'What about The Wise Idiots, man?' suggested Gabby.

Marcus and Barney looked at each other and laughed. Gabby looked hurt.

'Can I make a suggestion?' I asked.

The three of them exchanged glances and smiled knowingly. Perhaps they would humour the layperson. 'If I were you,' I said, 'I wouldn't worry about the name. What you need to do is practise actually writing songs and making music. Once you've mastered that, and got ten or so songs under your belts, you can record a few of them, and send your CDs to pubs. If they like it, they'll ask you to do a gig, and somewhere within this essential process for a group of musicians to become a band, a name will present itself.'

The three of them stood hands in pockets, then Marcus said, 'What about The Vegan Cleavers?'

'Shit!' spat Barney.

It was no good. They would ignore my sound advice. I was every bit as much of a Cassandra as Benny. Plus, I could see the prospect of success terrified them. It was so much easier to play around the ordered outskirts of an ambition than it was to plunge into its chaotic centre. Gabby handed me a piece of paper covered in messy handwriting. 'Tell me which band names you like, man. I've put stars alongside the ones I came up with!'

I took the piece of paper and read:

Anus Mirabilis
Oblivion for Little Lads
Works Access
The Sofas*
The Field Band
The Morbidly Obese Stick Insect Kings
The Tasty Scotch Eggs*
The Shiite Crew
Extrapolate To Vacuum
Raised Ironworks
The Milf Whisperers
The Adhesive Shoes

If Only It Would Stop Raining I Could Nip To The Shops for Mam*
Tie Me Up and Talk To Me, Sweetie Pie
French Kissing in the UAE
Reg Vardy and the Maestros
The Nice Men*
The Maltese Fulcrums
The Bivouac Kerouacs
The Seawater Trio
The Loony Rovers
The Dandelion & Burdicks*

Gabby hopped with anticipation. Marcus and Barney tuned up their guitars with expressions of concentration. 'What do you think, man?'

'I think they are excellent names,' I said, then whispered, 'But I think yours are the best.' Gabby gave me a hug, before asking Marcus and Barney whether they'd finishing tuning, to which they shook their heads. Then he went over to his drum kit and started to fiddle with a cymbal. I decided to intervene, and walked over to Marcus and Barney. 'Let me hear your strings,' I said to them. They each strummed their open strings. I was no expert, but I could tell they were basically in tune. 'Right, you're ready to go. Now plug in, and get playing!'

'My A string needs more work,' said Barney, craning over the guitar to listen.

'It doesn't,' I said. 'It's fine. Do you know that many more accomplished bands than yours—'

'The Sofas!' said Gabby.

'No fucking way!' said Marcus.

'Forget the bloody names!' I said. 'More accomplished bands than yours have recorded whole albums with slightly dodgy tuning – it doesn't matter, especially for a practice! Stop messing around, and actually play something together. Come on, guys!'

Gabby counted them in with his sticks, and they launched into a mess.

'Guys, guys!' I stopped them. 'What is that? Which song are you playing?'

'We haven't got any songs, man,' said Gabby.

'We have!' said Barney. 'I've been writing them since I was ten.'

'Great,' I said. 'Play one of those, then.'

Barney blushed, which I could tell Marcus thought extremely uncool as it made him blush too.

'Play one, Barney, man!' said Gabby. 'We'd love to hear it!'

Barney looked at each of us, and sighed.

'You haven't got any, have you?' I said.

Poor Barney shook his head. Marcus started to tune up again. Gabby broke into furious drumming which I quelled with a wave of my hand.

'Make one up, then,' I said.

'What, now?' asked Barney.

'Yes, now!' I said. 'This is as good a time as any. You will never live this minute of your lives ever again, it's gone, so use it!'

'Hey John, man!' said Gabby. 'They sound like lyrics!'

'What do?' I asked.

'What you just said about how many more minutes we have to live!' yelled Gabby.

'No, I wasn't talking about how many more minutes, I was saying you need to use *this* minute, this unique minute, just like any other minute in the history of the universe, but one that just happens to be now, this minute!'

Gabby again launched into a frenetic thrash metal beat. I surmised he was expecting me to rap over it. Marcus and Barney started to play along, if that's what simply sawing at the strings and putting your fingers anywhere on the fret board can be called. They all then looked at me. Why not? I thought, and took the microphone. I started to sing, following as best I could the poor timing of Gabby and out of tune playing of Marcus and Barney.

'GET LOOSE!' I shouted. Gabby thrashed away at his drums and shot me admiring glances as I bellowed a further selection of rock clichés. It felt great! Marcus and Barney were putting more effort into headbanging than playing. Gabby had an unusual drumming style, speeding up and slowing down at random, or stopping entirely for several seconds to take sips of lemonade from a glass on his windowsill. Still, we had fun – the footing of any worthwhile hobby. I tried a bit of headbanging myself, but was quick to stop because I was no longer a young man.

After twenty minutes or so of thrashing, we came to a crashing climax of sound and the song ended. I was dripping with sweat. I felt thoroughly cleansed. Gabby, Marcus and Barney were threatening to explode with excitement and pride at their accomplishment. They began to smash their instruments up – Gabby putting his disproportionately large white basketball boots through his drums, and Marcus and Barney using their guitars like sledgehammers upon their amplifiers.

'GUYS! STOP IT!' I shouted, trying to grab them and the tools of their trade. It was no good. Success had made them uncontrollably high. In the end I sat on a stool and watched. It seemed they wouldn't be satisfied until there were no pieces left larger than an average paperback. Once everything was smashed beyond recognition, they fell to the floor laughing. Gabby still wore two drums like a pair of unwieldy shoes.

Now I waited for the next stage. It didn't take long.

'Jesus, what have we done?' yelled Marcus.

'My mum will kill me!' shouted Barney.

'You've celebrated your first proper band practice by

smashing all of your instruments,' I said. 'Therefore, it is your first proper band practice and probably your last.'

'It's OK, man!' said Gabby. 'We're rich!'

I looked at Gabby for any sign of sarcasm, but found nothing. I wondered how he'd come to this conclusion. Did he plan to present this scene of devastation before Beryl as a business plan? It was my fault. I'd whipped them up into a frenzy, taken them too near their goal.

Barney and Marcus wept as they swept up the pieces of their guitars. I felt for them. Gabby stomped all over the room trying to remove the shoe-drums. In the end he sat and I pulled. It reminded me of assisting him with his footwear at the ice rink. I suggested to them that we go and buy a slice of cake each, which appeared to cheer them a little. Gabby asked me for his pocket money, so with a sigh I pulled out my slim pay packet and gave him a ten pound note. 'Jesus, you're rich, man!' shouted Gabby. I held my pay packet open, 'Gab, I have two hundred pounds to show for two weeks of back-breaking early-rising abuse-filled work. I'd hardly say I was rich.' All the way to the café, Gabby went on and on about what a fool I was to work.

'I'm never going to have a job,' said Marcus contemptuously. 'Work's for saps.'

'Rock is a job,' said Barney, seemingly over the fact that he'd recently smashed any hope of becoming a paid rocker.

'It's a luxury,' I said, then decided to shut up. It wasn't worth it. Only time would teach these young cretins that the world did not, and avowedly would not, owe them a living. They were still, I saw, labouring under the misconception that the universe cared about their existence. But for now, in this minute, it was all about cake. Gabby waved the tenner and kindly told us the cake was *on him*. I laughed bitterly, and Gabby smiled at me innocently. Not only was I buying the cake, I was facing the probability of being once again guarantor to local shopkeepers if Gabby decided to stock up on, say, light bulbs, because one of his metal tracks suggested we'd all be overcome by napalm Tuesday week. I kind of hoped we would.

21

THE SOIRÉE

Having indirectly provided Gabby and his friends with cake; having briefly returned home to wash and change, I walked up Dig Street, bound for Lois's. I clutched a bottle of Romanian Merlot which had been on offer at £2.99 from Mahmood's Hypermarket; specially imported, so he told me, from his brother's booze-cruise lock-up in Ashford.

The address Lois had provided was in Leytonstow's only posh enclave, known locally as The Village – the original country village Leytonstow had once been before being swallowed by London's unstoppable tide. Like many parts of the capital, in Leytonstow rich and poor lived cheek by jowl, yet somehow these worlds did not collide; something which always puzzled me – it was as though the poor were happy to preserve the rich, and vice versa. Thus, after a turn off Dig Street it took me less than a minute to leave the inner-city with its tramps, litter, tat shops, and pavements stained with revellers' sick, and enter a different world, like stepping back in time: pretty cottages, topiary, posh cafés, exclusive restaurants, and, somewhere, Lois.

I was dressed in my best attire: a dark green polo neck recently acquired from a local charity shop – I thought it might befit Lois's impression of me as a philosopher, and just maybe, a Milk Tray-style lover – and a pair of beige chinos from that same shop, still with rock-hard pleats. My outfit was completed by a pair of sensible brown shoes, and as the minutes ticked by I became aware that rather than looking like a lover, I more accurately resembled a long-established member of the local Sex Offenders' Register. I stopped by a well-kept "George Reigns" post box – George Formby flicked across my mind – then pulled out Lois's letter, afraid there'd been a terrible mis-understanding. I forensically examined each sentence, looking for anything I might have misconstrued. No, there it was, plain as day, *"Look forward to seeing you, about seven thirty!"* I glanced at my watch – seven fifteen – and felt dizzy. The Indian summer evening was warm, the low sun glinting through the stained glass of Leytonstow Village church. On this pleasant quiet street, entirely devoid of hashish smoke, angry bus drivers, sex shops, and general disorder, I felt dan-gerously outside of my *milieu* (I knew this word, just as Lois knew the word *Schadenfreude*). I took several deep breaths, and tried to convince myself that going to Lois's soirée was no dif-ferent from seeing her in the pub. But it was no good. I actually felt sorry for Lois, that she'd singled me out, because I knew that at my core lay a black hole of nothingness. Such thoughts didn't place me in the party mood.

I found a row of pretty cottages opposite the church, their front gardens alive with well-kept shrubs and colourful blooms. Birds and insects (nice ones; not pigeons or fleas), thin on the ground in the poorer parts, abounded. Number six lay at the end of the row. My breathing ragged, I opened the garden gate, resisting a powerful urge to go home. I knocked, and within seconds the door swung open.

'John!' said Lois. I fancied that, 1950s pin-up chic aside, she could have comfortably graced a Constable. 'I'm so glad you're here. Come in, meet the gang!'

'I found you all right,' I muttered.

'Evidently,' smiled Lois. Then she added, 'I like your polo neck.' I studied her blemishless face to see if she was teasing. 'Are you OK, John?' she asked.

'I'm fi-ne,' I said, the word *fine* broken by an involuntary gulp, and Lois laughed.

'Don't worry,' she said. 'Garden's this way.'

She took my hand and led me through the cottage – the walls floor-to-ceiling with modern art – and I wondered if she knew this had never happened to me before. I knew what the word soirée meant, but I'd never been to one. A barbecue was in full swing – at least ten young faces examining me, girls and boys with flaxen hair and colourful flip-flops.

'Everyone!' said Lois, holding my hand aloft like a boxing referee. 'This is John!'

'*No Way!*' said the young people, seemingly in unison.

'I'm from the pub,' I said, jerking a thumb in the general direction of The Edgar Evans, as if to anchor myself. Several of them tittered and glanced at each other. I became acutely aware I'd greeted this happy garden scene wearing the most severe of expressions. I was a good fifteen years older than most of them.

'John's a philosopher,' said Lois. There was a force field of silence you could have dipped a digestive into.

A ruddy-cheeked and athletic young man who wore red jeans and a blue rugby shirt with white turned up collars clambered out of a sun lounger, and removed his shades. 'Hey, mate,' he said – he pronounced *mate* "made" – and shook my hand with an iron grip.

'John, this is Rufus,' said Lois. 'I'll just get you a drink. We're on Pimm's, if that's OK? *Roofie*, will you look after John, please?'

I was desperately trying to work out what *Ompimms* was. Perceptive as ever, Lois laughed. 'Pimm's,' she said. 'A drink. You'll like it.'

Lois disappeared inside, and Roofie, a good head taller than I, and quite a bit wider – in the right places – stood looking at me. Then he turned to his friends, and said, 'No! Way!

110

This bloge's never had Bimm's!'

There came a chorus of more *Nooo Waaaays* from around the garden.

A new song started up on the ghetto blaster, and all at once the assemblage appeared to launch into space. 'TUUUUUUNE!' yelled Roofie, and began to perform what looked like mock-breakdancing moves in the middle of the lawn. The rest of the boys and girls, including an equally Adonis-like specimen tending the barbecue, began to shout 'TUUUUUUUUNE!!' too, and dance. Uncomfortable in my staid brown shoes, I realised I was witnessing a group ritual based around the repeated affirmation that the song in hand was indeed *a tune*. I felt as if I were in a washing machine. One of the girls – she wore blonde dreadlocks and her nose was pierced with a ring like a bull's – grabbed me by the hand, led me into the melee, and urged me to dance. I wanted to die, but began to wiggle a little, to the general amusement of those around me. I'd forgotten how to dance, and could only think of "The Birdy Song" or "Hands, Shoulders, Knees and Toes". I found myself doing a lacklustre "Funky Chicken" as the song abruptly came to a close, and the young people performed high fives and special handshakes, before re-occupying sun loungers or picnic blankets. Another song followed and although, to me, it sounded identical to the last, no one said *Tune*! It was quite the mystery.

Where the hell was Lois?

Done with his breakdance-lite, Roofie lay back down on his sun lounger, pointed at me, and said, 'Hey, made, gome and tage the weighd off.' I couldn't see anywhere to sit, so sat on the grass at Roofie's feet, as if I were his batman. 'So, made,' said Roofie. 'Whad are you in?'

'Sorry?' I said.

'Whad are you in, made?'

'A... a polo neck?' I said, fingering the sweaty green band around my neck.

Roofie laughed long and hard, then Lois reappeared with my drink. 'I'm sorry, John,' she said. 'My mum called.'

'I just asked him whad he's in,' said Roofie, 'and he said a boloneck!'

Lois handed me the glass, and said, 'He's asking what you do for a living, John.'

'Oh!' I said. 'I'm in DIY.'

'Nice one, made,' said Roofie. Then, more confidentially, 'One of the bloges at my place has a redail bordfolio.'

I had not the faintest idea what Roofie was talking about, but my wonderings were set aside as Lois seated herself on the end of Roofie's sun lounger, and took his hand. Of course. I looked at them. In time they would probably have children, bright brimming crumbs of confidence.

'Are you going to try your Pimm's, John?' said Lois.

I considered the glass in my hand, having forgotten I was holding it. A reddish colour, with fruit and leaves floating in it. Was it a joke? I took a sip.

'You like it?' she asked.

I nodded, and said, 'It's quite tasty.'

Roofie laughed, then hailed the young man tending the barbecue. 'Hey, Boner, bring me a hod dog, and gome and meed this top bloge!'

Boner put down his tongs, put together a hot dog, and ambled over, brushing thick blond hair out of his eyes. 'Do you want Dommy K?' he asked Roofie.

'Good call, made,' said Roofie. Boner returned to the barbecue, squeezed a strip of ketchup, returned, and handed the hot dog to Roofie.

'Hello, made,' said Boner to me. 'Whad are you in?'

Determined to be taken seriously this time, I told him I was in DIY, then asked what he did.

'Pensions, made,' said Boner.

'You work in a post office?' I asked.

'NOOO WAAAAY!' yelled Boner, and he and Roofie high fived.

'They work in finance,' said Lois. Then she added, 'John is an expert on polar exploration.' Then to me, 'Tell us about the time Sir John Franklin had to eat his boots, I love that one!'

Shamed in body and soul, I said, 'He and his party were so hungry they had to eat their boots.'

Lois looked at me, head tilted. 'You told it so beautifully in the pub, John. We were all in stitches.'

Boner pointed at my sensible brown leather shoes. 'Thad explains the brogues, made!'

'I'm unable to be myself,' I said, wanting to cry.

'Whad *are* you, made?' laughed Roofie.

'OK, enough!' said Lois, letting go of Roofie's hand, and standing. 'I told you to be nice to John!'

The need to be defended. I felt as small as it is possible to feel. 'I think I'll be off,' I said, and stood.

'Off to Greenland, made?' asked Boner. Roofie didn't laugh this time. Someone asked for another *hod dog*, and Boner returned to the barbecue.

'Come on, John,' said Lois. 'Let's go for a walk.' She took my hand and led me into the house. Roofie looked crestfallen – up until then I hadn't realised his face could pull such an expression.

Out on Church Road, the bells were ringing. I felt like a lovesick teenager, and Lois appeared to float in a mist over the tastefully worn old-world paving slabs.

'I'm sorry about them,' said Lois. 'They don't live around here. They don't know *how things are*.'

How *were* things?

'Don't worry,' I told her. We walked.

'He's not so bad,' said Lois. 'On his own he's not like that at all. But get him together with Boner, and they're a night-

113

mare. They don't know how to *be*. They boast, and belittle.'

I dropped the question. 'Why are you with him, then?'

She looked at me, and sighed. 'We were at uni together,' she said. 'My parents really like him. His dad is a High Court judge. Our mothers have become friends. I think they want us to marry.'

'Oh,' I said.

Lois stopped walking, turned to face me, and took me gently by the shoulders. 'What about you, John? Do you have someone special?' I thought about Gabby and Glyn, both of whom were pretty *special*, as they say. I told her I didn't. 'But you've so much to offer, John!' said Lois.

'You think?' I asked.

'Yes! You're knowledgeable and clever, and funny, and kind. Lots of women would like you.'

I looked into her eyes for a second too long and saw, suddenly, that she *got* it. Her face morphed into an expression of sympathy. There it was, plain as day: I was a charity case. The thought that she and I *might* hadn't even crossed her mind. The church bells rang out across the street.

'I'm a lot younger than you, John,' she said softly.

We stood facing each other. I was aware *this was the moment* – I should lean in and kiss her. My gut told me it was what we both wanted. Instead, I took her hand, and stood stock still amid the bells and birdsong. Little seed wisps floated between us.

'Do you love Roofie?' I asked.

'I should go back in,' she said. 'After all, it's my party.'

'Of course,' I said.

'I'm sorry,' she said.

'It's all right,' I said. 'I'm a fool.'

'We're all fools,' sighed Lois. She embraced me, kissed my cheek, and walked back to the cottage.

I walked home in tears.

TUESDAY

115

22

THE SACK OF
CLEMENTS MARKHAM HOUSE

My dreamless sleep was disturbed by the sound of splintering wood and shattering glass.

'Feck it,' said a voice.

I opened my eyes and saw someone standing outside the remnants of my window, grappling with a metal pole; someone I faintly recognised.

'So sorry to wake you, my friend, is that OK?' said the man.

The Gaffer of the tail-lift fiasco! Another face appeared, a younger man; the one who'd ruined his trainers by being pinned to the floor. 'Morning, mate!' he said.

'Morning,' I said, climbing out of bed. It then occurred to me that the men were apparently standing on thin air as my flat, number seven, was on the first floor.

I walked over to the broken window and peered out. Up and down, Clements Markham House was festooned with scaffolding.

'What's going on?' I asked.

'We're here doing a bit of work for The Big Man,' said the Gaffer.

'*The Big Man*?'

'Mr Kapoor,' said The Gaffer. 'Three more floors and a penthouse, is that OK?'

'Three?' I said.

'Maybe you'll be kind enough to put the kettle on for the lads?'

Still half asleep, I duly reached for my kettle and flicked the switch.

'Very kind,' said The Gaffer. 'We'll sort your window out, so we will, is that OK?'

'What do you mean by *three more floors*?' I asked, realising simultaneously I'd no mugs, tea, coffee, milk, or sugar.

The Gaffer pointed upwards with a hairy finger. 'Three more floors; six more studios, and a penthouse, is that OK?' he winked.

'What about the planning department?' I asked.

'They got enough floors already.'

'No, I mean planning permission. You can't just plonk three more floors on top of a beautiful Edwardian villa.'

'You'll have to ask The Big Man about that, so you will,' said The Gaffer. 'Now, we'll all have a nice brew, is that OK?'

I began to admit that I had none of the requisite ingredients for constructing anything other than a nice-hot-water-in-the-hand, when there was a knock at my door. In walked Glyn, wearing a singularly worried expression.

'Glyn?' I asked.

'Albert Speer last night,' he said, 'and now this.'

'Wasn't he...?'

'Hitler's architect, yes. He told me Hitler had decided Clements Markham House was perfectly positioned to allow the Hitlers to go *Up West*, while affording easy access to the Epping Forest, which Hitler admires.'

'Glyn, you *are* dreaming about these people, aren't you?' I asked.

'No, I'm afraid not,' he said sadly.

'I see.' I saw.

'It's weird, isn't it?' asked Glyn, a deep frown etched across his sizeable forehead.

'It's... unusual,' I said.

Gabby walked in, wearing an expression in direct counterpoint to Glyn's. 'John!' he yelled. 'They're fixing my hole, man!'

I thought about the "mirror-sized" hole Gabby had reported. 'Come here, Gab,' I said. We peered out of the window. 'Don't you think this is a bit excessive for mending your hole?'

Gabby had other concerns. 'Did they have scaffolding in Saxon times, man?'

I asked him what he meant.

'The men who built this place, man, back in Saxon times. Did they have scaffolding?'

'Clements Markham House is *Edwardian*,' corrected Glyn.

It is relevant to note at this juncture that Gabby's general education was born of his prolonged exposure to rock folklore; thus his appreciation of history and what happened when, where, and with whom, was rather sweeping, mixed up, vague, prejudiced, and a little bizarre.

'Gabby,' I said, 'these men are engaged in the process of effectively *destroying* Clements Markham House.'

'Destroying it?' said Gabby, his baby-blues widening. 'Aren't they going to move us out first?'

'Gab, who are *they*? Who are these kindly people who are looking after our best interests, and who might decide to move us to safety if matters reach a predetermined threshold of danger?'

'I dunno, man,' said Gabby. 'The Council?'

'Do you see any of their representatives here, to save us?'

Gabby looked at Glyn hopefully, who shook his head.

'The people in the Jobcentre?' suggested Gabby, pointing at its back wall across the railway line.

'Gab, their job is to find *you* a job, not gauge whether your living conditions are adequate.'

'Really?' said Gabby. 'But Beryl pays my rent.'

'Oh Jesus, Gab, we've been over this before. Where does Beryl get the money from?'

'The Council?' suggested Gabby.

'She gets it from me and Glyn, Gabby,' I said, indicating our respective heads.

'You two? I thought you worked in the DIY place?'

'We *did*,' mourned Glyn.

'Yes, we did, and we paid tax, and do you know where that tax went?' Actually, we hadn't paid tax, as we'd both earned well under the taxable threshold, but my point stood as I was perfectly willing to pay tax were someone to offer me an executive post.

'The Jobcentre?' asked Gabby.

'No, the government,' I said.

'But I don't get it from the government, silly!' said Gabby. 'I definitely get it from Beryl.'

'Where does Beryl get it from?'

'The Council?'

'Who in turn get it from the government, who are funded by tax paying individuals like Glyn and me!'

Gabby smiled. 'No, man, Beryl gets it from her computer. It's amazing! She presses a button and it goes into my account!'

I slapped my forehead, and reached out as if to shake Gabby to death, but Gabby thought I was giving him another hug – we looked like an exhausted couple at the end of a 1920s dance-a-thon. 'Forget it!' I shouted. 'JUST FORGET IT.'

'Man, I can't believe you thought Beryl got it from some government!' laughed Gabby.

'Back to the house, Gab,' I said, gesticulating at the poor proud masterpiece surrounding us. 'This building is already beautifully proportioned, a natural outcrop of human con-sciousness, a brick and mortar calling card of the requirements and dreams of our forefathers, little less than a mini-cathedral of purpose-built habitation demonstrating man's then self-ordained elevated placement of himself in the grand scheme of things!'

'But it's not fair that some of them lived in mud huts, and some of them lived in places like *this*,' said Gabby.

'Forget the bloody Saxons!' I yelled. 'The house is Edwardian, Gab, *Edwardian*. Not Saxon!'

'Cool down a tad, John,' said Glyn.

But Gabby wasn't done. 'So these Edwardithingys built the place for them, man?'

I bit my tongue, and attempted to pity poor Gabby. 'Clements Markham House,' I said slowly, 'was built in 1902, when King Edward VII was on the throne. This was a time of immense expansion. London was growing in all directions, indeed at times must have resembled one gigantic building si–'

'Any sign of that brew, now, lads?'

I turned to see The Gaffer once more leaning upon my windowsill. He was looking afresh at me. 'I thought I knew you, so!' he said. 'Amundsen Enterprises!'

I nodded.

'And what is it you do dere?'

I coughed the word *manager*.

'I thought you got the trollies from the car park?' said Gabby, helpfully.

'Yes, that too,' I said, reddening.

'It's a fine job, that,' said The Gaffer. 'It's a man's job, so it is.'

'Yes, I agree, it's an essential role,' I said.

'I bet girls could do that job, too,' said Gabby.

'Do you know Beardmore?' asked the pleasant gaffer.

'Yes, I do,' I answered.

'A dorty fecker, and no mistake!' said the perceptive

120

gaffer. 'We did a few jobs for him a couple o' three year ago. Did me up, down, and over, so he did.'

'Sounds like Beardmore,' I said.

'How about Douglas?' asked The Gaffer.

'He's still *in charge*,' I said, and winked, not lost on the quick-witted Irishman, who laughed heartily, slapped his thigh, and repeated *Is that OK?* several times.

'Now, if you lads could do a little thing for me, it would be grand,' said The Gaffer, a crafty look in his hazel eyes.

'Sure, man!' chirped Gabby.

'Gab,' I said, 'we don't know what it is yet.'

The Gaffer leaned upon the window frame, took a cigar from his top pocket, placed it between his lips, and at length lit it. He took a big puff and blew the smoke into my room. Glyn and Gabby coughed, and The Gaffer fixed my eye. 'You wouldn't do marble fire surrounds now, would you, lads, at Amundsen Enterprises?'

'Yes, we... *they*... do,' I said, perplexed, aware he was studying my body language.

'Grand. Now, do they ever get slightly... damaged?'

'Only when Beardmore chips them ever-so-slightly-on-purpose and squirrels them away to sell at a knock-down price for his own pocket,' I said.

The Gaffer chuckled. 'Now, does anything else get... damaged?'

'Yes,' I said, 'practically everything.'

'Terrible, terrible...' said The Gaffer, shaking his head. 'Well lads, I think I might have just the solution, is that OK?'

'We're all ears,' I said.

'And noses too,' said Gabby, gripping his.

'You see, Paddy's Poles – that's the name of this here firm, so it is – has decided to do a little more for the community, is that OK?'

'Really?' I asked.

'Now,' said The Gaffer, 'what's your favourite local charity, lads?'

'Adrian's Autos on Fairlop Road?' suggested Gabby.

'Gab, that's a second-hand car dealership!' I said. 'I can't think of a less charitable organisation.'

'The Council?' suggested Gabby.

'I like the RSPB,' said Glyn.

'My favourite charity shop,' I said, 'is the PDLA on Leytonstow High Road.' I'd recently found a fine biography of Fridtjof Nansen there.

'Ah yes, lads, a fine charity that... what did you say it was?'

'The People's Dispensary for Lonely Animals,' I said.

'What do you know, lads?' said The Gaffer, grinning. 'That's one of the charities on Paddy's Poles' list! Is that OK?'

'Is it?' I said.

'Now, lads, if you do come across any... damaged items, Paddy's Poles would be prepared to take them off you, to give to the People's Dispensary for Lovely Animals, is that OK?'

'*Lonely*,' I corrected.

'Bless you, laddie,' said the kind gaffer.

What was going on? I started to feel like I'd unearthed a giant black market based primarily on chipped marble fire surrounds. I told The Gaffer it was unlikely I'd come across such items, seeing as I'd quit. He seemed unconcerned, puffed contentedly on his cigar, and even expanded upon his tax affairs. 'Now, lads,' he said, 'there's method to me madness, so there is. You see, if you did come across any shop-soiled items in the near future, I'm proposing a win-win deal: Paddy's Poles buys them, gives them to charity, and the donations are deductible from our corporation tax, is that OK?'

'I don't know,' I said. 'Is it?'

'That's what the taxman says, so he does!' smiled The Gaffer.

First marble fire surrounds, and now *Her Majesty's Revenue and Customs*! I peered into the wily eyes of The Gaffer. Could it be that Beardmore had already dispatched his heavy?

'Giving to charity is a common form of tax evasion, and sometimes money laundering,' said Glyn.

'Glyn!' I said, which drew a surprised cough. Then I turned to The Gaffer. 'We'll think it over, Mr....?'

'Finnegan is the name,' said The Gaffer. 'But you can call me Paddy.'

With that, he flicked away his cigar, and went back to work. I felt dismayed that even a charity shop might be embroiled in this web of lies.

I thought back to what Glyn had said. 'Glyn? How come you know about tax evasion?'

He blushed. 'It was in a TV drama.'

I told Glyn I'd have a shower (in the sink) and we'd go to the Jobcentre to plot our next move. Gabby said he had some important music to play. When they'd both returned to their rooms, I sat on my bed and thought sadly about my resolution to change the world. The weight of freedom sat on my back like a sloppily-packed rucksack. My dreams now appeared paper-thin – I could no more change the world than peel the sun like an orange. I thought too about the scaffolding outside, Gabby's hole, Paddy's references to Mr Kapoor, a.k.a. *The Big Man*, Beardmore, and "shop-soiled" items.

But it was hard to think. Gabby was playing Sepultura so loudly that Paddy Finnegan again stuck his curly head back through my window and said his men were threatening strike action over it, so they were.

There was another knock at my door.

23

A LITTLE LIGHT ENTERTAINMENT

'What is it, Gab?' I said to the door, with a sigh.

'May we come in, Mr Torrington?'

Oh God. I went to the door and peered through the peep-hole. There stood the beatific Mr Kapoor and his shifty-look-ing little heavy (and nephew), Indeep, accompanied by a handful of my defeated-looking elderly neighbours.

'I'm in a state of undress!' I said.

'I'll give you five minutes, Mr Torrington,' said Mr Kapoor. 'You need to have the money ready.'

Rent day. As if we'd been sold down the river, all thirteen occupants of Clements Markham House had been sublet to Mr Kapoor by a much-pressed housing association eager to lose weight, and, it now struck me, quite possibly for tax pur-poses of their own. I'd have to run it past Glyn. If they were after a landlord who didn't mind receiving low rents, some-what infrequently, in return for supplying horrid bedsits ("studios") which were never cleaned, maintained, or certif-icated, they had hit the nail on the head with Mr Kapoor, who, excepting the irksome task of actually collecting rent from his tenants, was onto a pretty good thing.

He was, when he could prise it out of us, the indirect recipient of a small fortune in housing benefits, and lived in some style in a much-extended semi in Chingford. But word was that it wasn't enough. Old Brian, a sick ex-milkman and one of our neighbours, had led me to believe that Mr Kapoor had a plan; impatiently waiting out the demise of his long-term, and for the most part elderly, protected tenants, so he could then gather in a gaggle of young professionals at six times the rent. Mr Kapoor, according to Old Brian, was waiting for us to die.

Kapoor treated me with seemingly earnest-enough respect. He knew I was somewhat educated, and this appeared to impress him. In truth I'd once attended a minor polytechnic for the first term, only to be thrown out for having never once left my room. Whenever Mr Kapoor's path crossed mine, he would perform a sort of mocking bow and enquire, *How is my graduate?* Then he would set his pit bull-like nephew Indeep upon me to squeeze out money; a mixed reception.

Mr Kapoor and I enjoyed a voluminous correspondence. Currently I owed a total of £200, or four weeks' rent, which I had accrued by only paying £30 per week for ten weeks. In response to polite letters enquiring as to when I planned to make good my debt, I would write back in the most impressive scholarly terms, citing Freud, Jung, Tolstoy, and Pieter Bruegel the Elder's *Massacre of the Innocents*, cleverly suggesting the calculations were in error, and that fluctuations in the stock market, the alignment of the planets and the oscillating price of gold alone rendered it not really worth pressing.

This didn't wash with Mr Kapoor, who wrote back on paper with hand-coloured red borders, citing advanced calculations and enclosing photocopied receipts to back up his assertions. I would reply claiming that his photocopier was either faulty or his eyes were playing tricks on him, and had he considered getting a diabetes test? Strangely, this worked to delay things to a degree as long as I tacitly accepted that Mr Kapoor's little bruiser, Indeep, had free rein to assault me during their visits, as if I were paying the arrears back in pain, a hard currency in itself.

Gabby's music abruptly ceased. It could only mean one thing: Mr Kapoor had gained entry. Poor Gabby! I could see him cowering in the corner of his record-strewn room, whimpering like a neglected hamster. I picked up my slim pay packet, and flicked through the contents – £190 – everything I possessed in the world. Damned if I was going to give it to Mr Kapoor!

Shouts and squeals from above told me Indeep had got to work. I knew Gabby's style – he would be trying to throw them off the scent by telling them he knew someone called Beryl who would give them all the money they wanted. Soon, many pairs of boots clattering down the stairwell told me I was next. Sure enough, there was a firm knock at my door.

'Let us in, Mr Torrington, if you please!'

I searched the floor for a trapdoor I knew wasn't there.

'Just open the door, innit!' shouted Indeep.

I opened up and there stood a smiling Mr Kapoor and a scowling Indeep, a tearful Gabby, a mournful Glyn, and a shambling mess of our fellow tenants: yawning old boys with snow-white seven-day beards, wrapped in whisky-stained blankets. Indeep made to punch me in the stomach. I bent double like a circus man catching a cannonball, but his uncle raised a placating palm. 'Good morning, Mr Torrington,' he mock-bowed. 'How is my graduate?'

'Impecunious,' I answered.

'Bender!' spat Indeep.

'Due to my being impecunious?' I asked him.

'I see you haven't lost your sense of humour, Mr Torrington. Now, if we might come in for a few moments please, to discuss your arrears.'

Mr Kapoor leisurely walked into the middle of my room and rocked slowly upon the heels of his expensive shoes. Indeep darted about, inspecting what little I owned. Mr Kapoor again raised his palm, and tugged absent-mindedly at a spotted handkerchief tucked into the breast of his fine pinstriped suit.

'Nice weather we've been having,' I suggested.

'Ah, the weather, the weather,' said Mr Kapoor, now dabbing his nose with the handkerchief.

'John!' cried Gabby. 'Just give Mr Kapoor the hundred and ninety quid you've got, man! I'll look after you!'

Both Indeep and his uncle found this very funny indeed.

'Thanks, Gab,' I said.

'It's OK, man,' said Gabby.

An old duffer at the back of the little ensemble giggled.

Mr Kapoor returned the handkerchief to his pocket and pointed at the broken window. 'I see you've added some ventilation, Mr Torrington.'

As I attempted to relate the morning's events to my ever-attentive landlord, Indeep made another sweep of my belongings. I broke off my tale of woe as he began to delve into my little box of personal papers.

'What the fuck is this?' asked Indeep, holding up a ream bound with green elastic bands.

'It's John's novel, man!' wept Gabby. 'About what Captain Scott would have done if he'd found something weird at the South Pole!'

'Ah, the South Pole,' said Mr Kapoor.

'What are these ones?' asked Indeep, pulling out loose sheets of foolscap and throwing them into the air like over-size tickertape.

'My poems,' I said. 'You can take them in lieu of the rent, but it's your risk; they might be worth a million pounds, or nothing at all.'

'Or just a couple of quid, man,' added Gabby helpfully.

This also amused Mr Kapoor. 'Yes, Mr Torrington, I'll take your poetry as a down payment. Might you do us the honour of reading some?'

Gabby dropped to the floor, crossed his legs, and gazed at me. Glyn retched a couple of times before getting himself under control. Indeep spat in my sink. An old boy lit up a fag. Mr Kapoor folded his arms and tilted his head to one side. I retrieved a few sheets and cleared my throat.

'OK,' I said. 'This is a haiku, but it doesn't have the right number of syllables.'

'Shit!' said Indeep.

'I love it, man!' sang Gabby.

'That wasn't the poem!' I said. 'Just my little preamble.'

'Take your time, Mr Torrington,' crooned Mr Kapoor.

I took a deep breath, and let them have it.

I am like the Forth Rail Bridge
In that I must be constantly painted
With love.

Both Mr Kapoor and Indeep stared, before glancing at each other and roaring with laughter. 'Oh dear, Mr Torrington!' cried Mr Kapoor. 'Priceless! Another, please!'

Despite myself, I began to brim with pleasure. A gig was a gig. I read another:

A DIY store is like life
It contains everything one needs
But not in the same aisle

'Unless you're just after wood, man!' said Gabby, moved to tears.

Mr Kapoor laughed so much he had to take out his handkerchief again. 'More, please!'

When my landlord roars up, in his four-wheel drive
I think about the environment
And cry

128

'I told you he's a fuckin bender, innit!' said Indeep.

'No, no!' said Mr Kapoor. 'Tears are the mark of a man!'

Presumably bored with the arts, Indeep strode over and held out his hand in the expectation of hard currency. I picked up a saucer from the draining board and placed it neatly upon his palm, which my audience found quite funny – a coda to my recent performance. Indeep let the saucer drop to the floor, then actually did punch me in the stomach.

24

THE LITTLE BANKER

Having handed over all the money I had in the world, we left Paddy directing the sack of Clements Markham House, and commenced our monthly forced march to NatEast Bank in Leytonstow town centre. Indeep drove us like sheep down Erebus Road, and Mr Kapoor, hands clasped behind his back and apparently deep in contemplation, walked at the head of the convoy as if out for a gentle Sunday stroll. What a sight we were! – in various states of undress, bent double and moaning like a procession of flagellants – Indeep dancing up and down our ranks threatening martial arts performances worthy of the Olympics. Gabby wept loudly all the way, his lank hair hanging over his eyes, and frequently stumbling over his disproportionately large basketball boots. Glyn looked as if he were riding a D-Day landing craft. Our neighbours, the old men, moaned and groaned as if penning the soundtrack to a Hieronymus Bosch.

I watched over them as best I could, helping up the old and the lame (the majority), irritably ordering Gabby to stop crying, telling Glyn his retch mechanism was simply a state of mind, attempting to reason with the totally unreasonable Indeep, and appealing to Mr Kapoor's better nature. As such, I ran to and fro like a harassed infantry officer, barking here, cajoling there, sympathising and arguing by turns, and encouraging my fellows to sing heart-warming songs to keep their spirits up. Some of the older men had not seen daylight for a month, and peered nervously at the sky as if half-recognising an old friend. We were quite the spectacle, and I appealed to the shoppers of Leytonstow to find it within their hearts to intervene – that shaven-headed bruisers might repel Indeep, that old ladies might hit Mr Kapoor with their handbags – but my words went unheeded; rather they gawped or laughed, or both, at our shuffling misery. An evil-looking kid threw a coin which glinted through the air before felling a man at the rear.

'Mr Kapoor!' I shouted. 'We're being attacked!'

'Don't panic!' yelled someone.

Mr Kapoor raised his hand and the procession halted outside a fast food joint. Glyn stood some way off, looking at the sky. Gabby ceased wailing and looked on, terror-stricken, mascara running down his cheeks like Hiro-shima's black rain. I knelt by the man felled with the coin – it was Old Brian – and cradled him Nelson-like in my arms (or maybe it was a half-Nelson).

Mr Kapoor strolled over. 'What a beautiful day it is,' he said, smiling and taking deliberate breaths as if he were taking air on the sundeck of a cruise ship.

'Look what you've done!' I cried, dabbing the cut on Old Brian's head with the cuff of my cardigan.

'Gentlemen,' said Mr Kapoor evenly. 'Do you suppose I am your benefactor? Are you labouring under the mis-apprehension that it is my calling to provide you with free accommodation?'

'Isn't that what landlords do, man?' whispered Gabby to me.

Old Brian cleared his throat and delivered a large yellow globule which just missed Mr Kapoor's left foot. 'I paid my taxes, you bastard!' he said in his old man's warble.

Glyn took a break from staring at the sky. 'I don't think you've paid much tax in recent years, because you told us you've been on the sick since nineteen eighty.'

Old Brian blushed. 'I got banned from driving the milk floats. What was I meant to do?'

'Deliver lemonade, man?' suggested Gabby.

'No, Gab,' I said. 'He was banned from driving, and lost his job.'

'And my wife and kids, house, car, everything!'

'Taking a drink is a very risky business,' said Mr Kapoor.

Then Gabby began to bob up and down, and with sinking heart I made a wild guess that a free-money plan was being hatched. I wasn't wrong.

'I know!' he shouted. 'Let's *all* go and see Beryl in the Jobcentre!'

'Beryl?' said Mr Kapoor. 'And what might this Beryl do for me?'

'She'll give you all the money you want, man!' yelled Gabby, jumping on and off the kerb.

'Let me get this straight,' said Mr Kapoor. 'You are asking me to sign on at the Jobcentre in lieu of your rent?'

'Yes, he is,' I interjected, 'but he doesn't know what he is talking about.'

I decided to take matters into my own hands, and clambered onto a bench outside the fast food joint to address my bedfellows and the citizens of Leytonstow at large.

'My fellow residents!' I said. 'You might have noticed that Clements Markham House, our home, has today come under attack!' Ninety-five per cent of those gathered looked at me blankly, the other five per cent had cataracts. I went on. 'I propose that we carry on to the bank in an orderly fashion, give Mr Kapoor what he wants, then visit the planning office at the town hall to launch a protest!'

Mr Kapoor took out his handkerchief, wiped his eyes and chuckled. 'It sounds like an excellent plan, Mr Torrington.'

'Doesn't it concern you just a little?' I asked plaintively, stepping down from the bench.

'No, Mr Torrington,' said Mr Kapoor, 'because they will produce exactly what was sent to me only last week...' He removed a letter from his jacket pocket, and handed it to me. I quickly scanned it in disbelief: *planning permission granted – three extra floors – penthouse – renovation of existing studios...*

'We'll soon see about this!' I said, then realised that only myself, Mr Kapoor, Indeep, Glyn and Gabby remained, our colleagues having escaped into the fast food joint.

'We'll give them a breather,' said Mr Kapoor.

Our rest stop complete, we continued to the bank without further ado. I sensed a palpable nip of autumn, and despite all circumstances I began to interrogate the scene with interest, forgetting momentarily I was a prisoner. Re-exploring, I let my eyes roam freely, and observed birds going about their business from rooftop to tree to mobile phone mast. I saw schoolchildren flock around the local chicken shop bullying weaklings, old women dragging tartan shopping trollies overflowing with tired-looking root vegetables, workmen leaning upon spades cracking politically incorrect jokes, drug dealers standing furtively on street corners pretending not to be drug dealers and failing miserably, ill-tempered postmen stroking stubble while trying to decipher spidery handwriting, book-clutching pseudo-intellectuals watching the bustling street with sad expressions of historical dynamism, and beautiful

133

young ladies pouring all concentration into not falling off impractically high heels.

We were directed by Indeep to form a queue at the NatEast cashpoint and one by one optimistically inserted cards of all types in the vain hope that the bank might have made a decimal-point error and filled our accounts with money. Any cash dispensed was grabbed by Indeep and pocketed. The machine broke down after one of my colleagues inserted a scrap of paper upon which was written *Please can I have a few quid*. Indeep clipped the culprit, and shepherded us inside to do some personal banking, where all but one of the cashiers swiftly drew down their blinds, presumably deciding it was high time to grab lunch. One operative remained, a spotty youth. I approached, handed over my bank card, and wished him a good day.

'What can I do for you, sir?' he shrilled in his best voice, clearly rather excited at the prospect of holding the fort.

I turned to Indeep and told him I had less than zero in my account. Indeep looked around furtively and smirked at the cashier. 'He needs money, innit.'

'Yes, sir!' said the youth, before proudly showing us a drawer full of cash. 'How much do you want?'

Mr Kapoor chuckled and sauntered forward. 'Hello, my lad,' he said to the little banker. 'The security cameras are giving me a headache.' He gripped his temples and winced.

'Do you want me to switch them off?' asked the boy, clearly pleased his technical know-how might be useful.

'Would you mind?' said Mr Kapoor. The cashier walked to a console on the wall behind him, flipped a switch, and returned to his desk. 'Thank you so much,' said Mr Kapoor, and walked away, drawing out his mobile phone.

'Hundred quid!' snapped Indeep.

'But I haven't–' I said, and received a smack.

'Certainly, sir,' squeaked the youth. He pulled two fifties from his drawer and slotted them through the hole in the security screen.

Indeep and I stood there waiting. The young man stared back self-consciously, and went to pick his nose before settling upon scratching his blotchy neck. 'Will there be anything else?'

'Yes,' said Indeep, reading the boy's nametag. 'Kevin, can we have another hundred quid, please?'

Seemingly relieved to have something to do with his hands, Kevin once again opened the drawer and fetched out two fifties, handing them across as before.

'Wow, man, I didn't know that banks just give you loads of money even if you don't have any!' shouted Gabby from behind us. Indeep wheeled around and clamped a hand over Gabby's mouth.

I took my chance. 'You shouldn't be doing this!' I yelled at the lad. 'Why are you giving us money?'

Indeep dragged Gabby over and attempted to shut my mouth, too.

The young fellow looked confused and on the verge of tears, swivelling in his chair to look fruitlessly for lunching colleagues. 'I'm on work experience,' he cried. 'Isn't this what banks do?'

'Yes, yes,' reassured Indeep, 'this is exactly what banks do, innit. Give people money.'

'Are you sure?' asked Kevin.

'What else would banks do?'

'Nothing!' smiled the lad, much reassured.

'I never knew that!' yelled Gabby. 'I've been poor all these years, and I could have just gone to the bank!'

'Jesus, Gab, can't you see what's happening?' I cried.

'Yeah, man, we're paying our rent.'

'No! This young man has been hoodwinked into dispensing free cash!' I said, grappling with Indeep, who was trying to reassure the wavering boy while attempting to knock me unconscious.

Mr Kapoor returned to the desk. 'My lad,' he addressed the cashier. 'Please do not listen to the mad ramblings of this man. You are doing a fine job, keep it up!'

Indeep dragged Gabby and me to the rear of the bank while Mr Kapoor "processed" the other tenants, all the time sweet-talking the little banker into handing over more and more cash. Twice Kevin had to disappear behind a curtain to restock his drawer, and by the time the last occupant of Clements Markham House was being seen to, he was handing over wads of fifties as if they were napkins.

'This is terrible,' I said.

'Why is it, man?' asked Gabby. 'They can just print some more!'

'It's not as simple as that,' I said, desperately thinking of a way to save the boy's bacon.

Gabby was running his finger around a red button on the wall.

'They *can* print some, Gab, but if all we did was print money, the money would soon be worth nothing.'

'I doubt it!' laughed Gabby. 'They're nice, banks, aren't they, man? I always thought they were horrible.'

'Haven't you heard of inflation, Gab?' I asked.

'Like a Zeppelin?'

'No! In terms of money... Gab! Don't press that button!' I reached to pull his hand away from the red button with *Only Press in Emergency* clearly marked below, but then had a change of heart and pressed it myself.

'I wanted to press it!' said Gabby.

We all jumped as a high-pitched alarm sounded. The spotty youth was in the process of smilingly handing over another brick of fifties when all the shutters dropped like it was 1789.

Indeep lugged the bag of cash away, and Mr Kapoor strolled after him and outside. Everyone else followed, as much to get away from the piercing alarm as anything else. We crowded the pavement as a large silver Mercedes stopped at the kerb. Indeep clambered in, and Mr Kapoor turned to address us.

'Now, men,' he said with the gravitas of an Eisenhower, 'you have a clear choice. Your first option is to tell the police exactly what happened today. *This is very risky.*'

To emphasise the perilous nature of this first option, Indeep performed a variety of chopping movements from inside the car.

Mr Kapoor continued. 'The second option is to entirely erase today's events from your minds. *This is a wise option.* If you choose to be wise, I will not only deliver one hundred pounds in cash to each of you in the coming week, I will also allow you to live rent-free for a whole year. Good day, gentlemen!'

And Mr Kapoor stepped into the Mercedes, which sped off down the High Road.

'Wow, man, today is getting better and better!' cried Gabby.

Distant sirens began to peal like latter-day Bow Bells.

'Run!' shouted someone. My colleagues began to limp towards the friendly saloon door of The Edgar Evans.

'Oh, the humanity!' I shouted.

25

AN ELOQUENT HALLUCINATION

Glyn, Gabby and I followed our bedfellows into the pub. I found it hard to breathe, gripped with a singular feeling of utmost dread, not sure how to mentally file the fact that – there was no other way of putting it – we'd just robbed a bank.

Equally shocking, no one else seemed bothered. Over the moon at Mr Kapoor's "kindness", Old Brian, having related the good news and set up a group tab with Barry the Publican, stood everyone a drink, and another, and another, but whereas my fellows (excepting Glyn, who nursed a half pint dejectedly in a corner, and Gabby who drank mostly music) became jolly and emotional, I sank into terrible worry.

I had a palpable feeling that the world was falling apart.

I watched Lois, beautiful as always, and very busy, working her magic with the old men, charming them; refuelling them the very second they ran dry. I thought about her boyfriend, Roofie, and wove imaginings of their happy future together. What, I wondered, did my own future look like?

Glyn wandered over to me. 'John, we'd better get to the Jobcentre.'

The Jobcentre! 'Glyn, we've just robbed a bank, and the world is falling apart!'

'Indeep and Mr Kapoor robbed the bank, and I don't see any sign of the world falling apart, per se, John.'

'LOOK!' I shouted, grabbing Glyn's hand and dragging him over to a dirt-encrusted window. 'Look out there! Can't you see it? Everything is wrong! The world is in the process of ending!'

Glyn regarded the view. 'It looks like a normal scene to me.'

'Yes, but look *underneath,* Glyn!'

'Under the street?'

'No, *within*! The terrible strain everything is under! It's cracking up!'

'I think the drink might have gone to your head.'

'No! I don't think I've ever seen so clearly!'

'You might need a lie down.'

'Come on!' I cried. 'We're going to the town hall, or even the Houses of Parliament if we have to! We're going to make a counter-attack! We're going to save the world!'

'You're mad.'

'*I'm* mad?' I said. 'This coming from the man who entertains Nazis in the dead of night!'

'You do have a point,' said Glyn.

'You're damned right I do!' I said. 'Can't you see that your visitations are part of it? Part of the world's ending?'

'No, they're just my problems presenting themselves as eloquent hallucinations,' said Glyn.

I stared at him. It struck me that Glyn, as well as being a tax expert, might just have the answers to *absolutely everything* locked away within his problematic psyche.

'I think I know why you think the world is ending,' said Glyn softly.

'Really? Go on then, tell me! TELL ME!'

'I can't, it might hurt your feelings.'

'My feelings are hurt anyway, Glyn!' I said. 'You can hurt them a bit more, I don't think it will make much difference.'

Glyn regarded me, then began to speak. 'Firstly, you're traumatised after what happened in the bank. Secondly, you are very upset that your plan to resign from Amundsen Enterprises and change the world for the better is unrealistic and probably childish, and because you are almost pathologically convinced that you're special and unique, you therefore suppose that if you can't have your own way, the world must be ending.'

I began to weep. He'd struck a nerve as thick as a McDonald's milkshake.

'Sorry, John.'

'Glyn,' I said. 'Why didn't you say this earlier?

'You had to get to the point at which you'd be receptive to hearing it.'

I couldn't believe it. This was exactly what Benny had said to me, only more direct. Why was I so dense?

'What do I do?' I asked.

'Nothing.'

'*Nothing*?'

'Accept the situation. You are special, in so far as anyone can be, but it doesn't make you some sort of deity.'

The thought crossed my mind that Glyn himself might be experiencing some sort of lucid stage within his own cataclysmic breakdown.

'Glyn,' I asked, 'why do you carry on living?'

Glyn looked at me with his sad eyes. 'Because my genes are programmed to seek continued existence,' he said evenly.

'That's the reason?'

He nodded.

'Let's go and talk to the planning people at the town hall,' I said.

'John,' said Glyn.

'Yes?'

'Has it occurred to you that the world might be being born?'

It definitely had not.

26

WE MARCH ON
LEYTONSTOW TOWN HALL

Glad to be out of the pub, I walked along Dig Street with Glyn and Gabby, still thinking about birth and death, and wondering why I didn't seem to fit into life. It stood to reason that by the age of thirty-eight-and-a-half, pretty much halfway through, and certainly halfway or more through a life of poverty and sadness, a person should have developed some sort of comfortable persona to present to the world.

'Why don't I fit in?' I asked my friends.

'Because you might have a personality disorder,' said Glyn.

'Glyn, you're very judgemental today!'

'Sorry, John,' he said.

'That's a good name for a band, man!' said Gabby.

'*Sorry, John?*' I asked.

'No man, *Personality Disorder!*'

'It's tasteless,' said Glyn.

'You don't have to eat it, Glyn!' said Gabby.

They wittered on. The bloody band. I started to get angry about it all again. These green boys who'd just *tolerated* my sound advice.

I watched objects – post boxes, people, litter – slowly approach me and silently filter into my immediate past.

Was reality meant to feel like this? I had a strong sensation there was something wrong; something amiss, as if humanity had somehow crossed a red line, akin to the notion of peak oil. I'd *always* felt this, ever since I could remember – something badly wrong. With the world or with me? Or both?

We approached Leytonstow Town Hall, an imposing Modernist building, and Albert Speer popped into my mind once more. I turned to Gabby and Glyn. 'I have a strong feeling there's something wrong with the human race.'

'No, man, I don't like that name,' said Gabby.

'Oh God, Gab!' I yelled. 'Shut up about the bloody band!'

'Ahem!' warned Glyn.

I'd blown it; poor Gabby sat on the kerbside, and began bawling.

'The band is simply Gabby's way of making living bearable, John,' said Glyn.

'Have you swallowed a wise pill or something?'

'Not that I recall.'

We stood in uneasy silence, Gabby sobbing on the kerb, Glyn apparently studying pigeons sitting on the ramparts of the town hall.

'I'm sorry,' I said. 'It just winds me up that he and his little friends think success will just arrive, whether they work for it or not. It smacks of unbearable delusion, chaos, and sadness.'

'It's OK, John.'

'Is it?'

'He's just living, like us, in his way.'

'Why are things so hard to achieve?' I asked.

'Something to do with thermodynamics.'

I hadn't expected this response, and peered at Glyn.

'You can't make or destroy anything fundamental,' he added.

I told Gabby to be quiet so I could think. He looked at me with an expression that clearly said *I will if you hug me*. So I did. As he whispered sweet nothings, I looked at the town hall again – Albert Speer. 'Glyn, how come you're visited by Germans?'

'Mozart was Austrian. Hitler, too.'

'OK, and Austrians.'

'I'm not entirely sure, but I think it might be something to do with guilt.'

'Guilt?'

'Yes.'

'Can you expand?'

'No.'

'You were pretty forthcoming about *my* problems, Glyn!'

'Sorry.'

I eyed up Glyn as he watched the world from his sad eyes. Guilt. It was true that he did seem constructed of the emotion. That and the act of apology.

'Could it be,' I said, 'that you're feeling guilty about all the bad things human beings have done to one another in the past?'

'Yes.'

'And you're taking it all upon yourself.'

'Yes.'

'But why? You're not responsible for what happened before you were born. Or what happens now, for that matter.'

'Maybe I am,' he said, enigmatically.

I shivered. 'But how could you be?'

'I don't know. Perhaps I also have a personality disorder. Perhaps my ego is also enormous...'

143

'All right, Glyn!' I snapped.

But Glyn carried on. 'Maybe I feel responsible for all the bad things that ever happened in the world because I find I'm powerless to undo them, and this is a direct affront to my own elevated sense of self.'

'Look, a ladybird!' shouted Gabby, pointing at the floor.

'It's a woodlouse,' said Glyn.

We entered the cool atrium of Leytonstow Town Hall.

'It's a cathedral of bureaucracy,' I said.

Glyn coughed his approval, and Gabby did hopscotch across the tiles.

We were being watched from behind the reception desk by an elderly lady who looked as if she'd been set a task in 1947 and never debriefed.

'Hello, we'd like a meeting with the planning department,' I said brightly, before giving her a twenty-minute lowdown on the situation at Clements Markham House.

'So, we'd like to see the Queen!' said Gabby.

The geriatric receptionist pushed some papers towards me, then produced an egg and cress sandwich from a drawer and took a wet bite. 'Fill these in,' she said, mouth brimming.

'Have you got a pen?' I asked.

'Yes,' she egged.

'Can I use it, please?'

'Have you undergone Pen Training?'

'*Pen training*?'

'Pen Training.'

'I went to school, if that's what you're referring to.'

'If you haven't been on the Pen Training course, I can't supply you with a pen,' she said flatly, before opening the drawer and taking another egg-bound bite.

'What are you afraid of?' I said. 'That I might slip and the pen might pierce my heart? Or that I might inadvertently ram the bloody thing up someone's nostril?'

'Ahem!' warned Glyn.

'Glyn, it's ridiculous! I have every right to be frustrated!'

'Just give us the fucking pen, man!' shouted Gabby.

'Ahem!'

'Gabby!' I said. 'You sound like a yob!'

'Oh, John, man, I'm sorry, I'm sorry, I'm sorry!' yelled Gabby, clutching at my sleeve and trying to mount me.

'Can we use our own pen?' asked Glyn of the receptionist.

'*Yes*,' she said, in a very disapproving manner.

'Have either of you got a pen?' I asked my companions.

'No,' said Glyn.

Gabby rustled around in the many pockets of his death metal dungarees, and produced a small plastic spinning top, the type you get in a Christmas cracker. 'Will this do, man?'

'As a pen?' I said.

'Let's go and buy a pen,' suggested Glyn.

'I guess we'll have to,' I said, and faced the receptionist. 'But it's utterly ridiculous! I am here to report that our very heritage is being ripped asunder, and all you can focus on is your liability. The mind boggles.'

'Sir, I will be forced to have you escorted from the premises if you continue to be aggressive,' she said, and pointed at a sign. The sign said *Leytonstow Council does not tolerate threatening or abusive behaviour towards its staff*.

'That's equally ridiculous,' I said, trying to moderate my manner, which drew an encouraging little cough from Glyn. 'It is quite normal for a person to react with some frustration if completely unnecessary blocks are put in their way. Surely you can see that?'

'It's time for you to retire, man!' said Gabby.

It turned out the antique receptionist either couldn't

or wouldn't follow my reasoning. Having finished the egg and cress sandwich, she moved on to a banana, and just stared at us.

'Have you had egg sandwich and banana training?' I asked.

'No, that would be quite ridiculous,' she said.

There was a tatty parade of shops across the road. Gabby seemed unnaturally excited at the prospect of buying a pen, and mithered me to let him choose one. Feeling quite depressed, I irritably told him to get on with it. Glyn and I sat on a wall surrounded by constellations of dog poo. I gave Gabby fifty pence, and we watched him skip towards the shops. He disappeared into a Caribbean barber's shop.

'What!' I said.

'Maybe he's going to borrow a pen, to save you money.'

'We can but hope,' I sighed.

I took deep breaths of bus fumes, watched the world pass by, and wondered why it was so impossible to make anything happen.

'It would be different if we had lots of money,' said Glyn, as if reading my mind; I added this to his growing list of hitherto hidden skills.

'What do you mean?'

'You know they say that *money makes the world go round*?'

'Yes.'

'It does.'

'So, if we had loads of money, we could simply *buy* control?'

'Yes.'

I started considering whether or not it was morally justified to rob a bank in order to save our heritage, but then remembered that I had, effectively, done just that this morning.

'It would perhaps be morally justified to come by a lot of money in an immoral manner to ensure the greater good,' said Glyn, again following my train of thought perfectly, but crystallising it better than I could.

'But where do we get lots of money?'

This important question remained unanswered. At that moment Gabby came bounding back from the shop.

'What do you think, man?' he shouted, lifting up his hair to show something etched onto the side of his head.

'*The pen*?' I asked, not unreasonably, given the clear task Gabby had been set.

'Look, man,' said Gabby, 'he's shaved *Gabby* into my hair!'

I inspected the side of Gabby's head, then sat back down on the wall. I was ready for a good cry. 'Gab,' I said, 'it doesn't say *Gabby*.'

'No?'

'No. It says *Batty*.'

'*Batty*?'

'Yes, *Batty*.'

'Not Gabby?'

'No.'

'Why? Did he mistake me for a cricket bat or something?'

'I don't think so.'

'A battered fish?'

'No.'

'How weird, man,' said Gabby, 'I paid fifty pence for that!'

'Not for a pen?'

'No, for *Gabby* on the side of my head! And he's put *Batty*!'

147

'Come on,' I said, standing. We visited a newsagent next to the barber shop and purchased a blue ballpoint. It took thirty seconds.

We returned to the reception desk.

'What can I do for you young gentlemen?' said the receptionist. My heart sank.

'We have a pen,' I said, holding it up for her to inspect.

'Have you undertaken Pen Training?' she asked, slurping from a cup of milky tea.

'What?'

'Have you, or any of your friends, undertaken Pen Training?'

I stared at her in disbelief. 'As you well know, we've just been to buy a pen because you wouldn't let us use yours!'

'Ahem!'

'Oh, Glyn, shut up!' I shouted.

'Yeah man, fuck off, Glyn!' yelled Gabby.

'Gabby, I don't need your help!' I said, ready to strangle the little bastard.

Glyn began to retch. The receptionist picked up a phone, dialled and said, 'Jerry, I need security in reception.'

'Look, you don't need security,' I said. 'Just let us fill in the necessary paperwork, please, and we'll wait patiently. OK?'

She eyed me, took another sip of tea, then picked up the phone again. 'Jerry, I might not need security in reception.' She put down the phone. 'I can fit you into Pen Training at four o'clock,' she said, pointing at the clock. It was ten to.

27

PEN TRAINING

Gabby felt right at home at Pen Training, cracking jokes with a teenage boy with black teeth and a *Les Misérables* T-shirt. Glyn sat quietly at his desk, presumably for the greater good. I'd never felt so humiliated, and was so sorry for myself it was all I could do not to weep.

The door to the room opened softly, and in walked a middle-aged man with a benevolent smile and a bushy orange beard.

'Baldy!' shouted an extremely overweight young man at the front, who turned and grinned maniacally at us.

Gabby and the boy in the *Les Misérables* T-shirt guffawed and high fived.

'Yes, I'm a little lacking up top,' said the man softly, patting his bald pate.

Focus on Clements Markham House, I told myself.

Glyn coughed approval.

'Now,' smiled the man. 'For those who don't know me, my name is Tim, but you can call me Tim.'

The room erupted. I locked eyes with Glyn, who shook his head and mouthed that I should *keep it together*.

'Now I don't know what your key workers have told you about today, but we're going to be looking at the use of pens, pencils, and colours, and it will be a lot of fun,' said Tim.

'Excuse me,' I said, 'what do you mean by *key workers*?'

'Right...?' said Tim.

149

'John,' I said.

'Fatty!' shouted the grinning lad at the front.

'Right, John, your key worker is the person who helps you. They are a friend to you, when you need them,' he smiled.

'Look, *Tim*...' I said. The room erupted once more into laughter at the already concertinaed name.

'It's OK, John,' said Tim. 'All will become clear.'

'Look *T*... look *you*!' I shouted. 'I came here to visit the planning office, but the receptionist said I couldn't use her pen to fill out the necessary forms, so I bought a pen.'

'A fucking blue one!' shouted Gabby, high fiving the lad with the *Les Misérables* T-shirt once more.

'So, I came back to fill in the forms, but she said I couldn't even use my own pen, and that I had to attend pen training!'

'Yeah, man, we came to see the Queen!' yelled Gabby.

Tim smiled and slowly flapped his arms like one would slow an oncoming Morris Minor in 1972.

'I know it can be a *bit scary* to be in a classroom,' he smiled. 'Don't worry, John, you're among friends, *OK*?'

'What the hell are you talking about?'

'Prejudiced!' yelled the grinning lad.

'I'm outraged!' I continued. 'I come to the town hall on important business, and instead I find myself in a classroom with a bunch of village idiots being taught how to safely use a bloody pen!'

There was a shocked hush, save Glyn's rapid retching.

Tim looked distinctly upset. A girl at the front began to cry, and the big lad who had previously levelled insults stood and gave her a gentle hug (still grinning, I noted).

'I've never heard the likes of it,' said Tim, shaking his head. 'This is the kind of abuse some people have to face *every day of their lives*. This is a safe place, John, and you've damaged it with your nastiness and aggression. I'm ashamed on your behalf, I really am. Look, you've even made this fellow sick!' He pointed at Glyn.

'What?' I said. 'Glyn retches at the slightest provocation! Don't you, Glyn?'

'Raaagh! Yes – raaagh! – he's right – raaagh! – unfortunately – raaagh! – I do.'

'I would ask you politely to show us all a bit of respect now,' said Tim, 'and leave us to our training course.' Then he added, 'Or I'll get security.'

Threatened with security for the second time! 'Go on, then!' I shouted. 'Go for it! Get security and have them escort me off the premises!'

I sat back and folded my arms, experiencing the first tickles of regret. Looking a little worried, Tim shuffled out of the room.

'Raaagh! – Let's go – raaagh! – John,' retched Glyn.

'No!' I said. 'Look, I know what I said wasn't very nice, but I'm sorry, I'm absolutely *pig sick* of being mistaken for an imbecile!'

'Raaagh! – it's just the – raaagh! – big ego, John. You need to overcome it.'

'You want me to accept this grouping, do you? You want me to embrace *this* as my natural demographic!'

'These people have more in common with you than you realise, they are all – raaagh! – misunderstood and mocked.'

I glanced around the room at the faces staring at me.

Oh God. Regret hammered my brain like an atomic hangover.

I stood. 'I'm so sorry, all of you, I'm so very deeply sorry!'

'Gay!' yelled the grinning lad at the front, and Gabby and the lad in the *Les Misérables* T-shirt made it a hat-trick.

Tim returned with a security guard, and pointed at me sadly. The security guard propelled his wheelchair over to me. 'I'll have to ask you to leave, sir.'

'It's OK,' I said, 'I've realised that my previous behaviour was quite unacceptable. I'm sorry. I was... just shy about being in a classroom.'

The security guard looked at Tim, who shrugged, then smiled at me. 'John, I'm glad you've got over your initial nerves. We all get angry sometimes, don't we?'

'*Yes we do,*' I said.

'Thank you, Jerry,' said Tim. 'I think we're OK to carry on now.'

'As long as you're sure, Tim,' said Jerry.

The room erupted into laughter once more.

'Disabled!' shouted the grinning lad at the front.

I let myself undergo pen training, and, to my surprise, rather enjoyed it. Glyn was right; I felt comfortable here. These men and women were nice to one another. They weren't judgemental. They had no agenda. They were not trying to fleece me, or trip me up, or humiliate me. Towards the end, as Tim was demonstrating advanced crayon use, Glyn sidled over to me and smiled, something he almost never did. It transformed his face.

'I'm sorry, Glyn,' I said.

'It's OK, John. You know what you're doing, don't you?'

'Yes, I'm drawing a picture of a tree.'

'No, I mean you know what you're *doing*?'

'Eating humble pie?'

'You know you said that you wanted to re-explore the world and make people nicer to each other, more aware of others?'

'Yes,' I said, a little embarrassed by such wish-wash now my ego had been kicked into touch.

'That's exactly what you're doing, but first you're re-exploring yourself.'

So, I *was* following Benny's advice after all.

'In terms of the imprint we leave on the world,' Glyn continued, 'the only thing that matters is whether we were kind, or not.'

152

Tim wrapped up the session by producing a feather quill, which the group found exceedingly funny. I laughed, too; it was a quill, after all. Even Glyn managed a mirthful cough. Gabby thought it was hilarious.

'Now,' said Tim, handing out certificates, 'while I give these out I'd like to tell you about The Dig Street Festival.'

'Knickers!' shouted the grinning lad, proudly clutching his penmanship certificate.

'Yes,' said Tim, laughing. 'Now, The Dig Street Festival is something I've been planning for a little while. The idea is that this Friday lunchtime, we celebrate the changing of the season by doing little turns in the square outside Leytonstow Tube Station. The Council have granted us a permit for the occasion.'

'Al-Qaeda!' shouted the grinning lad, presumably, and worryingly, linking public transport to terrorism.

'Quite,' said Tim. 'Now the aim of us performing for passers-by is to help them to rediscover their surroundings with the help of a song, a dance, or some drama, and to make them happy and friendly. Does that sound appealing?'

I could not believe my ears!

A hot discussion immediately started regarding who would do what, who was good at what, who was shy, who wasn't, and who they could invite along as a special guest. In the end, that latter point was resolved; it was unanimously decided that David Beckham should attend, and recite a poem.

Why was *my* idea being presented at Pen Training?

'Right,' said Tim, 'now I'm not sure whether you're setting your sights a little...'

Rediscover their surroundings! Happy and friendly! Oh God. Basically, Tim had nicked my idea! I mouthed *I thought of this* to Glyn. Glyn shrugged.

'My band can play!' shouted Gabby.

'What's that, Gabby, you have a band, do you? Wonderful!'

'Yeah man, we're called The Sofas!'

'Hey, what a great name!' cried Tim. 'Very comfortable!'

'Anal sex!' shouted the grinning lad.

'And how about you, John?' asked Tim. 'Is there anything you'd like to do?'

'John can read his poems!' yelled Gabby.

'Wonderful!' said Tim. 'And you, Glyn? Any ideas?'

'Raaagh!'

'A freestyle rap! Oh Glyn, that's wonderful.'

And so Gabby, Glyn and I were signed up for The Dig Street Festival. Tim gave me his phone number, and explained to me in some detail how one might utilise a telephone.

I was numb.

And reception was shut.

28

LAND OF HOPE AND GORY

'Glyn,' I said as we walked down the town hall steps. 'I can't believe what just happened. That's *my* idea. He didn't mention corruption, but he's basically nicked it.'

Glyn turned to me and coughed. 'You thought of three things, John: one, rediscover familiar surroundings. Two, end all corruption. Three, make people generally nicer to one another.'

'That's right!' I said, impressed he'd taken note.

'I hate to break it to you, John...' said Glyn.

'What?' I asked, steeling myself for further revelations concerning my wrong psychology.

'They're pretty general,' he said.

'What do you mean?'

'I mean, I'm sorry to say this, but anyone could think of them. Gabby came up with one of them.'

'Did he?' I asked, glancing at Gabby who was prodding a dog poo with a twig.

'Yes; when he was explaining what he thought of the world to Lois, he said that he wished people would be nicer to one another. He said we should *pay* people to be nicer to one another, which, of course, would defeat the object.'

Outsmarted by Gabby. It was irrefutable.

Gabby began to mither me to go back to The Edgar Evans to rejoin the fun. Glyn said it wasn't his scene (I wondered what was), and went home. I escorted Gabby to the pub, not because I wanted to go, but because I wanted to taste oblivion.

The joint was jumping. They were pissed as farts. Lois was on top form, a Morticia-like spinning top as Barry chain-smoked from the shadows. As far as our cohabitees were concerned it was a famous night, where a multitude of increasingly flattering and chaotic toasts were bestowed upon Mr Kapoor *in absentia*, who, it was almost overwhelmingly agreed, was the single best landlord in the whole of Leytonstow, nay, East London. Old men had tears in their eyes recounting over and over how Kapoor had taken pity upon them, granting a year's free rent, and one hundred quid in cash each. They appeared to have conveniently forgotten the actual bank robbery – perhaps it reminded them of the good old days, when crooks was crooks.

Barry grudgingly lent us a calculator, and many painstaking one-eyed attempts were made to calculate exactly how much Mr Kapoor's package was worth. There were estimates of anything from £1 to £1million, but it was, after asking Lois to operate the machine, finally established that Mr Kapoor's bequest represented a benefit-in-kind of £2,700 each, which made visions of unlimited fags and booze (or mountains of Pot Noodles, CDs and basketball boots, in Gabby's case) dance before my colleagues' eyes in fantastic kaleidoscopes of promised oblivion and stupor. It was the alcoholics' version of Willy Wonka's Golden Ticket.

Weaving not a little, Gabby came over to the table where I'd sat miserably nursing seven pints of strong lager.

'What's wrong, man?'

'Something isn't right,' I said. 'I mean apart from what is quite obviously not right about the whole thing.'

'Man, I knew I shouldn't have played that Black Sabbath track!' said Gabby, slapping his stick insect's thigh and spilling the majority of his third lager-top upon the pre-war carpet. I regarded my little friend, all rosy from being the star of the jukebox. I had a nagging feeling that, somehow, I would be held wholly responsible for the calamity at the bank. Much went through my mind, from being told it was a *Candid Camera* stunt, to pondering whether, like Glyn, I was responsible for everything that had ever gone wrong in western (or eastern for that matter) civilisation.

I watched the old men, my neighbours, conga-ing painfully around the pub. How could they be so easily taken in after whole lives spent drinking-in the universe? Seeing that Gabby had safely vacated the jukebox, Barry took his chance to limp over and tap away at its keypad. Soon Edward Elgar's "Nimrod" was booming out of dust-topped speakers from all corners of the pub. The old men stood to attention, saluted the photograph of Jim Bowen above the bar, and shed tears of patriotic joy.

Observing this, Gabby moved towards me mumbling about his mam, arms outstretched in the asking of a loving grapple. With a sigh, I accepted his miniature frame into my arms, stroked his hair tenderly, and shed a little tear myself.

'Where are you now, Mr Kapoor?' I sighed aloud.

'Probably in Chingford, man,' murmured Gabby from the depths of my bosom.

WEDNESDAY

29

BEARDMORE'S OFFER

Lying in my pull-down bed I struggled to compose myself. Barely thirty-six hours into joblessness and I was without hope, like an ex-mining village.

'Oh God,' I said, listening to my own voice, and knowing God was dead.

'Ah, you checked in with The Father, is that OK?'

I started.

'Sorry, lad,' chuckled The Gaffer, leaning upon my window frame. 'How are you?'

I gave the stock English response. 'Not too bad.'

'Good!' said Paddy, sucking upon his cigar. 'All's well as long as you keep The Lord sweet, is that OK?'

'Are you going to fix my window?' I asked, changing the subject (I suppose strictly we were still talking about God's elements).

'We are that,' smiled Paddy.

'When?'

He brought forth a packet of custard creams and proceeded to tell me that the work was going apace; that *The Big Man* had finally honoured the next cash instalment this very morning, that they were breaking through the old roof tomorrow to start work on the first new storey, and that all was right with the world: the sun was shining, his football team had won at the weekend – even his wife was being nice to him, was that OK?

I was slow to catch on.

Of course Mr Kapoor had made the cash instalment!

There was a knock at my door. I opened it to find Gabby looking excited. 'John!' he said. 'Some dude called Beardmunch is on the phone!'

My chest tightened. So, here it was: Beardmore's knockout blow. My legs were leaden as I descended the communal stairs. The telephone receiver appeared to weigh several tons. I slowly pressed it to my ear.

'It's me,' said Beardmore. 'The place ain't the same without you.'

'Really?' I said.

'Yeah, you're not here,' said Beardmore.

'Oh.'

Silence.

'We'd like you to come back. But not just to mop and shift trollies,' said Beardmore. 'We're launching a new online... shop, and we'd like you to be our *Web Mobility Director*.'

'You can stick your job!'

'Whatever,' said Beardmore. 'So long, Torrington.' He hung up.

'Oh Gabby!' I shouted. 'What have I done?'

'Lots of things, man. Do you mean stuff you've done this morning, yesterday, or some other time?'

I lunged for him, but missed. Just before I could relaunch the assault, two letters plopped upon the dirty welcome mat. Gabby danced over to the door and picked them up like a dog fetching slippers.

'They're for you, man!' said Gabby, and immediately started ripping them open.

'Give them to me!'

I watched his face change from jubilation to outright shock as he studied the first letter, official looking.

'Blimey, man!' said Gabby. 'You're rich...'

I grabbed it from him. It was from the bank manager at NatEast. A brand new bank card was enclosed.

Dear Sir, it said, *I am pleased to inform you that you now have access to an overdraft facility of one hundred thousand pounds.* I read on – *valued customer* – *anything we can do, just let us know* – *nothing too much trouble,* etc. Then, at the bottom of the page –

Your Balance - £99,950 DR

'MY CARD!' I shouted, suddenly realising what had been niggling me ever since Mr Kapoor's silver Mercedes had raced off up the High Road. 'Oh God, oh God, Gabby! I left my bank card! The bank have it! They've pinned the lot on me!'

Gabby punched the air and screamed repeatedly, 'WE'RE RICH! WE'RE RICH!' Then he picked up the phone and started to dial.

'No, Gab!' I said.

'I want to tell Mam, man!' he shouted.

'Gab, we're not rich. Do you know what **DR** stands for?'

'Drink Ribena?' suggested Gabby.

'No...'

'Delicious Rabbits?'

'No, listen! It stands for Overdrawn!' I said, as my extremities began to grow numb with panic. 'It means that I owe the bank ninety-nine-thousand-nine-hundred-and-fifty pounds. It means the branch have hidden their mistake in leaving that little idiot at the helm by charging everything Mr Kapoor stole to *my account*!'

'You know what this means!' said Gabby, jogging on the spot.

'I'm going to jail?'

'No, man – it means we have fifty quid to spend!'

The very definition of the optimist – I had to give him that. I grabbed the phone and dialled frantically.

'I want to tell Mam!' said Gabby, trying to grab it back.

'Gab, I'm not calling your mum!' I yelled. 'I'm calling Beardmore to accept his bloody job!'

'Why, man, is he leaving?' asked Gabby.

'No, he's not leaving!'

'Wow, man, you're clever,' said Gabby, shaking his head with admiration.

'No I'm not!' I shouted. 'I have an awful choice – I either work for Beardmore or go to jail!'

'Yeah?' said Beardmore.

'Hi Eric, it's me again,' I said, cringing to my very follicles. 'I was a little hasty just now... I was joking... the fact is... I would love to take the *Web Mobility Directorship*.'

'Good lad. You know it makes sense,' said Beardmore. 'I'll see you tomorrow.'

'Thanks, Eric,' I said.

'I forgot to mention,' added Beardmore, 'you still need to mop the floors before we open. That's a part of the *Web Mobility Director's* job.'

'Really?'

'And collect trollies from the car park.'

'What?'

'And clean up spillages around the store during the day.'

'But that's my old job!'

'Take it or leave it,' he said.

I sighed. 'I'll take it.'

'Good lad.'

'Can I have a pay rise?' I asked, astounded at my cheekiness.

'The *Web Mobility Directorship* comes with a package. Talk about it tomorrow.'

'Oh, by the way, Eric,' I said. 'Can Glyn come back too?'

'The goofy homo?'

'Yes.'

'You can job-share,' and he hung up.

I felt sick to my bottom. Why, I asked myself, did I have to associate with such people? I made a mental note not to tell Glyn I'd just negotiated him a fifty per cent pay cut.

'Come on, man!' said Gabby. 'Let's go and spend that fifty to celebrate!'

'Celebrate what?'

'Everything!' said Gabby.

'Gab, I've just taken an eight grand a year job, if that, in a desperate attempt to pay off a hundred thousand pound debt! What's there to celebrate?'

'We could go and see Beryl at the Jobcentre!' suggested Gabby.

'Gabby, no...' It wasn't a bad idea.

'Anyway, man, I thought it was ninety-nine-thousand-nine-hundred-and-fifty pounds?' said Gabby.

'That makes it OK, then!' I said. 'Yes, you're right, peanuts; I'll pay it off within the week!'

'So what's the problem, then, man?'

'The *problem* is...' I said, almost crying, 'that you can't see past fifty bloody quid!'

For the second time ever (remarkably) I lunged at poor Gabby, pushing him up against the wall, sorely tempted to stave in his undersized head.

Thinking it was a hug (and perhaps it was), Gabby wrapped his arms around my ample trunk and held on for dear life, muttering such epithets as *John, you're the best friend ever*, and, weirdly, *I wish Mam could see us now*. I softened, and held him too.

I spotted the second letter on the floor, and *avec Gabby* slowly bent to retrieve it like a kangaroo with an overloaded pouch. It was my new PIN.

Gabby looked up at me, his eyes shining.

I held the PIN in one hand, the quietly moaning Gabby in the other, and thought further upon the fiscal chain reaction which had arrived unbidden at my door. I thought about what The Gaffer had said while leaning on my windowsill crunching his custard creams. Then, just like that, everything came together, causing me to drop both Gabby and the PIN: it was I bankrolling Paddy's Poles to destroy the Edwardian majesty of Clements Markham House!

'Oh God, Gab!' I yelled. 'I'm paying for the building works!'

'Oh John! That's really nice of you, man!'

Just then, another letter, less official, plopped onto the doormat. It was for me, and I recognised the writing. My heart began to somersault. I picked it up and opened it.

Dear John

I have been thinking about you. I'm sorry it didn't go well at my party. I'm sorry the boys were so rude. I keep thinking about how we stood looking at each other before you left. You asked me a question: I like Roofie, mostly, but don't love him.

Love, Lois

'Is that from *a girl*, man?' asked Gabby, his eyes wide with – what was it? – disgust.

Shaking from head to foot, I sat on the bottom stair, and tried to muster my thoughts and feelings. I couldn't.

'Do you want a hug, man?'

I nodded.

30

THE JOBCENTRE

Having learned that Lois did not love Roofie and that she wanted me to know it, and weighed down too with the knowledge that I was both bankrolling the rape of Clements Markham House *and* stooping to the depths of going to see Beryl, Gabby and I knocked for Glyn. He opened his door and stared at us from the gloom. 'Einstein, last night.'

'What did he say?' I asked.

'He was upset about Chernobyl. He couldn't stop crying. I had to slap him.'

'You slapped Albert Einstein?'

'I had to. He was hysterical.'

I looked at my two friends – relativity personified.

'Do countries really have atom bombs, man?' asked Gabby.

'Yes,' said Glyn sadly.

'Are you joking, Gab?' I asked.

'No,' said Gabby, his angry red spots linking up in a deep blush.

Oh to live in a world where nuclear weapons were fictional.

'Gab,' I said, 'I'm sorry to tell you this, but we have the ability to effectively exterminate ourselves at a moment's notice.'

'Ha ha,' laughed Gabby.

'It's true, Gabby.'

'Are you sure, man?'

'Absolutely,' I said. 'I'm afraid I'm one hundred per cent sure. It could happen this very morning,' I said. Would it be a bit of a relief? Stop this crazy game we didn't understand? The most notable thing about human beings was our ability to imagine the end, and take our lives should we desire, like mini-deities. It stood to reason that our greatest genii should come up with a fantastic method of mass suicide, a beautifully simple answer to the frustrating nature of being.

'Well, at least we have Beryl, man,' said Gabby, happy as a lamb once again. 'And at least atom bombs are really small!'

With thoughts of global extermination in mind, we traipsed to the Jobcentre.

I told Glyn that Beardmore was prepared to take him back. He threw up on the pavement, presumably recalling Beardmore's horrendous blood-black spit. It was decided that other options should be sought. My own choice was clear: prise £99,950 from Beryl, get another job earning something in that ballpark, or be forced to return to Amundsen Enterprises. Gabby was cautiously hopeful about the first option.

We three wound our away through a crowd of lost souls loitering before the entrance. Inside was uproar, like a re-creation of Dante's Inferno. Busy as a midday souk, the Jobcentre was packed to the asbestos rafters with all those citizens who had failed. Gabby, Glyn and I fitted right in. Evidently the budget did not stretch to air-conditioning or cleaning – I wondered if this was a conscious decision to try to encourage people out to work – the dead heat and sexual frustration of hundreds of unhappy bodies slapped one across the face, presenting instant prickly heat, and an instinctive wish to strip off and locate a cool river.

After learning Beryl was on her lunch break (I've no idea how Gabby made sense of the place to gather this information) we pushed our way through the crowds to study the boards where the jobs were pinned: cleaners, care assistants, labourers, dish washers (*plongeurs* as George Orwell would have said) and warehouse pickers.

'All the jobs people don't want to do,' observed Glyn.

'Why do people do these jobs anyway, man?' asked Gabby.

'Someone's got to, Gab,' I said. 'The world wouldn't work if they didn't.'

'Couldn't the Council do it?' asked Gabby.

I shot him an incredulous look, 'Gab, what do you think the Council is, other than a collection of individuals employed to carry out various essential services?'

'I dunno, man, it just *does* stuff.'

'Gab, I'm sure we've been here before!'

'Yeah, man, I come every week!'

'No, I mean we've covered this ground before. *People* do this stuff.'

'The Council is made up of people, just like you and me, is what John means,' said Glyn.

'Glyn, I'm pretty sure I was clear enough!' I yelled.

'Sorry, John.'

Not wishing to prolong this conversation, I moved to the next job board and studied the same sad list of nullifying jobs. I'd already had a go at most of them. I gazed at the ragged mass of my fellow human beings, moping slowly about the place, bumping into each other, depressed, or too excited, pissed, shouting, arguing, mock-restraining, and I surmised that if only they could form an orderly queue, pick a job from the boards, apply for it, get it, go home, sleep, then report for work on time the next day, the economy would sustainably boom out of all recognition, and the Jobcentre would have to shut – ironically shedding the jobs of folks like Beryl.

'God, it's irony, man!' yelled Gabby, busy trying to remove some chewing gum from his sleeve which he'd picked up while leaning against the cleaning jobs board.

'What?' I said, wondering whether Gabby too was developing Glyn's powers of telepathy, and worrying about how he would interpret my thoughts.

'Well, if all of this lot picked these jobs, then the people working here wouldn't have jobs!'

Rather snobbishly I seethed at the fact that not only was I forced to visit this hellhole, I was now also cosmically linked to one Gabriel Longfeather.

'It's quite ironic that Gabby sort of grasps the concept of irony, yet doesn't know how to use the word *ironic*,' said Glyn.

'Thanks, Glyn,' I said.

Beryl still on her lunch break, we joined a queue of jobseekers waiting to see a consultant. The one we were aiming at was a large unhealthy-looking fellow in his late fifties, with a pronounced squint, a grey liver-spotted pate, and numerous out-of-control hairy moles scattered about his large disgruntled face. He wore rimless glasses on a string as though he were CEO of a multinational and not a fat bastard paid a pittance to deal with smelly bitter losers all day long in East London's atmospheric equivalent of a rotting mangrove swamp.

The bloke ahead of us in the queue was a walking skeleton with a swastika tattooed upon his neck. His Adam's apple stuck out like a fin, and he reeked of booze and fags. He told the consultant that he couldn't perform manual labour due to polio, that he was a year shy of sixty-five, and what did the consultant suggest he do for the next year until his state pension came through? The poor consultant mulled this over. In doing so he doodled on a pad. He drew a swastika, then scribbled it out hurriedly. How on earth could he recommend an individual to a potential employer with an advert for ethnic cleansing and generalised intolerance permanently daubed upon his neck?

'Have you joined Job Club?' asked the consultant, which I took to mean *Go and ask someone else, please.*

'Fackin job club?' spat Swastika. 'I'm a fackin old man! I'm disabled! I don't want to work no more! I've 'ad enough!'

The consultant rustled among leaflets upon his desk and handed one marked *Job Club* to Swastika. Swastika held it like a gun, and they stared at one another. Then Swastika hobbled away. Now it was our turn.

The consultant blew his nose into a once-white handkerchief, coughed, took a swig of coffee from a bitten Styrofoam cup, and beckoned us forward – even the hand doing the beckoning looked depressed. I sat down, and Gabby opted to sit on my lap. I threw him off but he got on again so I threw him off again, but again he hopped on.

'Gab, get off!' I said.

'John, I'm really worried about what happened in the bank, man!' yelled Gabby, clinging to me. It had taken Gabby almost exactly twenty-four hours to process this information.

'Get off!' I yelled.

'WE ROBBED A BANK!' screamed Gabby, and mounted me once more. I decided to let him stay, on the grounds that he *shut up*.

'NI number...' drawled the consultant.

'NP4532...'

'Gab, I thought I was here to get a job?'

'Oh sorry, man.'

'It's...' I said. 'Oh. I can't remember it.'

'Do you want to use mine man? It's NP4532...'

'Stop,' said the consultant weakly. 'You can't use his.'

'I really don't mind, man!'

'The Inland Revenue *do* mind,' sighed the consultant.

'Surely it's not essential,' I said, 'I'm after a job, we can fill in the blanks later.'

The consultant eyeballed me.

'Why is he looking at me, man?' whispered Gabby.

The consultant rubbed his face, and took another gulp of machine coffee from the crumbling cup. Then he doodled again. This time he drew a palm tree.

'Let's start again,' said the consultant. 'What's your address?'

'Flat thirteen, Clements Markham Hou–'

'No, my address, Gab, not yours!'

'Why's he looking at me, then, man?'

'He's looking at us simultaneously,' I said. 'But he definitely wants my address, as I am the person looking for the job, OK?'

A vein throbbed on the consultant's pate. I gave him my address.

'And what kind of work are you looking for?' he asked.

'I'm not, man!'

'For Pete's sake, Gab! Get off my knee and go and get a coffee!' I tipped him off.

'Oh God, we're criminals, we stole all of that money!' shouted Gabby.

'Jesus Christ, Gab, shut up!' I yelled. 'Glyn, please take him to get a coffee, take him away!'

Glyn shepherded the white-faced Gabby in the direction of the coffee machine.

'Sorry about that.'

The consultant doodled a Star of David.

'Carry on,' I said.

'Is your key worker here with you today?' he asked.

'No, I don't have one!' I said.

'Are you disabled?'

'No.'

'Over sixty-five?'

'What?'

'Any dependents?'

'No.'

171

'Are you sure?' asked the consultant, glancing in the direction of the coffee machine.

'What the hell do you mean?'

'Do you suffer from mental illness?'

'Not that I'm aware.'

A clear 'Ahem' came from the direction of the coffee machine.

'Glyn, I heard that!' I yelled over my shoulder.

'Sorry, John!' yelled Glyn.

The consultant doodled a clock face.

'Are you taking psychoactive medication?'

'Why on earth is that relevant? I want a job, preferably something which doesn't make me continually want to die by my own hand.'

The consultant stopped doodling and sat back in his chair. Then he smiled at me – it changed his face dramatically, like the sun coming out on a wet day.

'This is a wind-up, isn't it?' he said, grinning.

'What is?'

'This, the three of you, it's a prank, isn't it?'

'No, of course not,' I said.

'You're very good!' sang the consultant, wagging his finger at me. 'Getting the little one to sit on your knee! Nearly got me, you know!' He heaved his not insignificant frame into a standing position and reached out to shake hands with me.

'Come on!' he laughed. 'Who put you up to it? Was it Nigel?'

'No,' I said.

'HERE, NIGE!' he yelled. 'YOU LITTLE BASTARD, HAD ME GOING THERE!'

Several stations away, a person whom I supposed to be Nigel slowly stood up, confused. He looked like Wally, star of *Where's Wally?*

172

'COME ON!' shouted the consultant. 'THE JOKE'S OVER! GOOD ONE, NIGE! WERE YOU IN ON THIS TOO, KERRY?'

A woman, presumably Kerry, shook her head and looked severe. The poor consultant's face fell. It was as if the Job-centre were observing a minute's silence.

'Come on, Nigel!' he pleaded.

'I'm sorry, Ken, I don't know anything about it,' said Nigel.

'Oh, God,' said Ken.

Kerry walked over. 'Take a break,' she ordered.

Ken shuffled off dejectedly. I offered Kerry an apologetic smile.

She sat and frowned. 'What can I do for you, sir?'

'I need a job,' I said. 'I am a regular guy who needs a job quite urgently.'

Gabby and Glyn returned with three coffees.

'It's a mocha, man!' said Gabby jubilantly.

'Cheers,' I said, and prepared to engage Kerry further.

'It's Italian!' said Gabby.

'What is?'

'The mocha, man!'

'No, it isn't,' I said.

'Ahem!'

'Glyn, it's evidently not Italian, it just came from that very Leytonstow-based machine!'

'Can we get on with it?' asked Kerry.

'It is!' yelled Gabby. 'There was an Italian flag on the machine!'

'There was,' affirmed Glyn, helpfully.

'That doesn't make it Italian, Gab,' I said.

'How do you know, man?'

'I haven't got all day,' said Kerry.

'Because I just know!' I shouted. 'The Italian flag is simply a marketing ploy to make you buy coffee.'

'Mocha, man!'

'God, mocha then!'

'OK then, clever clogs, man, where is it from?' said Gabby.

'Jesus Christ, Gab, how on earth should I know, some grotty industrial estate!'

'In Italy, man?'

'Can we just do this?' said Kerry.

'I'm sorry,' I said. 'So I recently worked in a DIY store, but...'

'Told you it's Italian,' said Gabby.

'GAB, JUST LEAVE IT!' I bellowed.

'Ahem!'

'LOOK. DO YOU WANT A FLAMING JOB OR WHAT!' shouted Kerry. A fleck of her spittle landed upon my lower lip, and I wondered at our intimacy.

'Yes, I do,' I said, drawing the shaking Gabby towards me for a cuddle.

'Are you willing to take a job?' asked Kerry, breathing heavily.

'Yes,' I said, stroking Gabby's cheek by way of apology.

'Does she know where the coffee's from, man?' asked Gabby.

'WHAT'S HIS PROBLEM?' yelled Kerry, pointing at Gabby.

'He's merely interested in where the coffee is from,' said Glyn.

'Where does this one fit into all this?' she asked me, pointing at Glyn.

'Raaagh!' said Glyn.

'It's a mocha,' said Gabby. 'From Italy.'

'RIGHT!' screamed Kerry. She picked up the phone and dialled frantically.

'What are you doing?' I asked.

'Probably phoning Italy, man,' said Gabby.

'I'M PHONING OUR VENDING MACHINE SUPPLIER!' she screamed. 'TO FIND OUT WHERE THE FUCK THE COFFEE COMES FROM!'

'It's mocha,' said Gabby.

'AAAAARRRRRGHHHHH!' screamed poor Kerry.

'Raaagh!' retched Glyn.

'YES, BILL! CAN YOU TELL ME WHERE THE COFFEE IN THE VENDING MACHINES COMES FROM?'

'I bet Italy, man.'

'JUST FUCKING TELL ME, YOU PRICK!' bellowed poor Kerry into the receiver.

'Raaagh!'

'AND FUCK YOU TOO!' she yelled, practically smashing up the poor phone.

'She's going to say Italy, man.'

'WIGAN!' she screeched. 'IT COMES FROM A SUPPLIER IN FUCKING WIGAN! NOT ITALY, THE COFFEE'S NEVER BEEN ANYWHERE REMOTELY NEAR ITALY!'

'It's mocha, man.'

Kerry reached across the desk to throttle Gabby, who screamed. Nigel decided to chance coming over to assist. He tried to restrain Kerry, who turned and slapped him.

'Is Wigan in Italy, man?'

'Raaagh! – no, it isn't.'

'So the mocha isn't from Italy then, man?'

'YOU FUCKING PERVERT!' screamed Kerry at Nigel.

Ken walked out of the toilets, observed the commotion, and went back in again.

31

BERYL SAVES THE DAY

'Hello, flower!'

We were approached by a jolly middle-aged woman wearing a leopard-skin-print blouse.

'Beryl!' sang Gabby, immediately dismounting me and wrapping his little frame around her.

'It's OK, you two, I'll take over from here!' she said to Nigel and Kerry. Kerry stomped off to the ladies'.

Beryl quickly tidied the desk with Gabby hanging beneath her like a baby monkey, then sat down, planted a kiss on Gabby's spotty forehead, disentangled him, and gently shepherded him in my direction. All with generous smiles. Lastly, she nudged Nigel with her vast bosom, and packed him off to his work station with a pat on the bottom.

'Gabby, how are you, my sweetie pie?'

'I'm great, man!' said Gabby. 'Aren't I, John? We're rich beyond our wildest dreams!'

'Gab, we're poor beyond our worst nightmares,' I said, which Gabby found super-funny.

'Oh, Gabby!' laughed Beryl. 'You won't be needing my money any longer, then, will you?'

'No, I won't, man!' shouted Gabby.

'Are you going to introduce me, sugar?'

'Oh, yeah, man. This is John, he likes Gilbert O'Sullivan. And this is Glyn, he likes Kraftwerk.'

'I do,' Glyn said.

Beryl and I locked eyes briefly. It was enough for truth to pass between us – about Gilbert O'Sullivan, and several other things. At that moment Kerry flung open the door to the toilets and strutted back to her desk. There was no sign of Ken.

'And how is your mam?' asked Beryl. 'I keep meaning to phone her. Tell her I will.'

'She's got athlete's foot, man!' said Gabby.

'I am sorry to hear that, Gabby.'

'It's OK, man, she likes it actually!'

'That's worked out well then, flower. Gabriel, is that an Italian mocha you're drinking?'

'Yes, from Italy, man!'

'WIGAN!' yelled Kerry from her desk. 'WIGAN WIGAN WIGAN WIGAN!!!!'

Truly I'd never heard that town used as an expletive. I was minded again of George Orwell, pies, and poverty.

'If you say a word enough it loses its meaning, and the artificial nature of language and what we call *reality* becomes more dubious,' said Glyn.

'So, John,' Beryl said. 'You're here to look for a job, petal?'

I nodded.

'Me too,' said Glyn.

'Right then, let's have a look for you boys.'

'I'm not, man,' said Gabby definitively.

'I know, flower, rock stars don't need jobs.' Beryl winked. I wasn't sure whether this kind of official rubber stamp to Gabby's musical aspirations was sensible.

'Work is for cats,' said Gabby.

We three looked at him, then the penny dropped.

'*Saps,* Gab, not cats,' I said.

'Oh! I *thought* cats didn't work, man!'

'Unless they're rat catchers, in which case they work in exchange for food,' said Glyn.

'Oh God, don't encourage him, Glyn!'

'Raaagh!'

'Have you got any jobs like that for John and Glyn, man?'

'Beryl?' I said.

'Yes, petal?'

'Don't you think it would be good for Gabby if he *did* work?'

'Don't think we haven't tried, my love,' said Beryl, looking fondly at the blushing Gabby, then addressing him: 'Haven't we, flower?'

Gabby nodded enthusiastically.

'Yes,' continued Beryl, 'we've tried all kinds of industries haven't we, pet? The vegetable industry, for one.'

'The *vegetable industry*?' I asked.

'We tried to get Gabriel a job as a potato rumbler, didn't we, sugarplum? And a verge cutter. What else? Streetlight cleaner, assistant typist, do you remember that one, Gabriel?'

'No, man,' said Gabby.

'Treasure, your job was to help a lady typist with repetitive strain injury in her thumb – you were given her space bar on a separate console, and your job was to press the space bar whenever she said *space*.'

'What happened?' asked Glyn.

'Well, that's the sad part, I'm afraid,' said Beryl. 'It so happened that Gabriel's first day on the job coincided with the woman having a complete nervous breakdown.'

'How unlucky,' said Glyn.

'And there was that mix-up on the streetlight cleaning job, remember, Gabriel?'

'Oh... no, man.'

'You misunderstood what the foreman said – instead of cleaning the streetlights, you unscrewed every single light bulb along Dig Street. It was sad, actually – caused seven separate car crashes that night. The court cases are still going on. There was another bit of confusion when you tried verge cutting, wasn't there, Gabriel?' Beryl chuckled.

'Was there, man?' grinned Gabby.

'Yes, sweetheart, don't you remember? Instead of cutting the grass verge, you used the long shears to cut down over five hundred rose bushes the Council had planted the week before.'

'Easy mistake to make,' said Glyn.

'That's what I said, Gary!' said Beryl.

'Glyn.'

'What exactly is *potato rumbling*?' I asked.

'Getting rid of excess soil from potatoes and peeling them,' said Glyn.

I couldn't help but laugh. Had I tried I could not have come up with a more suitable job for one Gabriel Longfeather.

'A very skilled job actually, sweetie pie,' said Beryl. 'But you didn't have much luck there either, did you, Gabriel?'

'Yeah, man!'

'No, you didn't, flower, don't you remember? You accidentally threw the wrong switch in an area you weren't meant to be in, and the whole workforce was smothered beneath thirty-six tons of potatoes. It was, and *is*, I believe, the only recorded example of a potato avalanche.'

'So I had another careers interview, man,' said Gabby, 'and Beryl decided I should be a rock star!'

Beryl winked at me.

Gabby winked at Glyn, and Glyn retched.

'Was that entirely sensible?' I asked.

'Have you not heard The Motherfucking Nice Chap Trio?' asked Beryl.

'The Sofas!' said Gabby. 'We're called The Sofas now, man.'

'That's a comfortable name!' sang Beryl. I wondered if she and Tim of pen training were married, or at least cohabiting with a strict fifty-fifty share of household duties.

'We've got a gig, man!' said Gabby.

'Oh, sweetheart! Where?'

'The Big Street Festival!' said Gabby.

179

'Dig,' corrected Glyn.

'Aw, you *dig it,* Gary, how sweet!' said Beryl.

'Glyn.'

'David Beckham is coming, man!' shouted Gabby.

'He's a local boy, sweetie pie!'

'He's going to read a poem, man!'

'After all he has a beautiful voice, buttercup.'

'Glyn's going to do a rap, man!'

'Raaagh!'

'Oh, he's doing it now!' said Beryl. 'Go on, flower, kick it!'

'Raaagh! – I'm not – raaagh! – I'm just retching – raaagh! – due to anxiety – raaagh! – disorder.'

'Told you, man!' said Gabby.

'That was groovy, Gary! Well done you!'

'Glyn.'

I decided to push things forward a little. 'So, jobs?'

'Right, my little Tinkerbell,' said Beryl. 'What kind of work are you looking for?'

I got right down to it, explaining to her precisely the fix we were in; with Clements Markham House, the bank, Amundsen Enterprises, my plans to fundamentally change the world, The Dig Street Festival and the fact that I needed to earn £99,950 pretty damn swiftly.

'OK, my love.' Beryl keyed her computer, Gabby balanced the empty mocha cup from Wigan atop his head, Glyn pawed at his mouth with a yellow handkerchief.

'What are your qualifications, sugar?'

She wasn't Mr Kapoor. 'I have an O Level in Art,' I said, blushing. 'C grade.'

'Well done, my love!' sang Beryl.

'But I've always been an autodidact,' I said hastily.

'Do you take medication for that, flower?'

'Tell me you know what *autodidact* means?'

'Ahem! The ego!' said Glyn.

'Oh Glyn, stop going on about it! Where are we? What the hell are we doing here?'

'You feel a need to elevate yourself above others by using big words,' said Glyn.

'If I'm honest, sweetheart,' said Beryl, 'I think we'll struggle.' She pulled out a calculator, and mouthed calculations while tapping at the thing with long pink false nails.

Gabby kept looking at me with a smile as if to say *She's great isn't she*? I ignored him, and he inched closer and closer.

'Well, flower, by my calculations, it would take you eight years to earn that kind of money, and that's without any overheads whatsoever.'

'Even if I were earning one hundred thousand per annum?'

Beryl looked at me, not smiling for once, but wearing compassion like a bright orange sash.

'I get it,' I sighed. 'What have you got?'

'Marlon Brando,' said Glyn. I do believe it was a joke. I didn't laugh. Gabby commented that *The Marlon Brandos* was a really good band name. I couldn't fault it.

'What would you *like* to do, treasure?' asked Beryl.

I was stumped.

'Go on, John,' said Glyn.

'No, it's ridiculous,' I said. 'Anyway, she's not likely to get me a job like that, is she? We're looking at the vegetable industry, or worse.'

'John wants to change the world,' said Glyn.

'Care assistant, then,' said Beryl. 'I've got a few jobs going; you'd need some training, treasure.'

'She's right,' said Glyn.

'So, you fancy *care* then, flower?' said Beryl.

'Work is for bats, man!'

'*Cats,* Gab,' I said.

'*Saps,*' said Glyn.

'Yes, that's what I meant... God almighty!' I shouted.

Beryl looked up from her console. 'What's wrong, treasure?'

'I don't *fancy* care! I don't fancy any of these unpleasant poorly paid jobs! Why can't I do something well paid, and with a bit of status?'

'Ahem!'

'Is it too much to ask, Glyn? I'm thirty-eight years old; surely I've graduated by now to something slightly more advanced than first base!'

'You're eleven miles from One Ton Depot,' said Glyn, somewhat spookily.

'Well, sugarplum,' said Beryl, looking at me over her reading glasses, 'firstly, you underestimate the importance of carers, and secondly to get a highly paid job you need to have professional qualifications and relevant experience. You don't seem to have either of these, my love.'

'Experience?' I yelled (suddenly aware that I was just another yelling visitor to the Jobcentre. All I needed to complete the act were bad tattoos).

'You need it, I'm afraid, *relevant experience*, my flower.'

'But I have experience coming out of my ears!' I said.

'In which field, my darling?'

'He's not a horse, man!'

'No, I don't mean that kind of field, silly!' said Beryl.

'A cow field?' suggested Gabby.

'Look, I know exactly what you mean,' I said. 'Don't get me mixed up with Gabby, OK? I know about life. Life is my subject, and I have studied it assiduously for thirty-eight point five years!'

'Oh, darling!' said Beryl sadly. 'Look around you, my love. There are men and women much older than you who have had life experiences to make your toes curl.'

I looked. She was right. The people around us wore their histories like cruel bridles. I imagined them all as beautiful pink newborns, once upon a time, blank little slates of babyhood, perfect fleshy blueprints of future purpose.

The mayfly had it right. Straight to the point. No philosophy, no naming things, no words for the universe, no morals; nothing but miraculous flitting locomotion, then forever stillness, in the lovely month of May.

It was the end of September.

'I don't mind what job I do, as long as no one spits at me.'

I needed the loo. I passed the scowling Kerry and went into the toilets, thinking hard about suicide. The frightening part was the act of moving from life to death, not death itself. Life was life. Death was death. Both states were immovably valid, for want of a better description, like Glyn's thermodynamics. Life was unbearable. Death was nothing. The problem occurred where these defining states met – the horror-gasket betwixt, the brief straddling.

Standing before a urinal, I began to imagine towering cliffs – the grand gesture of driving up to the edge, abandoning the car (even leaving it running) and walking... slowly. A state of tearful euphoria. Peace, the decision made, reality already decaying, becoming meaningless, perhaps reverting to infant perception. A step forward. Apologies to the child you once were; an averting of their eyes. Another step, the car purring behind you, still acting out its implacable old-world logic. One more step, and the body does what the brain envisaged and ordered. Gone! Not bungee jumping, but untethered, free. And regret! Something imagined and played with previously, now the rushing air, the physical reality of the unreal, just another now-event, but this one gutturally final. Bitter truth at last. The best ever thoughts, and the worst. An automatically composed wordless poem of being, a masterpiece. A wish to declare love, make fast. And then a moment of pain?

I rested my head upon the wall. Deep snoring sounded from one of the cubicles. I stood straight and laughed involuntarily. It was luxurious. I bent down, looked under the divide of the cubicle and witnessed Ken, slumped like Elvis on the toilet, a gentle smile playing about his significant chops, pants around his ankles. Ken was living. His snore told me that he was very much alive. He was doing his thing. I'd be willing to bet some fifty-odd years ago his mother had told a neighbour, "Ooh, my Ken ain't half a good sleeper!".

I stood again, somehow cheered by Ken's repose, and inspected myself in the mirror. Not exactly David Beckham, but no John Merrick either – somewhere between the two. Somewhere between birth and death. Alive still. Alive. Ken snored on. I thought about the advantages I enjoyed. My body, though out of shape, worked. My heart beat merrily away in the cavity of my chest. Wonderfully Alive.

The ego, John, the ego.

Glyn was right. We three, Gabby, Glyn, and I, were the proud owners of enormous buffoonish egos, quite unearned, ridiculous. But intact. After everything, we were still whole. I began to feel very excited. I thought of Beardmore, and a plan hatched. He wanted me back at Amundsen Enterprises, because he had a niggling worry that I might after all spill the beans to Mr Taxman. He needed me onside. This much I'd won. I would get onside all right. I would creep *inside*. I'd devote myself wholeheartedly to his dirty scheme – but the profits of iniquity would no longer line Beardmore's pockets – no, I'd fund The Dig Street Festival. Forget Beckham, I'd hire the entire surviving 1966 England Team to sing a song and tell a few jokes! I began to jump up and down on the spot as Ken snored on. Oh God, it was my time! It was *our* time! Time for the people of Leytonstow to rediscover their own intact egos! Time for us to live!

I left Ken doing his Elvis impression, and bounded out of the toilets to find Gabby crying bitterly, banging his puny fist upon Beryl's computer desk.

184

'What's wrong?' I enquired.

'Oh sweetheart, I'm afraid I had to give Gabriel some bad news,' said Beryl. 'The government aren't willing to support him anymore – he'll have to get a real job, flower.'

'But why, man?' asked Gabby, blinking at her like a just-rescued miner.

'I'm sorry, sweetheart...'

'Has the button broken, man?'

'The button, sugar?' she asked, fingering the buttons on her marquee-like blouse.

'The button you press to give me the money, man – has it broke?'

'*Broken*,' I assisted.

'Ahem!'

Beryl laughed lovingly at this innocent explanation of why the state might have chosen, after five or more years of fully supporting Gabriel Longfeather, to insist that he now make his own way in the world.

'No, the button is fine, sweetie,' she said.

'Does the fuse need changing in the plug, man?' asked Gabby.

'No, we checked that too.'

'THEN WHAT THE FILTHY ARSEHOLES IS IT, THEN?' demanded Gabby.

'Gabby!' I said, shocked at his unusual expletive.

'Look, sugarplum,' said Beryl, playing with his willowy white hands as one might absent-mindedly shuffle a deck of cards, 'we can't look after you forever. It's time you got yourself a job, and stopped relying on *mummy*.'

Gabby began to choke as if the Jobcentre had been injected with mustard gas, his little face a picture of wild confusion.

'Come on, Gabriel,' said Beryl. 'Buck up. Let's see if we can't get you a nice little job somewhere, darling.'

'A racing driver?' whimpered Gabby.

'We might be aiming a little high there, Gabriel.'

'How about an Italian Mocha Importer!' he said, brightening, and digging his sharp elbows into my side. I couldn't fault Gabby for his unique ability to bounce back.

'Are you Italian, sugarplum?' asked Beryl.

Gabby confirmed sadly that his family bore no Italian lineage.

'Sorry, poppet,' said Beryl.

'I could build a new bridge over the River Thames!'

I could see that Gabby's expectations of employment, though admirable, were somewhat unrealistic. Then, an idea came to me. 'Beryl...?'

'Yes, my treasure-bottom.'

'Gabby could help me to organise The Dig Street Festival!'

'The ego, John!'

'No, it's fine, Glyn,' I said. 'I have tamed the ego.'

'If you could pay him, I suppose it could work,' smiled Beryl.

'YES!!!' shouted Gabby. 'Beryl, can you belly dance, man?'

'Here's what we'll do,' I said. 'Gabby will come with Glyn and me to Amundsen Enterprises tomorrow morning and we'll job-share! When you're on, Gab, I'll organise The Dig Street Festival, and vice versa!'

'But when will I organise it?' asked Gabby.

'When your friend is working,' said Beryl. 'I think it's a cracking idea!'

'You'll slash your income in half, John,' said Glyn.

'Don't worry,' I winked, knowing full well I'd already done that for both of us.

32

THE BANK OF JOHN

'John, man!'

I opened my door to find Gabby, wildly excited, and clutching more letters.

'John!' he shouted.

'What, Gab?'

'You won't believe it, man!'

I took the letters. There were at least six, official looking. I began to open them.

'Oh my God,' I said as I read.

'Read them out loud, man!' shouted Gabby.

'Bank of Billericay,' I read. 'Dear Sir, we are delighted to offer you a two hundred thousand pound credit facility with <u>immediate</u> effect – your Einsteinium Card plus PIN is attached.'

The others were of the same order. Bank of Southend, Trusty Bank of Clacton, Pubclays Bank, Bank of Strood. Hands shaking, I totted up the credit on offer. It came to over a million quid. The vast overdraft I'd been granted by NatEast had clearly done something very major indeed to my credit rating.

'Gabby!' I cried. 'We're rich beyond our wildest dreams!'

'Don't get ahead of yourself, man,' said Gabby.

I grabbed my cardigan. 'Let's go.'

'Where, John, man?'

'To the cashpoint, Gabby!'

'But John, man, we haven't got any...'

'Any what, Gab? Money? Gab, we *have* money. We have *a lot* of money. We have *so* much money, that if it were cashed into twenty-pence pieces you'd be crushed to death if it accidentally fell on you!'

At the mention of twenty-pences, Gabby's eyes lit up.

'You mean...'

'Yes!' I said.

'Not...?'

'Yes, Gab!'

'We're going to Disneyland, man!'

'God, no!' I said.

Disneyland aside, I found that I very much wanted to *buy* something. Anything. Right now. I told Gabby to look sharp, and we made a run into town.

We stood before the same NatEast cashpoint our bedfellows had broken. Now fixed, it watched us cautiously with green LED eyes. Which card to use? I took the Bank of Billericay letter, drew out the card and PIN, and inserted it gingerly into the ATM, all the time looking over my shoulder. This felt like theft, and perhaps it was.

I inputted the PIN, and asked to see my balance. It was zero. Then I asked the kind ATM for one thousand pounds. It thought about it for a few seconds before whirring in a frenzy of counting. Then it presented the money. My money.

'You do the honours, Gab,' I said.

He stared at me. Then he grabbed the wad, and threw the lot up into the air.

'My God, Gab!' I shouted. 'What are you doing?'

'This is what they do, man!' he cried. 'When they're rich!'

'No they don't, Gab! They invest it wisely and avoid drawing attention to themselves!'

A breeze which bore the earthy odour of autumn carried the notes fluttering and somersaulting down the street. I ran to and fro grabbing what I could, aware that I found the act distasteful. Gabby had no such scruples and whooped and kicked bunches of banknotes like fallen leaves. It wasn't long before we had company. As if by magic, people appeared from all directions and began to chase the notes about the street, grabbing and stuffing what they could catch into their pockets. At the end of the feast, the money-grabbers disappeared as quickly as they'd appeared, leaving Gabby and I clutching, to my reckoning, two hundred quid at best.

'That went well, Gab,' I said.

'John, it did, man! I'm so happy!'

'Right,' I said. 'Rule number one: when we draw out money, DO NOT throw the lot of it up into the air. OK?'

'OK, John, man,' laughed Gabby. 'What's rule number two?'

'Rules numbering one to ten are all DO NOT THROW ALL OF OUR MONEY INTO THE BLOODY AIR, GAB!!'

'How about rule number eleven, then, man?'

We drew out another thousand. This time I retrieved it from the cashpoint, and distributed it between my pockets and those of Gabby's death metal dungarees. Gabby and I began to stocktake what we could buy. We wandered up and down Dig Street, and the adjoining Market Street. It looked something like this:

Dark Secrets, a sauna.

Wash n Feel Top, a coin-op laundry.

Chicken Hamlet, a fried chicken/kebab shop.

Dalzeel's Dos, an Afro-Caribbean barber shop.

Falguni's Fabrics, a sari and Indian fabric shop.

Serafina Sklep, a Polish deli.

Dirk's Sporting Store, a gun, fishing and general blood sports outlet.

Ghana Junction, an African newsagent/phoneshop/barbers/ money-transfer/funeral parlour.

Waris Meats, a Halal butchers.

Paddy Clout, a bookmakers.

Kashmir, a greasy spoon.

Interspersed between these shops were as many pubs. I had a feeling that spending the money on anything but booze, birds, and items we didn't need, was going to be an uphill struggle.

Gabby had disappeared.

'Gab!' I called. Where the hell was he? I ran to and fro peering into shops and pubs, wondering whether he wasn't getting something idiotic shaved into the side of his head again, or simply wasting my money on something we didn't want and couldn't carry.

I began to panic like a parent losing a toddler on a crowded beach. I tried to calm down and think. Where would Gabby go? *To Disneyland*.

I did a reconnaissance buzz on the Kashmiri café, and ordered a cup of tea to steady my nerves. The place was largely empty, just a few lost-looking souls dotted about nurturing cups of brown liquid. Badly rendered Technicolor paintings of what I assumed were Kashmiri landscapes festooned the walls. I needed to think. Gabby was out there somewhere, with about five hundred quid. What had I sent out into the world? I shuddered at the trouble this consignment of cash might herald for Gabby, a person normally and naturally barred from most adult experiences.

My own wad sat in my left trouser pocket. I began to shake with nerves. *Come on, John*! I told myself.

'I'm going to change the world!' I said to the café.

All eyes on me.

'Good luck, mate,' said an old man.

The old folks started to laugh. I did too. It was something about the way we were set out in the café, an archipelago of loneliness, and the red check of the tablecloths, the crumbs, the hairs, and the garish paintings on the walls. We laughed and laughed, wiping our eyes with napkins, a temporary community built on mirth and pain.

I dried my eyes, and sipped my tea. Then I saw Gabby emerge from Dark Secrets. Oh Christ! I bade farewell to my new friends, and ran out into the street.

'Gabby!' I shouted. 'Where have you been?'

He walked like an old cowboy too long in the saddle. 'Ohhhh, John!' he wailed.

'What, Gab? Are you OK?' I said, gathering him into my arms.

'John, man, they did things to me, in there!' He pointed to the plum-purple frontage of Dark Secrets.

I let him go. 'What things, Gab?' I asked softly.

'Really weird things, man!' said Gabby, then looked around himself and whispered, '*With bottoms and sausages.*'

'Oh God,' I said. 'Gab, where's the money?'

Gabby looked at me wide-eyed.

'You've spent the lot, haven't you?'

'They made me, man!'

'On bottoms and sausages?'

'Sorry, man!'

'Come on, Gab, it's time to go home.'

'I can't, John!'

'Why not?'

'I promised them I'd get more money and come back, man! Agnes is waiting!'

'*Agnes*?'

'Yeah, man, she said she'd tell my mam if I didn't get more money and go back!'

'Oh Gabby, they've played you!'

'No, John, I think...'

'Come on, Gab,' I said, pulling his black sleeve in the direction of home.

'John, man, I think I'm in love with Agnes!'

'What?'

Gabby didn't say anything but gazed at me with, yes, it

was unmistakeable, love in his eyes. He was in love with Agnes in the way an engineer might love a hydraulic pump.

'Gab, they just want your money!' I said.

'Agnes told me that if she was forty years younger she'd have my children. I told her I didn't have any, so she couldn't, man.'

I leaned my head upon a lamp post – probably one of those unscrewed by Gabby in his former employment – and mulled this over.

'Can I have some more money, man?'

What had Gabby done with his new-found wealth? Lost his virginity. Admittedly in a slightly niche manner, but nonetheless he'd gone and popped his cherry. It was time honoured. He'd used the money to change his life.

I totted up our finances. Thus far we'd spent a tiny fraction of my total credit. A drop in the ocean to move Gabby's life, I hesitated to say, *forward*.

'Come on, then,' I said, and walked towards a row of three cashpoints next to Paddy Clout.

'Agnes said she'd take me *downstairs* if I gave her two thousand, man!'

'*Downstairs*?'

'I thought she meant to watch telly with her if I couldn't sleep, man,' said Gabby, 'but she said *Oh no, not that*. So I said, "To have some toast and marmite?"'

'What did she say?'

'She laughed, man, and said that if we went downstairs she'd show me *The Dark Chamber*. I think I'm going to come here every day!'

I didn't comment further upon Gabby's potential two grand a day habit, but warned him absolutely under no circumstances to take up Agnes's offer of showing him *The Dark Chamber*. Gabby laughed, and said bottoms and sausages was fun enough for the time being.

Bottoms and sausages. My stomach churned.

My hand shook as I drew out another five hundred pounds for Gabby, who jumped up and down by my side as I tucked the money into one of the legions of pockets located around his death metal dungarees. He became sombre as we walked back across the road towards the cataract frontage of Dark Secrets. Then we were at the threshold, and he turned white; more accurately, he turned blue, as he was naturally white as porcelain.

'Oh God, John, man!'

'It's OK, Gab,' I said. 'You don't have to go back in. They won't tell your mam – they've no way of knowing anything about you.'

'But I told them my mam's number, man.'

'You did what?'

'And where she lives, man!'

'Gab, why on earth did you do that?'

'They said they'd tell my mam if I didn't!'

The mind boggled. I was entirely at a loss. Money had immediately corrupted everything. Why?

'Oh Jesus Christ, and God too!' yelled Gabby.

'What now, Gab?'

'The bottoms and sausages, man! They, well, you know, use them to…!'

Gabby began to loudly retch, as if to make up for Glyn's absence.

'What did you expect, Gab?' I asked.

'I DIDN'T KNOW IT WAS *THAT* BOTTOM!'

It had been a less than ideal introduction to the world of love and sex. I took out a twenty pound note and wiped poor Gabby's mouth with it. Then I hugged him tightly.

'Can we go home, man?' sobbed Gabby.

'Of course we can, Gab. Let's get you tucked up in bed.'

'But what about my mam, man?'

'She's probably already in bed,' I said, and winked at him.

Gabby laughed through his tears, and we abandoned Dark Secrets to the night.

There was one more surprise waiting for us upon our return to Clements Markham House, namely two envelopes waiting on the welcome mat bearing our respective names. Each contained one hundred pounds in cash, and a note from Mr Kapoor which simply said BE WISE.

I told Gabby I'd take care of his.

THURSDAY

33

GABBY'S TRUE CALLING

I don't know why it hadn't occurred to me sooner, but it was already on my mind as the alarm clock bleated its 4.45 reveille. I got out of bed and stuck my head out of the broken window. The eastern sky wore just the faintest skirt of light. I looked up and down the empty scaffolding, then at the overgrown garden rubbish dump, the train line, and the back wall of the Jobcentre beyond. I smiled.

At the first opportunity, I would buy Clements Markham House.

I showered in the sink and brushed my teeth. How much was Clements Markham House worth? Four hundred thousand? Forty per cent of my credit. An investment of course, bricks and mortar. Yes, I would be a model landlord. I would further spend money in restoring the building to its former glory. It would be my grand project. I resolved to contact Mr Kapoor that very morning and make him an offer. I would also phone Tim to give him the good news regarding our budget for The Dig Street Festival. Lastly, I would, somehow, make it quite clear to Lois that if she did not love Roofie, then... then what? This required further thought.

A freight train thundered past, shaking the building. Dressed, I went upstairs and tried to wake Gabby. I shook him for fully ten minutes, aware that he was unused to the world of commerce, and in particular the fact that, to allow business to occur on any given day, participants had to rise earlier than midday.

'Stop it, Mam!' bawled Gabby.

'Come on, Gab! We've work to do!'

'I've not wet, Mam, man!'

'Gab, it's John, come on!' I cried, shaking him violently. 'Look sharp, Gab! This is the first day of your new career!'

'I quit, man!' shouted Gabby.

'Gab,' I said, manhandling him into an Ivan Ilyich-like sitting position, 'you can't quit, you've not started yet!'

'AGNES!!' screamed Gabby, arching his back like a windy baby.

'It's time for some honest graft, Gab!' I said. Actually it was time for some very dishonest shady dealings; but for the greater good, of course.

'John, man, I don't want to work!'

'Jesus, Gab, who does? Do you think I *want* to work? Do you think anyone *wants* to work? Right now there are millions of people sleeping snug in their beds with perhaps an hour to go before they wake up and realise afresh that it's not the weekend, and they bloody well have to go to work! You are no different, Gab!'

Gabby ran a puny white hand through his coal-black hair, and watched me with wet eyes. I briefly thought about Agnes and bottoms and sausages, then acknowledged to myself that actually Gabby *was* a special case. He was different.

'Anyway, man, we have a ton of money, and Mr Kapoor said we don't need to pay any rent! Why do we need to work?'

It was a good question. I had to think quickly. I couldn't tell Gabby about my master plan. Telling him would be a one hundred per cent guarantee that Beardmore would know by the time the store opened. I reflected that perhaps *this* was rule number eleven – NEVER tell Gabby a secret. I scored a masterstroke. 'Gab, at work they serve Coco Pops in the café.'

Gabby leapt out of bed and reported for duty.

We went downstairs and knocked on Glyn's door. After

some shuffling and coughing it opened, and Glyn stood in the gloom staring at us with his sad eyes.

'Erwin Rommel.'

'Really?' I said. 'How was he?'

'In a bad way.'

'Sorry to hear that.'

'He was five minutes away from his forced suicide, and in a pretty reflective mood. He cried. I gave him a hug.'

'Right-o,' I said. 'Come on then, Glyn, we've work to do!'

'Glyn, man, we're rich!' shouted Gabby.

'We aren't,' said Glyn.

'That's a good joke, Gab,' I said. 'Now come on, those floors won't mop themselves!'

'But John, we've got a million pounds! We could go to Disneyland!'

Again, for the greater good, I reached out and flicked Gabby's left ear extremely hard. This shut him up, or more accurately made him change the subject, if screaming can be called a subject. Glyn eyed me steadily, before shuffling back into his stinking lair to get ready.

I felt happy to be outside walking along Erebus Road. There was again a palpable nip of autumn in the air, a sensation of what I could only describe as *things moving*: time, the world, our lives. The fresh air made me giddy.

'Where's Gabby?' asked Glyn.

We looked back down the road. He was slumped over a wheelie bin, fast asleep.

'Let's go get him,' I sighed.

We returned to where Gabby snoozed peacefully, his long greasy hair flirting with the embossed letters of the bin's proud owners, Leytonstow Council. I pulled at his Iron Maiden T-shirt and shouted things like, 'Gab, your mam will be really disappointed!' and 'I'm ashamed!'. Nothing. Poor

exasperating Gabby was so comfortable, so completely trust-
ing in the omnipresence of the Council's services that he'd
decided it was a good idea to let the kindly streets of Leytonstow take care of his little white body.

I returned to Clements Markham House and fetched a ball
of twine I'd bought from Mr Mahmood two years previously
but hadn't reason to use, until now. Back with Glyn and the
sleeping Gabby, I severed two decent lengths on the lip of a low
brick wall, and tied a length to each of Gabby's wrists. Next I
tied the other ends of the twine to Glyn's wrist and mine. Then
I delivered a kick up Gabby's arse, and we were away; Gabby
still largely asleep, fluttering behind us in the morning breeze.

Twenty feet down the road Gabby surfaced and let out a
scream.

'It's OK, Gab, we're off to work, remember?' I said.

'JOHN, I TOLD YOU I DON'T WANT TO WORK!' cried
Gabby.

'Gab, we've been over this!' I said. 'You have no choice,
you HAVE to work!'

'Who says?'

'Everyone! The Queen, The Prime Minister, The Bloody
President of the United States of America!'

'When did they say that, man?'

'Gab, they *intimate* it!' I said. 'They say YOU LOT NEED
TO WORK!'

'But what about Old Brian, man? He hasn't worked since
1980, and he's fine!'

This was debatable in the extreme. I pictured Old Brian
wearing his most commonly worn expression, a pitiable
visage of bitter regret and complex health requirements.

'Do you want to end up like Brian?' I asked.

'Why do you have to be so horrible about poor Old Brian?'
said Gabby. 'He's a nice old man, man!'

Of course he was nothing of the sort. Until I'd been unable

to stand another second of it and had politely banned him from visiting my room, Old Brian had taken great pleasure in sharing a glass of Romanian Merlot and regaling me with diverse tales from his *interesting* life – highlights of which included petty cruelty to dogs, betrayal of impecunious women, self-righteous beating of little children, and thieving of swimming pools of milk.

'He's OK,' I said. 'But he's sad, Gab, and I don't want you to be like him. He's sixty-three, and has nothing to show for it, except for general congestion of all systems.'

'Like the M25,' observed Gabby, wiping away chunks of mascara.

I leaned over and gave him a tight hug.

'Come on, Gab,' I said. 'Let's go to work.'

'What's the point, John, man?'

'There isn't a point, Gab.'

'Oh right, man! Come on, then!'

I broke Glyn from his cloudy reverie, and we recommenced our trek. Within five minutes Gabby had again fallen to complaining bitterly about anything and everything which came to mind – that was when he wasn't falling asleep. I delivered another kick up the arse, and mentioned Coco Pops again, and for several minutes he skipped merrily beside us like an organic sidecar. But five minutes later he was snoring once more. Glyn and I man-hauled him onward.

I was thinking about how I would make my offer to Mr Kapoor when I tripped and fell, hitting my head upon the pavement. Gabby found this very funny. Glyn again paused to consider the sky. Then Gabby looked disgusted.

'What, Gab?' I asked.

'Oh John, man, you've sat in dog poo!'

I stood up quickly and craned my neck to inspect my bottom. Indeed it was caked in fresh dog poo. Not only was this utterly disgusting, it gave the impression that I'd soiled myself on the way to work. I told Gabby to get some leaves, and a search ensued. We looked high and low, but couldn't find even the smallest patch of greenery. Finally, Gabby plucked a weed from a crack in the brickwork of a betting shop and brought it to me. I thanked him, and tried to wipe the poo away, but the weed only decomposed, the poo went all over my hands, and was now smeared to an even greater extent over the seat of my slacks.

I shook a poo-coated fist at the sky and roared my disapproval.

'It's a test,' observed Glyn.

I made an executive decision, and removed my trousers, using the unsoiled parts to wipe my hands. I retrieved my bankcards and keys, then dumped the trousers in a bin.

'Come on!' I ordered, 'I've got more important things to think about!'

'But John, man,' said Gabby, 'you aren't wearing any trousers!'

I strode on manfully.

'Gabby's right,' said Glyn.

I wheeled upon them. 'Do you think I am not aware of this fact?'

'Which one, man?'

'The fact that I have, at this precise time, got no trousers on!'

Gabby found this especially funny. I'd really brightened up his morning. Even Glyn cracked a smile, said I was *legless*, then apologised.

'Gabby, stop laughing!' I shouted, as he jogged at my elbow muttering the word *trousers* over and over.

'Oh, John, man!' said Gabby. 'I'm sorry, it's just so funny!'

I exploded, and in one clean sweep, like a magician removing a tablecloth without disturbing the crockery, ripped away Gabby's own trousers, threw them over my shoulder, and stared into his shocked eyes.

'Oh God,' said Glyn.

Now it was my turn to laugh. Gabby wore no underwear. His child-sized appendage shifted a little, as if turning towards the morning sun like a little flower. Gabby screamed, ran at me, and with unexpected strength ripped the shirt from my back, buttons flying in all directions. In retaliation I cleaved his Iron Maiden T-shirt down the front, threw it to my feet and stamped upon it with a ferocity until that moment not imagined by mankind. It was like the worst porn film of all time.

'Raaagh!' retched Glyn. Wordlessly, Gabby and I turned on the poor fellow and in five seconds flat had removed and torn up every stitch of clothing he wore.

Panting, and amid a symphony of retching on the one hand and wailing on the other, I sat on a post and performed a quick inventory. I wore only sensible brown shoes and socks. Glyn, puking in the gutter, wore a pair of maroon boat shoes. Gabby, screaming and scampering to and fro like a just-uncovered woodlouse, wore only his disproportionately large white basketball boots.

Five thirty. Where to find a clothing retailer at this time? I grabbed Gabby, clamped a hand over his mouth, and told him and Glyn the plan. We would leg it to work, and dress in health and safety gear. Gabby's bulging eyes assented, and Glyn retched an OK. I gave the sign, and both of them sprinted in the general direction of Clements Markham House. Kicking myself at not explaining the plan clearly enough I gave chase, and forced them to about turn.

The street was getting busier. Drivers tooted their horns and lobbed witticisms at us. A car containing four sober-looking businessmen slowed – they wound down their windows and laughed so hard, red-faced, pointing, tears rolling down their cheeks, that the driver lost control, mounted the kerb and ploughed into a bus shelter advertising carpet cleaner. Doors opened and the men clambered out wearing a broad selection of expressions, evidently not knowing whether to laugh or cry. They gave chase, ties of all colours fluttering in the morning breeze. Luckily for us, decades of sitting behind desks had rendered our pursuants rather unfit and wheezy. One of them quite lost his balance and finished up-ended in a litter bin, the soles of his expensive brogues waving at the sky. I wasn't sure whether to laugh or cry either. Gabby was evidently enjoying himself now, ducking and diving around the big men like a featherweight boxer. Glyn seemed to have lost his appetite to run, and wasn't chased either – instead he stood at the kerb studying the sky while bus drivers leaned from their cabs and swore.

I thought of a way out. 'Gentlemen!' I shouted to the businessmen. 'Thank you for your co-operation! You have just participated in a work of art called *Chaos and Conformity in the Urban Setting.*'

This appeared to bring them round.

'Come with me, gents, and I will reimburse you for your trouble.'

Having resumed their composure, and commenting that in any event our antics had significantly brightened up their morning and company cars didn't matter, the men followed me to the cashpoint, chatting. Given a structure, I noted – in this case an artistic performance – our nudity had suddenly become quite acceptable. I looked at Glyn, still standing at the kerbside staring at clouds and being shouted at by drivers, and I realised he was fully immersed in a sub-performance of his own.

'Glyn!' I shouted as I drew out five hundred pounds to give the grinning men. 'It's wonderful! It's stupendous! It's called *Oh, Morning Sky, I am Nude Like You.*'

'You're insane,' said Glyn.

Perhaps he was right. I didn't care. We bid the men farewell; they disappeared laughing into a burger joint, presumably to recoup what the running might have worked off. I gathered Gabby and Glyn and we set off again up Dig Street. I was so excited. I couldn't wait to tell Tim.

Gabby spotted three black bin bags by the door of a charity shop. We tore them apart. Baby clothes in one. Toys in another. Ladies' clothes and shoes in the third. I fished out a yellow summer dress and held it against Gabby.

'Put this on,' I said, finding also a pair of white cotton knickers and handing them over.

'This is alarming,' observed Glyn.

Gabby looked horrified. 'John, man, these are girl dresses!'

I pulled out a larger dress for myself, white and sporting a nice pattern of red roses and green leaves.

'Gab,' I said, pulling mine over my head, 'you have a clear choice. You can continue to be nude, or wear that dress and those knickers.' It reminded me of the choice Mr Kapoor had given us outside the bank.

Gabby cried and held the dress and knickers at arm's length. Glyn cried too. I didn't know what all the fuss was about. I rustled around further in the third bag and pulled out a black and white striped figure-hugging pencil skirt and floral blouse for Glyn. I fished around some more and produced a fetching pair of yellow strappy heels for Gabby – presumably cast off by the same teenage girl as the little yellow dress. Lastly I spotted a nice embroidered handkerchief which I handed to Glyn, who coughed and wiped his eyes with it.

Weeping, Gabby slipped into the dress, pulled on the knickers, and slid his feet into the heels. I zipped him up at the back. Then I assisted Glyn to squeeze into the black and white pencil skirt and floral blouse.

We stood and studied our reflections in the shop window.

'John,' said Glyn, 'you and I look utterly ridiculous, but... Gabby looks *nice*.'

'FUCK OFF, Glyn!' screamed Gabby.

'Gabby, there's no need for that,' I said. 'Never tell some-one to *fuck off* when they give you a compliment.' Perhaps this was rule number twelve.

Glyn was right, Gabby did look nice. I don't think I'd ever seen his legs before. They were slender and quite hairless, with pleasing contours. The heels gave his calves and bottom a worryingly fetching shape.

'It's rather confusing,' said Glyn.

It was a bit.

'It shows our bias for visual stimuli,' said Glyn.

I gave Glyn *a look*. Glyn coughed and blushed.

'I'm a man, man!' shouted Gabby, as he fished a tube of mascara from his shredded trousers and began delicately applying it to his pretty lashes.

Make-up reapplied, he performed a slow-motion toss of his just-out-of-the-salon hair and strutted towards Amund-sen Enterprises. Oddly, Gabby's whole persona appeared to have morphed. Whereas Glyn and I were quite obviously hairy flat-footed blokes wearing badly-fitting dresses (I was minded of Fred Flintstone and Barney Rubble), Gabby assumed a distinctly feminine air (our Wilma or Betty). His walk was different. Now, he kind of swung his hips. His bare arms turned out slightly at his elbows. *He had a waist.* I could not dispute the fact that Gabby made a cracking girl.

I found myself shooting little glances at him. Glyn kept grunting and sighing. Gabby suddenly figured on the univer-sal stage of the male gaze.

'Bloody hell, Glyn,' I whispered. 'We've got a beautiful girl on our hands!'

'Raaagh!'

'Quite,' I said.

Gabby sauntered gracefully up Dig Street like a *débutante* amid wolf whistles and dirty propositions from tired-looking men. Glyn and I lagged a few paces behind struggling with our loins and our consciences. Any women we encountered shot daggers.

'Girls are great, aren't they, man!' cried Gabby.

It was true. Though I was nowhere near as convincing as Gabby, my own mind swam with the weight and mystery of what it meant to be female. This was never-before-experienced power! A motorist whose tongue lolled from his mouth like a randy lion's crashed into the rear of another goggling male. Amid blaring horns and rising steam both drivers ignored their predicament and gawped at Gabby, dangerously intense lust etched across their sweat-beaded faces. They had just one aim in life, and that was to mate with Gabriel Longfeather.

'John, we should have got boobs, man!' Gabby said.

'Gab, we're late!' I said.

There was no stopping him. He retraced his steps, bent over the charity bags in a worryingly suggestive fashion, and fished out a bra and several pairs of socks. He put it on, stuffed them in, and returned to Glyn and me with an impressive pair of bouncing bosoms.

More minor car crashes ensued. Some men looked suicidal. Gabby now looked so stupendously attractive that Glyn took to staring again at the sky wearing a worried expression, perhaps fearing this sucking vortex of sexuality would fell aircraft or even spacecraft.

'Oh John, it's so great being a woman, man!' yelled Gabby. 'Why weren't we women before?'

'Because we're male,' said Glyn.

I had to agree with Gabby. Although Glyn and I were the ugly sisters, I found myself very much enjoying being a woman. To be male (and plain to boot) was to be invisible. And what a practical garment a dress was! My lower body had never felt so ventilated – it was like dipping into a magical lake. I told Gabby this, and he drew out a fan to hide his blushes.

'Where did you get that, Gab?' I asked.

'It was in the bin bag, man!' said Gabby.

Yes, I was a fat friend, largely ignored by the myriad gentlemen on the street sucking toothpicks and fingering rusty switchblades in sweaty pockets – but Gabby! How proud his mam would have been! Having been covered in heavy metal paraphernalia for as long as I'd known him, it was fitting and right (and strangely ironic) that on this day, his first day free of Beryl's petticoat strings, he should find his true calling: to be a beautiful lass. It was poetic. My mind whirling, I began to wonder if I shouldn't smash confectioners' windows and grab armfuls of chocolate to present to him! Just then, the love-boat mood was somewhat compromised as Gabby hiked up his dress and did a wee on a road sign suggesting that vehicles over six tons might wish to find another route.

34

AMUNDSEN ENTERPRISES RELOADED

'Fackin time you call this?' spat Dave Lofthouse, standing at the fire door puffing on a roll-up.

'Hello, Dave,' I said. 'Nice to see you again.'

'Fack we got 'ere, then?' he asked, peering over his horn-rimmed bifocals.

'We had... a couple of issues on the way here,' I said.

'What fackin issues?'

'Did Eric tell you we were coming back?'

'Yeah, 'e did,' sighed Dave, wringing his battered red-top with bony hands as if trying to free the ink. 'You're gonna 'elp 'im flog all the fackin knock-orf.'

'John?' asked Glyn.

'Fack's 'is problem?'

'He doesn't have a problem,' I smiled. Glyn had, of course, too many to count.

'Did Eric tell you I'm going to... job-share?' I asked. Dave looked at my friends. Gabby performed a curtsy. Glyn exposed his large yellow teeth and moaned like Chewbacca.

'Fackin job-share 'e says,' muttered Dave, shaking his head and relighting his extremely short roll-up. 'What's with the fackin dresses anyway? Is it the new fashion to be a fackin puffter?'

'Not that I'm aware,' I said.

We followed Dave into the store, through the gardening section, and to the mopping storecupboard. He rifled through a box of consumables and gave us Marigolds and detergent. Next he provided three stout mops and a wheelie bucket each. Having filled his, Glyn shuffled off with his equipment to start mopping the screw aisle. Gabby started laughing, presumably at the realisation that he was expected to work.

'Gab!' I warned.

'What's this silly stick-thing with a shaggy dog on the end he's given us, man?'

Without warning, Dave slapped Gabby hard across the face, so swiftly and nonchalantly that had Gabby not begun to wail I might have doubted anything had actually happened.

'HE SLAPPED ME!' screamed Gabby.

'Nuffink funny about mops,' said Dave.

'What's a mop, man?' asked Gabby, holding one. I could see I'd have to start with the basics.

This display of moronic stupidity earned Gabby another tart slap.

'HE SLAPPED ME AGAIN!' cried Gabby.

Dave waited, hands on hips, looking at Gabby.

'Where can I get a mop?' asked desperate Gabby, gesturing with his mop, trying his best to look like a self-starter.

Dave again whacked him around the head, and Gabby tumbled to the floor exposing his little white cotton knickers. Dave whistled. Conscious that I too would receive some tough love were I to intervene in the wrong manner, I said, 'Dave, it's OK, I'll look after Gabby.'

'Watch the thick little bastard like a fackin 'awk,' said Dave, before flicking his dog-end at Gabby and taking off down the store on his spindly legs.

'He hits girls, man!' sobbed Gabby.

This hadn't occurred to me. Did Dave or did Dave not think Gabby was a girl? He certainly wasn't one to play along.

He wasn't playful at all. I reasoned that perhaps Dave simply classified people as *worth hitting* or not – perhaps a species of unconventional feminism?

In an approximation of possibly the second worst porno movie ever made, I stood behind Gabby, put my arms around him, whispered into his ear what a mop was, and showed him the basics. Gabby began to emit little sighs of pleasure.

'Wow, John, what a good mop you are!' said Gabby, batting his eyelids and softly biting his lower lip.

'Mopper,' I corrected.

'What, man?'

'This is a mop,' I held up his mop, 'and you are a mopper, Gab.'

'Is it time for Coco Pops, man?'

'Not yet, Gab,' I said, 'you have to do some work first. You have to mop the floors.'

Gabby started laughing again.

'Gab,' I said, 'you really must stop laughing about mopping. If Dave catches you, you know what'll happen.'

'He'll give me another mopper, man?'

'No, Gab, if you laugh at mopping or mops, and Dave catches you, he'll slap you again!'

'But why, John?'

'Because keeping this place spick and span is his life's work, Gab. Laughing about it is disrespectful.'

Gabby laughed. 'You mean that old man has wasted his whole life here?'

Dave arrived from the rear and boxed Gabby's ears, sending him once more to the floor like a yellow anvil.

'Make this little bastard useful in the next thirty seconds, or it's out the fackin door,' said Dave.

I pulled myself together, spotted Dave's forklift, and by way of distracting him asked a question about why the forklift didn't topple forward when lifting a heavy weight.

Dave stopped, and looked at me.

'Why the fack are you still 'ere?' he asked me.

Something Glyn had said about thermodynamics flashed across my mind.

'Well,' I swallowed, 'the way it looks to me, the forklift should topple over if you lift something heavy.'

Dave's face softened, and he chuckled. 'It's all about counterweight and centre of gravity, innit.'

'Oh, right,' I said, madly gesticulating to Gabby that he should get on with it while Dave gazed lovingly at his forklift truck.

'So, if you lift something heavy you need *less* counter-weight?' I asked.

'No you fackin banana!' cried Dave. 'Come 'ere, let me show ya.'

Dave and I walked off.

I got the full works. Dave explained everything there was to explain about forklift trucks, or at least that's how his treatise appeared to me, knowing nothing whatsoever about the subject. We talked about counterbalance, negotiation of corners, maximum loads, frequency of servicing, their history and staggering variety – he was just telling me about *Guided Very Narrow Aisle Order Picking Trucks* when, to my considerable relief, his phone rang. Dave sighed and answered.

It was Alan Povey. They immediately started bickering. I inched away, praying that I would find Gabby mopping away in his little yellow dress. Needless to say, I didn't. Where was he? I ran to and fro, hoping Dave and Povey's professional disagreement would last the course of my search. Where would Gabby go? Home? I was divided in my feelings for this outcome. On the one hand, it would be quite a relief if Gabby were to get out of my hair. On the other this would simply compound his trouble growing up, plus I was scared he'd be raped and killed *en route*, if he even knew the way.

I ran to the front of the store. The sun was just coming over the remaining island of houses, throwing its rays down Glyn's completed wet aisles. No sign of Gabby in the car park. I looked back across the store, and ran to see if Dave was still on the phone. He wasn't. Perhaps Glyn knew where Gabby was. I found him mopping an aisle which was currently barbecues and the like, but would soon be restocked with Christmas decorations.

'Glyn, have you seen Gabby?' I asked breathlessly.

'Yes,' said Glyn.

We eyeballed each other.

'And?'

'I saw him pass five minutes ago.'

'Jesus, Glyn, come on, tell me more, in which direction? Was he OK?'

Why the hell was he so bloody tongue-tied at work?

'He was riding a sit-on lawnmower. He was laughing.'

'Christ, Glyn!' I shouted. 'Didn't you do anything?'

'Yes.'

He looked at me like a large dozy animal wearing a pencil skirt and blouse. 'Seeing he was unwilling or unable to contribute, I increased my mopping rate to twice that of normal.'

I stood thinking, hands on hips in my summer dress with the red flowers and green leaves. I watched Glyn dancing with that mop, showing it the moon and the stars, a world expert in his field. I could have wept, he was such a cracking mopper.

I crept up to Dave's broom-cupboard-cum-office and carefully looked inside. He was sitting at his desk, smoking a roll-up and staring intently at Page Three. Then I ran to the only part of the store I'd not yet checked, the builders' yard outside. I heard voices out there and hid behind a rack of brown plastic drainpipes. I spotted Gabby sitting on a petrol lawnmower, chatting ten-to-the-dozen with Brendan, the buffer who never said a word.

What on earth was Gabby telling him? Probably about the money, Dark Secrets, Beryl, his mam. Ready to apologise and scoop Gabby up, I walked into earshot.

'*Master of Puppets* is the best Metallica album, man!' shouted Gabby joyously.

'And what about Iron Maiden, what's your favourite one?' asked Brendan. He was Welsh!

'It has to be *Powerslave*, man!' cried Gabby, punching the air.

'I love that one!' said Brendan.

Heavy metal! Of course! Oh, thank God!

They were so engrossed that I remained unspotted. I thought about what to do. Part of me was exceedingly proud – here was Gabby holding a perfectly relevant two-way conversation with another adult. It occurred to me that perhaps Gabby was not a *doer* at all, but an *enabler*. Apart from various discussions I'd had with Benny, this was the first joyful conversation I'd ever witnessed in Amundsen Enterprises.

I thought back to Glyn and his hard-edged utilitarian drive. Gabby was fine. Dave was fine staring at tits in his office. I too had a plan – why wasn't I working on it?

The lawnmower was a problem.

I took a deep breath and walked up to Gabby and Brendan.

'Hi, Gab!' I said brightly. 'I'll just take the lawnmower, and leave you to it.'

'Oh, John, man!' shouted Gabby. 'You'll never guess what! Biggy B is in a hard rock band! They're doing a gig at The Edgar Evans tomorrow night, and Biggy wants The Sofas to support!'

Biggy B blushed.

I was just about to warn Gabby that The Sofas weren't ready at all for their first gig, but... I didn't. What was the point? The greater good. So, Gabby had hustled a gig. So what? We'd just have to ensure The Sofas were ready for it.

'Gab, that's great!' I enthused. 'Just hand me the lawn-mower keys and I'll leave you to it.'

'God, I love working, John, man!' shouted Gabby as he plopped the keys into my hand.

'Gab, you're doing really well!' I said, and with that bid a farewell to *Biggy B*, mounted the lawnmower, and took off into the store.

I laughed as I progressed along the aisles, nudging the lawnmower back home at its quietest pace. I trusted Biggy would protect Gabby if Dave were to tire of breasts.

35

A CALL TO MARBELLA

Having safely stowed the lawnmower alongside its shining friends, I headed to the front of the store. It was seven fifteen – easily enough time to make a couple of calls ahead of the arrival of *The Mob*, as Dave liked to put it.

I walked on tiptoes to the empty customer services desk, took out my wallet, and drew out a scrap of paper with Tim's number on, and the yellowed business card Mr Kapoor had given me when I'd first moved in. Who to call first? I decided upon Mr Kapoor, that being the more difficult. I'd call Tim for dessert. The ring tone struck me as odd; more of a buzz. It went on for some time before someone picked it up.

'Yes?' said a far-away voice.

'Hello,' I said, 'it's John Torrington, from Clements Markham House.'

'John!' said Mr Kapoor. 'How is my graduate?'

'I'm OK.'

'What can I do for you, Mr Torrington?'

'It's about Clements Markham House.'

'How are the building works progressing? Do you like the design?'

'I was thinking, what I'd like to do...'

'Hang on a second, Mr Torrington...' I could hear him in the background ordering coffee, croissants, and orange juice.

'Sorry, Mr Torrington,' said Mr Kapoor. 'Where were we?'

215

'Where are *you*, Mr Kapoor?'

'Marbella,' he said. 'So, Mr Torrington, what can I do for you?'

This threw me – as well having realised I was bank-rolling the building works, it was now also clear I'd secured Mr Kapoor a city-break in the sun. I continued. 'I... I want to buy Clements Markham House.'

'You do?' said Mr Kapoor. 'Hang on a second, Mr Torrington, let me just put my phone on loudspeaker so we can discuss this further with my associates.'

The call wasn't quite progressing as I'd imagined. I realised now that I hadn't imagined the call at all. But had I, it would have been a simple case of me telling Mr Kapoor that I wanted to buy the house – Mr Kapoor would say yes, and I would thenceforth be the proud owner. I grew hot and embarrassed at the hard light the actual call was throwing upon my poor knowledge of how the world worked. How did people find this stuff out? Why didn't I know it? I knew lots of other things. I knew, for example, that one of Kaiser Wilhelm II's ministers died of a heart attack while performing a *pas seul* for his master, wearing a tutu.

'Would you repeat your offer for my associates, please, Mr Torrington?' asked Mr Kapoor.

I cringed. 'I was just saying that I'd quite like to... make an offer on Clements Markham House. Please.'

There was a torrent of laughter.

'He did say *please*!' said someone.

'Is it the one with the poems?' asked someone else. Mr Kapoor said it was.

'And how much are you willing to offer me, Mr Torrington?' asked Mr Kapoor.

'Three hundred,' I said, thinking leaving off the *thousand* might be talking their language.

More laughter.

'Three hundred pounds?' said Mr Kapoor. 'Mr Torrington, I shall have to consider your offer very carefully!'

'*Thousand*!' I supplied.

'Oh. But I had not yet rejected your earlier offer, Mr Torrington!'

Another waterfall of laughter.

'No!' I said. 'I am offering three hundred thousand pounds!'

'You are?' said Mr Kapoor. 'Well, this *is* interesting!'

'So... how about it?'

'I will consider it long and hard, Mr Torrington!' said Mr Kapoor. 'On the proviso you read me another of your fine poems. Think of it as a down payment.'

'What, now?'

'Yes, of course! Your audience is waiting!'

I thought about it. Of course I knew now that Mr Kapoor had no intention of taking my offer seriously. It was, however, one of those situations where some well-chosen words might just turn the tables – shut those up who thought they could mess with Mr John Torrington.

'We're waiting,' said Mr Kapoor, pleasantly.

It was time to pull something out of the bag. My mind was a blank.

Then it came to me! I would borrow something from a fellow poet. I was sure he wouldn't mind – it was one troubled soul helping another. I chose "Home Is So Sad" by Philip Larkin. I just hoped they didn't know it was by him. I recited it in my best voice, and the party grew silent. Very silent. No laughter, just silence.

'Home Is So Sad

Home is so sad. It stays as it was left,
Shaped to the comfort of the last to go
As if to win them back. Instead, bereft

217

Of anyone to please, it withers so,
Having no heart to put aside the theft

And turn again to what it started as,
A joyous shot at how things ought to be,
Long fallen wide. You can see how it was:
Look at the pictures and the cutlery.
The music in the piano stool. That vase.'

After a pause, someone in the background said, 'What fackin vase?'

'HOLD YOUR TONGUE!' shouted Mr Kapoor.

More silence. Did this mean I was now the owner of Clements Markham House?

'Well, Mr Torrington,' said Mr Kapoor. He was weeping, I was sure of it! 'This is an extremely beautiful poem. You appear to know absolutely nothing about money, about *business*. But, my dear fellow, you clearly have more than the average man's insight when it comes to *life*.'

I started to feel guilty about stealing the poem. It has been said that Philip Larkin was something of a xenophobe. He might have found the idea of my airing his poem to a group of Indian gentlemen breakfasting in Marbella a little irregular, to say the least. Perhaps it served him right.

'You have moved my associates and I this morning, Mr Torrington. You have moved me to tears.'

'Fackin bender, innit!' said a voice.

'As I have pointed out to you more than once, Indeep, tears are the mark of a man!'

'If he's a fackin bender,' said Indeep.

'I must apologise for my earlier jocularity, Mr Torrington,' said Mr Kapoor. 'Please let me take you out to dinner upon my return, to make amends, and hear some more of your fine poetry.'

'Really?'

'Yes. Tomorrow afternoon. You interest me greatly, Mr Torrington.'

'What about my offer...?' I said.

He'd hung up.

36

THE CHINOS, TIMOTHY?

Checkout staff were arriving, and going straight to the café for their breakfasts.

I took the phone from where it sat, and rested it upon my knee under the desk. Then I dialled Tim. It was answered immediately.

'Yes, hello?' answered a woman.

'Hello, is Tim there?' I asked.

'TIMOTHY!' shouted the woman.

'Coming, Mum!' shouted a distant voice.

'So what're you wearing, love? Chino pants?' I heard the woman say. 'Look, dear, I've ironed one of your dad's shirts for you, the lovely turquoise one!'

'Thanks, Mum,' I heard Tim say. 'I really appreciate it. Well done.'

'You don't need to congratulate me, son!' said Mum. 'After all, I'm your mum, and it's my job to look after you, isn't it? Now your dad's gone...'

'Tim?' I said.

'I know it's hard, Mum,' said Tim. 'But we agreed Dad's in a better place, didn't we?'

'Yes, in bloody Clacton, with that hussy!'

'Mum,' said Tim, 'can we chat about this later? I think there's someone on the telephone for me.'

'I'm sorry, love, but I'm not coping!' cried Mum. 'I can't get over it!'

'But Mum, you were always complaining about him, weren't you, remember?'

'Sometimes; I mean which wife doesn't complain about her husband now and then, I ask you?'

'Tim, I've only got a few minutes,' I said.

'Mum, you complained about him day and night, remember? You said he held you back, that it had been the biggest mistake of your life to marry him, and you should have married that Wayne when you still had the chance, remember?'

'He was dishy, that Wayne!' brightened Mum. 'But I couldn't have trusted him – he was a ladies' man, was Wayne, a lost cause.'

'And Dad was dependable, wasn't he, for the most part?'

'I'll grant you that, he was reliable, your father, apart from in the end when he ran off with that jezebel!'

'Do you think it's possible, Mum, just a tiny wee bit possible, that you might have driven Dad away?'

'How?'

'The constant complaining, perhaps? The day-and-night nagging? I mean (and this is just one argument, Mum), do you think it's possible that he might just have got so sick of it that he decided to end his days with another? One who might give him an easier ride? Be less critical?'

'Come on, Tim!' I yelled. I expected Beardmore's SUV to arrive at any moment.

'What?' yelled Mum. 'Now you listen here, Timothy! I cooked and cleaned and swept after that man for forty-five years! I tolerated his bedroom antics, lay there like a bloody stuffed doll and let him have his wicked way! I won't have it, Timothy, I was a good wife!'

'I'm sure you were, Mum,' said Tim. 'But do you remember when Dad had his triple bypass? Do you remember, when he came to, the first thing you said to him?'

Silence. I assumed she shook her head.

'He opened his eyes and you said, tartly, if I may add, "The lawn needs mowing, Roy".'

'Did I?'

'You did, yes.'

'Did it need mowing?'

'Probably, but that's not my point, my point is–'

'The bloody grass *did* need mowing, then! Who was meant to do it? Me, shackled to the bloody kitchen? Me, on my back, legs akimbo in the bloody bedroom?'

'Mum, I take your point, but–'

'So, what's it to be, Timothy?' asked Mum. 'The chinos?'

'Yes,' sighed Tim.

'And the turquoise shirt?'

'Yes, thank you, Mum.'

'Good lad,' said Mum. 'Now what are you waiting for, get the bloody phone, Timothy!'

'Hello, Tim speaking,' said Tim.

I was lost for words.

'Hello? Anybody there?'

'Hello,' I said.

'Who is it, please?'

'It's John Torrington,' I said. 'You might remember me from a recent Pen Training session at Leytonstow Town Hall?'

'I'm not sure I do...'

'There was a misunderstanding. I was at the town hall to pay Building Control a visit, but the receptionist put me into Pen Training in error. I caused a bit of a stink, and you had to... unfortunately... call security.'

'Got it!' said Tim. 'A classroom can be a frightening place, can't it, John?'

'I suppose so,' I said, grasping something as yet undefined with a sinking heart.

'Have you tried the out-of-hours number, John?'

'The out-of-hours number for what?'

'Didn't I give you a pamphlet, John?' asked Tim. 'There is a number you can call at any time, day or night, even Christmas Day if you didn't like one of your presents! No, well actually it's not for that – that's my little joke – it's for when you're feeling lost, or sad, or when you just need a shoulder to cry on, or when–'

'Tim, I'm not calling with regard to any of those things.'

'Have you contacted your key worker, John?'

'Bloody hell, Tim! Look, I'm sorry you've got problems at home, but please listen to what I am saying! I don't need to call anyone for advice, and I haven't got a bloody key worker!'

'Oh,' said Tim.

'I have good news, Tim! There's something I didn't tell you when we met.'

'If you've done time, John, it's OK.'

'No, I haven't done time! Tim, listen, it turns out that I am really rather rich! And I want to spend my money on The Dig Street Festival!'

Silence, save Tim's mother singing Phil Collins' hit "Two Hearts" in the background.

'Tim,' I continued, 'I want to rip *everything* wide open! We'll rediscover The Garden of Eden! It'll be the very first day the world has ever seen, Tim!'

'Where are you, John?' asked Tim.

'At work. Why?'

'Where's that, John?'

'Amundsen Enterprises.'

'Now, John,' said Tim. 'Can you find a nice quiet place to have a sit down?'

'Why?'

'John, I'm going to make a couple of phone calls and send some nice people to help you.'

'Bloody hell, Tim!' I shouted. 'You don't understand, The Dig Street Festival has already started! Just this morning a friend of mine stood naked on Dig Street staring at clouds! It was wonderful!'

'That's nice, John,' said Tim. 'Get yourself a cup of tea, sit tight, and we'll be with you as soon as we can.'

Now Tim's mum was singing "Bright Eyes" by Art Garfunkel.

I felt really angry at Glyn. I shouldn't have heeded his warning retches at Pen Training. I should have steamrollered the whole bloody thing – thrown over tables – somehow suspended Tim from the ceiling, pushed the security guard and his wheelchair down the sweeping staircase...

'Tim, why on earth do you assume that I require assistance? I DO NOT!'

'John, there is nothing wrong with needing a little help now and then. Don't worry.'

I took several deep breaths.

'Look, Tim,' I said. 'I really am rather rich, and I do want to make something of The Dig Street Festival.'

I heard Tim sigh. 'It's very kind of you, but to be honest I'm not sure what money could add to our little festival.'

'But Tim, the money is purely a conduit to the greater good, a necessary evil. I could compare our situation to that of a pressure group who decide they can only succeed by working with the system they hate.'

'Can you give me some examples of what the money could do?' asked Tim.

I... couldn't. I could only think that the money could buy us all a nice fish supper once the performances were done.

'T-shirts. I can buy us all T-shirts proclaiming our objectives!'

'Nice idea, John,' said Tim. I could tell he was just being kind, kindness being Tim's number one skill. I couldn't fault it.

'I could buy us some Personal Representation!' I cried.

'I'm not sure I have much truck with that kind of thing.'

'Why not, Tim? If it gets us what we want?'

Tim said carefully, 'I'm not actually sure we want the same thing.'

'I think we do, Tim!' I said, a little too vociferously. 'At Pen Training you said you wanted The Dig Street Festival to enable people to "rediscover their surroundings", and be "happier and friendlier"! Remember?'

Thinking time for Tim. In the background Mum sang "Scarborough Fair".

'John, I know I *said* those things...'

'You didn't mean them?'

'Yes, I did,' said Tim. 'But we appear to be talking at cross-purposes. You seem to be planning to change the world in some definite manner – perfectly admirable of course – but I simply want to enable the group to collaborate in a little performance, outdoors, to help build their confidence. To be honest I think presenting them with some sort of extravaganza would scare them witless. Me too, I might add.'

God, I felt foolish.

Tim had entirely succeeded in dragging me back down to earth. Why was I so ridiculous? What was wrong with simply *living*? I was a mopper. A mopper. *A mopper.* There were worse things to be.

'Are you all right, John?' asked Tim.

'I'm not sure,' I said.

'Look, I won't make any phone calls, but why don't you simply join us for the... well, I only called it a *festival* to make it sound exciting. Why don't you join us, and read your poems? It's tomorrow lunchtime, outside Leytonstow Tube Station.'

'I will,' I said weakly.

'I heartily look forward to it, John,' said Tim.

We said goodbye, but just before Tim put the phone down I could hear his mother weeping.

Poor Tim.

37

A LETTER TO LOIS

Poor John. Nothing had been achieved. Lois popped into my mind. She did not love Roofie. Why had she taken the trouble to write to me to answer my loaded question? I caught my reflection in a zigzag shaped mirror which was on fifty per cent special reduction. Last week it had been twenty-five per cent, the week before that ten per cent No one wanted it. I watched myself thinking about no one wanting the mirror or what it reflected. I would write back to Lois.

Again, I passed a surprised and worried-looking Glyn in the car park. Again, I crossed Whitehorse Road and went into the newsagent. Again, they only had writing paper with love hearts in the corners. Perhaps these were apt. I wasn't sure I could love anyone, apart from the grand gesture (or aim) of loving humanity; but if I could, then I loved Lois. The knowledge throbbed within my breast. And the hopelessness.

Again, I walked a little further up Whitehorse Road to the small park which had once been William Morris's garden, and, again, perched on the bench next to the lake.

'Hello again,' I said to the ducks and Canada geese.

Again, "Bread?" said their faces.

'I'm sorry,' I said. 'I haven't got any bread this time, either. I'm going to write a love letter to a barmaid called Lois. I haven't got a chance, but I can't help myself, now I know she doesn't love Roofie.'

'Quack,' said the duck nearest.

'Quite,' I said.

I took out the love heart paper and a pen. No pen training required here.

Dear Lois
Thanks so much for your note about not loving Roofie.

No, that wouldn't do. She knew what she'd said in the note, I didn't need to rub it in.

Dear Lois
Thanks so much for your note. I think I love you, and I can't stop thinking about us holding hands outside of your house. I should have kissed you (or tried, at any rate) but I lost my nerve, and I was too hot in that green polo neck, I shouldn't have worn it. Do you think we might have a chance, you and I?

No! I was rambling in a short note. And I was begging, practically. She wouldn't respect me if I begged. I scrunched up the second try and had another go.

Dear Lois
Thanks for your note. Thanks for answering my question – but you needn't have. I knew it already. I hope you find the happiness you deserve, Lois.

All My Love, John.

p.s. sorry about the writing paper, it was all they had.

I sealed it in the envelope and wrote out Lois's address. I looked at the ducks and Canada geese. Every single face still said "Bread?". 'Sorry, guys,' I said. Then I popped back to the news-agent for a stamp, dropped the letter in a post box, and went off to help Glyn with the trollies. Gabby had showed up too.

38

DO NOT ASK HIM FOR HUGS

We three were shunting trollies in circles when Beardmore's dangerous-looking black SUV glode across the car park and pulled up in the best disabled parking bay. Gulping, I tossed Gabby some quick advice regarding this gentleman:

Do not ask him for hugs.
Do not tell him jokes.
Do not ask him whether he likes heavy metal (he doesn't, he likes Gilbert O'Sullivan).
If possible, don't speak to him at all.

'Aw, he sounds nice, man!' said Gabby. 'Apart from the Gilbert O'Sullivan!'

'He's a monster,' said Glyn.

'Glyn's right, Gab,' I said. 'In any given circumstance, you should never assume that Beardmore will be anything other than absolutely horrible.'

'Like Alice Cooper, man!' yelled Gabby.

'No, Gab,' I said, 'Alice Cooper is just pretending to be evil – he's actually, by all accounts, a thoroughly nice man. Beardmore is just the opposite, I'm afraid.'

'More like Lemmy from Motörhead, man?'

A crack appeared in the driver's tinted window, releasing plumes of smoke and "Nothing Rhymed" by Gilbert O'Sullivan. I couldn't see Beardmore, but was well aware we were being scrutinised. I quickly directed the boys to finish clearing the car park of trollies arranged about us like a Wild West wagon camp.

Oddly, guiltily, I felt a certain pride. Even though I planned to use my new role as *Web Mobility Director* to scupper Beardmore, it was still recognition of sorts. I found myself rather looking forward to seeing him, much as a hostage may begin to foster amiable feelings towards their captor. The door opened and Beardmore clambered out, the car suspension popping up with what one imagined was relief. Cigar clamped between his thick lips, he waddled our way. It was 9 a.m. – the armpits of his enormous blood-red shirt were already ringed with giant sweat patches. He looked like Demis Roussos's evil twin.

I glanced at Gabby, who wore a singularly terrified expression – I didn't think there was much risk a hug would be solicited.

'Gents,' said Beardmore.

'Hi, Eric,' I warbled. 'This is Gabby, I'm going to job-share with him if you don't mi–'

'When did yer become a fackin bender?' interrupted Beardmore, stroking a wooded chin with a fat greasy hand.

'It's a long story, man!' said Gabby. 'You see, me, John, and Glyn, were walking to work this morning and we ripped off our clothes by mistake, so we–'

'What the fack 'ave you brought this little cant for?' asked Beardmore, pointing at poor Gabby.

'Gabby. Very useful,' I lied. 'I thought he could mop and collect trollies while I'm at the Internet café, selling.'

'For the same fackin pay as one?' stated Beardmore.

'Yes,' I said.

'One pay packet for the three of you little cants?'

'Ahem!' observed Glyn.

I boiled with anger but tried manfully to hide it – of

course Beardmore spotted my inner disquiet and I could see that it pleased him greatly. He commenced snorting.

'Eric,' I said, 'it's a deal!'

'Good lad, let's spit on it,' said Beardmore, and after a gargantuan hawk, delivered his disgusting mess into Gabby's pixie face.

As Gabby wiped himself clean of gunk and tears, a lorry towing a scrap car arrived. As it neared, I could see the car was none other than a canary yellow Ford Cortina saloon Mark III. It took me right back to my childhood. A real beauty. Our difficult conversation was put on hold as we watched the driver jump from his cab and start to unhook the car, which, once disentangled from its web of chains, fell to the tarmac with a great thump. The driver waved at Beardmore, who chuckled and tilted his cigar back, before returning to his cab and roaring off, leaving the Cortina in the middle of the car park.

Alan Povey came running out of the store waving his arms and shouting something about *Ruddy Authorised Treatment Facilities*. Almost before the lorry had turned into Whitehorse Road he began plastering the Cortina with red health and safety stickers. Once the car had been consigned to health and safety damnation (it looked like it had chickenpox), he stood back, hands on hips, and looked quite pleased. I could see clearly that the "risk" the Cortina presented was not one of potential hurts to human beings, but more, for Povey, an unbearable emblem of unexamined freedom; just too wild a non-standard object for his nerves. Povey had hunted the beast down and tamed it with regulatory damnation – it no longer sat out there in the clear air of an asphalt wilderness, but had been disciplined and domesticated by well-thought-out directives. The car still had sharp edges, I noted, but no matter, because Povey was sated. It seemed to me this was a version for health and safety professionals of the philosophical conundrum regarding whether or not a tree in a remote forest makes any sound when it falls unobserved.

Povey scuttled across the car park to we four.

'Are we reet?' he grinned.

''e's brought this little bender, Alan,' said Beardmore, pointing at poor Gabby, who pinched his yellow dress and curtsied.

'She's a pretty lass, all right!' sang Povey. 'She appears to be perspirin. 'ave you worked 'er too 'ard, Eric-lad?' he winked.

Beardmore laughed.

''ave yer showed 'er oo's boss then, 'ave yer?' leered Povey.

Gabby blushed and batted his eyelids. To my mind he was becoming a little too good at being just the kind of girl these men expected a girl to be. I made a mental note to introduce Gabby to the concept of feminism.

'And what 'ave we 'ere with these two in dresses?' laughed Povey. 'What is it, *Gay Day* or somethin?'

'You are quite wrong to directly associate men in female attire with homosexuality,' said Glyn.

I gawped at him. Out of the blue it was the bravest thing I'd ever witnessed.

'And in doing so,' continued Glyn, 'you reveal an extreme lack of social awareness, worldliness, and indeed intellect.'

Povey looked puzzled. I wondered if he was considering whether Glyn's opinions put anyone in harm's way. Beardmore, a sporting man, was clearly enjoying where this would go, and watched Povey intently.

Then the penny dropped. Beardmore could not spit in our faces with Povey present!

'You're an entirely closed person, Alan. You expend your energies on anything which will not add value to any given situation, and you are intolerant of other human beings to the point of psychosis.'

Povey appeared deep in thought. He was entirely unable to *listen*. For Povey, all social interaction was an exercise in thinking about what *he* wanted to say next.

'Is 'e drunk?' asked Povey at last.

'Probably,' said Beardmore. 'Come on, Alan, let's get this fackin day on the road.'

''e can't bloody well work if 'e's drunk, Eric-lad!' said Povey.

'I'll sort it, Alan,' said Beardmore.

'You'll sober 'im up?' asked Povey. ''ow?'

'I'll fackin well sort it.'

'You'd better move that car, Eric,' said Povey, pointing at the now polka-dot Cortina. 'It's a bloody death trap that is!'

'We'll fackin move it all right,' laughed Beardmore. Then he turned to me. 'See *you* in my fackin office.' The two men shuffled off through the entrance into Amundsen Enterprises.

'Jesus, Glyn!' I said. 'That was amazing!'

Glyn grinned at me. I was so unused to this I almost found it embarrassing.

'My fear appears to have deserted me, John,' smiled Glyn, 'because I know that if the going gets tough, unless I'm actually killed, I'll end up feeling very much better for suffering.'

God, Glyn was fun.

'Would you strike me, please, John?' asked Glyn.

'Strike you?'

'Yes, if you wouldn't mind,' said Glyn, presenting his round face.

Not knowing quite what I was doing, I raised my hand and gave him a little slap.

'Punch me, if you will, John,' said Glyn. 'Hard.'

'Glyn, I really don't want...'

Gabby suddenly leapt forward and, with surprising strength, delivered a glancing blow which sent Glyn reeling.

Glyn shook his head, bent over for a second, then

straightened up. 'Many thanks, Gabby,' he said.

'Gabby, you mustn't hit people!' I said.

'But John!' said Gabby. 'Glyn asked!'

'It's fine,' said Glyn. 'When I was staring at the sky this morning, I realised that I really rather like rough treatment and humiliation.'

'You like it?'

'More specifically, I feel purged,' said Glyn.

'Purged?'

'Yes,' said Glyn. 'Fun doesn't have to be fun to be fun.'

'Pardon?' I asked.

'Fun,' said Glyn. 'It doesn't have to be *fun* to be fun.'

He recommenced mating trollies, and I understood that our revelatory conversation was over. I turned to Gabby. 'Are you OK, Gab?'

'Yeah man, of course!'

'*Of course.*'

Glyn took Gabby's hand and dragged him along. I watched them go, and completed a quick inventory of where we were:

1. Mr Kapoor would not take my offer seriously, and Clements Markham House was probably lost.
2. Tim wasn't faintly interested in taking The Dig Street Festival to the next level.
3. I'd negotiated a 66.6% pay cut with Beardmore and was over £100k in debt.
4. Fun did not have to be fun to be fun.
5. I had access to just shy of one million pounds sterling.
6. I'd sent a letter covered in love hearts to Lois.

39

THE CHRISTINE KEELER

Highly conscious of body language, I sat in Beardmore's foul elevated office waiting until he'd finished pretending he had something more important to do. He stumbled about picking up various items of desk furniture, weighing them in his hands like cricket balls, shooting me occasional glances to make sure I was feeling appropriately discarded.

My counter-attack consisted in avowedly avoiding Beardmore's glances while whistling the theme tune to the *Antiques Roadshow*. This was a smokescreen – I felt anything but cool and collected – fear and joy seared through my system in equal measure. Wild Technicolor images of birth and death assaulted my mind: babies, rivers, empires, mountain ranges, solar systems, and stars themselves.

I pondered Beardmore's likely reading of my body language; of course having to factor in also the white summer dress with green leaves and red flowers. I figured it went something like this:

DEMEANOUR	NORMAL PERCEPTION	BEARDMORE'S LIKELY PERCEPTION
Arms and legs crossed	Defensive	Gay
Prim, straight back, knees together	Respectful	Gay
Lounging, feet on the table	Disrespectful	Gay
The Christine Keeler	Sexy	Gay

Having previously experienced a chink in Beardmore's armour, I didn't wish to appear intimidated. I placed my feet on his desk, which made him suffer a coughing fit. Worried for his heart, I removed them. Beardmore sat down with a snarling chair fart. We eyeballed each other.

'Let's talk business,' I said, breaking the seal of our wary dance.

Beardmore laughed. But he didn't quite achieve nonchalance. With not a little effort, he rose, turned, opened a cupboard and dragged out a large metal box with green canvas straps and a mass of wires connected to an old-fashioned telephone receiver. I half wondered if he was about to ask me to be a suicide bomber.

'This is your mobile phone,' he puffed, pushing the army-green equipment across the desk; in the process upsetting the large full ashtray, which further soiled the thing.

'Stand up,' ordered Beardmore.

I did not. Then I did.

'Turn around, you little cant,' he said.

Affecting total detachment, I complied and Beardmore humped the "mobile" phone onto my back. It was heavy. I groaned – this cheered my foe.

'Put your fackin arms through the straps.'

I allowed this.

'Now you're connected,' he chortled.

'How do I make a call?' I asked.

Beardmore again lifted the weighty equipment from my back and set it with a heavy clank upon the desk. Then he opened a flap in the box, reached inside and pulled out the sort of crank one would associate with a Model T Ford. He began to turn it, and the thing sputtered into deafening life.

'JESUS, IS IT A PETROL PHONE?' I shouted, a little concerned that gasoline and mobile telephones weren't good bedfellows, or so signs in most petrol stations claimed.

'WHAT'S IT FACKIN MATTER?' spat Beardmore.

'HOW DO YOU DIAL?' I yelled.

'I'LL CALL THE SPEAKING CLOCK,' shouted Beardmore, and proceeded to dial behind another flap in the metal box. 'PICK UP THE RECEIVER, YOU LITTLE SHITE!'

I didn't like the way I was addressed, but went along in the knowledge that in order to scupper him and his nice little set-up I needed to appear grateful and, moreover, mysterious. I smiled a little, and picked up the receiver, which was covered in what looked like frying grease. I carefully placed it to my ear while Beardmore continued to crank.

'OH YEAH! WE NEED TO DO THIS, TO GET RECEPTION!' cried Beardmore, violently pulling out a thick black aerial from the top of the box. I watched it go up and up until it punctured the polystyrene ceiling tiles above our heads and disappeared into the black void.

Somewhere in the far distance I heard, 'At the third stroke...'

The demonstration complete, the atomic telephone was switched off.

'One more bit of kit,' said Beardmore, opening another cupboard. 'A camera to take pictures of the... soiled stock... to e-load onto the fackin Webinet.'

He produced a genuine antique, a vintage Polaroid camera, and handed it to me. I weighed its chunkiness in my hands.

'I'm not sure,' I said, 'that having a physical copy of the photo will actually assist me to upload the image.'

'What are you on about, you little cant?'

'Eric,' I said, 'the image needs to be in a digital format in order to upload it to the Internet.'

'Thick bastard,' spat Beardmore, tapping the side of his wrecking ball head with a cigar-brown finger. 'Watch this.'

Beardmore pointed the Polaroid at me and took a snap. We waited, and when the photograph was ejected, waited some more for my image to materialise. Once it had, Beardmore straightened the 1970s computer console on his desk (it looked like the computer and the phone might have come as a package), held the Polaroid within its field of vision (had it eyes) and said, 'Compooter, e-load this photo onto the fackin Webinet,' before turning to me with a grin. 'There. Easy fackin peasy!'

I wondered whether Beardmore thought he was commanding the bridge of the Starship Enterprise. I wasn't an expert, but nonetheless briefly considered pointing out a few technical issues regarding what I'd just witnessed. I made a mental note to procure a digital camera.

'You're all set,' said Beardmore. 'If you can be... *trusted*, all you need to do is photograph the gear, put it on the fackin Webinet, sell it for as much as you can, deliver to the buyer, and give the proceeds to me, so I can... send to 'ead Office.'

'Sounds fine,' I said.

'So?' asked Beardmore, licking his blackened lips and coming nearer.

'I can be trusted,' I said.

Beardmore's fetid mouth was now a couple of inches from mine. He whispered, 'If you *can't be trusted*, some very bad things might 'appen, whether I'm in fackin jail or not. Do you understand, you fackin cretin?'

'Yes. I understand.'

'And?' asked Beardmore, his shark's teeth within biting distance of my chin.

'Thank you,' I cringed, 'for the opportunity to work again at Amundsen Enterprises, and for the... benefits package.'

'Good,' allowed Beardmore, withdrawing, eyeing me and farting down again into his leather-effect swivel chair. 'Now fack off, you little toerag!'

With some effort, I picked up both the immobile phone and antique camera, and made to leave.

'One more thing,' said Beardmore – damn it, he'd said *one more thing* before I'd got the chance!

237

'Yes, Eric?'

'Company car,' he held up some keys attached to a dog-eared piece of leather.

This I hadn't expected!

'Really?' I asked.

'Yeah, it's that pile of shite in the car park!'

'Does it drive?'

'Fack knows.'

40

NICE WHEELS

Beardmore couldn't have known I'd be pleased as punch with the car – but I was. Clutching the Polaroid camera, the immobile phone strapped to my back, I struggled down the green metal stairs and headed outside. Still "parked" askew where the lorry had dumped it, and covered in health and safety warnings, the car, *my* car, sat reflecting the late summer sun and drawing what might after all have been envious glances from valued customers. I could tell it was as out of place in the world as I.

Glyn was soldiering on, collecting trollies in his floral blouse and figure-hugging pencil skirt. There was no sign of Gabby – I assumed he was once again engaging the previously mute in conversation. I approached my company car and proudly stroked its red sticker-covered utility contours, being careful not to cut my hand on rusty edges. Glyn ambled over.

'Nice wheels,' he said without sarcasm, a mode of expression entirely absent from his repertoire. I took the key, its edges like worn pebbles, and popped the boot to stow the camera and immobile phone. As it sprung open, I could have sworn joyful cries of children playing at 1970s English beach resorts wafted into the car park, along with the odour of cigarettes, fish and chips, and sun cream. I half expected to find buckets and spades made of thick old-fashioned plastic, corners white with age, and rough still with timeless specks of sand.

'The tax disc ran out in nineteen eighty,' said Glyn.

'The year Old Brian ran out of free milk,' I said.

I lumped the tools of my trade into the boot, worried for a moment the chassis might simply give way – but no, despite Glyn's worried expression, it held. Now to turn the thing over. I cleared the beige-beaded seat of Wimpy detritus, and clambered in. The suspension gave a low moan akin to the cry of a humpbacked whale. The wheel nearest me was visible through the rusted front wing, the ashtray full of cigarettes smoked to their butts. The passenger seat boasted a well-shuffled set of dirty playing cards – Summer of Love ladies depicting lascivious Confessions-Of-A-Window-Cleaner poses. What became of these women? Some dead, some now grandmothers with barely the living memory of a poor decision taken in youth. I gathered them from the seat and handed them to Glyn, who retched, looked around with a wild expression, then produced an elastic band to bind them, finally tucking the naughty pack up the sleeve of his floral blouse – their final resting place.

I turned the key, and with a high-pitched yelpa-yelpa-yelpa the Cortina's starter motor gladly fulfilled its sole purpose, to harry the engine into spluttering life. Thick black smoke issued from the rear and underside of the car, to the extent that day turned to night. I disengaged the hand brake – in doing so realising the car didn't possess one – depressed the clutch, and began fighting with the gear stick amid sounds reminiscent of one of Gabby's band practices. The head of the gear stick was a yellowed golf ball with no indication of which gears were where, but finally I found one, slowly raised the clutch, and prepared for my first expedition across the car park.

The Cortina lurched backwards, and Glyn bellowed with pain. I killed the engine and leapt out coughing into the black veil. When the smoke cleared I spotted poor Glyn's head sticking out from underneath the chassis, his body entirely eaten, soft blond hair covered with soot.

From the floor, Glyn smiled. 'John, you knocked me over.'

'God, I'm so sorry, Glyn!' I yelled, grabbing at his pretty lapels in an attempt to drag him out.

'It's OK, John,' said Glyn. 'I rather enjoyed it.'

'Enjoyed being knocked over?' I asked, aghast. 'Your new-found liking for suffering extends to nearly being killed?'

'It appears so.'

I squatted to survey our predicament. Glyn's pencil skirt appeared to be hooked. Push or pull, I could not dislodge him.

'Hang on Glyn, I'll have to try something.'

I jumped back into the car, started it once more amid so much black smoke I was terrified Glyn would asphyxiate, and desperately searched for any other gear except reverse. The problem was I couldn't remember where reverse had been. What to do? The clock was ticking. I was in danger of gassing Glyn Hopkins to death. At last I found a gear. Assuming there were four forward gears and one reverse, I surmised the odds were in Glyn's favour and mine that, upon lifting the clutch, the car would move forward, thus releasing my poor friend from its grasp. I lifted the pedal – the car performed a squealing wheel spin and shot backwards again. I cut the engine and rested my head on the steering wheel, preparing to weep.

'Are you OK, John?'

I snapped my gaze to the right to find a chimney-sweep-like Glyn Hopkins staring at me.

'Oh, thank God!' I said. 'I thought I'd killed you!'

'You didn't.'

'Are you hurt?!' I asked, searching his blouse for puncture marks.

'Yes, thanks.'

'Badly?'

'Adequately.'

241

41

RUG-TESTING AND
A CATCH-UP WITH BENNY

Glyn thanked me again for knocking him over, and limped off to resume rustling trollies. Business was in full swing at Amundsen Enterprises. Benny snoozed in the arms of a heavyweight hammock; soft meringues of smoke sifted into the store from beneath Beardmore's elevated door; the checkout girls manned the tills yelling at each other nasally and teasing valued customers who happened to glance at the contents of their low cut tops; Povey dashed from colleague to colleague like an unpopular *maître d'*, urging them to look lively; Dave bombed up and the down the aisles on his favourite forklift truck chewing the end of an unlit roll-up; and consumers milled about, imagining themselves fulfilled for buying all the tat Amundsen Enterprises had to offer.

I thought I'd best locate Gabby, increasingly worried he'd come a cropper at the hands of Dave, who surely now had his card firmly marked. I searched high and low – wheelbarrows, hods, cement, treated wood, creosote, vinyl, plasterboard, subtle lighting, in-your-face-lighting, mirrors, plants, toilets, taps, kitchens, bathrooms – and finally, in passing the fluffy rug and cushion aisle, spotted two pairs of feet sticking out from under a shelf, one clad in patent leather ballroom dancing shoes, the other in strappy yellow heels. I changed course with some trepidation.

'Oh, hello!' said Douglas Dauphinoise, painfully getting

up from the fluffy purple rug upon which, unless my eyes were deceiving me, he and Gabby had lain *in flagrante*.

'Oh my God!' I shouted. 'Jesus wept! Gabby!'

Gabby's pretty yellow dress was up around his bony hips, and his little cotton knickers were not quite straight.

'I was just... assisting Gabriel with this rug,' mumbled Douglas, playing with his cuffs and straightening his orange kipper tie.

'It's true, man,' beamed Gabby. 'And he said he'd give me a ride in his Rolls Royce, and show me some little puppies he has at home! Isn't that nice? Oh John, man!' sang Gabby. 'I'm so glad you brought me here, it's a lovely job!'

'Gabby, what would your mam think about... *this*?' I asked, pointing at the site of the debauchery I'd just uncovered.

'She'd think it was a great job too, man!'

'Gabby,' I said, 'don't you see what's going on?'

'Yes, Douglas is helping me to test out this rug, so that customers don't buy it and find out it's not good for lying down on, man.'

'I'm sure you can manage now, Gabriel,' said Douglas. Then he ambled back down the aisle whistling "I loves you Porgy".

I straightened Gabby's knickers and pulled his dress down before setting him on his feet. 'Gab, you really need to stay away from Douglas.'

'He's a nice old man, man,' said Gabby.

'Gab, I don't know how to say this...'

'What, man?'

'Douglas *took advantage* of you.'

'Like in tennis, man?'

'No, not like in tennis, Gab.'

'I can't believe I've been getting money from Beryl for so long, man!' yelled Gabby. 'I was born to work, it's wonderful!' He danced down the aisle after Douglas.

243

Gabby's talents were staggering. What to do about this? I watched him go and reflected that he was, after all, twenty-six. Was there anything definitely wrong about having a quick fumble, if that's what both of them desired?

I walked back down the aisle and found Benny having a sit down on the supersize hammock. 'Hey, John!' said Benny. 'It's good to have you back!'

I told Benny everything, blurted the lot out. I told him about my threats to Beardmore, my initial attempts to re-explore Leytonstow, Gabby's rock star delusions, the soirée and my unrequited love for Lois, the sack of Clements Markham House, the bank robbery, the sensation I'd had that the world was ending, Glyn's suggestion that perhaps I was witnessing a rebirth, my endeavours to draw Leytonstow Council's attention to the history-theft in their midst, pen training and my first baby steps toward humility, our unconventional visit to the Jobcentre, and my revelations upon hearing Ken snore, the process by which I became the most creditworthy poor person in history, my idea to play Beardmore at his own game and divert his ill-gotten proceeds to The Dig Street Festival, the hard immediate lessons drawn from my super-abundance of money, including Gabby's niche deflowering, our difficult walk to work and our realisation and joy at the crazy power of womanhood, my unsuccessful attempts to buy Clements Markham House and also convince Tim that he needed a PR budget, nearly killing Glyn but this being OK because *fun doesn't have to be fun to be fun*, my sad realisation that anything I thought was clever and inspiring was simply a rehashing of clever and inspiring stuff much cleverer, more inspirational, people had said and done before, and finally my uncovering of Gabby's abuse at the banana-fingered hands of Douglas Dauphinoise.

I took several deep breaths and wondered what Benny would make of it all. I felt deeply ashamed of my idiocy.

During my diatribe, he'd simply nodded slowly and dabbed his broad forehead with a handkerchief.

He began to giggle. Then he threw back his head and roared with laughter. 'John! What a tale!'

'I'm an idiot,' I stated.

'Far from it, John!' said Benny, putting a vast arm around my shoulder. 'Far from it, my friend!'

'You're just being kind,' I said.

'I'm not, John,' said Benny. 'I apologise for laughing, but you have to admit, you've had some *interesting* experiences out there in the desert! It seems to me like you've done exactly what you told me you'd do!'

'Does it?'

'Yes!' said Benny, his mirthful eyes flashing. 'You've changed the world!'

'Have I?'

'You've been on quite a journey with those friends of yours, haven't you?'

'I suppose I have.'

'It sounds to me as though you've single-handedly stuck with them and shown them the path to righteousness!'

'Are you sure?'

'You've allowed them to *see* themselves, John!'

'Really?'

'John,' said Benny, tucking in the back of his enormous beige shirt. 'You've been on a seldom travelled road, one few dare to tread. You've been further into the desert than just about anyone else I know. And on these daring travels, you met the devil, my friend!'

'Beardmore?'

Benny laughed. 'No, not him. Eric is a lesser devil. He's a learner devil, who needs to work on his consistency.'

'Who, then?'

'You've met the most seductive devil of them all – the

245

devil within your own heart. You've stared him in the eyes, John. And do you know what?'

'What?'

'You scared the living daylights out of him!'

'I did?'

'Yes, John, you did. He poked you in the eye – you gave him a tissue. He tried to break your legs – you found him a pair of crutches. He called you names – you recited a beautiful poem. He told you nobody cares – you sent him a love letter.'

'Benny?' I said.

'Yes, my friend?'

'You mentioned going out into the desert, and meeting the devil, and all these acts of kindness…'

'I did!'

'So, are you saying…' it felt too ridiculous and embarrassing even to consider, '…are you saying I am somehow like Jesus?'

'Yes, just that,' said Benny, his handsome face fired in the kiln of sincerity. I began to stutter, and Benny laughed louder and harder than ever. 'Oh, John!' he cried. 'You really are fantastic! You really do make me laugh!'

'Then you're not saying I'm like Jesus?' I asked, cringing. This was the antithesis of the impossible social situations Beardmore was apt to conjure – if I *was* Jesus it was ridiculous, and if I wasn't Jesus then I was ridiculous for thinking it.

'John, I'm sorry,' said Benny. 'I couldn't help laughing. It's lovely how seriously you considered whether you might be Jesus.'

'Oh.'

Benny grew grave. 'What I'm saying is that only he who confronts evil with love can *really* know Jesus. And I think that you really *know* Jesus.'

'Benny,' I said. 'What about the other, you know, gods?'

'What do you mean, John?'

'I mean, you know I'm an atheist?'

'You say you are,' said Benny.

'Why would I go through these trials and only discover *Jesus*? What about Buddha and the rest of them?'

'There's no such thing as an atheist,' said Benny flatly.

'Of course there is!' I said, and rattled off what I knew about the history of religion, Darwin, geology; all stuff I'd read, or heard on TV.

Benny waited patiently. When I'd finished he said, 'You didn't mention love.'

'I could have mentioned it,' I said, then had a think. It came to me. 'I could have mentioned that love is simply a vehicle for propagating genetic information, whether by the need to mate repeatedly or not abandon children, nothing more.'

'Very impressive.' Benny winked. 'Does it feel like that?'

'It just *is*!' I said.

He raised an eyebrow and smiled.

'OK, no. It doesn't feel like that.'

'What does it feel like, John?'

'Love?'

'What does living in the world feel like? Forget what it's fashionable to think, or what you think you're meant to think. What does it feel like to be alive?'

'A bit lonely?'

'Tick,' smiled Benny.

'Sometimes sad?'

'Tick.'

'Occasionally funny?'

'Got that one for sure! Tick. Those are very human feelings, John. Hardly the cold logic you were talking about earlier.'

'But how can you say atheists don't exist, when they patently do?'

'It's quite simple,' said Benny. 'I believe atheists are borrowing the robes of Jesus. They stand on God-shaped stools.

They forget that our drive to understand comes from the heart, the unprejudiced dreams of childhood where reality and unreality are perfectly intertwined. Though they don't remember it, the first rung on the stairway to knowledge is to understand this – understand God if you will – be licked by his love. There is not a man or woman alive who hasn't felt the power of God as a child, and those who feel it keenest – they are the ones who achieve most, they are the ones who change the world. It doesn't matter what they call themselves.'

I was astounded.

'Can you see why Jesus liked little children?' smiled Benny.

'Benny?' I asked.

'Yes, my friend.'

'Are you God?'

Benny laughed. 'Would you like me to be God, John?'

'Yes, I think I would.'

'OK,' said Benny. 'But you know, John,' he winked again, 'I'm more of a Buddha.'

I laughed.

Benny said, 'So, do you feel a bit better?'

I nodded.

'Now you're Jesus, what would He do next?' said Benny.

'I think He'd do what I'm doing, but with the courage of His convictions,' I said.

'You're a wise man, John,' smiled Benny. 'But while you're at it, why don't you try being nice to Eric. Remember, he's only a learner devil.'

'I'll try,' I said, not quite sure my compassion stretched that far. 'But what about the money? Should I just give it back, and cut up the debit cards?'

'You know,' said Benny, 'God has been around the block a few times. He likes pretty flowers, but he's also quite, shall we say, well acquainted with money. He's not afraid to speculate. So, John, use the money. Use it wisely, and for good.'

I patted the cards in the little pocket on my white summer dress with green leaves and red flowers. 'But what if the people I give the money to don't end up using it for good?' I asked.

'Let them wander into the desert with their money and meet the devil.'

I thought about telling Benny he could be a bit corny, but decided against it.

42

LUDWIG HOPKINS
DEBUNKS PHILOSOPHY

I went to the café, something I'd never normally do mid-morning for fear of a figurative ear-bashing from Povey, or a literal one from Dave.

A strange kind of peace had come over me. I felt sunny, and given to smiling at those I passed. Apparently it was infectious – even Tracy gave me a quick grin as she plonked my "coffee" on the counter.

Mug in hand, I looked out at the car park and saw Glyn struggling on with trollies and handcarts. I rapped on the window. He spotted me and coaxed his trolley-train to a halt.

'Come and have a coffee!' I mouthed to him, lifting the cup and grinning.

Glyn just stared open-mouthed, presumably in disbelief at my new-found freedom.

I made gesticulations that he should dump the trollies and come right away. He stared some more, shook his head and started up his caravan again.

I rapped more insistently.

Glyn again stopped the train before bending forward, hands on thighs, and opening and shutting his mouth like a large fish. Ritual performed, he straightened and glanced at me, then tipped back his head to consider the sky. To my surprise, he mated one last trolley, and began to limp across the car park in his figure-hugging pencil skirt and frilly blouse.

Soon, Glyn was seated opposite me. I asked, 'What were you thinking about when you looked at the sky?'

'Nothing.'

'*Nothing at all?*'

'Yes.'

'Are you sure?'

'Yes, I'm sure. We do our best thinking when we don't think about anything.'

I took the opportunity to relate to Glyn my conversation with Benny. Tracy tutted as she marshalled sausage rolls on the counter.

'Benny's wrong,' said Glyn.

'Didn't you dream of God as a child?' I asked.

'Yes.'

Silence. One could hardly call Glyn forthcoming. I got the impression that if he weren't prodded he would never open his mouth again, except, say, upon passing Dark Secrets, and only to retch.

'Glyn, don't you agree that an intellectual (for sake of argument a successful scientist) can only achieve her potential as a result of that initial dreaming process? Perhaps we could call it "multidimensional thought"?' I was pleased with that. 'So, isn't it fair to say that the scientist's subsequent decision that God doesn't exist is essentially based upon the fact that something resembling God showed her the way?'

Glyn said, 'Those words are logical.'

'What?'

'What you said does not defy cod logic,' said Glyn, 'if we accept the limitations of the human language game.'

'You've lost me.'

Tracy's frequency of tutting increased to perhaps one tut every ten seconds as she scrubbed the oven in her yellow Marigolds.

Glyn didn't appear in any hurry to explain to me what he

was on about, but instead stared mournfully at the train of trollies he'd abandoned in the car park.

'Don't you find it a lovely idea though, Glyn, that God might guide us in our childish dreams?'

Glyn didn't have time to answer my question because at that moment Dave walked into the café. My insides tightened, and Glyn commenced machine gun retching which, dubbed over Tracy's rhythmic tutting, sounded like heavy rain on a tin roof.

I thought of Benny and calmed myself; after all, this was only the visitation of another minor devil. I turned to look at Dave, forced a smile, and even chuckled.

A quick and perceptive person, Dave took all of this in. He looked a bit confused, and deeply pissed off. A smile wasn't in the script, never mind a chuckle. He took a pew at the counter, viciously shook out his red-top, and barked his order at the tutting Tracy.

Perhaps comprehending this sea change, Glyn's rapid retching lessened to a closing grunt. It was interesting to note that although Glyn grasped intellectually that he rather enjoyed and was willing to endure pain and humiliation, his wider self wasn't necessarily in on the act and reacted with fear, just as my gut had clenched upon Dave's entrance, even though I now suspected I possessed superhuman powers.

'Einstein believed in God, you know,' I said, loudly.

'He was being dogmatic and mysterious,' said Glyn, 'part of his New York party turn.'

'Why is Benny mistaken, then?'

'So far as we can talk of such things at all, it's meaningless to measure the performance of a half-formed machine.'

'Not sure I follow,' I said. This was an understatement.

'The definitive measurement of the validity of thought should start when the human being is fully developed, and preferably at their peak. Anything else is meaningless static,

252

just as a half-built computer will only produce erroneous data. An adult cannot simply appear fully-formed, it's against the laws of chemistry – there is of necessity a period of organic growth, but just as an adult poet disregards juvenilia, so should an adult at their peak disregard any half-baked conclusions reached on the way up.'

I stared at Glyn. I'd never known him so forthcoming!

Dave kept throwing us glances. Good as he was at hiding feelings after a lifetime of dangerous toil, I could decode his micro-body language quite clearly. He had not a clue what was going on, and this bothered him greatly.

I stared some more at Glyn, and he reddened.

'Why are you blushing, Glyn?'

'Why not?'

'It suggests to me that you're not entirely convinced by what you're saying.'

'It is impossible to be one hundred per cent sure about anything, so far as that statement can be made. The blushing is simply a physical reaction to my anticipating that if I *did* blush you might suspect that I'm not convinced by what I said.'

Fun doesn't have to be fun to be fun.

I wondered how Benny would address Glyn's position. I suspected he might chuckle and let Glyn wander free in the desert.

'Glyn, why do you keep saying things like *so far as that statement can be made* or *if we accept the limitations of the human language game*?'

Glyn scratched his nose and coughed. 'I suggest you read Ludwig Wittgenstein,' he said. 'He will explain everything to you, so far as anything can be meaningfully explained.'

'Who is he?' I asked.

'An Austrian philosopher,' said Glyn, now blushing distinctly.

'Who's visited you?'

'A few times, yes.'

'What does he say?'

'He says that all philosophy has been barking up the wrong tree in asking questions of the universe which, essentially, it can't and won't answer.'

'I see...' I said, not really seeing.

'So really the question *Does God exist*?' continued Glyn, 'cannot really be asked of the universe, because the universe simply doesn't require interrogation. It just *is*. So although *Does God exist*? is a perfectly natural question for a human to ask, it's actually meaningless, and ultimately pointless. Indeed the concept of *actually existing* is meaningless too. Even to describe the universe as *being* is unhelpful. In itself, the universe is akin to the experience of not yet being born, or being dead. Any discussion is a race to meaninglessness.'

You didn't mention love.

I said, 'But if language is so meaningless, then all of our efforts to explain to one another how to manipulate matter would simply fail, and not result in, for example, a successful trip to the moon and back?'

'That is a Newtonian encounter,' said Glyn. 'Simply a matter of linear mathematics, harnessing thrust and making things airtight. It's building upon the theme of a trebuchet.'

If only Gabby, Marcus and Barney were here, I thought! I wanted to start a band called Building on the Theme of a Trebuchet immediately!

'Whatever we do,' continued Glyn, 'just as a spacecraft is airtight, human beings are hermetically sealed into humanity. Talking about it is pretty poetry, and passes the time of day, nothing else.'

I thought about Captain Scott, all-too-British in the meaningless Antarctic wastes. 'But doesn't Wittgenstein basically negate his own arguments?'

'Ahem!'

'Glyn, I'm allowed to disagree with you. That's what philosophy is about, isn't it?'

'Sorry, John.'

'I mean it's not like Wittgenstein could step out of *the human language game* as you put it, make his pronouncements, and then come back, is it?'

I thought again of Scott and his pals, sealed from civilisation in the last tent, their deaths perhaps the most apt comment on the nothingness outside.

'So what was Wittgenstein like when he visited you?' I asked.

'A little joyless,' said Glyn.

Dave drained his cup, stood, considered us for a few jittery moments, then walked quickly from the café, muttering.

43

SUGAR-COATED BOLLOCKS

I caught up with Dave to check that my newly acquired confidence had not rattled the old boy too much. He was in his office staring at Page Three and snapping pencils in two.

'Are you OK, Dave?' I asked.

'Am I fackin OK?' spat Dave, shaking his head.

Mandy, twenty-two, from Epping, Essex, winked at us from Page Three.

He rolled the newspaper up, stood, and commenced whacking the air with it. The fact that he didn't assault me was progress indeed. 'What was all that shit you was sayin in the fackin café?' he demanded, pointing his baton at me as if mid-relay.

'Glyn and I were philosophising, that's all,' I said.

'Philosophy!' said Dave. 'It's about as useful as an ashtray on a motorbike!'

I smiled at this nice simile, and resolved to tell Glyn about it.

'It's not fackin funny!' said Dave. 'Do you know, I started work when I was thirteen years old.'

'That's young,' I said.

'You're fackin right it's young! It's sixty-two fackin years ago! I've been graftin ever since! I ain't stopped once! And do you think that in them sixty-two years I've 'ad time for fackin philosophy?'

'I'm guessing you haven't.'

'I 'ave fackin not! I've been too busy payin my fackin taxes! I've kept the fackin NHS afloat! I've paid for them to empty the fackin bins, and keep all them lazy fat bastards sitting on their arses on the fackin dole! And you think I've 'ad time to fackin philosophise?'

'Dave, you've lived a long time,' I said.

'I fackin 'ave!'

'Why?'

'Chance,' said Dave, quick as a shot.

'What have you learned in that time?'

'That you just need to fackin get on with it.'

'Is that all?'

'Course it's not fackin all!' yelled Dave, then he sat down again and shook his head. 'Do you think I'm gonna waste my breath telling a kid like you about life?'

I was a little taken aback.

'You don't like that, do yer?' said Dave. 'You think you're the fackin bee's knees, don't yer? Well yer not! Come back in forty fackin years and tell me something about life! Now fack off and do some work!'

I thought about Glyn's assertion that no conclusion we came to on the way up was worth anything.

'Dave, what's the point in only becoming wise at the age of seventy-five? Wouldn't it be better to say we're wise when we're still young enough to build upon it?'

'I give up,' sighed Dave. 'Do you know, I could've died at any point when I was a young man, surrounded by 'eavy machinery all day long. I used to see men mangled, ripped to shreds, brains spilled all over the fackin shop floor. It could've been me – nearly was, many times, and probably should've been. So don't talk to me, son, about philosophy, all right?'

'Where did you work?'

Dave coughed and said something inaudible.

'Pardon?'

'A fackin chocolate factory!' said Dave.

I couldn't help but smile. This angered Dave immensely but again, somehow, my levity gave me a stay of thrashing.

'Do you know, son, all the fackin crap you can buy in the shops is made somewhere. Some poor bastard's gotta make it! Same goes for fackin sweets – someone's gotta stir up all the shit and pour it into the fackin moulds all day long! Can you imagine giving up your fackin life for a chocolate bar?'

I supposed it was all done by machines now, but I didn't say this.

'Do you believe in God, Dave?'

'Don't fackin tell me you're one o' them?'

'No, I'm not,' I said.

'Why are you asking me then, son? If you're asking me whether I think I'm gonna die and go up to 'eaven, then no, I'm not. There's no God, so don't waste your time thinking about it. You see, the trouble with your generation is that you think you're important, that the world owes you a fackin living, and that you can 'ave just about anything you want if you just put your mind to it. I'm tellin you, son (and you might as well listen because I'm right) that you are *not* important, and 'ow ever 'ard you try you will *not* get what you want. Fackin Disney sugar-coated bollocks.'

'Why does my generation think like that?'

'Shite on the telly. Do you know, when I was young, you just lived, and you fackin died too. You got on with it, like the next bloke. We didn't fackin philosophise.'

'Dave,' I said, 'I've really enjoyed philosophising with you.'

Dave opened his mouth, presumably to berate me... but didn't. He just stood there with it open. And then he smiled. I smiled back. He'd been a harder nut to crack than Tracy at the café, but I'd done it.

44

SHOBBING, SWEEDIE?

I walked away from Dave's broom-cupboard kingdom casting about me for Glyn and Gabby, when I spotted none other than Lois enter the store, followed, languidly, by a smirking Roofie. Shocked and confused, I hid behind a pillar and watched as they made their way through the electronic entrance barrier and into the first section of the shop floor; being a crossroads of lampshades, pound buckets, and powertools on reduction.

Lois, dressed in her customary goth-chic, picked up a bright orange handbasket. Roofie, clad in red trousers, white shirt, with a pink woollen jumper casually draped about his neck, carried some sort of crimson cushion under his arm. They looked like they'd taken a dramatically wrong turn in Knightsbridge.

I felt spectacularly shy, especially so in my white dress with the red flowers and green leaves, and, sick with jealousy, stalked them at a safe distance.

They arrived at the paint section, and I stole down a parallel aisle – it was anti-mould sealants – and eavesdropped through the shelves.

I heard Roofie say to Lois, 'Hey, Shordy, look; they've got these baint-names for blebs. Sex On The Beach Bink. Sunday Roast Teak. Oh, loog at this one! Gosta Del Sol Yellow!'

Shorty? I boiled with anger at his dismissive nickname. Lois was, after all, about five feet seven.

'Roofie, they are perfectly good paints,' said Lois. 'Not everyone can afford Barrow and Fall, you know.'

They were approached by the guy on the paint section: Afonso.

'How can I help you two youngsters?' he drawled.

'Roofie, pass me the cushion, please,' said Lois. Then to Afonso, 'We want to match the colour of this, please.'

'It's high-end,' said Roofie. 'And that's not the name of a Tube stop.'

'Don't boast,' said Lois.

'I'm just giving this oberative the necessary information,' said Roofie. '*This* is a Coralie Baptiste hassock, made. Trés chic in barts of Hants.'

'Hants?' repeated Afonso.

'Would you able to mix a colour to match this?' asked Lois.

Afonso took the cushion from Roofie, inspected it, and gave it back. 'Yeah, I got this colour. I'll get it.'

As Afonso wandered down the aisle in search of the right shade, Roofie put his arms around Lois's waist and tried to kiss her.

Lois pulled away. 'You think you're above all this, don't you?' she said.

'Above whad?'

'This...' she gestured at the shop. 'You think the people who work here are far below you. You're mistaken, Roofie.'

'Why do you live around here, anyway?' asked Roofie. 'And what about that geek you invided to the bardy? What was that all aboud?'

The *geek* cowered in the sealant aisle, wondering whether Lois remembered where he worked.

'You mean John?'

The hairs on the back of my neck rose, and I held my breath.

'He was a screamer. He thought Boner worked in a bost office!'

'You and Boner were horrible to him,' said Lois. 'Couldn't you see he was shy, and not used to it? You picked on him, just because he doesn't speak the formulaic language of finance.'

'Chill out, Shordy,' said Roofie.

'Don't tell me to chill out,' Lois snapped. 'John is... John is off the beaten track. He's creative. He's unique. When he speaks, he says things I've never heard before.'

Roofie stared at her. 'It sounds like you have a crush on this bloge.'

Just then, Afonso arrived back clutching a pot of paint. 'Here,' he said. 'Perfect match.'

Lois took the pot, and examined it.

'Budget paind,' said Roofie.

'I don't think this is quite the shade,' said Lois. 'The cushion is more of a vermillion. This looks like cinnabar.'

Afonso sighed, took the pot, and read the label. 'This is our red,' he said. 'It's red, like the cushion.'

'It's a hassock, made,' said Roofie.

'Do you have Barrow and Fall?' asked Lois.

'Say what?' asked Afonso.

'Barrow and Fall,' she said. 'They make paint.'

Afonso sighed again. 'I'll go and find out,' he said, and ambled off down the aisle.

'Shordy, you *do* have a crush on that weird bloge you brought to the bardy,' said Roofie. 'I'm sure your barents would love him, especially if he wore the bolo neck.'

'That's enough!' said Lois. 'John is a special man. And *you* must be threatened by him, because *you* keep going on about him.'

'Take a chill bill, Shordy,' said Roofie. 'If you wand to dade weirdoes, it's up to you.'

'Maybe I will date him,' said Lois. Roofie's face fell; it was the second time I'd had the opportunity to enjoy such an event.

Afonso reappeared. 'We don't carry it,' he said.

Lois thanked Afonso, threw the cushion at Roofie, and made for the exit. Rather less languid, Roofie followed.

'Idiota,' I heard Afonso say to himself.

45

ENTER DIAMANTÉ

Still processing what Lois had said, I found Gabby and Glyn sheltering from rain near the entrance to Amundsen Enterprises. I told them we needed a digital camera, and quick. Gabby immediately began to compile a shopping list.

'I want a new dress – a black one with zips, man!'

'Shush, Gab!' I hissed.

'And some platform shoes to make me six-foot-seven!'

'I don't think shoes with one-foot-three soles exist, Gabby,' said Glyn.

Across the car park, large drops slapped the dirty sycamore leaves clean, jousted with patches of engine oil, danced on car bonnets, and ran in great black moss-strewn swathes down the gable end of the lonely island of houses. This now was a world where Lois might consider dating me. We three ran for my car.

I got in to find Gabby already sitting in the passenger seat.

'How did you get in, Gab?'

'Through there, man!' said Gabby, pointing to what could only be construed as a missing passenger door.

'Oh God, someone's made off with the door!' I yelled.

'How inconsiderate,' said Glyn.

'It's like *The Dukes of Hazzard*, man!' shouted Gabby.

'It's not really, is it, Gab?' I said. 'They had doors, only the doors were welded shut for some unknown reason, and they got in through the windows.'

'And they slid across the bonnet, man!' yelled Gabby.

'*The hood*,' said Glyn.

Gabby got back into the rain and flung himself across the bonnet (hood) and managed to bang his head. He lay in a puddle crying.

'Are you OK, Gab?' I asked, picking him up.

'They must have left those bits out, man,' sobbed Gabby.

'Glyn, can you be Daisy Duke?' I asked.

'No.'

I let it be understood that for health and safety reasons – perhaps I was learning from Alan Povey – Gabby and Glyn must sit in the back. I picked Gabby up and installed him. The rain had washed most of Povey's red stickers away. Glyn coughed and clambered in next to Gabby.

My Cortina started after a prolonged period of coughing, and again filled the air with thick black smoke. I wrestled with the gear stick amid crunching sounds one would expect to hear only in a wrecking yard, found a gear, and hit the gas. We had zero visibility. It was a vicious circle – the smoke would only clear if we got up enough speed to throw it in our wake, but to achieve the required velocity would entail extreme peril.

Gabby and Glyn began screaming the moment we moved. At first the only way I could tell we *were* moving was by noting the g-forces experienced; which, right now, unless the laws of physics had recently flipped, strongly suggested we were reversing at high speed.

The smoke began trailing in our wake. Miraculously we found ourselves racing backwards, bumper to nose, amid honking traffic up Whitehorse Road. Gabby and Glyn still shouted and screamed but I floored it like Burt Reynolds, whooping and draping my arm out of the window. We must have looked like a dirty yellow comet, hurtling along, bumping between kerbs and frightening and amusing by turns the citizens of Leytonstow.

263

'ARE WE NEARLY THERE YET?' screamed Gabby.

I spotted the Internet café and slammed on the brakes which, I discovered, were just mock-ups of brakes. There was nothing for it – I aimed the Cortina at a brand new black Range Rover parked outside the Internet café and kindly allowed it to stop us, figuring it was a case of die or run the gauntlet of the Range Rover's owner's wrath. With a horrible crunch we ploughed into the big four-wheel drive. I switched off the ignition, and waited.

'That was special,' said Glyn, wiping sick from his blouse.

A small fat man ran out of a nearby hairdressers with a towel still wrapped around his neck, and half a haircut. He knelt by the front wheel of the now arguably ruined Range Rover and wept, crying that I'd killed his baby.

At that moment it stopped raining and the sun came out. I felt immediately cheered, and quickly embraced my shaken companions.

I knelt down and hugged the little man. Pretty soon we were joined by other folk, all howling and tear-strewn, whether in mirth or lament I couldn't readily establish. People stared at my white dress with the red flowers and green leaves.

I stood, fetched a scrap of paper from the Cortina and wrote out Beardmore's details, before thrusting it into the little man's wet hand, stalwartly insisting that all would be sorted, the Range Rover repaired, and Beardmore would likely chuck in some free stuff for his considerable trouble.

Somewhat placated, and evidently a little scared of we three staring at him in our dresses, the little fat man stood and took a note of the Cortina's number plate – OMG 642R. Then he insisted that I both photograph the evidence and put him through to Beardmore to confirm the company would take liability.

I took the Polaroid from the boot and began to snap the

damage. The barber sauntered out and began to snip at the little fat fellow's hair while he inspected my photography.

'Dude, I love a retro camera!'

I turned to find a natty-looking fellow in his mid-forties, who went on to announce himself a reporter from the *Leytonstow Log*, the local rag.

'Bobby Diamanté,' he cheesed, gripping my hand extremely tightly and flashing his pearly whites. 'Dude, I wanna run a piece on you!'

'*Me*?' I gushed.

'Yeah, dude, I mean, what's all this about, friend? Are you a *Boeing* fan?' is what I heard.

I tried to answer his question as best I could, referencing the aeroplane manufacturers, citing that I'd never been on a 747, but had once flown in a 737 from Teesside airport. This left Diamanté looking confused, but evidently ready to give me the benefit of the doubt.

'I meant the dress, the cross-dressing, dude; it's so fucking cool. Did you get the inspiration from *Boeing*?' is what I again heard.

Racking my brains for some link between the very manly business Boeing were engaged in and wearing ladies' clothes, I again launched into my answer – I managed to indicate that I'd always rather liked airline stewardesses, but that this had not directly influenced the morning's course of events.

'*David Bowie*,' said Diamanté.

'Oh God,' I said.

'You don't know who David Bowie is, dude?' asked Diamanté, casting worried glances at the crowd.

To relieve him I immediately lifted my face to the sky and commenced singing the chorus of "Starman", to which Diamanté nodded his head and shuffled about the pavement. Then he turned to the crowd and encouraged others to join in. No one did, save the little fat man of the Range Rover who was evidently a Bowie fan (and, who knows, maybe a Boeing fan too), and Gabby, who began to headbang furiously. Glyn continued to regard the sky.

'Dude, what is it you're trying to DO HERE?' yelled Diamanté, busting a few more shapes as I continued to sing.

'THE DIG STREET FESTIVAL!!' I screamed. 'THAT WAS THE OPENING CEREMONY OF THE DIG STREET FESTIVAL!!'

'Oh my God!' said Diamanté.

'A put up?' said the little fat man. 'This Beardmore, is he part of it?'

I confirmed that Beardmore was indeed part of it and invited Diamanté to send some more questions my way.

'Dude, is The Dig Street festival going to be very *street*?' asked Diamanté.

'Very what?'

'You know, dude, *street*?' repeated Diamanté, folding his middle-aged arms like a gangsta rapper.

'Yes,' I said, understanding. 'Yes, it's so *street* that the word "street" is included in its name!'

'Whoa, dude!' blew Diamanté. 'Just you involved?'

'No, there's Gabby, and Glyn. You're involved too, and you, and you, and you, and you, and you...' thus I began to point to every human being I could see, until an old fellow shouted me down, telling me I was a bloody disgrace, that it made him ashamed to be a man, and that in his day I'd have earned a damn good thrashing at the hands of the local constabulary.

'You see?' I said to Diamanté with a grin.

'See what, dude?' he asked, looking about wildly like a meerkat.

'That was another Act of the Dig Street Festival! It was entitled *The Personification of the Generation Gap by Human Animals Living Nonetheless, Geologically Speaking, at Exactly the Same Time.*'

I wasn't sure where this was coming from, but it got Diamanté very hot indeed.

'Oh my God, dude, it's the fucking SCOOP I've been looking for since I was in college!'

'Can I speak to Beardmore now?' said the little fat man with the hairdo-in-progress and dented Range Rover. He and the barber stood side by side laughing good-naturedly.

'Sure!' I said. 'Let me get the phone from the boot.'

I popped it and lifted out the hulking immobile phone. I solicited the assistance of a very excited Diamanté to put it onto my back. Then I asked the barber to extend the twelve feet long antenna, before inviting the little fat man to open the flap, take out the crank and wind it as fast as his little arm would allow, while simultaneously dialling the number for Amundsen Enterprises, which I shouted out to him over the noise of the thudding telephone. Finally I gave the little fellow the receiver.

It was hard to hear the conversation between the little fat chap and Beardmore, but I got the basic gist: '... very funny... some damage... man in a dress... Cortina... all covered, he said...' then his expression very much changed. '*Really*?'

The little fellow handed back the receiver. 'Beardmore's coming down here,' he said miserably. What a talent for unhappiness Beardmore had. Great raindrops again began to fall, as if we'd upset the sky.

It was contagious; the barber's eyes began to fill with tears. Indeed mine did too. Gabby began to wail. Diamanté was transfixed by this sea change in our demeanour, and began himself to get hip with it and loudly weep, taking photographs all the time on his slightly more modern camera than mine. Even the old fellow who had berated me and thus helped create the most recent Act of the festival (of which this was certainly the next instalment) grew misty-eyed and morose, surely thinking back to the good old days, when men were men and coppers beat people up if they were puffters. The tears spread, and pretty soon men, women, and children, were crying, clutching shopping bags full of items all priced at a pound. It appeared that one only had to walk past to be infected – I watched a large skin-headed gentleman with an SS badge on his lapel become overwhelmed with emotion as he witnessed these many lifetimes of pent-up sentiment erupting at once. It was extremely cathartic, and I hoped it might help him realise he'd backed the wrong horse. Glyn continued to stare at the sky.

Thus the majority of the local population were sobbing as Beardmore's sleek black SUV pulled up. As was his modus operandi, Beardmore sat for a while hidden behind his tinted windows surveying the scene, figuring whom he could best bully.

The door opened and out he clambered. He made the little fat man look like a supermodel. Fully aware that this was yet another Act of The Dig Street Festival, and winking this madly to Diamanté, I stepped up to Beardmore, smiling, amazed at how brave I'd become, and regally shook him by the hand, claiming loudly for all to hear that this was *The Great Beardmore*, and that he alone was the mastermind and patron of The Dig Street Festival, which elicited cheers and a roar of enthusiastic applause from the crowd. The little fat man seemed especially moved, and knelt in a puddle before my mammoth boss as if he were being knighted.

Beardmore started snorting, and I did something naughty; I suggested to Diamanté that Beardmore was here to discuss the Festival, and that Diamanté might wish to grab the opportunity to interview him immediately. Diamanté leapt at the chance, and fronted up to Beardmore with the most pleasant of airs. His opening gambit was to say, 'Dude, you must be so proud...' before Beardmore let forth a cannonball of muck, which pretty much covered Diamanté's face in its entirety. Reeling, and holding onto his fragile hipness for all he was worth, Diamanté staggered backwards, treading on the toes of the still-kneeling little fat man, who gave a piglet scream, which the crowd appreciated with another round of applause.

'Jesus, this is like Vietnam,' spluttered the poor Diamanté, who was clearly too young to have been involved in the war. Perhaps he was referencing a bad holiday experience.

'I'll cut you a deal,' said Beardmore to the little fat guy, no longer kneeling.

'You'll cut *me* a deal?'

'Take it or fackin leave it,' said Beardmore impassively, leaning over the little chap like a vast fatberg.

'What's the deal, then?' asked the little fat guy, intimidated as per the plan. The barber also looked suitably apprehensive, his scissor fingers twitching.

Beardmore leaned in and put his face so close to the little fat chap's that their very noses touched. I leaned in too, as did the admirably-recovered Diamanté. Beardmore whispered, 'The deal is, if you fack off now, I won't get my boys to sort you and your whole fackin family.'

Initially a flicker of doubt passed over the little fat chap's face, as he presumably wondered if the rest of Beardmore's *boys* weren't just like me, before I saw him crumple under the weight of the menace, and figuratively retreat. He proffered a sovereign ring to the emotional barber, who kissed it, before yanking open the door of his Range Rover, starting the engine, and with a terrible sound of ripping metal disentangled the two cars and roared off down Dig Street in a haze of spray.

'You gents are looking a little fluffy at the back,' said the barber.

'I'll 'ave a trim,' said Beardmore. 'On the 'ouse.' Then he added, to me, 'Get to work, you little cant.'

Beardmore waddled off with the barber. Diamanté and I drew breath under a shop awning.

'Shit, dude!' said Diamanté. 'This is BIG!'

'I'm glad you think so,' I said, wondering if he was referring to the festival or Beardmore's ability to expectorate.

'I'm going to break this thing!' shouted Diamanté. 'Dude, I'm gonna break it bad!'

'I'd rather The Dig Street Festival was broken in an entirely positive manner,' I said, again dicking with the fellow. I'd learned to do this somehow as a result of wearing ladies' garb.

'Oh no, dude, I'll make it beautiful!' said Diamanté. 'I'm going to file this motherfucking report, and the world is going to know about The Dig Street Festival!'

'Load of shite, if you want my opinion,' said the old fellow who'd berated me about geological time.

Bobby Diamanté winked at me, pointed his sharp fashionable shoes in the direction of the *Leytonstow Log's* offices (which I knew to be on Market Street) and said, very self-consciously but nonetheless in a pleasing and sincere manner, 'Keep it tight, dude. Stay focussed.'

'I will,' I promised him. God, I liked Diamanté.

'John?' asked Glyn, wet hair sticking to his large forehead. 'I would like some money, please.'

'Me too, man!' yelled Gabby.

'What for?' I asked.

'To spend,' said Glyn.

'I gathered that, Glyn!' I said. 'To spend on what?'

'Various things,' blushed Glyn.

'To spend on a dress with zips, man!'

Not wishing to appear miserly, I assented and we found a cashpoint.

'How much do you need?' I asked Glyn.

'Raaagh!'

'Would fifty quid do?'

270

'A – raaagh! – thousand.'

'God, that's a lot of money, Glyn!'

'Not in the context of gross domestic product.'

'What?' I asked.

'The economic output of the UK.'

I eyeballed Glyn and reflected that I did have the makings of a miser.

'I need two thousand, man!' yelled Gabby.

'No bloody way, Gab!' I said.

I inserted one of the cards and withdrew a thousand for Glyn and twenty quid for Gabby. This seemed appropriate.

Glyn took the money, coughed some thanks and lolloped down the wet street in the direction of home. Gabby asked me if I could change the twenty into twenty-pence pieces, thus solving that mystery. We watched the enigmatic figure of Glyn retreat.

'Gab, what do you think Glyn will spend it on?' I asked.

'Clouds,' said Gabby, before sprinting to the nearest pub.

Enormous drops pelted the pavement, clearing away the living memories of my Free Festival.

46

BEARDMORE'S REVELATION

It was hard to focus upon the job-in-hand now that The Dig Street Festival was so firmly launched and just about to break bad in the *Leytonstow Log,* thanks to irrepressible Vietnam Vet Bobby Diamanté.

Nonetheless, I pressed on and walked into the Internet café. Maybe they knew a camera shop. Flushed with my recent successes, and perhaps touched by the supreme confidence of either Beardmore or God, I stridently announced myself as the new Amundsen Enterprises *Web Mobility Director,* and immediately commandeered a work station, loudly demanding a cup of coffee (milk, one sugar) for my trouble.

A studious-looking fellow at the opposite work station stood and told me he thought I'd acted despicably? (He supplied the question mark, and raised his eyebrows to further confirm it.) I apologised with a grin, and stated that one could hardly compare my entrance to truly despicable acts like genocide. The manager, a slight fellow who barely looked old enough to walk, never mind man an Internet hub, walked over and asked what he could do for me? He too raised his voice, Australian-style, at the end of his sentence, and I began to wonder if the whole Internet might be Antipodean-themed.

'So, what's that on your back?' asked the manager, pointing to the still-steaming box, mindful of the twelve feet long antenna which still stood proudly erect, though rather bent in accommodating the low ceiling – in fact, it stuck out of the door.

'I'm connected,' I winked; it was becoming a bad habit. The kindly little manager shuffled off to put the kettle on, and I stood and announced my overall plan to the room at large, that I planned to organise the most fantastical festival Leytonstow had ever witnessed. The studious-looking fellow began to shake with excitement, and apologised for formerly accusing me of being despicable, now proclaiming (with another question mark) that I was, in fact, one of the most remarkable human beings he'd ever encountered? I confirmed this and we shook hands.

'Are you a time traveller?' asked the studious chap, regarding me very seriously.

'We are all time travellers after a fashion,' I said, which evidently impressed him as he snorted and grabbed a tissue to blow his nose.

'Personally,' I continued, wondering if some wag had spiked me, 'I have travelled from nineteen sixty-seven to the present day in what now appears to me to be the blink of an eye. Similarly, I will travel on into the unimagined future, before expiring, when time will no longer exist.'

The little Internet hub manager had returned with a nice cup of coffee for me, and said, 'Oh my God, are you really from nineteen sixty-seven?'

'Entirely,' I spake, taking up the cup, burning my upper lip and pouring half of the coffee upon the console before me, which slightly detracted from my assertions that I was a Time Lord.

'Bro!' shouted the little manager. 'My dad's gonna kill me!'

Having put the computer on the radiator to dry off a bit, and having assured the little manager that a man called Beardmore would pay his dad for all damages incurred, I set about explaining my visit, and my need to locate a camera shop to buy a digital camera in order to photograph a large number of shop-soiled items. They sniffed and smirked, and suggested I use things they called "stock photos".

Thenceforth the little manager and the studious chap with the moustache set about creating me an account on something called "eBay".

Just as things were going so well, I had a heart attack – my torso shook violently, and I couldn't breathe. How immensely cruel, after taking care of my body as I had, ensuring a regular antiscorbutic onion ring intake, and washing it down with bathtubs of Romanian Merlot, supposed to be good for the heart. I tried to put myself in the recovery position and prepared to meet my maker, sad that my own solipsistic demise would render the little manager and the studious chap non-existent, and beckoning them with my last ounce of strength not to fight it.

'I think your phone's ringing?' said the studious chap, pointing to the bouncing bomb upon my back. Thank the Lord, I wasn't dying after all! The world was safe for another day! I picked up the receiver.

'What the bloody 'ell's goin on?' shouted Alan Povey.

'Oh hi, Alan,' I said. 'I'm at the Internet café selling the... shop-soiled items.'

'We've got some paint spilled in aisle five! 'oo's gonna clean the stuff up? Somebody's gonna break their ruddy neck!'

'What colour is the paint?' I asked, by way of playing for time.

'What ruddy colour?' shouted Povey. 'What does it matter what the flaming colour is?'

I imagined Povey trying to coat the paint in red health and safety stickers – perhaps I didn't want a clash.

'Where's Glyn and that little girl you brought along?' yelled Povey.

'They're helping me,' I said. Actually they *were* currently assisting me by being out of my hair.

'I ask you again: 'oo's gonna clean the ruddy stuff up?'

'Just tell me the colour so I can bring the relevant cleaning equipment,' I said, and added, 'so I can clean it in a safe manner.'

'Right!' said Povey. I heard him shouting into the store, *What's the ruddy colour of the paint? We don't bloody sell that colour! We do?*

'John, I'm told it's myrtle green!' puffed Povey.

Then I heard him respond to some distant cry – *What? The ruddy car park's flooded? I'm on my way!*

'I'll be right there,' I said, and hung up, which was lucky as I suspected the petrol immobile phone was just about to explode.

'Listen,' I said hurriedly to the studious chap with the small brown moustache, and the little manager, 'I have to attend to some business. I will pay you both twenty quid if you put a slightly chipped marble fire surround onto the Internet and put it up for sale! I won't be long!'

They looked extremely happy with my offer. I set the immobile phone on a table with a giant clank, and hurried across the rain-drenched street to find Gabby.

I ran into the pub and wound my way through the familiar throngs of mottled old men supping pints. Gabby was at the jukebox headbanging to Status Quo.

'Gab!' I said. 'I need you to go back to Amundsen Enterprises to clean up aisle five!'

'OK, man!' said Gabby.

'Great!' I said, surprised.

We waved goodbye to the old men, and were out again on rainy Dig Street. We sheltered briefly at a bus stop.

'See you later then, Gab,' I said.

'Where is it, man?' asked Gabby.

'Aisle five,' I said. 'A spillage of myrtle green paint. Scoop it up with lots of tissue then mop it clean.'

'No, that funny place we work, man,' said Gabby. 'Where is it?'

I noted that Gabby was searching exactly the opposite horizon to where the superstore lay, so with a sigh turned him one hundred and eighty degrees and gave directions. Gabby nodded.

'Have you got it?' I asked.

'Yeah, man!' cried Gabby, and ran off.

'Gab!' I shouted. 'Didn't you listen to a word I said? It's the other way!'

'I'm going home to have a sleep first, man!' said Gabby.

'What?'

'I'm a bit tired!'

'You haven't time for a sleep!'

'Sleep is good for you, man!' said Gabby. 'Mam says!'

'I'm not saying sleep is bad for you, but just that at this moment you *do not* have time to catch a sleep before you go and mop up the paint! It's very simple!'

'Where did you say it was again, man?'

I sighed and leaned on the glass of the bus shelter.

'OK, Gab,' I said. 'Let's go.'

I took his puny hand and dragged him across the road to the yellow Cortina, still parked where we'd crashed. The windscreen was covered in soggy parking violation notices.

'Oh God, more debt!' I cried.

Gabby slid once more across the wet hood, this time with slightly more aplomb than his previous attempt.

'Well done, Gab,' I said.

I installed Gabby in the back and fastened his seat belt.

'Oh man, this is fun!' shouted Gabby, whooping and enjoying the mirth of passers-by.

I gave him a hard stare. 'It's not so much fun, Gab, as really bloody annoying!'

'It's not, man, it's fun!'

'Gab, fun would consist of me bring able to trust you to walk the pretty short distance to the store, clean up the paint, and return here!'

Fun doesn't have to be fun to be fun.

I reflected that perhaps this was a test of Glyn's mantra, and resigned myself. I glanced at the Internet café – it had not exploded. Neither had the barber shop where Beardmore sat getting a trim.

Eric is a lesser devil, a learner devil, who needs to work on his consistency.

Benny's unbidden words gave me an idea.

'Gab, wait here!' I said.

'What, here, man?'

'Yes. I'll be two ticks!'

I ran down Dig Street for a block or two and into the arcade where I knew there was a record store oft-frequented by Gabby. I searched the O section and found what I was after. I paid the owner and, clutching a CD, ran to the barber shop.

'Eric!' I puffed, leaning on the doorframe in my white dress with the green leaves and red flowers.

Beardmore and the barber studied this apparition.

'What the fack you want?' asked Beardmore.

'I got you a present, Eric,' I said, and handed him the CD – *The Greatest Hits of Gilbert O'Sullivan*.

Beardmore opened the CD case. Then he looked at me again. A tear slowly made its way down his left cheek.

'Bloody corny, that is!' laughed the barber, before coughing and shutting up.

I smiled at Beardmore, left them to it, and ran back.

The Cortina had gone.

Of course it had!

Of course, of course! How could I have been so stupid? So neglectful!

Gabby was now surely dead. I sat in the middle of the wet road and cried. Cars and buses honked at me, drivers yelled for me to get out of the way, or words to that effect.

'The festival is still a pile of shit!' shouted the old man

who'd previously cast aspersions upon my grand enterprise. He was under a bus shelter, watching me.

'Gabby! Oh Gabby!' I cried. My poor little man! I shuddered to consider how mangled he would be in his pretty yellow dress.

'I'll take you back to the fackin store.'

Beardmore!

'What you waiting for, you little bastard?' he said, and held out his enormous hand to pull me up. He clutched *The Greatest Hits of Gilbert O'Sullivan* with the other.

Was it a trick? I raised my arm slowly, aware that we were reworking Michelangelo's *The Creation of Adam*.

He helped me up; we walked to his black SUV.

Beardmore inserted the CD and we pulled away down the wet street. It was the very definition of an unforeseen situation. The first song he put on was "Matrimony".

I scanned the route looking for poor Gabby and the yellow Cortina.

'Fackin good one this,' said Beardmore. 'We played it at our wedding.'

I looked at him. He was crying again. I went to hold his left hand, but he glared at me. A bridge too far.

'We called our daughter Clair after one of his songs,' he said.

'It's a lovely name,' I said.

Beardmore sniffed, then said, 'A marble fire surround fell off the wall and killed them both.'

I wanted to laugh! I desperately held my breath.

Beardmore glared at me.

'I started 'acking the shit out of every fackin marble fire surround we 'ad in stock,' he said. 'I wanted to batter the fack out of 'em, make 'em fackin extinct. Then I started damagin everythin else what came in. Don't tell fackin Alan. The amount of "accidents" we 'ave at the store, he thinks the place is fackin cursed.'

I looked at him wide-eyed.

'Then I started drinkin and gamblin,' said Beardmore. 'I gambled everything. The fackin lot. I got desperate, and started to use the money from the fackin knock-off. If you tell the fackin taxman, it's the end of me, and Alan too; Amundsen Enterprises is 'is fackin life.'

I'd managed to get hold of myself. 'It's a sad story, Eric.'

Indeed it was. Everything now made sense. An inconsistent devil indeed.

We pulled into Amundsen Enterprises, and I was exceedingly relieved to see the yellow Cortina in one piece (or at least in the same condition it had left Dig Street).

We drove through giant pools to get to his favourite disabled parking bay, and stepped out into ankle deep water, rain hammering down.

Povey was standing at the sliding doors wearing a terrified expression and directing staff in placing sandbags.

'Where've you bin, Eric-lad?' he yelled. 'We've a bloody flood on our 'ands!'

'Not yet we 'aven't, Alan,' said Beardmore.

'If it keeps rainin like this we'll be up to our ruddy necks!' shouted Povey, slashing his own with his hand as if to order an execution.

I ran past them into the store to search for Gabby.

'Oh, Gabby!' I cried, running down aisle five.

He was covered top to toe in myrtle green paint, while the mop and kitchen roll stood spotless by him.

'I slipped, man!' said Gabby.

'Yes, and rolled around a bit!' I said. 'Oh, Gabby, I thought you'd died!'

'I didn't die, man,' said Gabby through a green film.

'I can see that, Gab.'

47

THE SPRINTER

I cleaned Gabby up as best I could, installed him in the café, then mopped the myrtle green paint in aisle five, the potted plant aisle. It looked as if the conifers and mini palm trees had melted and oozed out across the floor.

Then I went back to the front of the store to see if we'd been breached.

No sign of Beardmore. Instead I found Povey staring with worry at sandbags and sky. The car park resembled an Olympic swimming pool, but the rain appeared to have stopped.

'That were a bloody close shave!' said Povey, poised with his red stickers, to coat, one supposed, every single drop of a flood. I could sense the painful extent to which the chaotic elements dug into his very soul, challenging his nature with their laissez-faire attitude to person and property.

'There's muwer forecast fer tomorrow!' he said. 'Muwer bloody watter!'

'Has the store ever flooded before?'

'Never, lad!' snapped Povey. 'It's this ruddy global warmin. These days it doesn't just bloody rain, it absolutely poo-wers!'

'Where's Eric?' I asked, fishing for a way in. I'd hardly had time to process our recent conversation. The overriding effect thus far was to make me feel very guilty. Guilty for assuming he was a devil, born that way, and not, as I now knew, bent into bitter shape by experience. Of course, I reflected, this tale might have been a ruse to ensure I wouldn't report him to the taxman. If this was the case, Beardmore was an extremely good actor.

''e's int' ruddy office, isn't 'e,' sighed Povey. 'If the watter gets any 'igher 'e'll come out and 'ave a word wi' God!'

In this moment of levity I went in for the kill.

'Was Eric ever married?' I asked, in as offhand a manner as I could muster.

Povey turned and looked at me. 'Why d'yer want to know that, lad?'

'I just wondered,' I said.

'Listen, my lad,' said Povey, 'it doesn't do to go pokin yer nose around other people's business.'

'It's just... I noticed he doesn't seem to like marble fire surrounds,' I said, cringing.

''oo's bin talkin to yer?' asked Povey.

'No one,' I lied.

'If someone's bin tellin tales about Eric, then I need to know.'

'I was talking to Eric,' I said, 'and he mentioned his marriage.'

Povey's eyes widened. 'And marble fire surrounds?'

'Yes.'

Povey sighed, sat down on the wall of sandbags, and stared at the floor.

'It were a bad *do,* that were,' he said. 'A very bad *do*.'

'It did sound it,' I said.

''e adored 'is missus, and that little lass, 'e did,' said Povey, still staring at the floor, which was scuffed with years of fork-lift abuse.

'How long ago was it?'

'Ooh, must be twenty year now, lad,' said Povey, 'but feels like yesterdee. Poor lad, and 'e *were* but a lad back then, 'ardly out o' short trousers. It were a *bad do*.'

'And he hasn't married since?'

'Oh no!' said Povey looking at me. 'She meant the ruddy world to 'im she did, and the little lass. No, it did fer poor Eric, it did. Do you know 'e used to be a great sprinter, did Eric.'

I must have looked surprised.

'Wouldn't think it, would yer, lad? But yes, 'e were a sprinter. A bloody good sprinter with a big smile. That's 'ow I remember 'im best, when 'e first came as apprentice, and that must be, bloody 'ell, thirty year back. You see, back in them days, Amundsen Enterprises weren't just a place to buy stuff. Oh no, we did things fer people! We 'elped 'em choose, and then we fitted it for 'em. Them were the bloody days!'

Povey pulled out a handkerchief and dabbed his eyes.

'It were a service,' he said, 'something to tek pride in. We used ter be a social 'ub – Saturday morning all the local fellas used ter come down and talk tool. It were great. Wid put on bacon baps.'

'Sounds lovely,' I said.

'Not like now, mind,' said Povey, standing once more to regard the heavy sky. 'Youngsters 'aven't a bloody clue about the art of mekin' tool. They're all too busy flippin bloody burgers to care, or tappin away all day long on ruddy compooters. All them muscles put to waste. All them fine specimens sat behind bloody desks.'

Povey wore a faraway expression and pursed his lips, presumably recalling the tool-toting specimens of his youth.

'Is there any hope for Eric?' I asked.

'Eric?' said Povey, glancing at Beardmore's closed door. 'We can but 'ope, lad. I know 'e's a little gruff, but 'e's a good lad at 'art, and you should've seen 'im ruddy well sprint.'

I opened my mouth to ask another question, but bottled it. Instead I studied Povey as he stood regarding the flooded car park, one foot upon the wall of sandbags as if he were an explorer surveying an entirely new landscape. I took a deep breath, and said, 'Alan, you know how you are very keen for everyone to observe health and safety regulations?'

'Yes, lad,' said Povey, now staring at me.

'Do you think you sometimes observe them a little *too* stringently? I mean, do you think that perhaps... sometimes, you overdo it a little?'

'Are you 'avin a nervous brekdown, lad?' cried Povey.

'No, I'm not. It's just that... remember that run-in you had with that Irishman and his lads about the tail-lift? Well, I needed the loo afterwards, and...'

'Spit it out, lad!'

'I think I heard you crying in a cubicle, and I just wondered whether you'd regretted the rigour with which you'd tried to apply the regulations?'

'Bloody 'ell, lad!' cried Povey. 'Them's some bloody flowery words for a trolley-dolly!'

'Yes... sorry,' I said, 'but my question stands.'

'*His bloody question stands,*' sighed Povey, folding and refolding his arms.

'I hope you don't mind me asking,' I said.

'Listen you,' said Povey. ''Ow old are yer? Forty?'

'Thirty-eight,' I said.

'Well let me put a question to you, lad. What're you doin, a clever boy like yerself, with all them flowery words – what are you doin still pushin trollies and clearin up messes at thirty-bloody-eight? What I'm askin, son, is *what went wrong*? Why aren't you at the top of bloody Canary Wharf printin money? Or do you like this life? Do you like the fact that nobody gives a bloody damn 'oo you are, or what yuv got ter say?'

'I find it... a challenge,' I said.

'I bet yer bloody well doo!' said Povey, nodding vigorously. 'So if yewer askin me what went bloody wrong in *my* life, then respectfully, son, I ask you to mind yewer own bloody business!'

'You make a very good point, Alan,' I said, 'but all you've done is throw a difficult question back in my face. My question still–'

'*Still stands*!' laughed Povey. 'Ee, you are a daft bugger. Listen son, what I'm sayin is that we both 'ave our bloody crosses to beyer. Me, you, Eric, Dave, Douglas, Benny, Tracy, and the rest of 'em, even that bloody miserable bugger 'oo's yewer mate – yer know, the one 'oo bloody well coughs before sayin anythin, and 'oo's sick if yer so much as ask 'im the time of day!'

'Glyn.'

'Ay that's 'im, bloody weirdo!'

'I just thought you might want to talk about things,' I said.

'I thank you fer that, son,' said Povey, 'but fer some of us talkin just won't do. It's gettin on with it that counts. Someone's gotta bloody well run this stuwer, an' that person 'appens to be me.'

I admired Povey's dignity. I wanted to tell him that I knew all about his arduous "leaving home" routine, but most of all I wanted to tell him about Beardmore's pilfering (not to mention his spitting). But I knew I couldn't. I also realised just then that I really couldn't tell the taxman about it either. I became aware that the society of Amundsen Enterprises was balanced as precariously as any of nature's ecosystems, and quite beautiful in its own way.

We'd run out of things to say, and both stared at the gloomy clouds. Then Povey coughed, and seemed to be looking for a natural way of parting. I became suddenly self-conscious of my white dress with the green leaves and red flowers.

'If you ever do want to talk about things...' I said.

'Oh, don't be such a big girl's blouse!' said Povey, before mincing off in the direction of the toilets.

Girls' blouses got me thinking about Glyn. Where the hell was he?

284

48

FUN DOESN'T HAVE TO BE FUN
TO BE FUN

I popped into the café to check on Gabby. He was laughing with Tracy about something or other, another grump he'd turned inside out. It seemed I'd underestimated my little friend.

Next, I went back past the peacefully snoozing Benny to look in on Beardmore's knock-off. I ran my hand along the top of a slightly chipped marble fire surround and reconsidered its meaning. I cast an eye over the dizzying array of items.

'Listen,' I said, addressing the items. 'Here was I thinking you were just stuff to line Beardmore's pockets. But no, each and every one of you represents a tear shed for the loss of his missus and little lass.'

The shop-soiled items said nothing. Perhaps, like Glyn, they'd read Wittgenstein.

I put my foot on the first rung of a bent ladder, and reflected that I couldn't very well divert Beardmore's revenues having heard his tale of woe. Unpleasant as Beardmore was on a day-to-day basis, his demise (for surely my actions would cause an avalanche of thugs to kill him) would clearly crush Povey who regarded him as a son, and in turn upset the fine balance of the store. There was so much going on "under the hood" of Amundsen Enterprises, so much of which I'd been entirely unaware: wars, grief, envy, hatred, love, lust, and much more – in a word, anything a human being *could* feel, every possible nuance, was felt somewhere and by someone within the *society* of the store. The world is all that is the case.

Somehow, gaining an insight into these goings-on had... what? *It had humanised me.* Yes, I could feel it. I laughed out loud! Thirty-eight-and-a-half years of waiting in the wings, waiting for life to start, wondering where all the action was, forcing my own ridiculous constructs of made-up meaning upon unsuspecting audiences. I'd been wandering lost in a jester's desert, a fool's badland. For thirty-eight years I'd wanted everything to be perfect and, in the event, nothing was, and it turned out this was good. All I'd needed to do was to embrace it. I was flawed, and it was OK. This didn't just apply to me:

Beardmore was not perfectly bad.
Povey was not perfectly crazy.
Benny was not perfectly wise.
Brendan was not perfectly silent.
Dave was not perfectly cynical.
Tracy was not perfectly miserable.
Beryl was not perfectly kind.
Gabby was not perfectly idiotic.
I was not perfectly unsuccessful.
I wasn't sure what to say about Glyn.

The working day was drawing to a close. I shut the door to the knock-off department and walked slowly back to the front of the store. I knew what I must do.

I found Gabby and told him we'd be leaving soon.

'Aw man, do we have to?' he cried.

'You've changed your tune, Gab!' I laughed.

'Douglas asked me to go with him to the pub tomorrow night, man!'

'Really?'

286

'Yeah, man! He said he'd take me to the pub, give me all the twenty-pences I can carry, get me really drunk, then take me home to show me his puppies! Isn't that nice of him, John?'

'You're going on a date with Douglas?'

'A what, man?'

'A date, Gab. A potentially romantic meeting.'

'No man, he's just a really nice old man, man!'

'Gab, you need to be careful...'

'Why, man?' asked Gabby, his face betraying absolutely no suspicion whatsoever.

I left it. Who was I to ban Gabby from dating Douglas? Plus, I would be at the pub. I'd watch over him.

I told Gabby to meet me at the front of the store in ten minutes. Then I walked to the green metal stairs to Beardmore's elevated office, mounted them, and with each step hardened my resolve to do what was perhaps not strictly ethical, but necessary. I resolved to get on with it, like Povey. I knocked.

'Come!' shouted Beardmore.

I opened the door to see him seated at his desk. It was covered with screwed-up tissues.

'What do yer want?' he grunted. 'If yer want more fackin waterworks you've come to the wrong fackin place.'

'No, I don't want that,' I said. 'May I?' I indicated a plastic chair by the wall. Beardmore stared at me, then nodded.

'What then?' he said. He took up a cigar and lit it with a trembling hand.

This time I paid no attention to body language. I held the aces. Beardmore, fully aware of this, was bent out of shape.

'It's OK, Eric,' I said.

'What the fackin 'ell you on about?' he shouted. It didn't matter – his eyes told me what I needed to know.

'I'm not going to tell the taxman, Eric,' I said. 'And I am resigning from the position of *Web Mobility Director*.'

'I knew you was a fackin pussy!'

Again, the mouth said one thing, but the eyes another.

'I was very moved by what you told me in the car,' I said.

Beardmore's eyes moistened again.

'So I'm going to turn a blind eye, on one condition.'

He stared at me.

'My condition is that you stop threatening people. And that, in particular, you stop spitting at people. It is unspeakably horrible, disgusting, and cruel. It is your way of saying "Look world, I'm a disgusting animal, and this is all I'm worth". You are worth more, Eric. I know that you were a fine young man, a sprinter with a big smile. Yes, a terrible thing happened to you. An awful thing. But you are still that bright young man, Eric. And you still mean a lot to people in your life.'

'Like fackin who?' barked Beardmore.

'Alan, for one,' I said.

'Fackin puff.'

'He *cares* for you, Eric!' I said. 'He thinks of you as a son.'

Beardmore eyed me.

'I loved 'er,' he said. 'The baby. Both of them. The world ended when they ended.'

'But *you* didn't end, Eric,' I said. 'You're still here! Look at you chain-smoking those cigars! And look at the shape you're in! You are doing everything you possibly can to kill yourself, save actually attempting suicide. It's pointless, Eric! And it's incredibly hurtful. Alan really loves you, and all you do is pilfer from the store he's given his life to, and drive him frantic with anxiety! You need to make some changes, right now. You can bring this back from the brink, Eric. I know you can. I believe in you. You're still that bright smiling sprinter inside. You haven't changed.'

Tears ran freely down Beardmore's cracked cheeks. He started to sob loudly with great hulking movements, bouncing up and down in his farting chair.

I stood and slowly moved towards him, gingerly placing a hand on his shoulder. Beardmore immediately turned and locked me in a fierce embrace. He wept for all the pain and injustice in the world.

'That's it, Eric,' I said. 'Get it all out. This is the first step.'

The embrace went on and on, and on, and neither did the force of Beardmore's grief abate. The front of my white dress with the green leaves and red flowers was soaked in his tears.

I heard a noise, and looked back at the door. Gabby! His eyes were wide with wonder. Heaven knows what he was thinking – something about puppies, I imagined.

Beardmore also became aware of Gabby, threw me away, and violently straightened up, wiping his eyes with the back of his hairy hands.

'Don't mind Gabby,' I said to Beardmore. 'He only has good thoughts.'

'Little pixie bastard,' said Beardmore, then smiled.

We both laughed at what a little pixie bastard Gabby was, standing there in his once yellow, and now myrtle green, summer dress. Luckily Gabby also thought it was rather funny, although on what basis, I couldn't say.

'Thanks, John,' sniffed Beardmore. 'I'll think about what you said.'

I mimicked, 'You know it makes fackin sense, you little cant.'

Beardmore smiled some more, and Gabby looked per-plexed.

'Now fack off!' said Beardmore.

'No, you fack off!' I said.

'I will fack off after you've facked off!' laughed Beard-more.

'I can't fack off until you've fackin shut up!' I said.

'You are both dirty bastards, man!' yelled Gabby, perform-ing what looked like star jumps.

'And you can fack off an all!' shouted Beardmore to Gabby.

Gabby began to sob.

I shook Beardmore's hand, grabbed poor Gabby, and we took our leave.

'One more thing,' said Beardmore. Bugger, he'd done it again!

'What?'

'You can keep the fackin car!'

49

THE TIME TRAVELLER

Inasmuch as my plans had changed, I thought it only fair to revisit the Internet café to pay the studious chap with the quivering moustache, and the little manager, for their trouble.

The rain had held off. Gabby and I waded across the car park and clambered into the Cortina. I strapped Gabby in, started it up amid more dense black smoke (it reminded Gabby of Deep Purple's "Smoke on the Water", so he said), struggled with the gear stick, carefully raised the clutch, and much to my pleasure we began to move in a forward direction. I pulled out onto rush-hour Whitehorse Road, chucked a right onto Dig Street, draped my arm over the sill, and felt very much a man of the world, more at ease with myself than I could ever remember.

'Where's Glyn, man?' asked Gabby.

I had forgotten he was missing.

'We'll find him, Gab,' I said.

'Oh, good, man,' said Gabby.

Having no brakes, I estimated the distance we would require to slow to a stop, and we glided into a space outside the Internet café and the barbers, just nudging the dented black Range Rover which had also returned.

We drew very little attention. Though admittedly at the extreme end of the spectrum, the Cortina was just another clapped-out car in a street of unroadworthy, untaxed, uninsured bangers, driven by (apart from the little fellow with the Range Rover) unlicensed individuals with not an asset in the world.

291

I unclipped Gabby's seatbelt, scooped him out and closed the driver's door, which fell off into the gutter with a clatter.

'Man, it's a soft-top now!' yelled Gabby.

'It's not, Gab,' I said. 'It just doesn't have doors.'

A little bird swooped and flew straight through my car.

'Rock and Roll!' shouted Gabby.

We walked into the Internet café.

'I wondered where you were?' said the studious-looking chap, his little brown moustache quivering with concern. The little manager walked in from the rear.

'Yes, sorry,' I said. 'We had a few things to–'

'We've sold a thousand fire surrounds?!' yelled the little manager.

'What?' I asked. 'How?'

'So, we put a stock photo on eBay?' cried the studious looking chap. 'We described it as having been reclaimed from an old country house, a bargain at ten pounds, and we've sold a thousand?'

'So, it was my idea to say it came from an old country house?' beamed the little manager.

Oh God. I was in hock again, and this time to the tune of one thousand marble fire surrounds.

'But I only have, at best, ten,' I said. 'And they were all made in Indonesia less than a year ago.'

What a strange situation. I'd been *Web Mobility Director* for less than a day, and had tendered my resignation, but in this time it seemed I'd been wildly successful. The thought struck me that this could be a semi-kosher business for Beardmore. He would, of course, have to manage his distrust towards marble fire surrounds in order to make it a viable proposition.

'How far afield have they sold?'

'Aberdeen?' said the studious-looking chap.

'Penzance?' said the little manager.

'Wow, that's in America, man!' yelled Gabby.

'Right!' I yelled, full of entrepreneurial zest, and patting the bank cards in my pocket. 'I want you to order nine hundred and ninety antique marble fire surrounds from Indonesia!'

'I'M ON IT?' shouted the studious-looking chap, his little brown moustache looking as if it might start spinning like a clown's bow tie.

'And order me a little black dress, with zips! A leather one!' yelled Gabby.

'What the hell!' I shouted. 'Yes, order that too!'

I took out two twenties and paid the pair of them.

'If you manage to order nine hundred and ninety marble fire surrounds from Indonesia, I'll pay you a thousand quid each!' I cried. 'I'll be back tomorrow to see how you've got on! Goodbye!'

I grabbed Gabby and made to leave, but the little manager called me back.

'You left your time machine!' he cried, pointing at the immobile phone still standing like an alien monolith upon the desk.

'You can have it!' I said. 'It's all yours! I'm off to buy something from the future!'

'Oh my God!' said the little manager. 'I'm going to travel back in time to nineteen eighty-four and buy a brand new Atari!'

'It's not actually a time... hang on,' I said. 'If this really was a time machine, that's all you'd do?'

'I thought you said it was a time machine?' he said.

'There's no such thing as a time machine,' I said.

'But you said you'd travelled from nineteen sixty-seven?' he said.

'Yes I have, but it's taken me thirty-eight-and-a-half years to get here!'

The studious-looking chap with the brown moustache and the little manager looked extremely disappointed.

'I would go back to Saxon times, man!' said Gabby. 'To see them build Canary Wharf!'

I looked these three young men up and down, two heartily disappointed, the third inspecting the immobile phone for a button called "Visit Saxon Times", a button perhaps as lovely and useful as Beryl's "Put Money in Gabriel Longfeather's Account" button. I decided to change my tune. Just as being a tad eccentric had not caused Gabby to die in the last twenty-six years, I observed that the little manager and the studious-looking chap with the brown moustache had too lived effectively believing that time machines did exist – neither of them wore their trousers back to front, nor were they mal-nourished from their beliefs rendering them unable to eat.

'Actually,' I said, 'I was joking. It probably is a time machine.'

My companions brightened significantly.

'But don't just go back to nineteen eighty-four for an Atari,' I continued. 'Indeed, you could have some *serious* fun with this! On the theme of nineteen eighty-four, I would think about going back to nineteen forty-seven to tell George Orwell about the *actual* nineteen eighty-four, to see what he makes of it.'

'Who's George Orwell?' asked all three simultaneously.

A feeling of intense loneliness swept over me. My instinct was to bark at them for an hour or so about how they really needed to know who George Orwell was, in order to be able to say that they'd experienced a fully-rounded human existence.

'Don't forget to order the marble fire surrounds!' I said, and grabbed Gabby and walked out of the shop, leaving the little manager and the studious-looking chap with the brown moustache to use the time machine for a retro shopping spree.

Angry black clouds were once again forming above our heads.

50

GUILTLESS GLYN

I decided to leave the car on Dig Street, hoping some avid collector would entirely renovate it overnight in the manner of *The Elves and the Shoemaker*.

Glyn. I'd given him one thousand pounds, and where the hell was he? This amount of cash was clearly not enough to disappear and start a new life. My imagination was filled with images of him struggling to breathe beneath a collapsed mountain of magazines of a certain genre.

'Let's look in all the pubs, Gab,' I said.

Gabby immediately began to jiggle in his hand a very large pile of twenty-pence pieces. I was about to upbraid him for caring more about jukeboxes than Glyn, but supposed that Gabby could put on a tune while I checked the toilets – actually this was a good working model of our respective roles in life.

Thus we wove our way from pub to pub, Gabby placing a tune in each as our calling card, creating waves of sound-memory as we progressed down Dig Street. Not a sign of Glyn. We were getting perilously close to home. We passed the pound shop where I'd attempted to find out the number for directory enquiries. The aubergine-purple frontage of Dark Secrets stared at us, and I thought of bottoms and sausages.

'Gab, what do you think Glyn would do?'

'I think he'd work as a mop, man,' said Gabby, making a half-hearted and ultimately failed attempt to leapfrog a post box.

'Jesus, Gab!' I said, pulling him up from the cracked pavement. 'I need to teach you the art of inference!'

'OI, WANKERS!' shouted someone.

Gabby and I whirled to behold the shouter exit Dark Secrets, and advance in our direction, a man in a striped pencil skirt and flowery blouse. Glyn? It *was* Glyn, but wearing an expression I'd never seen before!

'Glyn, what's going on?' I asked.

'I've been hanging upside down all fucking afternoon, being whipped by Mistress Gladys!'

'Glyn, what's happened to you?' I cried.

Gabby cowered behind a bus shelter like a chilly chihuahua.

'I'm free, that's fucking what!' shouted Glyn, pulling out a pack of cigarettes and lighting the wrong end of one.

'Free of what, Glyn?' I asked, as he coughed and threw the thing away. 'What have they been doing to you in there?'

'They've whipped me. They've gagged me. They've waterboarded me. They've taken cigarette lighters to my bits, they've inserted things, and they've repeatedly threatened to extract my incisors. It's been the best fucking day of my life!'

'What's wrong with Glyn, man?!' yelled Gabby, wrapping himself around my middle.

'I think, Gab,' I said with trembling voice, 'Glyn's been down to *The Dark Chamber*!'

'Does it make you swear, man?'

'It looks that way, Gab,' I said.

'Let's go and get fucking arseholed!' shouted Glyn, having now managed to light another cigarette in the proper manner, which also made him cough.

'Glyn doesn't smoke, man!' cried Gabby.

'Glyn, what's happened to you?' I again asked.

'I just fucking well told you, cloth ears!'

'No Glyn, what's *happened* to you? You seem to have become someone else entirely!'

'Fuck that!' said Glyn. 'I've just had the whole of human history surgically extracted! I'm fucking free. Let's go to the cunting pub!'

'He's horrid, man!' cried Gabby.

'Oh, Glyn!' I cried. 'They've brutalised you in an afternoon!'

'Go fuck yourself,' said Glyn.

'John, Glyn told you to *go fuck yourself*, man!'

'You too, you little imbecile,' spat Glyn. 'The pair of you, go fuck yourselves!'

'How do we fuck ourselves, man?' asked Gabby.

'ENOUGH!' I shouted.

Then I got down on my knees before our altered friend. 'Where are you, Glyn Hopkins? Where is my sensitive philosophical friend? Glyn, I need you to come back!'

'Glyn's dead,' spat Glyn.

'He can't be!' I cried. 'Can't you see, Glyn, you can't just throw off human suffering in an afternoon! The world needs you to carry it in your heart! It's your job, Glyn! You are a curator of souls! Without you, we're nothing! I'm begging you, please come back! Hitler still killed millions of people! Stalin still executed his closest comrades! Pol Pot still decimated a generation! Kitchener still sent the flower of England into the trenches! Glyn, oh, Glyn!'

If ever I'd witnessed a proper inner battle (and I hadn't) I witnessed one now. Glyn dropped to the floor and ran horizontal windmills about the pavement, screaming and cursing. Gabby found it funny, and I had to tell him tartly that it wasn't. On and on it went, the volume of Glyn's shrieking never abating.

Gabby popped into a newsagent for a lolly, while I watched poor Glyn wear holes in his pencil skirt.

'I DON'T WANT THEM TO VISIT ME!' he bellowed.

'Who?' I asked.

'The GERMANS!' he yelled. 'AND THE AUSTRIANS!'

'Glyn, you look after their souls!' I said. 'You're a responsible archivist of evil! Without you, the world would spin into a black hole!'

Then he stood, and brushed himself off. Gabby returned sucking on a lolly.

'It's not strictly true about the black hole,' said Glyn.

'Oh, Glyn!' I said, and hugged him for all I was worth, laughing so hard I thought I'd burst. 'You're back, my lovely friend, you're back!'

'I thought it wasn't funny, man,' observed Gabby.

'It wasn't, and it's still not. I'm laughing with relief, with happiness!'

'Are we still going to the pub, man?' asked Gabby, again jiggling his coins. I hugged Glyn all the way home (he just about tolerated it), and in turn Gabby hugged me, a bit jealous. As we turned into Erebus Road, Glyn apologised unreservedly and admitted he'd enjoyed the bondage session so much that it might have driven him temporarily insane. I was hard-pressed not to agree. Gabby put forward the powerful theory that bottoms and sausages gave one a funny feeling in one's tummy.

Our words dried up and our feet drove piles as we arrived home to what was once Clements Markham House. It was actually quite difficult to interpret the plot we stood before. This was where it should have been, I was sure of that. The top floors were entirely gone and in their place stood a multistorey towering glass edifice, so gross, so distasteful, and so unbefitting of a period property that I nearly vomited. Indeed, I leaned over to do just that, but nothing came out, and I almost felt like apologising to our once-lovely home on account of not being able to express fully my searing disgust.

'God, it's beautiful, man!' shouted Gabby, dancing up and down.

'Gab, it's awful!' I yelled, wringing my hands with anger, and stamping my feet on slabs crazy-paved from the support legs of mobile cranes.

'It's a moral vacuum,' said Glyn, somewhat enigmatically.

The space between the garden gate and the front door was covered by an enormous dark blue tarpaulin, which spewed black smoke from a hole at the apex. I pushed open the gate, parted what served as the door to the tarp, and peered into the interior of the makeshift structure.

The bleakest scene! Rows and rows of tired blackened faces stared back at me – all of our elderly neighbours, cowering over a pathetic fire.

As my eyes became accustomed to the inky blackness, I began to pick out among the men scores of empty bottles: beer, spirits, and super-strength cider. A sea of cigarette butts littered the floor (and indeed every surface) like an evil orange carpet.

'What have they done to you?'

No response, except one of the gentlemen started to sing a very shaky "Mull of Kintyre".

This was Mr Kapoor's grand plan, written in blood, that his gift would allow his tenants to drink and smoke themselves to death; he had played his part, and now these gentlemen were only too happy to fulfil their side of the bargain.

Old Brian hobbled up to me. He didn't look too *clever*, as Povey would have put it.

'What's happened, Brian?' I asked, steadying him.

'Fackin Asians came down 'ere and frew us out didn't they!' he spluttered.

'The dairy industry doesn't tolerate racism,' commented Glyn.

'Mr Kapoor?' I said. 'But he's in Marbella!'

''Ow the fack d'you know?'

'Oh, just a guess,' I said. 'So it wasn't Mr Kapoor, and Indeep?'

'Nah it was some other fackers, wannit, they all look the fackin same anyhow!'

Much as I felt sorry for Old Brian, it was very difficult to like the fellow.

I turned to see Gabby puffing sadly upon a brown cigar, and sipping from a half-full plastic bottle of suspiciously yellow "cider". I told Old Brian to sit tight (he was tight in any case), made Gabby drop his refreshments, and ordered him and Glyn to join me in entering Clements Markham House to observe and record the full extent of the wrongdoing at hand. Glyn seemed unmoved, but I was willing to forgive him, he having only recently been insane. We three waved to the old men, and shuffled through detritus towards the front door.

Seemingly untouched and eternal, the myrtle green front door swung open dutifully, sweeping away a snowdrift of choking dust. What destruction! The inside was a shell; the staircase simply not there, the internal walls and ceilings disappeared, replaced with a spider's web of scaffolding and Acrow props. To my horror I realised that Clements Markham House had been all but demolished. Only the external skin of bricks remained; an architect's twee trick in an otherwise entirely modern structure. Among the mess, a single ladder stood, which disappeared upwards into darkness and dust.

'Hey, John man, look!' shouted Gabby, lifting reams of letters from the dust. 'They're all addressed to you!'

Gingerly I took them, wondering what further species of madness they would herald. I blew on the envelopes and studied them closely: official-looking, and, as Gabby had said, every one of them addressed to me. My heart sank, and I opened one.

More offers of oodles of credit. Useless. I was now richer than a marginally successful oil magnate, but had I succeeded in saving Clements Markham House? No, I had not.

'It's *so* nice of you to pay for all this, John, man!' yelled Gabby.

Ah, yes! How could I forget! It was I funding the wholesale destruction of history. Glyn was lobbing history into a vault of forgetfulness, and I was paying for the manufacture of a vast cement plug to choke the entrance. Gabby tested the payphone to see if it still connected to his mam. It didn't.

Everything except my credit rating was in ruins: Clements Markham House, the gnarled arteries of the old men, Gabby's maiden honour, Glyn's no-nonsense sanity, Beardmore's emotional life, The Sofas' instruments, Dave's Britain, Povey's order, my Ford Cortina, the studious-looking fellow with the brown moustache's and the little manager's sense of science fiction – even philosophy itself had been breached by a dam-busting uppercut from Ludwig Wittgenstein.

You didn't mention love.

I threw the offers of more credit into the dust. Horrified, Gabby kneeled to retrieve them.

'Leave them, Gab!' I said. 'Money cannot help us now!'

'But John, man!' yelled Gabby. 'What am I going to wear to the pub tomorrow, with Douglas? I want a black dress with zips! A leather one!'

'Jesus, Gab!' I shouted. 'Here we are surrounded by a vision of ruin not witnessed since Stalingrad, and all you can think about is the pub!'

'I love the pub, man!' said Gabby.

'You like the jukebox within the pub,' observed Glyn, pointlessly. It was fabulous to have him back.

'Come on, guys!' I said, digging to the very soles of my sensible shoes for courage. 'Let's rally together! What shall we do? Give me your ideas!'

'Oh, God, man!' cried Gabby, his face etched with what appeared to be a powerful realisation.

'What is it, Gab?'

301

'MY STEREO, MAN!'

Gabby sprinted towards the lone ladder, and in a flash disappeared into the inky blackness above.

'Gabby!' I shouted. 'Come back!'

'His stereo will almost certainly be destroyed,' said Glyn.

'Glyn, don't you think Gabby's actions confirm the distinct likelihood of just that theory?' I asked irritably.

'Sorry, John.'

'Have you considered that your magazine collection might be mangled?' I asked.

'RAAAGH!'

Oh yes, it was nice to have Glyn Hopkins back. He ran on his flat feet into the darkness to investigate.

Pattering on the dark blue tarpaulin told me that it was raining again. I pictured poor Povey, and recalled his forecast of another deluge.

I listened to Gabby creaking and banging his way up our corrupted home. Then I heard him scream, and the worst was confirmed.

I mounted the ladder and climbed, arriving coughing and covered in dust, at a platform which used to constitute the floor of Gabby's room. Gabby was slumped, crying over his broken stereo. I walked over to him and offered sympathy.

'It'll be OK, Gab. We'll fix it up somehow.'

Gabby stared at me with wet eyes and shook his head, drawing back his dusty hair with a hamster's fist.

I bent over the thing to take a better look; it was smashed into a jumbled mass of wires reminiscent of the innards of an old-fashioned telephone exchange. Outside, the rain intensified. Drops began to fall silently from above, fizzing when they landed in Gabby's ex-stereo. The odour of ionisation filled the room, as if we'd just tested a tiny atomic bomb.

I walked over to Gabby's huge record collection and pulled a few out, blowing off the dust. 'Gab, your records look

OK, and I'll buy you a new stereo tomorrow,' I said.

'Will you, man?' he asked, wearing a little smile and wiping his eyes.

'Of course, Gab,' I said. 'I'll buy you an even louder one, when we go and buy some more instruments.'

'Cool!' yelled Gabby, jumping up and down on the platform and creating worrying percussions.

'Can I have two stereos man, and link them together, so it's even louder?'

'No.'

'Aw, man!' pouted Gabby.

'Look, Gab, let's rescue your records, and I'll get you a brand new top-of-the-range player. OK?'

Gabby smiled and nodded. I realised immediately that I'd made a grave error. I'd been so concerned with the stereo that I hadn't really considered the scale of his record collection, and moreover how we would safely lug this tonnage down the rickety ladder to the hallway.

Gabby had no such qualms, grabbing armfuls and lobbing them straight down the hatch. After watching him for a minute, I came to the conclusion that it was the way forward.

I joined him in grabbing records and tossing them into the gloom. In the event it was quite therapeutic as I thought of all the days and nights I'd been forced not only to listen to them, but to learn by rote their terrifyingly crass lyrics.

We were flinging away the contents of the last bin when I heard a shout from downstairs. I grabbed Gabby's arm and told him to be still.

'Are you there, lads?' the voice called.

It was Paddy, The Gaffer.

'I'm just here to see if you like it, is that OK?' he called.

Gabby and I descended to find Paddy standing knee-deep in heavy metal records.

'So, lads,' he grinned. 'You like it so?'

I was speechless.

'I love it, man!' said Gabby.

'Ah, good lads. It's not quite finished yet, but it'll be grand, is that OK?'

All of a sudden I recalled that earlier in the week, leaning in through my broken window puffing a cigar and smiling, he'd somewhat enigmatically asked me about marble fire surrounds.

'Why did you ask me about marble fire surrounds, and Eric Beardmore?' I demanded.

'What's that you say?' asked The Gaffer, his face blanching.

I enunciated slowly, 'Marble fire surrounds, and Eric Beardmore,' and watched him squirm.

'You must have been talking to someone else so, lads, is that OK?' said The Gaffer unevenly.

'It's fine, man!' said Gabby.

'You know what I'm talking about,' I said, calmly. 'What do you know about it?'

I watched The Gaffer try to smile. His eyes grew wet. He fumbled within his coat, drew out his pack of cigars, and lit one with an unsteady hand.

'I'm listening,' I said.

'What to, man?' asked Gabby.

'Ah, lads,' sighed The Gaffer. 'I was wondering if you knew. Earlier in the week, well, I was doing a bit of *fishing*, is that OK?'

'I told you man, it's fine!' smiled Gabby.

'Gab, shut up!' I said. He whimpered and hugged me.

'It's like this, lads,' sniffed The Gaffer. 'You see, me and Eric, we go back a long ways so, and... I was doing a bit of work at Eric's house once, and I was short on time...'

'Go on,' I said.

'Well, lads, I fitted a marble fire surround in Eric's house so I did, is that OK?'

'Is it, John, man?' asked Gabby.

'Shush, Gab!' I hissed, then met The Gaffer's eye. 'Go on, Paddy...'

'I didn't put enough bolts into the wall, and that night, well, it fell off, and...' The Gaffer broke off and broke down.

'Paddy,' I said. 'You didn't do it on purpose.'

The Gaffer took a deep breath, puffed out his chest, and straightened up. Then he took out a large green handkerchief and wiped his eyes.

'There's more, is that OK?' said The Gaffer. 'You see, I was great friends with Alan Povey too, so I was.'

My mind began to whirl.

'Eric lost his wife and bairn... that was bad enough so it was. But, well, they pinned the lot on Alan.'

'They blamed *Alan?*' I said.

'You see, lads, it was poor Povey designed the instructions for fitting the fireplace, and the judge... the judge said he was *negligent.*'

'*Negligent?*'

'The instructions didn't carry any health and safety regulations so they didn't, is that OK?'

The missing link. Povey, blamed for health and safety negligence. The real subject of the argument about the tail-lift. Weeping in the toilet cubicle.

I felt deeply sorry for Povey then, and Beardmore, and The Gaffer too, who looked desperately sad and guilty. Gabby whistled the theme tune from *The A-Team*.

In a perfect storm of pathetic fallacy, the rain began to thunder down upon the dark blue tarpaulin outside. More water to flood Povey's fears.

I had an idea!

'Paddy, what would you say if I told you there is something you could do for Alan and Eric; something which would not rewrite their pasts, but would make their futures a whole lot brighter?'

It was a shame that Glyn, presumably still rooting for jazz mags in his ruined room, hadn't been with us in the hallway to hear my heartfelt words.

'I'd bite your arms off, is that OK?'

'No!' said Gabby.

'Amundsen Enterprises was very nearly flooded today,' I said, 'and just look at the weather now...'

We looked outside at the soaking tarp, and the wet pristine bins, and the mini-rivers running down the gutters carrying leaves and crisp packets.

'Could you build flood defences around the store, tonight?' I asked.

The Gaffer's eyes opened wide. He pursed his lips and took a sharp intake of breath.

'You can do it!' I said, stamping my foot in heavy metal.

'Do what, man?' asked Gabby.

'Save everything!' I shouted. 'Make something good happen for a change!'

'Lads...' said The Gaffer. 'It would be grand... if we could do something... if, if we had the means, is that OK?'

Crafty old man! I patted my side, and winked at him.

'Did I mention I was a millionaire?'

The Gaffer grinned.

'Right!' yelled The Gaffer. 'I'll grab the lads right now, and we'll get on it, is that OK?'

'It's OK,' I said.

Paddy The Gaffer stood in the hallway with Gabby and me, leisurely finishing his cigar, while I deconstructed the phrase *I'll grab the lads right now*. But finally, with a glint of his hazel eyes, he once again shook our hands and disappeared into the wet dusk.

51

GOODBYE TO ALL THAT

What to do now? I was pondering whether to gather up the old men and take them to a hotel, but given their state I supposed they might have to make do with a rather low-class establishment, indeed it might almost exactly match their current living quarters at the front of Clements Markham House, and if these were our prospects, what was the point of moving them at all? I was the newly-appointed general of a ragtag army on a battlefield of architectural outrage.

My reveries were broken by coughs and the loud swishing of much paper. Gabby and I turned to see Glyn struggling through the dust, carrying a tower of magazines of a certain genre.

'They're not wrecked, then?' I asked.

Glyn said nothing. Bent at the knees, and struggling through heavy metal records like black piles of autumn leaves, he delivered his tower to the floor, before standing for a few seconds in concentration to check all was balanced. Then he wordlessly returned to his room. Gabby went bright red, and threw me glances.

More rustling and coughing; Glyn returned with another lofty column of magazines, which he deposited as neatly as possible next to the first. Several more trips, and Gabby and I had to start inching out of the front door to make way for this naughty behemoth. What a thing to save from the jaws of historical destruction, I thought, a life's work of furtive top-shelf purchases! And how much hot guilt was represented by this solemn collection?

At last Glyn, having added yet another pile, didn't return to his room, but stood leaning on one of his rude buttresses, panting.

The hallway was transformed, containing as it now did a pile of sexual tofu upon a bed of hard rock salad. I laughed. So did Gabby, immediately and raucously, copying me.

'Raaagh!'

'Oh, come on, Glyn!' I laughed. 'I can't believe it's come to *this*!'

'Raaagh!'

'Women do have funny bodies, man!'

Now I laughed even harder at Gabby's perception of why I was laughing, and Gabby, his eyes never leaving me, snorted and bellowed, holding his sides. Even Glyn started to chuckle, then grew serious once more, which pricked my hilarious bubble.

'What?' I asked.

'What about *your* stuff?' he asked.

My poems! My half-finished novel! I'd completely forgotten my room was surely also destroyed!

I ran to the ladder and climbed once more into the gloom.

I found the entrance to my room and paused upon the ladder, suddenly nervous at what I might find in this crucible of wrecked dreams, my former hiding place from the world. I took a deep breath, dismounted the ladder, and walked into what remained of my home.

The first thing I noticed was that my broken window had been fixed. I was cheered a little by this – Paddy had been as good as his word.

I searched for my little desk, the piece of worktop offcut where I'd oft and unsuccessfully tried to pour the world out onto paper. I found it among the dust, snapped in two. I paused, recalling happier times in Clements Markham House.

But I was already rewriting history. Times hadn't been happy at all. In reality this room had been my jail, my solitary confinement, where I'd thought that if only I could weave beautiful-enough webs of meaning in the foul air, the world's soul would somehow know it, and send out a search party. It embarrassed me to think of it – mopping aisles by day and, by night, imagining I was somehow cosmically coupled.

I found my polar exploration books in a jumbled pile in a corner, and shouted for Gabby to come and help. He appeared at the top of the ladder like a gothic hod-carrier, and I loaded him up. Next I searched out my box of writings, and found it dumped upside down in the ruins of the sink. I thought about the totality of what was saved from Clements Markham House, and reflected that this box of ridiculous daydreams was possibly the most regrettable artefact of them all. I delved inside as if it were an end of the pier lucky dip, and drew forth a few sheets. Haikus, the type with which I'd amused Mr Kapoor, Indeep, and the old men. I read a couple and sighed, so daft were they, so light of meaning, so poorly picked and workaday were the words. I alone knew how I'd sweated.

Gabby reappeared at the top of the ladder, smiling, and I remembered how sweetly he had appreciated my verse. I decided he was the essence of a haiku. I picked up the box, gave it to him to carry down, and placed a kiss atop his head. Then I took one more look at my room, said *Goodbye*, and mounted the ladder myself.

52

ASK THE WHALES

Night had fallen. Glyn, Gabby and I sat in the hallway with our belongings, listening to the rain patter on the tarpaulin. Every now and then the old men would strike up a song. Among others:

"The Green Green Grass of Home"
"Tie a Yellow Ribbon"
"The Most Beautiful Girl"
"It Never Rains in Southern California"
"The Night They Drove Old Dixie Down"
"My Sweet Lord"
"If You Leave Me Now"
"Sweet Caroline"
"Love Is In The Air"

We explored our piles of belongings, Gabby talking ten to the dozen about Ozzy Osbourne, Glyn standing stock still and shooting desperate glances at a magazine which had fallen open. For myself, I took up *The Worst Journey in the World* by Apsley Cherry-Garrard, the classic account of Captain Scott's last and fatal expedition by one of his surviving party, and read about the mad winter journey undertaken by Cherry, Bowers and Dr Wilson in the sub-zero polar night with the sole aim of collecting penguin eggs, a quite ridiculous undertaking, delivered with the utmost seriousness of man's permanent struggle to learn. It got me thinking.

'Glyn,' I said, 'let's march on Dig Street.'

'*March*?'

'Yes!' I said. 'Let's occupy Dig Street!'

'You want us to live in Dig Street?'

'No. Well, kind of,' I said. 'Let's take the old men and the tarpaulin, and our belongings, and camp in Dig Street, near the Tube. We'll protest.'

'Protest about what?'

I wasn't sure. Gabby was singing "Iron Man" by Black Sabbath, so it was a little hard to think.

'Let's protest about... being forced to live our lives entirely unseen, whether by God, or our fellow men.'

'Your ego is certainly resilient,' Glyn observed.

'It's my best asset!' I said. 'And we can see how Paddy and the lads are getting on with the flood defences.'

Constant action was required of any human being to chase off a nagging sense of our certain demise. I felt immediately better. I told Glyn, and he grunted. Gabby was headbanging and screaming the words to "Welcome to the Jungle" by Guns N' Roses.

'GABBY, BE QUIET!' I yelled.

Gabby gave me an odd little smile. Glyn coughed, while still glancing at the open magazine, and I told them what we'd do.

'Let's go to the supermarket, get as many shopping trollies as we can, bring them back here, and load up. Then we'll man-haul to Dig Street!'

It was nine o'clock. There was a twenty-four-hour supermarket in the direction of Stratford. We set off immediately in the pouring rain.

We got lost several times, tramping up and down suburban cul-de-sacs, or finding ourselves walking on roads too major to own a pavement, our faces coated in the spray of a thousand wildly spinning wheels.

'Someone should invent some sort of handheld navigation device!' I shouted to Glyn as we tried to cross a loud main road, only half-sure where we were. 'Not a map, I mean something to actually tell you where to go!'

'Someone has,' said Glyn, 'it's called a sat nav.'

'*Sat Nav*?'

'A Satellite Navigation system,' said Glyn.

'I can see the supermarket, man!' shouted Gabby. We crossed the road safely, and headed towards familiar illuminated signs some way down the road.

A Satellite Navigation system! It jogged my memory, but I couldn't think where I'd come across such a thing. What a useful item! I resolved to buy one. Why hadn't I known about this? I thought about the last few years, and it started to make sense. Essentially, this is what I'd done over this time period:

1. Sat in my bedsit dreaming bad dreams/writing bad poetry/mournfully looking out of the window at passing trains, with no television, or access to the Internet (I did know the Internet existed, but had never been entirely sure what it was for, apart from flogging marble fire surrounds).

2. Sat in the pub talking to old men, Glyn, Gabby, and women with fading looks and low self-esteem, when they'd let me, and not about modern navigation systems.

3. Mopped floors.

4. Collected trollies from car parks.

5. Bought food and wine in local shops such as Mahmood's Hypermarket, which didn't sell navigation devices.

6. Sat in local cafés feeling decidedly lonely, not thinking about navigation devices, but thinking instead about where and how humanity had gone wrong.

7. Read books about the heroic age of polar exploration, where, in retrospect, they really could have done with modern navigation devices.

We were nearly at the supermarket. I thought about how pristine earth's orbit had been before Sputnik 1. I also wondered whether I'd been too quick to judge the pair in the Internet café. What else existed that I didn't know about?

'How do these devices work, Glyn?'

'They require contact with three or more satellites.'

I pictured women with bright red lipstick and World War Two hairstyles sitting up in space plugging wires into switch-boards.

'Each satellite knows its exact location. The time it takes for the signal, which travels at a set speed, the speed of light, to come back from the three or more satellites enables the device to accurately establish its position upon the earth's surface.'

I was dumbstruck! To think you could utilise actual sat-ellites blasted into orbit at a cost of trillions to find your way to the local shops.

'How does the satellite know where it is?' I asked.

'Raaagh!'

'What?'

'Raaagh!'

'Glyn, if you don't know, just say so!' I said. 'There's noth-ing wrong with admitting you don't know something.'

We were outside the petrol station linked to the supermar-ket. I waited for Glyn to admit he didn't know how they did it. No such luck. He appropriated an extremely severe expres-sion and lolloped off grunting towards the trolley park.

'Do they ask the whales, man?' asked Gabby.

'Yes, Gab,' I said, following Glyn. 'They do.'

Glyn was rustling trollies from the trolley park with such exquisite skill that Gabby and I had to stop and admire it. Years of pushing and pulling these meshed steers in all weathers and all seasons had paid off, and now we were witness to a man in his element, a man at the apogee of his ability.

'God, you're good!' I said to Glyn.

''t'would be better could I paint like a Rembrandt,' said Glyn.

We performed a quick tally of the amount of gear we must lug to Dig Street – I suspected Glyn was not enamoured with my plan, but also guessed that he would go along with it, given the fact that Dark Secrets and its *Dark Chamber* would be close at hand. We required three large trollies alone for Glyn's after-hours collection, and three for Gabby's records and my polar books and box of writings. We added to this four more trollies for the belongings of the old men. Thus we mated ten trollies, and set them in motion in the direction of the ex-Clements Markham House.

All was progressing well; Glyn was again conducting the trolley orchestra like a maestro, when disaster struck. Just outside the store, the trollies stopped dead, and could not be shifted. It was as though a lorry had shed a hundredweight of superglue on the pavement. Gabby and I pushed and pulled, but move they would not. Glyn stood back, arms folded.

'Come on, Glyn!' I cried. 'Lend a hand!'

'I prefer not to,' said Glyn.

'TOSSERS!' shouted a blurred head from a passing car.

'Why, Glyn?'

'It's pointless.'

'This is hardly the time for an existential crisis!'

'The wheels to the trollies have been locked, because we've taken them off the premises.'

'*How*? Is someone watching us?'

'No.'

Silence, save the wet passing of heavy traffic.

'Glyn, why can't you be a little more forthcoming? Here we are, soaked to the skin, trying to do something to save our most treasured possessions, and the old men, and all you can do is fold your arms and give one-word answers!'

'Raaagh!'

Gabby continued to struggle with the trollies.

'Gab,' I said. 'Did you hear a word we said? Stop trying to move the trollies, for God's sake!'

Gabby desisted, and looked at me with his "sad face". Glyn watched me with his own much-practised version.

'Come on, guys,' I said, more softly, drawing Gabby in for a cuddle. 'You mustn't let *problems* beat you so easily.'

This was rich coming from me, when, over the years, every single one of my problems had politely queued up, said a quick hello, then annihilated me.

'Gab,' I said, gesturing at the stuck trollies, and looking down at him clutching me. 'What is the problem we're faced with?'

'My stereo is smashed, man!' cried Gabby.

'No, I don't mean *that* problem, Gab,' I said, pointing very clearly at the trollies with my free arm.

'Glyn will never get a girlfriend?' suggested Gabby.

'Raaagh!'

'No, Gab!' I yelled. 'Well, yes, that *is* a bit of a problem, but I'm sure we can solve it, *but not now!*'

'All I require is punishment,' said Glyn, happy as the day is long.

'I give up, man,' sighed Gabby.

'Gab, the problem is, we want to take these trollies home, load them up with our possessions, then push them to Dig Street, where we will camp and show the world what poor fate has befallen us.'

'FUCKERS!!' screamed a voice from another passing car.

'Can you help us, man!' shouted Gabby to the car, waving as it disappeared into nebulous spray.

'To call for help would be one solution, Gab,' I said, 'but I'm not sure the occupants of that car are in a charitable mood. No, we need to overcome this problem ourselves. Glyn, any ideas?'

'We need to override the system by which the wheels have been locked.'

'What, you mean it's *a system*?'

'Yes.'

I waited for Glyn to expand, but the annoying bugger just stood there. Could it be that each and every trolley was fitted with one of these satellite navigation systems? The mind boggled at the expenditure. Was there anything which didn't talk to satellites these days? Were we effectively controlled by extra-terrestrial agencies?

'We need to ask the whales to let us use the trollies, man!' shouted Gabby.

I was impressed – his train of thought had clearly followed mine, albeit with an aquatic flavour.

'How does it work, Glyn?' I asked.

I expected a rasping retch, but was equally impressed when Glyn shifted his stance, unfolded his arms, and was clearly about to explain all. Of course! He was a black belt in the trolley world!

'The brakes are tripped by sunken-wire technology. There is a wire in the ground around the perimeter of the store. Crossing this wire puts the brakes on. If we took the trollies back into the store car park, the brakes would be released.'

I was both relieved and disappointed that the trollies were not being controlled from earth orbit.

'So how do we overcome it?' I asked.

'I know, I know!' yelled Gabby. 'We can dig up the wire, man, and hold it in front of the trollies all the way home, and then to Dig Street!'

'It's a bad idea,' said Glyn.

But Gabby was unfazed, and started to claw at the ground like a dog burying its poo. I grabbed him and made him face me.

'Gabby, your plan is excellent, *to a certain extent*. The only problem is that the wire is presumably of a set length.'

'Even if it was infinitely long, it's still a bad plan,' said Glyn.

316

'Glyn, can't you see I'm letting him down lightly?' I said.
'Raaagh!'
'Come on then, clever clogs, what's your idea?'

Glyn told us there were several options. He listed them, and we rated each. Gabby chipped in more ideas, too, which I was pleased to see Glyn patiently tolerated. I came up with one also.

Options Discussed:

IDEA	OWNER	RATING
Ask the supermarket manager to switch off the locking system.	Glyn	Unlikely
Make the trollies float, thus overriding the need for moving wheels.	Gabby	Entirely unfeasible
Dig a hole and cut the wire, thus breaking the current, and presumably the wheel locking system.	Glyn	Possibly dangerous
Get the whales to change their policy on trollies.	Gabby	Bizarre
Live in this spot for the rest of our lives.	Gabby	Undesirable
Leave the trollies and hire a man-and-van to take our belongings to Dig Street.	John	Raaagh! On account that the man would judge Glyn for the nature of his belongings
Overcome the trollies' group friction by splitting them into three groups – 3/3/4 – buy some rope from the supermarket, and each man pull a group home.	Glyn	Boring, but do-able
Beam the belongings to Dig Street, like on *Star Trek*.	Gabby	No rating given

Feeling more and more like Captain Scott, I felt proud of the ingenuity of my men, but it was in the end decided by a vote of two to one that we would split the trollies, procure some rope, and man-haul them home with their brakes on. Gabby held out for an immediate trip to the seaside to change the whales' minds, but I promised him a lolly when we bought the rope, so he was happy too.

As we couldn't budge them an inch, the trollies didn't need guarding, so we three sallied forth to buy some rope. We crossed the threshold of the supermarket; I grabbed a basket, and started shopping.

Gabby ran to the confectionary aisle. Glyn loitered around the magazine section, and I made for the DIY aisle – a selection of the things we sold at Amundsen Enterprises all squeezed into a few shelves.

We were in luck. They had rope, not particularly thick, but rope, and we could always double it up if necessary. I took forty metres of the stuff, and went to find my companions.

Having fetched Gabby from the confectionary aisle with a lolly, and having grabbed Glyn from the magazine section clutching a copy of *Impractical Photography*, we headed to the checkouts.

Once outside we roped up our wet trolley trains. With a great heave-ho I commanded our party to start hauling. It took all my strength to get mine moving, but once in motion they dragged pretty much adequately. Unequal paving slabs were a problem, with the whole train shuddering to a halt frequently, necessitating the arduous task of going back to the trollies and lifting stuck wheels over impediments.

After a hundred metres or so, I stopped to look back. Glyn was right behind me, tugging away. Gabby was right where we started, repeatedly running at the rope's slack, but unable to shift his load an inch.

Glyn and I left our loads and went back to him.

'Mine must be really really heavy, man!'

I exchanged glances with Glyn, and we got to work. Firstly, we reduced his load to two trollies. No dice. Then we untied the second, and tried that. Poor Gabby, foaming at the mouth with effort, could not get even one trolley to shift. I started to wonder if his one remaining trolley was especially heavy, or actually stuck to the pavement in some fashion. Glyn evidently wondered the same, picked up Gabby's rope, tugged it lightly, and easily made it move.

We wondered what to do.

'We'll have to leave him here,' said Glyn.

'No, man!' said Gabby. 'I can sit in one of your trollies!'

I thought upon it. I would not desert a man. Yet I needed that man to have some practical input in the undertaking, and we did need to get back to Clements Markham House soon to rescue our housemates.

'Baskets,' said Glyn.

'What?' I asked. I thought he'd broken down in brain.

'Gabby can tow a stack of shopping baskets, and those back at the house can use one each to carry their things.'

Genius. I told them to wait, and ran back to the supermarket. I only hoped they were not linked to some even cleverer anti-theft device.

I stole some baskets from outside the entrance, and soon Gabby was all set.

'LET'S GO!' I shouted.

We were off, Glyn and I towing five trollies each, and Gabby with his hand baskets. It started to rain again, which succeeded in lubricating the ground slightly, but the going was tough, and my shoulders hurt. Glyn grunted and occasionally let loose an effort-fart and an apology at my rear. Gabby cantered by our sides, his baskets clattering along in his wake like wedding cans, laughing at how much effort

Glyn and I were expending to keep things moving. It was very difficult not to blow our tops but we managed it, somehow; and finally, even wetter than before, we arrived back at the remains of Clements Markham House.

A party was in full swing beneath the dark blue tarpaulin as the old men boozed away Mr Kapoor's gift, but I alone knew it was a dance with death, and that I must break it up.

53

THE DARK BLUE TARPAULIN

We parked the trollies and baskets by the pristine bins. New Orleans jazz thudded from inside the dark blue tarpaulin. There was a night-time chill to the air, but Glyn and I stood panting like perverts, laced with dirt and sweat. Gabby stood by us, retelling the fun he'd had dragging his tower of baskets, terrifying cats, and rebuffing kind offers from men wishing to take niche photographs – it was trippy.

Once my composure was regained, I gritted my teeth, parted the flaps of the "tent" and marched inside.

I found a scene reminiscent of a Hieronymus Bosch painting.

An old woman with a mouth like a red slash gyrated to the jazz, semi-clothed, loudly making unspeakable suggestions to the old timers (Mr Wittgenstein again shot across my mind like a flicking tongue).

The old boys were variously stripped, aggressively up-ending evil-looking bottles of dark spirits, pawing at the polar regions of the old professional only to be kicked free with such oaths as to make Casanova blush. The air was fetid, the odour unmistakable – I presumed what in youth had been watertight had been replaced in old age by uncontrollable leaks.

My senses scrambled, I peered from whence I'd come to find the disembodied heads of Glyn and Gabby gazing through the curtains like Morecambe and Wise, one wearing an expression of guilty longing, the other of utmost terror.

It wasn't long before the lady cordially invited me to join the fun. We began a seat-of-the-pants waltz around the outer reaches of the pissed tarpaulin.

'I need to take these men to Dig Street!' I shouted amid the din of the jazz and the whirling weapon of her yellow feather boa. What she replied I cannot bring myself to repeat.

Someone tapped me on the shoulder.

'Glyn!' I said.

'May I cut in?' he asked, staring longingly at my partner.

Shocked, and a little relieved, I stood down.

She kicked Glyn in the nuts. He scooped her up, shouted 'Fuck this!' and immediately they fell into what can only be described as *sex dancing*, for to call it *sexy dancing* would be too feeble a term. It seemed my friend had reverted to his *guiltless* alter ego.

Now I felt arms encircling my middle. Fearing I was about to be again ensnared, I was relieved to look down and find Gabby quivering harder than Shakin' Stevens in his prime, his face whiter than the wing tips of an Arctic tern.

'Look at Glyn, man!' Gabby cried. 'He's doing something strange with his tummy!'

'I know, Gab,' I said. 'I'm sorry you have to witness it.'

Now *Guiltless Glyn* was viciously slapping her bare buttocks and whooping like a rodeo star, while she scratched out his eyes and screeched with laughter.

I cast about for a way to bring the party to an early close. Old Brian stumbled over to me looking fit to die. I struggled to think he'd ever been a morning person.

'Brian, we've got to leave this place!' I shouted above booming Dr John.

'We'll fackin leavvve it when wis rready,' slurred Old Brian, unmistakably interpreting *leaving* as exiting this mortal coil.

'No, Brian!' I yelled, Gabby vibrating at my middle. 'We are leaving right now! This party is over! I am not letting Mr

Kapoor get his way! I am not letting you all drink yourselves to death!'

'Lighten up, yer little cant!' shouted a voice from the gloom.

''ave a fackin drink and belt up!' yelled another.

I shed a protesting Gabby, and ploughed blindly through the stinking mess to seek the source of the thudding music. I was shutting the place down. Povey would have been proud. I was shutting down death itself.

'I'M SHUTTING DOWN DEATH!' I cried, waving my arms and kicking all impediments.

'I'm doin a fackin jive!' yelled another voice.

Bottles were thrust into my hands, but I let them smash upon the ground. I was as unstoppable as *Guiltless Glyn* was inappropriate.

Leaning down in one wet corner, I found the source of the music – an over-large evil-looking ghetto blaster, covered in ash. I felt at the rear for a lead, yanked it out, and the din abruptly stopped.

All functioning eyes were upon me. The lady stood wearing a half-smile, casting glances around her, pretending to be coy. Gabby cowered behind her. Glyn stood next to Old Brian looking very ashamed indeed.

I took my moment and addressed the tarpaulin at large.

'Men!' I said, as impressively as I could muster. 'And lady.'

'Ain't no fackin ladies 'ere!' quipped an old boy.

'Turn the fackin music back on, yer little bastard!' shouted another.

'Men, I beg you listen to me!' I said.

'No,' said several voices.

'Mr Kapoor might have destroyed Clements Markham House,' I said, 'but I will not let him destroy you too. You, our grandfathers...'

'Must be drugs,' I heard one of the men say to another, who nodded.

'No, I am not on drugs,' I said. 'I am perhaps, right now, the most sober being in the universe!'

They all laughed, including the lady, who shrieked in the manner of an overacting Shakespearian crone.

What did I want to say? I kicked myself for claiming I was the most sober individual in all of reality. I'd lost them, having barely had them in the first place. I was ridiculous. I began to panic and stutter, which they enjoyed. But just then Gabby strode up to me, swept a frail hand through his plastered hair, and turned to the crowd.

'You lot will all die soon, man!' he yelled. 'Because you're old.'

Cringing to my very hind teeth I waited for the rotten tomatoes, but amazingly Gabby's audience looked expectant, and interested. Even the old hag stopped corpsing.

'I am not old!' Gabby continued. 'I am twenty-six, man! Soon I will be twenty-seven, and I will have lived for exactly 14,199,840 minutes!'

They looked at him in wonder.

'You are all about ninety years old, man! That means you will have lived for about 47,335,680 minutes!'

'I'm sixty,' said someone.

'About 31,557,600 minutes, man!'

Silence. I hoped to God Gabby had a point.

'I will die when I'm twenty-seven, man, because I'm a rock star! But you aren't rock stars, so you have lived until you're nearly dead because you're so old! But I ask you, how many of those thirty-one million minutes have you spent at the seaside, man?'

Gabby turned to me, arms outstretched, and I understood that it was time for me to congratulate him wholeheartedly upon his oratory. I didn't want to.

Old Brian stepped forward, wiping his eyes. 'It's fackin ages since I went to the seaside!'

'Them were the days!' reflected another. 'When we was kids.'

'I do miss my old man!' wept Old Brian. 'I can still see 'im, larkin about, buildin sandcastles!'

I watched in disbelief as the tarpaulin was gripped by holiday fever – man showing man how they used to roll up their trousers for a paddle; how Dad would wear a knotted handkerchief on his head; how Mum would gossip with her sisters; and how they would play, as children, tearing up and down the beach, burying long-departed relatives in the sand, riding donkeys, meeting neighbours, eating sandy egg sand-wiches, everyone in their Sunday best, or on a public holiday, whole trainfuls of them steaming to the coast and singing songs, and being happy.

Notwithstanding the rain, there wasn't a dry eye in the house.

The lady slapped a mottled thigh, and struck up "I Do Like to be Beside the Seaside", slowly at first, elegantly. The years peeled away from her. She strutted up and down, the song picking up speed like a locomotive topping an incline, until the whole tarpaulin shook with glee, the old men sticking out their elbows and prancing up and down with bandy legs, *oh I do like to be beside the seaside, oh I do like to be beside the seaaaa*!

54

CAPTAIN SCOTT MAKES A STRANGE DISCOVERY AT THE SOUTH POLE

Midnight. Keenly aware I must use this outpouring of community spirit to engender the move, I energetically gestured for Glyn to join me in urgent conference.

He lolloped towards me, weaving in and out of dancing men, grasping a scrap of paper and a pencil. With relief I gathered that *Guiltless Glyn* had again been set to slumber.

'Glyn!' I said. 'We need to get packed right now, and go!'

'Ahem,' said Glyn, holding before me the piece of paper, which appeared to be covered with calculations. 'Gabby accounted for leap years.'

'What?'

'When Gabby told them how many minutes they'd lived, he accounted for leap years.'

I gawped at Gabby.

'Gab,' I asked, 'what is a leap year?'

'Is it a year for frogs, man?' he answered gravely, chin pinched between forefinger and thumb, and lightly bouncing up and down.

I said to Glyn, 'He's amazing, that's all there is to it.'

'Raaagh!'

'You just can't admit it, can you, Glyn?' I said. 'There's no accounting for it, it doesn't appear to follow logic, and you just need to accept it.'

'He's faking imbecility!' said Glyn, baring his large teeth.

'For what, and for whom?' I said. 'He's not. He's the real deal, aren't you, Gab!'

Gabby nodded enthusiastically.

'All I need you to do, Glyn, is to admit there is a nugget of mysterious wonder locked somewhere within our little friend, which is entirely unaccounted for. We might say it's magical; godly, even.'

'With respect, John, you're talking rubbish,' said Glyn.

'Is it so different from your night-time liaisons with Germanic historical figures?'

'I told you, they're just–'

'I know,' I broke in, '*your problems presenting themselves as eloquent hallucinations.*'

'Raaagh!'

'I'm sick of doubting the world,' I said. 'I'm tired of being told that nothing is real. I for one am prepared to believe wholeheartedly that Gabby *is* magic, just as I'm prepared to believe that you really are visited by famous Germans.'

'And Austrians.'

'Yes, them too. I mean, look around us,' I continued, pointing to the holidaymakers. 'These people are, right now, joined together by the memories of folks and places which simply do not exist any longer in the universe, other than as beautiful Bayeux tapestries of the mind.'

'Science is responsible for everything you take advantage of at all times of the day.'

'What, like using a satellite blasted into space for trillions to find the shops?'

'Raaagh!'

'You might well retch, Glyn,' I said, 'because you know I'm right!'

'Science and reason cannot be described as boring or dull. It's like saying "my foot is dull". Science and reason do not

327

ask of such comment. You cannot meaningfully tack such comment to them.'

'I just did!'

'And you contradict yourself, John. You told The Gaffer to construct flood defences around the store, but you might as well have told him and his men to perform a sacred dance to make the rain go away! You reap the benefits of hard logic when it suits you!'

I studied Glyn Hopkins in awe – this was the most forthcoming I'd ever seen him, with his sane hat on. The irony was that it was inexplicably wonderful to see him so dominantly espousing the sanctity of the explicable.

You didn't mention love.

'Glyn,' I said, 'if I were so wedded to rationality would I be taking great earnest pleasure at seeing my friend so animated, at seeing him so achieved and fulsome in this minute of his life? Would my heart be throbbing so? Answer me that, Glyn!'

I became aware that the singing had ceased, and we were being watched.

'It's definitely drugs,' I heard a man say.

'Come on!' I said to the crowd. 'Let's pack up and go to Dig Street!'

'No!' said several.

Knowing what I must say next, I shot Glyn an apologetic glance.

'If you come with me, I'll buy each of you a bottle of anything you want,' I said, cringing at being reduced to bribery.

'Ribena, man!' shouted Gabby.

The men looked extremely keen to get going.

The rain held off for long enough to enable us to haul the soaking dark blue tarpaulin from its moorings, shake the water away, and place it in one of the immobile shopping trollies. The moon came out, and cast an eerie light over the scene.

I dispatched men in all directions. Half of them returned to me immediately, looking confused and having achieved nothing, but I sent them away again, and soon in the indistinct silvery light we looked like a mass of wriggling maggots, an amorphous orgy of life beneath the towering mineral monolith of Clements Markham House Mark II.

Everything touched delivered large dark droplets of water. The wind whipped up and the urban canopy dumped sheet after sheet upon our heads. I stood, soaked to the skin, barking orders at all, fumbling through chaos like a blind man, trying my best to impose some order, some organisational structure upon which we could build our dreams.

I dispatched Glyn and Gabby with several trollies to pack their things. They disappeared through the myrtle green front door, Glyn clattering the trollies over the step, but within ten seconds Glyn was again standing before me, wearing a look of horror.

'What is it?' I asked.

'Bags!' he cried, tugging at his thinning blond hair.

'You have trollies,' I said.

'They're see-through!'

I grasped the problem. To my rough estimation, Glyn would require at least fifty carrier bags to conceal his naughty stash.

'Glyn, are the magazines *really* that important to you?' I asked. 'Isn't it too much trouble? Why don't you just leave them here and free yourself? Let them go! It'll be cathartic!'

'Raaagh!'

'You could buy some more,' I said. 'How about I buy you a whole new collection once we've found somewhere else to live?'

'But who would look after these?' said Glyn, pointing at the house.

'I'm sorry, Glyn, I don't follow,' I sighed, starting to feel

329

irritated and wondering whether *he* wasn't now feigning imbecility too.

'Have you ever noticed...?' said Glyn. The moon's light was not good, but I could clearly see that he was blushing an electric pink.

'What?'

'Have you ever noticed which ones I buy?'

Now I felt embarrassed. 'Do we have to talk about this now?'

'I never buy... *those* which feature... *professionals*. I mean those who have a whole career doing it, and are... comfortable within their trade. I buy those which feature... everyday women.'

'That's nice, Glyn,' I said, 'now *please* can we get on!'

'I haven't mentioned this to you, John,' said Glyn, avoiding my eye.

'What?'

'I'm not just visited by notable Germans and Austrians at night.'

'No?'

'No.'

We stared at each other. The mind boggled.

'*They* visit me too.'

'*They*?'

'All the women.'

'The women?'

'We cuddle all night long in my bed, me, and... up to ten of them at a time. I think it's half the reason the Germans visit me.'

'And the Austrians,' I said.

'Yes.'

I wasn't sure how to respond. I thought of the time when Tim had almost called on me the men in white coats.

'But it's just your problems presenting–'

'No,' Glyn cut in. 'I don't think it is.'

330

Where did this leave us? We were playing hopscotch with the roles of rationalist and surrealist, logician and madman.

'What do they want, Glyn?' I asked.

'They ask me to give them back their innocence and self-worth. They long to be fresh hopeful strong young women once more. They beg me to let them cross in reverse the Rubicon of male corruption, hypocrisy and emotionally-stunted cruelty which caused them to bare to the world their secret beautiful fragrant places, and thus denude the true meaning of the universe.'

I felt like I might faint. He was crazy as a crouton.

'My God!' I cried. 'So you're telling me that not only are you the keeper of the world's military guilt, you're also stock-piling the regrets of the world's glamour models! What else, Glyn? What about all the kids bullied by other kids to the point of suicide? What about the people-traffickers? How about the drug cartels? Where does it stop?'

Glyn didn't get a chance to answer, because at that moment Gabby came running from inside the house.

'John, man!' he shouted, terrified. 'A woman!'

Glyn turned white as a fresh doily. I felt time slow down, as if reality were splitting and splintering like the hull of a ship locked in ice. The magazines of a certain genre had come to life!

Wearing Gabby like a belt, I grabbed Glyn's upper arm. We three slowly shuffled towards the myrtle green door, hardly daring to breathe.

Gulping, I reached out, pushed it open and peered inside. I saw something move. Nameless forms shimmered and shifted in the gloom. Then a shape moved towards us.

'You naughty little boys!' it yelled, followed by high-pitched laughter.

Oh, the relief!

I laughed. 'It's the stripper!'

''oo you callin a fackin stripper?' she cried. 'Exotic dancer's what I am!'

At once I loved the world. I loved my senses. I loved my brain which could sort and sift like a magical cauliflower. It was comparable to Dostoyevsky's brush with execution – I knew what it was for reality suddenly to break off its friend-ship, but then return, deeply regretful, begging forgiveness and swearing never to abandon me again.

As for Glyn, I was comfortable enough with his being insane, as he carried it off beautifully.

'Ooh 'ere's a fackin light!' said the exotic dancer, massa-ging the wall. The hallway was lit by a builders' arc hung from scaffolding criss-crossing the ceiling. All our belongings were highlighted in perfect resolution. She cackled at what she beheld.

'Fackin 'ell, boys!' she said, leafing through piles of mag-azines of a certain genre, and garish record covers more often than not depicting groups of ageing men clad in tight leather trousers – a potpourri of sexual peculiarity.

I wondered how my poems fitted in.

'You wanna get out more, boys!' laughed the exotic dancer. 'You don't need all this crap, 'andsome beefcakes like you!'

'Told you, man!' said Gabby, before darting behind me to hide.

'Is her soul saved?' I asked Glyn, inclining my head towards the exotic dancer.

'You're purposely trying to embarrass me, John.'

''ere, don't you two speak nice!' she giggled, before turn-ing back to the stashes. ''oos is 'oos, then?'

'The magazines are his,' I pointed to Glyn. 'And the records are his,' I said, pointing behind my back at Gabby.

'What's yours, then?' she asked.

I pointed at a cardboard box in the corner.

'Travellin light are ya, big boy?' she laughed, and climbed

over mountains of media to get to it, before reaching inside and pulling out my papers.

'It's John's novel about what would happen if Captain Scott–!' shouted Gabby, before I gagged him with my hand.

'A fackin writer, eh?' she said, weighing it in her hands. ''oo's it like, then? Fackin Floor-bert?'

'Sorry?' I said.

'Madame fackin Bovary!' she said. 'One of me favourites. Can you write like fackin Floor-bert?'

It was my first literary discussion, albeit not in the circumstances I'd dreamed about.

'I don't think so.'

'More like Anna fackin Karenina then?'

'I'm not sure,' I said, reddening, and noticing that Glyn was rather enjoying my own idiot's exposé.

'Think I'm fackin stupid, don't ya?' she said, peering at my manuscript. I shook my head.

'You do, mate,' she said. 'All young people think all old people are fackin stupid.'

'No, *I* don't!' I said. 'I know that it's young people who know nothing, but think they know everything!'

'This is interestin!' she said, reading. 'Listen to this!'

'Please don't!' I said, but she silenced me with a wave of the hand.

Bowers, possessed of excellent eyesight, had spotted it two days before through the telescope, but now even Dr Wilson with his recurrent snow blindness could see it unaided – a perfect silver sphere sat alone upon the horizon in the direction of the pole. By their calculations, they were just one day's march away.

They camped, to discuss the find, but no one wanted to talk. It could only mean one thing – they'd been beaten. Scott watched his four companions trying to put a brave face on things, but it was obvious they were devastated. He felt it him-

self – it was as though his energy had drained away into the ice, and moreover he felt the cold. Scott thought about what to say. He knew he must break the silence.

'I think,' he began, 'that you have probably reached the same conclusion as me, that we've been beaten.'

Bowers, Wilson, Oates and Evans watched him, but said nothing.

'But I propose that we carry on to the pole. I've every faith that you will see our journey through like English gentlemen.'

Not much else was said, but counter to expectation, and even though the cold seeped mercilessly into their reindeer sleeping bags, all five men enjoyed a better than average night's sleep.

In the morning, the silver sphere still perched upon the horizon; they packed up, got into their traces, and began to man-haul their sleds. The going was good, with no sign of the rough ice crystals which had so impeded their efforts in previous days.

All day, the sphere grew, and in snippets of discussion mid-haul they began to doubt their navigation and their senses. They stopped for lunch.

'We've covered seven miles this morning, sir,' said Bowers, 'and I estimate we've another four to the pole. The odd thing though, sir...'

'What is it, Bowers?' asked Scott.

'By my estimation, the object we can see does appear to be at least four miles away, and if this is the case, it must be at least fifty feet in diameter. It would be impossible to carry such an object to the pole.'

'Might it be a trick of the light?' asked Evans.

'If it is, it's an entirely new phenomenon,' said Wilson.

'I think we can all see that this is a solid real object,' said Oates. 'Yes, it looks as though we've been beaten to the pole, but by whom?'

'Or by what?' said Scott.

The exotic dancer paused. 'This is fackin great!' she said. 'What the fack is it at the pole?'

'Aliens, man!' shouted Gabby.

I could have strangled him. The ultimate spoiler, and it wasn't even accurate. For the first time in my life I'd held an audience spellbound, and Gabby had given the *flavour* of the bloody game away!

'You've nicked that from Arthur C Clarke!' said the exotic dancer. 'They found their monolith on the fackin moon, but you've put it at the saaf pole!'

It was entirely true. One more segment to add to the body of evidence that I did not possess an original bone in my body.

'You're right,' I said, as deflated as Scott and his pals had been upon first spotting the sphere.

'It don't fackin matter,' she said. 'There ain't nothing new, mate, we're all a pease puddin of stuff what people have thought and said before. Let me get the fellas, I'll read more!'

She hurried outside to get the old boys, and pretty soon they shuffled into the white light blinking like neurasthenia cases, being peppered with the flak of her hurried retelling.

Soon, the men seated on piles of records and magazines along with Glyn, Gabby, and me, she started where she'd left off:

There wasn't much more to say. The five men packed up, and started their journey once more. The weather was excellent, a perfect deep azure sky, and a helpful northerly before which they gladly raised their sled-sails. They made excellent progress, and within two hours were standing at the base of a towering silver sphere, perfect as a vastly scaled-up polished ball-bearing.

'There's certainly nothing comparable at the North Pole,' said Dr Wilson. 'In any case, it is beyond the realm of credibility that this... thing... could be natural.'

'Could it be due to the earth's rotation?' asked Bowers. 'An igneous outcrop of some sort?'

Their discussion was broken by the sudden commencement of a low hum. Each of them involuntarily backed off a few feet, and listened. The hum grew in intensity, and was accompanied by–

'Arthur C Clarke made the fackin monolith hum on the moon, too!' laughed the exotic dancer.

'I know, I'm sorry,' I said.

She continued:

The hum grew in intensity, and was accompanied by a sensation that the giant sphere was shimmering, as if emitting visible shock waves.

'It's opening!' shouted Dr Wilson.

'Don't panic!' yelled Scott.

The five men watched as a vertical crack appeared along the whole diameter of the sphere–

'A tenner little green men come out!' said Old Brian to a mate.

The sphere opened like a vast American refrigerator to reveal countless shelves of dizzying complexity and action. The men struggled to comprehend what they saw – the contents of the shelves, if that is what they could be described as, throbbed and shape-shifted; music they didn't recognise boomed, tiny human beings danced, or sat in gatherings, in parliaments, rested in parks, rode odd machines in a miniature sky, and a million other occurrences all at once, every human dream brought into terrifying reality only to change, change, and shift, be remembered, forgotten, matter and not, every illness, famine, marriage, birth and death. Countless atomised wars raged, and pointed projectiles rocketed into microscopic skies–

'Where's the fackin green men?' asked Old Brian.

Scott and his four companions stood rooted to the spot, unaware of their freezing extremities, each lost in this cornucopia of dizzying sensory overload. There was no need to think – their conscious thoughts could not have kept up in any case. Each became aware that they were being filled with the most acute sense of intangible knowledge.

'My God!' cried Dr Wilson, the most fervently religious of the five men. He kneeled in the snow and bowed his head.

Each man began to understand that, all along, this had been their overall goal, in coming to Antarctica, in seeking out the southernmost extremity of the globe – to know the true essence of the universe, a universe consisting of everything that is the case, of all actions and reactions, the past, the present and the future, the time before time and the time after–

'It's just like the bit at the end of *2001: A Space Odyssey*, when the last remaining bloke goes through that psychedelic 'ole,' said Old Brian's mate.

I hung my head in shame.

''e's got a really fackin bad drug problem,' said another.

'It's the same as little green men. I still won my tenner!' said Old Brian.

'No, you fackin ain't!' said his mate.

The exotic dancer threw the manuscript back into the box. 'It fackin ends there,' she said.

'Sorry,' I again apologised.

'What happens next, man?' said Gabby.

'Nothing,' I said.

'He shot 'is bolt too early,' said the exotic literary critic with a wink. 'Once you've made everyfink go magic, there's no fackin way back.'

A picture of Dig Street flashed across my mind. There was something waiting for us there.

'There might be a sphere of sorts waiting for us in Dig Street,' said Glyn.

'What, like in the fackin story?' asked Old Brian.

'Bollocks,' said his mate. Most of the other old boys were taking a nap.

'Cam on then!' said Madame Bovary. 'Let's get down there an' see!'

'Shall we, men?' I said, noting that reality was much more interesting, much more nuanced, than anything you could make up.

'Go on then, yer silly bugger,' smiled Old Brian.

'Glyn,' I said. 'Run back to the supermarket and get as many carrier bags as you can! We'll pack the rest!'

Glyn retched at the implied mention of what the bags would carry – a laughable gesture seeing as we were using his grotty collection as chairs. He then lolloped off into the night.

I stuck my head out of the myrtle green door and peered at the sky. Towering clouds covered the moon, and more heavy drops began to fall.

55

THE MARCH ON DIG STREET

Wearing my white summer dress with the green leaves and red flowers, brimming with thoughts of the impending Dig Street Festival, the fact that if Bobby Diamanté was as good as his word we'd be "broken bad" in the *Leytonstow Log*, that my actions would save Amundsen Enterprises from the terrible business interruption of a flood, and that the world would soon behold the fate that had befallen its grandparents, its architecture, and its historical sanctity, I bellowed out orders to my men and one exotic woman, and we packed up everything except the magazines of a certain genre in our stolen useless shopping trollies and hand baskets. We looked like an equal opportunities road crew, working under the glare of the builders' lamp, navvies in the night.

Soon, Glyn returned, to a roar of encouragement from the men, at which he dropped his enormous billowing consignment of nearly-opaque carrier bags, and suffered a retching fit so fierce that it seemed he was giving birth. Not in all of history could I think of a time where so many souls (if we were to believe Glyn's assertions regarding the magazines of a certain genre) were transported in an entirely positive manner. It was ground-breaking; again, if Glyn were to be believed, we were literally carrying the souls of our fellow human beings to a place which had become sacred, in order that they be cleansed of their pain and suffering.

I hurried inside to tell Glyn all of this, and found him

stuffing the carrier bags and apologising to each and every cover girl for his haste.

'Glyn, it's magical!' I said.

'If you're happy with your life, as lived at this moment, then that's a good thing, and should temporarily outweigh the fact that what you're doing, and have done now for the last week, is entirely idiotic, and almost certain to prompt you to kill yourself at some juncture in the future.'

'Cheers, Glyn,' I said stiffly; thereafter I held his carrier bags open while he poured in his treasured collection. Soon, we were dragging three supermarket trollies piled high with grot over the threshold of Clements Markham House, and onto the figurative ice of the pavement, to man-haul to Dig Street and our presumed sphere of everythingness.

Now we were on the pavement, with the world as it stood, and all was ready. These were the travelling arrangements:

Load to Man (or Woman) Haul

GLYN:
- 3 trollies bagged magazines of a certain genre.

JOHN:
- 3 trollies heavy metal records (plus a handful by Gilbert O'Sullivan).
- A small box of poems (mostly haikus with incorrect number of syllables).
- An unfinished plagiarised novel about what would happen if Captain Scott had discovered a strange sphere containing Absolutely Everything at the South Pole.
- A small library of second-hand books all pertaining to polar travel.

GABBY:
- 1 hand basket containing the exotic literary critic's yellow feather boa.

OLD BRIAN:

- 1 trolley of his possessions, namely:
- 4 double-breasted suits dating from 1962, in blue, green, grey, and fawn, for wearing "on a Sunday" to the pub (in actuality each time he went to the pub, which was all day every day).
- 4 ruffle shirts in black, yellow, turquoise and pink, to go with the suits.
- His milkman's cap.
- A biography of Margaret Thatcher.
- Water/sun-damaged photo album of his long emigrated kids, ex-wives, favourite dogs, and happier times at Clacton-on-Sea.

THE EXOTIC DANCER:

- 1 hand basket containing copies of both *Madame Bovary* and *Anna Karenina*.

THE REST OF THE OLD BOYS:

- 7 hand baskets, and 3 trollies containing all of their worldly possessions, plus the dark blue tarpaulin, including, but not limited to:
- Retirement carriage clocks.
- Several globes (one depicting the earth as known in the time of Portuguese Dominance).
- £50 in premium bonds which had never come up.
- The late wife's ornaments.
- A book about Dreadnoughts.
- *Guinness Book of World Records*, 1975.
- Several hundred kipper ties.
- Unopened and expired Wedding Ale, brewed especially for the occasion of the marriage of Charles Windsor to Lady Diana Spencer in 1981.
- Army Medals (Suez).

We set off!

I was minded of scheduled visits to the bank, courtesy of Mr Kapoor and Indeep, except this trip wore an entirely positive hue. It brought tears to my eyes.

We stopped for a hot dog and a shake at an all-night takeaway at the corner of Erebus Road. The proprietor had Parkinson's disease (by his own admission – he talked of it for fifteen minutes straight), and afterwards my fellows laughed long and hard at the fact that our shakes were truly shook. I ran to and fro telling my army that such jokes were inappropriate.

Rain poured upon our heads. We were all soaked together. It gave proceedings a wartime concentration, a martial law of being, which suited us nicely. We pressed on, clattering and grunting through the night. I was aware that this part of our quest was just as joyous as anything our destination might offer. I said as much to Glyn.

'Given the multiplicity of our past regrets,' answered Glyn, 'we should not enjoy the present, or look to the future with any hope whatsoever.'

'Bloody hell, Glyn, nothing would ever happen if we thought like that!' I said.

'Nothing *does* happen, really,' said Glyn. 'Not in the last few billion years, anyhow.'

'Christ, Glyn, what's this if it's not *something happening*?'

'It's playing tectonics,' he said.

At least it was a more ambitious version of the saying "rearranging the deckchairs on the Titanic", and I told him this – he showed me his slightly over-large teeth. There was a rarity in the air.

'John, man?' asked Gabby, skipping by my side as I lugged.

'Gabby,' I puffed.

'How did the *Pier* get to the South Pole, man?'

'*Sphere*,' I corrected.

'Pier?'

'*Sphere.*'

'Pier?'

'S-P-H-E-R-E Gab! *Sphere!*'

'Did you make that word up, John? You're very clever!'

'Gab, a sphere is a three-dimensional circle, like the earth, or the moon, or a football.'

'Wow, man!' said Gabby. 'They should make up a word for that kind of shape!'

'I don't know how the sphere got there, Gab,' I sighed, returning to the second of my trollies to help it over some sidewalk sastrugi.

'Who does then, man?' he asked.

'No one, Gab, it's not yet written.'

'Wow, man, so it's sitting there right now at the bottom of the world, and no one knows why, or how it got there?'

'No, it's not sitting there, Gab. I made it up, it doesn't exist, except in my imagination.'

Actually, it existed more solidly in the imagination of Arthur C Clarke, but I didn't feel like going into that with Gabriel Longfeather.

'So there's nothing at the South Pole then, man?' asked Gabby, crestfallen.

'Yes, there is a permanent base there.'

'Whoa! Rock and Roll, man!!' he shouted.

'No Gab, not *that* kind – not a bass guitar – a *base* b-a-s-e meaning a permanent settlement, of scientists.'

'And penguins!'

'No penguins. They only live at the coast, hundreds of miles away. At the South Pole there is no life whatsoever, except the scientists who live there.'

'Do they have telly, man?'

'Probably... but I don't think they are there to watch TV.'

'So what do they do?'

343

'They study Antarctica, and learn about the earth, history and space.'

'Why, man?'

Glyn lumbered up. 'For military purposes.'

'No, I don't think it's just that, Glyn,' I said.

'Do they watch DVDs, man?'

'It is,' said Glyn. 'Governments are only willing to fund scientific study which ultimately leads to military development.'

'I need a wee, man,' said Gabby, and darted down a garden path.

'I think that's a little negative, Glyn,' I said, halting my train of several thousand heavy metal records. 'Yes, there's a military aspect to it, but surely you can't deny that human beings also have a unique inquisitiveness about the world around us?'

'The only truly remarkable thing about human beings is that we've developed the ability to exterminate ourselves.'

'Glyn,' I said, placing a hand on his shoulder. 'I've noticed that you've... you've become increasingly negative of late. Are you OK?'

He watched me with such sad eyes. His own two spheres of nothingness.

A giant clunk briefly made me wonder if reality was again threatening to denude. I looked at my train and saw that a man with whom Gabby was happily in conversation had just placed a washing machine on top of my second trolley.

'What's going on?' I asked.

'John, this man's given us his old washing machine! Isn't that kind, man?!'

'Cheers, mate,' said the man, and disappeared back down his garden path.

'Gab, I don't want a washing machine!' I said.

'Really, man?' asked Gabby.

'Really!'

'He asked if we take stuff, and I said we did! We do take stuff, John, don't we?'

'Yes, our stuff, Gab! Come on. Help me get it off...'

The man returned to his front gate. 'Mate, you're not dumping that outside my gaff!'

'Look, there's been a mix-up,' I said. 'Gabby here thought that we took anything, but we don't, I'm sorry but can you take it back, please?'

'What's wrong with it?' he asked.

'There's nothing wrong with it, just that we are carrying *our* things, and we don't take *other* people's things. Sorry.'

'Listen,' said the man, 'it ain't my problem, I saw you was rag and bone, I asked your little circus friend 'ere if you take stuff, and 'e said yer did. So 'ere it is,' and he disappeared again.

'Sorry, man!' cried Gabby, stretching out his arms for a cuddle.

'Come on, you lot!' shouted Old Brian, now some thirty yards ahead of us with the main party.

'Jesus, Gabby!' I exploded. 'Not only am I carrying your bloody ridiculous immature records, you've also needlessly added an enormous cube weighing probably seventy kilos!'

If it wasn't spheres it was cubes. What other geometry awaited?

'I think I must be depressed,' said Glyn.

'Have they got washing machines at the South Pole, man?' asked Gabby, once again skipping towards Old Brian and the gang, holding his basket with the yellow feather boa.

'YES!' I screamed.

'What about microwave ovens, man?'

I took deep breaths.

'Perhaps I should see a doctor?' said Glyn.

'You're not depressed, Glyn,' I said. 'You're just much more sensitive than most.'

'John, why are we doing this? Why are we going to Dig Street?' he asked.

I wasn't good at exactly pinning down motivations. Lois popped into my mind. It struck me that having abandoned Clements Markham House to throw our fates to the wind, I would not have an address for Lois to reply to my letter.

'I'm not sure, Glyn,' I said. 'But don't tell anyone.'

'Perhaps *you're* depressed?'

'I'm not, Glyn,' I said. 'I'm just naturally upset that Gabby has caused me needlessly to lug a washing machine.'

'Come on, John,' said Glyn. 'I think there really might be something waiting for us at Dig Street.'

I wanted my bed. I leaned against the traces, cracked my load from its stasis, and tried to catch the rest of the party.

'You don't really think that, Glyn,' I puffed.

'Sorry,' he sighed.

'Thanks anyway.'

56

A Clean Kebab

At length we arrived at Leytonstow Tube Station, bone tired, soaked by squalls, hungry, and not knowing what to do next.

In the manner of Mr Kapoor, I raised a hand to bring our caravan to a halt, and sat upon a bench to gather my thoughts. The wind got up, sending hard rain horizontally. Shop signs banged. Tramps huddled shivering in doorways. Empty red buses droned up and down. Fluorescent ants threw the remains of yesterday's commerce into yawning refuse lorries. The air was filled with dogfights of litter. Nightwalkers, drunks and small groups of late night party-goers wandered in and out of the station.

I marshalled my thoughts, and made a mental to-do list, while my troops sought shelter:

1. Feed my army.
2. Check the progress of the flood defences around Amundsen Enterprises.
3. Check up on the Internet café and the Indonesian marble fire surround order – tell Beardmore about his new kosher business plan.
4. Redistribute my wealth to the citizens of Leytonstow.
5. Prepare for the Dig Street Festival.
6. Check in with Bobby Diamanté and the *Leytonstow Log* coverage.
7. Enable the citizens of Leytonstow to:

a) Re-explore their immediate environment.

b) End corrupt/underhand behaviour.

c) Be nicer/more sensitive to one another.

8. Buy Gabby, Marcus and Barney new instruments, and practise for the gig.

9. Get Gabby a black dress with zips. A leather one.

10. Buy Gabby a new top-of-the-range stereo.

11. Chaperone Gabby on his date with Douglas.

12. Enable Glyn to let go of the entire guilt of the human race, without causing him to morph into *Guiltless Glyn*, and find him a life partner who is not a picture upon a printed page.

13. Find our *Sphere*, and figure out what it is, where it came from, and what it means.

14. Provide Lois with an alternate address, should she wish to write back.

'John, John, John, man!' cried Gabby, still holding his hand basket with the yellow feather boa, and dancing on the spot. 'I'm really hungry, man!'

I filed my mental to-do list and left the wet bench.

'OK, Gab,' I said. 'Let's eat.'

I did a quick headcount of our colleagues. They were now rather spread out. Some were begging at cashpoints. Others huddled together on benches. The exotic dancer was talking to a red-faced boy in a doorway.

We parked all our worldly belongings, plus the broken washing machine, outside Leytonstow Tube Station, where Dig Street and Market Street intersected. I thought it might be quite nice to have a sit-down meal, and decided to reconnoitre Market Street. I told the old boys to sit tight, and set off. Glyn and Gabby came too.

'Wouldn't it be nice to have a proper sit-down meal, somewhere warm and friendly?' I said. 'And have a really good chat with everybody about life, the universe and everything, over several glasses of wine?'

'It's two in the morning, John,' said Glyn.

'Let's be optimistic!' I said.

Glyn coughed. Perhaps it was an optimistic cough.

'So, what do we fancy?' I asked.

'Pizza, man!' yelled Gabby. 'Or curry! Chinese! Fish and chips at the seaside!'

'A greasy box of low-quality fried chicken wings and soggy chips, made in a mouse-infested environment,' suggested Glyn.

'That's what you fancy, Glyn?' I asked, my mouth watering at Gabby's more appealing suggestions.

'What I fancy is irrelevant, as the only option we have is to eat a greasy box of low-quality fried chicken wings and soggy chips, made in a mouse-infested environment. Or a kebab, but not a clean kebab I'm afraid, if there is such a thing.'

'You don't have to eat the box too, man,' said Gabby.

Initially I poured scorn upon Glyn's depressing aspirations, but soon it became perfectly obvious that every food outlet in the vicinity was closed, their security grilles pulled down to reveal garish graffiti and many scars from repeated late night ram-raid attempts.

We stood a while, as empty crisp bags and anti-littering leaflets whizzed past our ears, my eyes still scanning up and down the street in the vain hope that I still might spot a nice friendly restaurant, and trying to ignore the garish neon lights of what now looked like our only option: Chicken Hamlet.

I shuddered to think how many times over the years I'd been poisoned in the small hours of the morning by the smiling operatives of this last-ditch takeaway. We arrived to find most of our colleagues gazing through the glazing like moths drawn to the moon. The sign featured a brightly coloured cartoon of an extremely happy-looking cockerel giving the thumbs up and winking. "Go on, please eat me", it might have said.

The interior was not designed to be welcoming or inspiring, but perfectly unbreakable. All surfaces were smooth and hard, and everything which could conceivably be removed was bolted to the floor.

Chicken Hamlet boasted a night-time society of its own. Currently (and this accounted for the fact that my colleagues had chosen to cower outside) it was populated by a gang of ten or so tall young men, all wearing hoodies and brand new training shoes. They were in constant motion, laughing and cracking jokes, occasionally half-hugging each other in that stiff-elbowed minimal-contact manner trainee alpha males do, bumping fists, scanning the street for passing girls, and walking with faux limps back and forth across the dirty floor.

'Those big boys look scary, man!' said Gabby, hiding behind me.

'Don't worry, Gab,' I said.

'They love their mothers,' said Glyn, seemingly moved. 'Individually, they're sensitive young people, unsure of their role in the world or indeed how the world works and how they might go about getting what they want from it. They're aware that as large and physically strong as they've so recently become, they are still very far away from wielding the balance of power, wealth and influence, and right now, individually, privately, they doubt that they could ever be equal to exerting it. They are scared and confused little lads in beautifully proportioned men's bodies. Indeed their physicality is *so* impressive that–'

'Yes, thanks, Glyn,' I said.

'Raaagh!'

'Sorry, Glyn,' I said, 'I'm not sure that focusing upon their overwhelming strength and underdeveloped judgement will reassure Gabby and our colleagues that they can get at the food without being assaulted.'

As leader of our rabble, I knew I must act. I took a deep breath. Oddly, the thought crossed my mind that I could wear the broken washing machine on my head as a crash helmet. I dispelled this thought, and entered the shop.

It was only then I remembered what I wore – namely the white summer dress with green leaves and red flowers. I'd become remarkably used to wearing a dress, and rather liked it; but, judging by the immediate reaction of the young men within Chicken Hamlet, I had to acknowledge that, to them, my appearance was quite novel and likely to cause a ripple or two, the first being that all ten or so of them turned to me bellowing with laughter and snapping their forefingers, shouting "OH NO!" or just "OOOOO!" and photographing me with their mobile telephone devices.

I tried to effect a manly demeanour, and set my face in what I thought was its most statesman-like aspect, but this only caused them to laugh so hard that they had to hold on to the counter or one another to avoid falling over. The din was incredible. They were yelling at one another in somersaults of concussive sound, ten test pilots and ten sonic booms, fighting among themselves to record for posterity the definitive version of the atomic fashion outrage in their midst.

The Turkish fellows behind the counter looked on with a mixture of impassivity and mirth. I threaded my way through the barking young men as if walking across a crowded dance floor and leaned upon the counter, panting. One of the Turkish fellows inclined to hear my order, and I was just about to give it when the din notched up yet again. Now it was almost as loud as Gabby's ex-stereo. I looked over my shoulder to see Glyn lolloping into the shop with wide eyes and baring his teeth, Gabby hugging him from behind. Driven in by naked hunger.

The noise within Chicken Hamlet was deafening. I backed away from the counter and reached through seas of track-suits and waving baseball caps to grasp Glyn's hand. I pulled him and Gabby towards me, and turned my attention back to the Turkish fellow.

'FIFTEEN BOXES!' I shouted, unsure if I was using the correct parlance.

'BOXES!' bellowed the young men.

'What?' said the Turkish fellow, cupping a hand to his ear.

'FIFTEEN BOXES!' I again yelled.

'BOXES! BOXES!' again laughed the young men.

Having heard this time, the Turkish fellow nodded, and started to prepare our fare.

I turned around. 'WHAT ARE YOU MEANT TO SAY, THEN?'

'BOXXXXXESSSSSSS!' they all screamed.

While our order was processed, Glyn, Gabby and I stood stock still at the counter, trying our level best not to draw any more unnecessary attention, and by and by the young men tired of us, finished their food, threw their empty boxes on the floor, and filed out into the night.

Blissful silence, save the wet sizzling of chicken and the whirr of the grease-encrusted extractor fan.

'Been to gay club?' asked one of the Turkish fellows, pleasantly.

'Yes,' I sighed.

The danger having passed, Old Brian and the boys plus the exotic literary critic filed in and pretty soon we were each clutching a hot cardboard box with the picture of the winking cockerel on the lid.

Famished after our man-hauling, we attacked the boxes. Contrary to my low expectations, the hoosh was beautiful – the fried chicken melted in the mouth, and the smart saltiness of the chips sent pleasure-waves of satisfaction to our very cores.

As soon as the primary concern of hunger had been dealt with, our bodies demanded sleep, urgently. Yawns passed around Chicken Hamlet like a craze.

'Come on, men!' I commanded. 'Let's find somewhere to sleep!'

'And woman, man!' said Gabby.

'Thanks, love,' said the exotic literary critic.

'John,' hissed Gabby in my ear. 'Can I not sleep near her, man?'

'I'm fackin beat!' yawned Old Brian.

We thanked the Turkish gentlemen for their hospitality, and walked out into the rain, wind and darkness. My feet felt like cannonballs. I could happily have slept where I stood.

We found our worldly belongings largely untouched, except that approximately half of Glyn's collection of magazines of a certain genre either lay in puddles or span in wild vortexes of wet ticker tape.

'RAAAGH!!!'

Poor Glyn. It was the cruellest fate. He ran to and fro grasping at air, desperately pulling bunches to earth. But it was no good – the wild wind had deposited them far, wide, and high – many were stuck to the wet windows of offices above the shuttered shops. Careful not to be observed by Glyn, I allowed myself to chuckle at the strained small talk of office workers come the morning.

'Let them go, Glyn!' I said. 'After all, you still have several hundred in the trollies.'

'Bye-bye, my loves!' cried Glyn. 'I'll never forget you!'

'You dirty boy!' said the exotic literary critic.

We picked a spot around the side of the Tube station in an overgrown car park, took out the dark blue tarpaulin, arranged the trollies in a circle and stretched the tarp over the top, anchoring it with broken bits of concrete. Thus we all crawled into our makeshift home and used various items

353

from the old boys' belongings to paraphrase beds and pillows: old towels, bundles of clothing. In the end it was all rather snug, the rain pattering on the tarpaulin, passing buses droning, an occasional fight breaking out in the street.

The exotic literary critic gave us a bedtime story by reading her favourite excerpts from both *Madame Bovary* and *Anna Karenina*. Just as the normally horrid fried chicken had tasted delicious, in our weary state our new home began to approximate a five-star hotel, as our exhalations fugged up the atmosphere, and the lady's well-crafted words massaged our ears. I lay between Gabby and Glyn, the former snuggling in and telling me how happy he was and what a great friend I was, the latter quietly sobbing at the loss of his jazz mags.

My last thought was of Lois walking towards me, reciprocal love in her eyes. Or maybe it was a dream.

57

THE VISITORS
(NOT THE ABBA ALBUM)

Something pressing against my face. Something warm and giving.

There is a murmur, low talking. Hushed female voices, but distinct is Glyn's, even and soothing. Then another man's voice; an old voice, with a thick accent.

I surface a little more. The wind is still up. A streetlight casts light through waving branches and the skin of the tarpaulin to reveal soft blue shapes in stop-motion. I realise I am entirely surrounded by naked women.

Those nearest watch me, smiling. Dotted in-between and gently snoring are the old men and the exotic literary critic. Seeking Gabby, I lean over the smooth warm navel of a woman to my left and find him sleeping on her, wearing a little smile, his head lodged between two giant bosoms.

Where is Glyn?

I sit up – there he is, talking in low tones to a handsome old man with a resplendent beard. Glyn holds the hands of women surrounding him.

The handsome old man is stroking his beard, and shaking his head. Perhaps he is crying. Now Glyn and the women embrace him.

I lie back down. Fragrant skin enfolds me, and I snuggle down into the deepest humanity.

FRIDAY

357

58

LOVE BREAKFAST

When I awoke, the memory of my strange dream was already brittle and breaking. The sun streamed into our makeshift shelter in exit-wounds of dappled light. Some of my fellows slept on, others were seated cross-legged on piles of pornography and heavy metal records, gently smiling at the new day. Gabby still snored by my side, hair spread over his pillow like a mare's tail. Glyn was sitting up, knees tucked under his chin, wearing a thousand-yard stare.

'Morning, Glyn,' I said, 'I had the oddest dream.'

Glyn snapped from his reverie and turned to me. 'Without dreams there are no days. Without days there are no dreams.'

It seemed a little heavy for an opening gambit to this festival day. But he wasn't done. 'Dream life is a mode of living unencumbered by the pressing needs of the flesh, freed of the sensory overload of our senses. We are most ourselves when dreaming. Life is but an uncomfortable interlude to an infinity of dreaming sleep...'

'Give it a fackin rest, mate!' yawned Old Brian, cracking his arthritic knuckles. ''oo fancies a bacon sarnie?'

'Karl Marx last night,' said Glyn, watching me with sad eyes. 'And all the women who blew away in the wind.'

It hit me like a freight train! The handsome fellow with the giant grey beard and thick accent! And the women!

'Oh God, Glyn!' I said. 'I *saw* him! I saw them all! I woke up in the middle of the night surrounded by naked women, and I saw you giving Karl Marx a hug!'

'Fack me, they're on a permanent trip!' said an old fellow to a mate.

'Their fackin mainframes are shot.'

Glyn stared at me with alarm. I could feel his thoughts fighting it out. 'A coincidence!' he said, baring his over-large teeth.

'No,' I said.

'Marx told me he wished they'd buried him somewhere like Leytonstow, and not Highgate with its rock stars and champagne socialists.'

'That... makes sense,' I said.

'He said he thought George Orwell was an accomplished writer, but lacked a sense of humour. He very much likes Fidel Castro.'

'These... visions?' I asked. 'I mean, they weren't...?'

'*Our problems presenting themselves as eloquent hallucinations*? No, I believe not,' said Glyn.

'How do you explain it, then? Am I likely to bump into, I don't know, Vincent van Gogh today?'

'The intensity of this last week has enabled you to see beyond the end of your nose, John.'

Involuntarily I touched the end of my nose.

'Reality is a game of the senses,' Glyn continued. 'It's like a rock streaked with igneous veins of human meaning.'

'Are you gettin the fackin bacon sarnies or what?' said Old Brian.

Gabby awoke.

'Morning, Gab,' I said.

'I dreamed about my mam, man!' he said. 'But she had two massive pillows up her cardigan!'

I glanced at Glyn, who sighed. Gabby had seen the women too.

Our party was mostly awake. The exotic literary critic applied more mascara to yesterday's sediment. Old Brian repeatedly asked everyone in the tent whether they required red or brown sauce, casting glances at me to ensure I knew exactly what the score was – i.e. that I needed to go outside and fetch breakfast without further delay.

I stood and stretched.

'And grab us a cuppa tea, son,' said Old Brian with a wink.

I parted the flaps and walked out into the world. The day wore a balmy brightness akin to what I imagined the earth had basked in on its first ever solidified day. Men and women streamed into the Tube station clutching cups of coffee. Kids with oversize blazers and short ties walked to school in giggling groups. On Market Street, bronze-armed traders unloaded racks of clothes and pallets of only slightly bruised fruit from dirty white vans. Buses dumped thoughtful commuters upon cracked paving slabs. The ground shook as hot trains thundered through the depths. Women strutted stiff-legged in work heels, negotiating labourers' admiring glances. Old Pakistani gentlemen shuffled ruminatively in their slippers. Humanity was everywhere. The street was still saturated by damp excerpts from the magazines of a certain genre.

I considered all of this. It was high time to make some ripples of my own.

I marched to the nearest cashpoint and made it a thousand pounds lighter. Then I accosted a market trader yet to unload his van.

'Good morning,' I said. 'I want to use your stand as an impromptu free breakfast outlet!'

'You what, mate?' he asked, sleeves rolled up and fag drooping from his mouth.

'Don't unload yet!' I said, and handed over a hundred quid. He shrugged, smiled, and sat upon the stoop of the van to smoke his fag and blink at the sun.

I rushed down Market Street to a café, went inside and handed the harried-looking proprietor five hundred pounds.

'Fack's this for?' she asked, holding the money as one might handle a live hare.

'Listen,' I said, 'I want you to make one hundred breakfasts, please! Just keep them coming!'

'Yew gonna fackin eat 'em?'

'No, I'm going to feed the citizens of Leytonstow!'

And with that I practically cartwheeled around the café's tables collecting sauces, salt and pepper, napkins and newspapers, before again darting up the street to my makeshift outlet, where I met a group of toothpick-chewing traders standing over the one I'd given the hundred quid to, friendly enough, and wondering what the hell was going on, quipping that I was the perfect wife in my dress.

I stood the condiments on the table and grinned at them.

Then I dashed off through the market to an Indian fabric stall already set up. I waylaid the lady at the helm, and asked her with great smiles for a length of beautiful red silk. She commented upon what a nice day it was after yesterday's storm, apart from the rude pictures, and cut me a good bolt of lovely cloth. I liked it so much that I asked for some more lengths, of blue and yellow. She provided these, and I thanked her, thrust her one hundred pounds, invited her to breakfast and shot off again to my stand, around which had now gathered a decent enough crowd.

The market trader with the drooping fag was explaining to them with exaggerated bronzed-arm movements what had happened. Squawking white-limbed seagulls swooped overhead among telephone cables. Groups of office workers peered at us from their grot-plastered windows. I spread the lovely red silk across the table and looked towards the café, outside which stood the proprietor, grinning at me, pointing inside, and giving thumbs ups.

Glyn, Gabby, the old men and the exotic literary critic now joined the throng of interested passers-by. I quickly dispatched Glyn and Gabby as waiters, before calling them back to bunch around their waists yellow and blue emblems of silk respectively. Ah, they did look lovely.

Minutes later, breakfasts were arriving from the café in great steaming batches. Glyn and Gabby deposited the food upon the blood-red stand and it was whisked away and eaten with outdoor relish, boundless grins, and cries of thanks which ricocheted around the street like friendly gunfire. The proprietor said she and her staff had never been so busy – she kept running outside to shake me warmly by the hand. The market trader whose stand I'd borrowed happened to be selling T-shirts emblazoned with the legend *Fill Your Boots*, and this happy coincidence meant that *he* now also enjoyed a roaring trade selling T-shirts to those who'd enjoyed my breakfast and wanted a memento of the joyful club they'd joined.

It didn't take long for word to get to the *Leytonstow Log*, whose offices were hard upon us, and specifically Bobby Diamanté, who came strutting up the cobbled street in his fashionable brogues, tight gusset pants, and pin-sharp shirt. He was clutching a stack of newspapers, grinning fit to burst.

'DUDE!' he cried. 'What's happening?'

I found myself high fiving him like a rapper.

'Look, dude!' he said, fanning copies of the *Leytonstow Log* across the red table.

I was dumbfounded!

A LEYTONSTOW LOVE REVOLUTION
TODAY JOHN TORRINGTON
IS CHANGING THE WORLD
WITH THE DIG STREET FESTIVAL

...ran the headline, with a photograph of me in my summer dress with the green leaves and the red flowers addressing the crowd outside the barber shop. I looked like a cross-dressing Lenin at the oratory box in Sverdlov Square.

It was happening. After the storm of the past, I'd emerged into the bountiful glare of a sunlit present. And Glyn and Gabby still rocketed stand-to-café-to-stand bearing breakfast after breakfast. True, each time Glyn returned to the red table he reminded me, 'You're paying for this, therefore it's sullied.' But did it matter? I was passing paper to my fellow human beings so they might bridge the gap between themselves and joy. *Did it really matter?*

'Glyn, does it really matter?' I asked as he dumped more breakfasts at my outlet.

'Yes,' he said.

'You've changed your tune!' I said.

He fixed my eye. 'Dreams are only beautiful when viewed from a distance. Get too close and you'll see they have troublesome cogs.' Then he was off to the café to porter more steaming hot grub.

Bobby Diamanté began hawking copies of our own *Pravda* to the crowd, and soon The Dig Street Festival was big news.

'I've called the BBC, dude!' shouted Diamanté. 'I know a journalist lives in Wanstead. He was my dealer.'

Sure enough, before long a BBC radio van with a rooftop satellite dish parked outside Leytonstow Tube Station, and dispatched a young woman presenter and cameraman.

As Glyn and Gabby rushed back and forth in their beautiful sashes, the reporter began to harvest commentary from the crowd. The trader whose stall I'd commandeered told her with great smiles, "They're cross-dressin 'ippies, but good sorts."

Glyn took a breather and sidled up to me, grunting.

'Isn't it great, Glyn!' I said.

'Must be a slow news day.'

'Oh come on!' I said.

'Raaagh!'

I turned my attention back to the young reporter, who was speaking to camera, a backdrop of citizens munching breakfasts and giving repeated thumbs ups.

'The inhabitants of Leytonstow awoke this morning,' she said, 'to the whole of the town centre littered with pornography. We understand this was a stunt aimed at drawing attention to The Dig Street Festival, also being hailed as The Leytonstow Love Revolution.'

'I thought of that last bit, dude!' shouted Diamanté.

The cameraman started to wave me *on camera*.

'The man behind The Dig Street Festival is John Torrington,' she continued, 'and he joins us here. Mr Torrington, hello, you're live on BBC breakfast television.'

I thought I might faint.

'The Archbishop of Canterbury is already saying that the pornography stunt was immoral and obscene,' she said. 'How do you respond to that?'

I glanced briefly at Bobby Diamanté, who stared back at me in expectation of wonderment.

'We don't believe it's obscene,' I said. 'We believe it is a far greater obscenity when nudity and sexuality are considered shameful. We believe the sex industry should be regulated, like in France. "Give sex workers rights!" we say.'

I thought Diamanté might choke with excitement.

'Fackin baguette-eatin frogs!' shouted someone, which sent pleasant laughter wafting up and down the street.

'Get 'em off, then!' yelled someone else from the crowd.

I did just that! I pulled off my dress and underpants, and stood stark naked on live national TV. I could see the reporter desperately thinking on her feet. Her cameraman appeared to find it very funny.

'Put 'em back on!' yelled another wag from the crowd.

So I did, and the reporter looked relieved.

'The stunt has also been condemned by feminist groups,' she went on, 'and your approach to spreading love via fried breakfasts has been criticised just now by a Junior Health Minister. How do you respond?'

'You simply would not believe me if I told you the truth about the stunt,' I said, 'and anyway, look at us, we're wearing dresses, we love the power and truth of all women!'

The reporter looked at me with what could only be interpreted as admiration – I was sure her expression had been caught for the nation.

'As for the Junior Health Minister's comments,' I said, 'I always thought that a good fry-up was essentially our national dish. I ask him, does he not enjoy an English breakfast, and if not, *why not*? Isn't it good enough for him? Would he prefer a croissant?'

The crowd cheered.

'I love a fackin good fry ap!' shouted someone.

'I hate croissants!' yelled another.

'I love porn!' cried yet another.

'Raaagh!'

'What's that?' asked the reporter of Glyn, stuffing the microphone into his face.

'Raaagh!' said Glyn.

'Please can you expand? Are you part of The Dig Street Festival?' asked the reporter.

'Every one of the women depicted in the photographs littering Leytonstow this morning was known to me personally.'

'You dirty bastard!' shouted a woman from the crowd, but I could see the male onlookers weighing up our Glyn with a new respect.

'I am the keeper of their souls,' said Glyn. 'I remember them and celebrate their womanhood, when everyone else in the world has consigned them to the dustbin of debauchery.'

I felt the need to chip in, so that Glyn's manifesto would not be *entirely* weird.

'Look, he believes in safeguarding the sanctity of women so wholeheartedly that he's even wearing ladies' clothes!' I said. 'In memory of all the mistreated women throughout history!'

God, I was quite good at this! I had no idea whatsoever where it was all coming from.

'And so we see that this Friday morning,' said the reporter into the camera, smiling people behind her still stuffing British sausages into their mouths, 'there is a unique… movement beginning in East London, one which appears to espouse love, English delicacies, and women's liberation. This is Jenny Suckling, reporting from Leytonstow. We'll be back later…'

Once the cameraman indicated to her with a wave of the hand that she was off, Jenny Suckling exhaled and smiled at me. Bobby Diamanté sidled up to her. 'Very nicely done, sweetheart!' he smarmed.

'Was it?' she asked.

'Oh yeah!' he said. 'What a sign-off, English delicacies! You're on fire! This could be your big break, you know!'

'You think?' she asked, noncommittally.

'Trust me, sweetheart,' he said with a wink, perfect teeth glinting, and handing her a business card (in the process touching her hand unnecessarily, I thought).

Jenny Suckling thanked me, said they'd some work to do in the van, and that she'd be back in half an hour to get another update, *unless things develop*.

I watched them thread their way through the crowd, wondering what this meant.

'Hey, do you think she likes me, dude?' asked Bobby Diamanté, looking a little sad.

'Oh yes, I'm sure,' I said.

'She thinks you're creepy,' said Glyn.

'Creepy?' said Diamanté.

'Yes.'

'Oh, come on, Glyn,' I said. 'Bobby, I'm sure she thought you were perfectly nice.'

Bobby Diamanté looked unsure.

Just then, an unmistakable large black SUV pulled up alongside the BBC van. Suddenly I remembered the flood defences. And here we were basking in beautiful sunshine, not a drop of rain.

59

THE FLOOD DEFENCES

Alan Povey jumped from the passenger side. He stood there looking wildly in all directions before spotting me, sticking out his elbows in the manner of Buster Keaton, and mincing towards Glyn, Diamanté, and me, with haste.

He was already shouting as he arrived. 'What the bloody 'ell's going on?'

'Hi, Alan,' I said. 'Want some breakfast?'

'I'll give you ruddy breakfast!' he yelled. 'There I am, stood in the stuwer at seven this mornin, lookin at my bloody watch, wonderin where my bloody moppers are! Then someone comes up to me, tells me yuwer on the ruddy telly, so I switch on, and there you are throwin a ruddy party!'

'Oh God!' I said. 'I'm sorry! I totally forgot about my job!'

Povey looked shocked to the core. 'Forgot you 'ad a ruddy job!' he shouted. 'What would 'appen if I forgot I 'ad a job, or the blokes 'oo drive the ruddy ambulances?'

'I'm really sorry, Alan,' I said.

'That's only 'alf of it! It appears that someone's played a bloody practical joke on me an all! An a little birdie tells me yewer behind it!'

'What kind of joke?' I asked, knowing exactly what he meant.

'A ruddy fence!' he shouted, purple with rage. 'That's what! A ruddy six-foot fence around the whole stuwer, and a badly installed one at that!'

'Christ, I'm sorry,' I said. 'I thought I was doing a good deed. I asked Paddy to build some flood defences. You looked so worried yesterday, I just had to act.'

'Flood defences?' shouted Povey. 'That bloody Paddy couldn't erect a mole 'ill!'

I thought back to the fact that I'd asked Paddy to make the defences just after he'd admitted it was his shoddy workmanship which led to Beardmore's tragedy. I'd felt sorry for him.

'Flood defences!' laughed Povey bitterly. 'Come with me, yer little numptie!'

Wondering if I was about to make another series of poor decisions, I fumbled in my pockets for a bank card, whispered a PIN to Diamanté, and hissed at him that in my absence he should:

1. Redistribute wealth to the citizens of Leytonstow.
2. Get Gabby to tell Marcus and Barney about *both* gigs (for it had just occurred to me that The Sofas were to play first at *Tim's* version of The Dig Street Festival! – oh God, and remembering my phone call with Tim, what the hell would he make of all *this*?)
3. Buy them some instruments, and ask Gabby, Marcus and Barney to practise URGENTLY!
4. Continue to give Jenny Suckling and her cameraman positive sound bites, and highlight the plight of the former Clements Markham House, the old men and the exotic literary critic.

At this juncture, Old Brian hobbled up and reminded me that the condition the old men had set for accompanying me to Dig Street was that I would furnish them with a bottle of their choosing. So, regretfully, I added to my hastily composed list:

5. Buy Old Brian and his colleagues a bottle each of whatever they fancy.

Thus I followed Povey through the crowd, smiling like a politician arriving at Downing Street knowing he is about to be fired, waved at Jenny Suckling sitting in her open-sided van, and clambered into the back of the black SUV.

'Look at the car! He's workin for the secret service!' I heard someone yell.

'Who is?' I heard Jenny Suckling ask.

'Right, Eric, back to the stuwer!' cried Povey.

Beardmore slowly turned to face me from the driver's seat.

'Mornin, John,' he said. 'I see you've bin 'avin fun.'

He lit a cigar, and we drove towards Amundsen Enterprises, Povey in the brace position.

'I see you on the fackin telly,' said Beardmore as we waited to turn left down Whitehorse Road, 'wiv yer fackin bent friends.'

We arrived, and made our way through a mass of uncollected trollies. I tried to convince myself that everything was virtually the same as yesterday: the row of dirty sycamore trees, the burned-out motorbike in the corner, the blank patient wall of the outcrop of houses, and the shabby light industrial plots surrounding Amundsen Enterprises.

Beardmore started to cough with laughter as we parked. Povey was almost in tears. Having tried to convince myself that everything was more or less the same, I turned my attention to the store itself, and had to admit that it was entirely encircled by a six-foot tall wooden fence, held up by sporadic concrete piles roughly driven in at all angles to the surface of the car park, surrounded by jagged chunks of backfill.

'Flood defences, my arse!' said Povey.

Povey was right. It looked as if a bunch of toddlers had been given heavy plant and told to crack on. As if to underline just how poor the *defences* were, a neat hole had been easily cut at the bottom of one panel, through which customers who still wanted to shop crawled in and out.

''oo the bloody 'ell are they?' cried Povey, pointing at a vehicle pulling up next to us.

'Oh God, we've been followed,' I said.

'It says bloody BBC on the side of that van!' yelled Povey. 'Oh my giddy aunt! If you've not done enough damage to the good name of this stuwer, now you've told the ruddy BBC to turn up! Well, that's it! I'm 'angin up my ruddy dancin shoes! I'm finished!'

Beardmore chuckled.

With a sinking heart I watched as Jenny Suckling, and her cameraman, clambered out of the satellite van, followed by Glyn, then Diamanté! Only Glyn was not roaring with unbridled laughter.

I got out of the SUV and ran across to them in my white summer dress with the green leaves and red flowers. I had but one question:

'WHO'S MANNING DIG STREET?' I shouted.

'Your little friend Gabby is, dude!' yelled Diamanté. 'Hey, what a cool cat!'

'And the bank card, and the PIN?' I cried.

'All dealt with,' said Diamanté with a wink. 'Gabby knows exactly what to do!'

My God, I had war on both fronts.

Meanwhile, Jenny Suckling and her cameraman were busy linking back Live to the Nation. 'In a bizarre turn to what seems to be some sort of peaceful cultural revolution in East London,' she began, 'we've followed John Torrington's blacked-out SUV to a local DIY store, where it appears he's paid to have it entirely encircled by a six-foot-high fence.'

She walked over to me. I was still wrestling with the knowledge that, providing he could remember the PIN, Gabby was currently on the loose with a virtually unlimited amount of money.

Perhaps seeing I was indisposed to think clearly, Diamanté stepped in.

'This is performance art, baby!' he said to Jenny Suckling, winking at me. 'John feels that the world would be a better place if only we could measure our success not so much by the bottom line, but by the bottom of our souls.'

I had to hand it to him, I couldn't have bettered it.

'So what we're doing here, Jenny – do you mind if I call you Jenny?' asked Diamanté.

She shook her head, and rapidly made *hurry up!* circles with the hand not holding the microphone.

'So, Jenny, what we're doing here is making it physically impossible for people to shop, to show the world that *not* shopping does not cause them to immediately perish.'

'Hang on...' said Jenny Suckling into camera, 'we're getting reports of what witnesses are calling an *unprecedented spending spree choreographed to heavy metal music* in Leytonstow town centre. Can you comment, John?'

'Yes...' I said, thinking as quickly as possible. 'We've forcibly closed this superstore, but purposely upped the rate of spending in the town centre, firstly to demonstrate the sanctity of our town centres versus American-style out of town shopping outlets, but also, importantly, we've set the spending frenzy to heavy metal to give a kind of medieval aspect of hell to it, and to indicate that the act of shopping in itself does not feed the soul, just as religion did not feed the masses, just as heavy metal does not feed one's sexual maturity.'

'Boom!' shouted Diamanté.

'Jenny, you're anchor!' shouted the cameraman. 'They've got the Chancellor of the Exchequer on the line from Westminster!'

Jenny Suckling reddened, smiled at the sky, then assumed her camera face. She recommenced her broadcast to the nation.

I spotted a helicopter.

'Chancellor,' she said. 'What is your response to this powerful and daring piece of economic engineering?'

'Our pre-election manifesto committed to increasing investments to town centre infrastructures, and we're delivering on these promises; we've invested two billion pounds more than the previous government did, and we're going to...'

I glanced inside the satellite van. There was a bank of screens upon which coverage of the fenced-off Amundsen Enterprises aired on at least six different networks. The Chancellor's words faded, and I wandered closer in amazement. Several of the pictures switched to coverage of Dig Street, and Market Street. Telephone wires were festooned with brightly coloured silks of red, yellow and blue. Groups of young and old alike appeared to be headbanging in sync, men sported dresses of the brightest hues, whole toyshops had been emptied out upon the cobbled street, Frisbees tossed back and forth; and there was Gabby, wearing a little black number, with zips, installed behind the largest drum kit I'd ever seen, knocking the living hell out of it.

After thirty-eight-and-a-half years of obscurity, insults, depression, bad food, and loneliness, here I was: mad, good, and safe to know!

But what did I want?

Lois flashed across my mind.

Apart from Lois, I didn't know what I wanted. I had no idea, even less of an idea than I'd had before my meteoric rise to fame.

I was tapped on the shoulder.

'Dude, we've done it!' grinned Diamanté. 'We're bloody famous! Where shall we go on holiday?'

'I think you've missed the point, Bobby,' I said, walking back to Jenny Suckling and her cameraman.

'Dude, I'm cool with that,' said Diamanté, evidently not.

Jenny Suckling was wrapping up her report. 'In this extended programme, we'll be looking later at the roots of this charismatic cultural revolution. For now, I'm heading back to where it all started to report on what sources say will be a highlight of the Dig Street Festival: a live musical performance outside the Tube station at midday – on a day where we've come to expect the unexpected, we're *all ears...*'

'Oh my God, sweetheart, you're sooo good!' said Diamanté, but Jenny was pressing her earpiece to her head, listening intently.

'...this just in,' she said. 'Four members of the Cabinet have been spotted dining out this morning. Not so unusual you might think, but we're not talking the Ritz – they've been spotted at what appear to be carefully choreographed photo opportunities, eating full English breakfasts at traditional cafés in central London. This of course spurred by John Torrington's earlier assertion that it was in fact unpatriotic for a Junior Health Minister to have commented that the nation's favourite breakfast meal was an unhealthy choice.

'And this just breaking... we're getting reports that a well-known supermarket chain says their sales of sausages, bacon, eggs, hash browns, black pudding, and baked beans have surpassed all known records. The National Association of Farmers is holding an emergency meeting to try to keep up with demand, but a spokesperson for NAF said, and I quote, "Most farmers are over the moon about it, and wish to thank John Torrington for highlighting what a fabulously nutritious breakfast option meat really is". The spokesperson went on to announce that a special consignment of black pudding was being delivered to Number 10 Downing Street at two o'clock this afternoon, a move that is likely to see the Prime Minister himself accept the delivery, and hold a press conference off the back of a much needed positive story. This is Jenny Suckling, BBC News, at a walled-off DIY superstore, in East London.'

'Will you marry me?' asked poor Diamanté.

'No,' said Jenny Suckling, before heading back to the van.

60

A DEVELOPING SITUATION

Having begged Glyn and Diamanté to go back to Dig Street with Jenny and her cameraman to *monitor events*, I watched the BBC van pull out into Whitehorse Road, narrowly missing an arriving bulldozer, which was followed by Douglas's royal blue Rolls Royce.

'Thank the bloody Lord!' cried Povey, running to intercept the arrivals (and pulling out his pack of red health and safety stickers).

Beardmore laughed, lighting another cigar.

'I'm really sorry about all this, Eric,' I said.

'Fack it,' dismissed Beardmore with a wave of a giant mitt. 'There's more to fackin life than worryin about shit.'

It was a sea change. I'd done it.

'Yer know, John,' continued Beardmore, 'I feel about a thousand fackin times better now than I 'ave for years. Even went for a fackin walk around the block this mornin. Put me fackin jogger bottoms on!'

'I'm so glad, Eric!' I said.

'I knew you was a gay little bastard,' said Beardmore, chewing upon his Cuban, 'but you've shown me the fackin way. I even 'ad fackin Alan over to dinner last night. We 'ad a laugh about old times.'

'I'm not homosexual,' I said.

'Listen, mate, I don't give a fack what you are. You could

be the biggest bender in the fackin universe, I couldn't give a shit. You done me a favour, and I won't forget it.'

True, a walk around the block in his jogger bottoms had been a start, but I could see there was a way to go yet, in all departments. I was just glad Jenny Suckling hadn't sought additional commentary from my politically incorrect friend.

'Listen, Eric,' I said, as Povey talked to the bulldozer driver and plastered the blade with red stickers.

'What, mate?' said Beardmore.

'I have a business proposition for you. No, it's not that kind of thing,' I said. 'I think you'll like it, but... I'm afraid it involves *marble fire surrounds*.'

Beardmore took the cigar from his mouth, and the humour disappeared from his face.

'I know you don't believe in *therapy*, Eric,' I said, 'but—'

'It's for fackin gaylords,' he said.

'Quite,' I said, 'but look, I tried to sell one of the slightly damaged fire surrounds at the Internet café, and ended up selling *one thousand* of them to punters all over the UK.'

Beardmore was speechless. The bulldozer clattered past us towards the poorly installed fence, with Povey yelling at customers to stay exactly fifty feet away, and wear dark glasses if they had any. Douglas appeared to be searching his car for an exit.

'I've ordered a thousand of them to be made in Indonesia immediately. They'll be shipped over in a week or two, and all they need is delivering. The mark-up is immense. You'll easily cover postage and packing, as it were, and make a tidy profit. I'll pay for the first batch. What do you think?'

'We'll need some quality fackin builders to install 'em,' said Beardmore.

The bulldozer attacked the first sections of the fence. True to shoddy appearance they simply fell over, which made Beardmore chortle. I thought this boded well.

We watched the bulldozer make mincemeat of the *flood defences*. It was all over in ten minutes, to a hearty cheer from the crowd of waiting customers and inquisitive souls from other light industrial plots. The blank gable end of the island of houses looked on impassively.

I heaved a sigh. I wanted to take up my therapeutic mop, and lose myself in its rhythmic sway, to forget all this madness.

I spotted Benny. He stood just inside the store, and waved at me. We exchanged gazes, and wordlessly He imparted to me, *reassured* me, that there was no going back.

Eleven o'clock.

I told Beardmore about his two new charges at the Internet cafe, and he said he was keen to meet them. I guessed this meant he'd accepted my business proposition. We agreed we'd return to Dig Street.

First, I walked up to Douglas's Rolls Royce and lent him a hand by opening the door, out of which he tumbled.

'Much appreciated, Gareth,' mumbled Douglas from his upside down position.

I couldn't help noticing that he was wearing a twinset and pearls.

'You look… nice, Douglas,' I said.

'Oh, thank you, Gareth,' said Douglas. 'I wonder, have you seen young Gabriel?'

I shook my head, and scarpered.

61

THE DIG STREET FESTIVAL

We parked next to the satellite van. As was Beardmore's habit, he cut the engine, lit up a cigar, and surveyed the scene. It was a nicer habit than spitting.

There was only one way to interpret what we saw. I began to sweat.

'It's fackin wild!' said Beardmore.

I couldn't have made a more acute observation.

I peered through the tinted windows, and gawped. All my doing. Had I wanted *this*? I wasn't even sure what *this* was.

'They're 'avin a fackin good time, at any rate,' said Beardmore.

This was undeniable.

'Listen, mate, you'd better get out the fackin car, or *them lot* are gonna tip it over,' said Beardmore.

He was right. People from all directions were sprinting, walking, limping and Zimmer-framing it towards us. Film crews, among them Jenny Suckling and her cameraman. Men, women, and children, holding hands and trailing behind them streamers of red, blue, and yellow. Skinheads in tight-fitting dresses. Young people sporting ♥ *Meat* T-shirts. Old men in Second World War uniforms, their rows of medals and ribbons glinting in the sun. Buses and cars standing still. Smiling policemen dancing with old dears. Traffic wardens and tax collectors exchanging high fives.

378

'I'm not fackin jokin, mate, get the fack out!' said Beardmore.

'Oh God, what've I done?' I asked him.

'You've gone and made the whole fackin place gay!'

And gay it was. I clambered out of the car and was shot-blasted by a tumultuous roar of voices. Beardmore's car lurched backwards in a cloud of smoke and a second later the crowd enveloped me, kissed me, rubbed my head, pinched my bottom, and hoisted me up, up, up, into electric air. Borne along by countless hands, floating as if performing a space-walk in the orbit of an entirely new world, I could see that every conceivable surface, wire, post, window and shop was festooned with the brightest varieties of red, blue and yellow, the colours I'd happened to pick out at the Indian fabric stall. Balloon murmurations of the same hues floated high above our heads. Billowing streamers twisted and turned in the blue sky, bed sheets were waved from windows, and white-teethed women exposed painted breasts from tower block balconies.

My senses scrambled, I was lowered, and found myself standing in the middle of a stage which nearly bridged Dig Street, emblazoned with the same tricolour as the balloon-filled sky. Blazing heavy metal thundered out of enormous stacks of speakers. Gabby, Marcus and Barney stood behind me, Gabby in his little black dress with zips behind the mammoth drum kit, Marcus and Barney clutching sparkling guitars.

'Gabby, what's going on?'

Gabby immediately launched into an ear-splitting cacophony of percussive noise. Marcus and Barney began to claw at their guitars, adding to the tsunami of uproar belching from the towering speakers with a force akin to the back-thrust of a climbing jumbo jet.

The mind boggled at Gabby's powers. Just as he'd coaxed Brendan to talk, somehow he'd managed to turn a free-breakfast stall into a rock concert to rival Live Aid. There was even a barrier at the front, with bouncers!

A microphone was handed to me by a grinning man wearing only spectacles, pink knee-length socks and sandals. I understood that I was to sing, and proceeded to yell badly paraphrased rock star lyrics.

Led by a blushing Glyn, beautiful young women wearing only red, yellow and blue sashes began to mount the stage and walk across it to Gabby's somewhat unpredictable thrashing beat. I swung the microphone by its cable and grinned at Glyn, who paused after each step to retch, which the young women copied, presumably thinking it was a new dance. The crowd caught on, and soon people as far as the eye could see were repeatedly taking to their knees.

Next, David Bowie mounted the stage in full Ziggy regalia. I walked towards him in awe, that Gabby could have brought a bona fide rock star to the party!

'Hey, dude, it's me!' shouted Bobby Diamanté.

Abruptly – you could have called it his *defining drumming style* – Gabby brought the song to a crashing end halfway through a bar.

Something was thrown onto the stage. I picked it up. It was a ♥ *Meat* T-shirt.

'Put it on!' shouted someone from the crowd.

I pulled it over my summer dress with the red flowers and green leaves, and the crowd roared its approval.

'Say something, then!' someone else shouted, and a ripple of laughter went around.

No pressure.

'Ask me anything!' I yelled into the mic.

They liked that. Flanked by virtually naked girls, Ziggy-Diamanté, and unlikely trendsetter of the minute, Glyn, I scanned the audience, and spotted Jenny Suckling.

'Jenny!' I said. 'Ask me a question!'

One of the bouncers behind the barrier handed her a microphone.

'Jenny Suckling, BBC News,' she said. 'John, why did you choose Romania?'

''e fancies Gippos!' shouted someone, which got a laugh.

'Yes I do,' I said, seriously, to pour scorn upon the tasteless quip, but mostly to buy time.

I smiled at Jenny. She read me right, thank God, and saw that I didn't know what the hell she was talking about. 'John, cultural activists are citing your choice to use the national colours of Romania for the Dig Street Festival's theme as a masterstroke,' she said, indicating the sea of red, yellow and blue around us. 'Other sources tell me that Romanian wine is your favourite tipple?'

The penny dropped.

'Romania!' I said, holding both hands in the air. 'What a place!'

This brought a round of applause, but I was nervously aware that I'd have to add a little more meat – after all, as my T-shirt proclaimed, I ♥'d meat.

Luckily, Jenny again came to my rescue. 'John, at least twenty other suburbs in London are following your example,' she said, 'and are holding themed festivals with the national colours of diverse states. Is this a comment upon immigration?'

My God! I'd set off a chain reaction of festivals! I was kissed on both cheeks by two nearly naked girls, and made my response.

'I'm pro-immigration!' I shouted.

The crowd gave this a mixed reception.

'I know that we're a small, crowded nation and we haven't much room left. But in a nutshell, if we deny rights of access to our brothers and sisters then we only deny ourselves the greater pleasure of our humanity. I am proud today to be a united nation. We, Londoners, we are the real United Nations!'

The crowd went wild chanting UNITED! UNITED! UNITED! They sounded like football fans.

Then, in what I thought an act of extraordinary bravery, Glyn gently prised the microphone from me. 'Ahem...'

The crowd laughed.

'Not to mention the fact that in the days of Empire,' said Glyn, 'Britain and our European neighbours invaded practically every corner of the globe, appropriated all and any resources which took their fancy, forcefully imposed European values, language, architecture, and in doing so destroyed the fine balance of previously perfectly functioning indigenous cultures (that is, in all their glorious imperfection) which actually set in motion the population migrations that many are now so dead-set against allowing.'

The crowd were silent, apart from an old Asian man at the front with a long orange beard who waved his walking stick at Glyn and said, 'Good on you, son.'

Poor Glyn. It was the low point of the festival. I could see faces in the crowd peering at him in perplexity – one almost imagined they were wondering how the inventor of the newest dance craze in London could say something so obviously tasteless and uncomfortable.

Glyn had another go. 'As for us being overcrowded, we aren't. Our areas of social deprivation are overcrowded and stretched to the limit, but our affluent areas have plenty of space to spare. Millions of affluent middle-classes live in largely empty houses with millions of spare rooms, and acres of gardens. I suggest that immigrants move into these areas, so that the liberal rich can put their social consciences into practice!'

This time he'd fared better. The crowd applauded.

'Let Travellers live on Hampstead Heath!' shouted a voice.

'Move all the Romanians to Knightsbridge!' yelled another.

I took the mic from Glyn. 'And to answer your question, Jenny,' I added, 'yes, I love Romanian wine!'

The crowd thundered, up-ending their own various tipples – I could see Gabby had furnished more than Old Brian and his pals with a bottle of their own choosing.

62

THE REAL DIG STREET FESTIVAL

The clock perched atop Leytonstow Town Hall (the building itself draped in red, yellow and blue) struck twelve. I glanced to the side of the stage, and did a double take.

Tim!

He was standing there with his merry band; but if truth be told, he didn't look particularly merry. He gently beckoned me to join him at the side of the stage.

'Now for their next song,' I said to the crowd, 'I present once again, The Sofas.'

Amid much applause, I asked the band what the next song was called. They disagreed, but after fighting it out, told me. I returned to the mic.

'This one's called "It's Not Nice to Use the Word Spastic, Unless You're Ian Dury". Enjoy!'

Gabby and the boys rocketed into another train-wreck of an anti-song – luckily most of the audience were pissed enough to think the Beatles had reformed – and I walked nervously over to Tim and the gang.

'Hi, Tim,' I said. 'Are you all ready to sing a song or two?'

The group again guffawed at Tim's already abbreviated name.

Tim glowered at me, in an accommodating manner.

'Transvestite!' shouted a young man in his charge, the one of considerable girth who'd grinned maniacally from the front row of Tim's class.

'John, I know it can sometimes be difficult to understand what is being said to you when using the telephone...'

'It can be...' I accommodated back.

'Tim?' said a rake-thin teenage boy with bottle-bottom glasses. 'Didn't you say that people *should* wear clothes? What about on a Friday?'

'Paedophile!' shouted the grinning chap, and high fived the teenage boy with black teeth still wearing his *Les Misérables* T-shirt.

'John,' said Tim, 'it seems that you've come up with some sort of circus, an extravaganza, but I do recall saying to you quite clearly on the telephone that the plan was for the group to just sing a few songs by the Tube, to... *build confidence in a social setting.*'

'I'm sorry. Things do seem to have got a little out of hand.'

We paused briefly to watch poor Glyn retching his way across the stage once more, followed by a gaggle of half-naked young maidens, ducking and straightening in his image.

'Yes, things do appear to have got out of hand, a bit...' mused Tim.

'But the stage is all yours!' I said, gesturing to Tim's slightly apprehensive-looking crew (all apart from the large lad who still grinned like the devil incarnate).

'I don't know, John,' said Tim. 'It's very easy for some people to drop the social mores of everyday life, to enjoy wild abandon for a little while, before simply picking them up once more, like a bunch of keys. What you're doing here – I'm afraid it goes against everything I've tried to instil in these vulnerable people, in order that they might fit into a society which, for most of the time, has some very inflexible, but not actually visible, rules, which it can be very dangerous to break – for example, that one should, at all times, wear clothing when out in public, and as nice as it would be if we could mix and match gender when choosing what to wear, many people – especially those of a violent nature – take strong exception if we get it wrong. And however artistic it might be to decorate the town centre with pornographic images, it is not, as a rule, acceptable to read such material in public. And importantly, that as tasty as a full English breakfast is, one should strive to eat a balanced diet.'

'Arteriosclerosis!' shouted the grinning lad.

'Quite,' said Tim.

Of course Tim was entirely right. I was beginning to realise there were some inviolable laws of the human universe. I thought back to what Povey had said about what a pickle we'd be in if paramedics didn't come to work. Even something as seemingly insignificant as deciding to stay in bed, and not turn up, would actually have the effect of breaking down society.

I looked over the wild crowd, and my stomach churned at what disarray, what lawlessness I'd engendered! By breaking the normally cast-iron rules of society, by sticking a crowbar into a chink of magic I'd spotted in the armour of reality, I'd set off a chain reaction of dysfunction and disintegration.

All of a sudden I saw Leytonstow as a desperate plague village. Our crops lay unharvested. Babies lay unsuckled. We were burning everything we had in one orgasmic feast, but what did tomorrow hold? *We'd gone magic*, as the exotic literary critic had said, and there was no way back. Leytonstow had gone magic, and its essential services were essentially in ruins.

Then it occurred to me that perhaps this was what Benny had told me with his eyes when we'd exchanged gazes at Amundsen Enterprises.

At that moment, the teenage boy with black teeth and the *Les Misérables* T-shirt invaded the stage to join Gabby. They met with a high five, after which Gabby's friend grabbed the microphone and started to bellow into it in the manner of a death metal "singer".

'Oh dear,' said Tim.

'I want to sing too!' yelled the skinny lad with the pebble glasses. 'Can we? Oh please, can we?'

Poor Tim had to assent, in the full knowledge that all his good work was being pulled apart like a gradually unravelling jumper.

He nodded sadly, and the group took to the stage.

Tim and I followed them. I took the microphone from the lad with the *Les Misérables* T-shirt, and waved at Gabby to end the song, which of course he did immediately, regardless of whether the satisfactory end of a particular bar had been reached.

'Let's hear it for The Sofas!' I shouted, 'London's premier... *avant-garde* musical outfit! Now, ladies and gentlemen! For something really special! I'd like to welcome to the stage...'

Oh God, what were they called?

Hurriedly I asked the very worried-looking Tim, and he told me.

'I'd like to welcome to the stage, to sing some songs, Tim's Life Skills Group!'

Tim's charges lined up, and prepared to sing.

'Awwwwww!' said the audience. I bristled, thinking it very patronising.

'My brother-in-law's friend's got one of them!' shouted a voice from the crowd.

'Your brother-in-law is one o' them!' shouted another.

'Ain't they sweet,' said a woman's voice.

'Ain't it past their bedtime?' said another.

Poor Tim's face grew beetroot.

I felt deeply ashamed in my ♥ *Meat* T-shirt.

Then Tim took the microphone from me. He was crying.

'I want to say something about these people you are so keen to mock!' he said, wiping his eyes with his sleeve.

'Go on then, baldy!' shouted a voice.

'They carry themselves with a great deal more dignity than most of you do! I want to say that every single day is a struggle for these people, a struggle to understand the workings of a mad, sex-and-shopping-obsessed society, a struggle to fit in, a struggle to avoid being mocked or assaulted, a struggle to please their parents, a struggle to...' and at this moment poor Tim could not continue. I embraced him. He let the microphone fall to the red floor. It was quickly picked up.

'AL-QAEDA!!!' screamed the portly grinning lad.

There was an immediate hush in the crowd. A woman screamed. I could see journalists at the front of the crowd hurriedly filing reports.

Jenny Suckling caught my eye and grabbed a microphone from one of the bouncers.

'Jenny Suckling, BBC News. John, do you think it is appropriate for someone to yell Al-Qaeda at a public gathering, in London, so soon after an atrocity perpetrated by people sympathetic to that very organisation?'

It was a cruel question. I wondered if perhaps Jenny's careerism had caught up with her, too.

'That's a tough one to answer,' I said. 'Perhaps if we could have another question, and I'll have a think about it.'

Jenny smiled at me, and handed back the microphone, but it was taken by a beautiful young woman with very long dark hair.

'My name is Corina,' she smiled. 'I work for Romanian embassy here in UK. May I introduce to you, John Torrington, the Romanian Ambassador!'

At that unexpected turn of events, Gabby gave perhaps the loudest drum roll in history, and a smiling plump middle-aged man with rosy cheeks and an oiled moustache clambered up onto the stage, followed by two young men carrying a small box and a wooden crate.

Finally, a whole troupe of what looked like Morris Dancers

in skirts and straw hats sporting red flowers mounted the stage, and took their places amid the almost naked women, Glyn, Ziggy-Diamanté, Tim and his Life Skills Group.

The Ambassador embraced me, and took the microphone.

'I love English breakfast!' he shouted, to renewed roars of approval.

The Ambassador then motioned for the two young men to join him. First he took the crate, and lifted the lid to reveal twelve bottles of red wine.

'Romanian wine for John Torrington!' he smiled at the crowd, and they clapped.

I exchanged further glances with Jenny Suckling. I knew she could tell I wasn't happy, and that perhaps I was busy regretting the whole thing. She was right.

Now the ambassador took the smaller box from the other young man. I wondered if he was about to give me a cigar. He opened the lid carefully, and drew out not a cigar, but a large silver key.

'This is a present from the people of Romania!' he said, 'May I present to John Torrington a key to the city of Bucharest!' he smiled and handed me the object.

'Where the fack's that?' shouted several voices.

'Let's hear it for Romania!!' yelled the ambassador.

Immediately, frantic Slavonic folk music began to pour from the stack of speakers, and the troupe of strange Morris Dancers each took a British girl and began to spin her around the stage, manfully crying Hey! Hey! Hey! between each agitated beat. It went on and on, faster, wilder, the British girls evidently enjoying themselves immensely. Tim's Life Skills Group also danced with much joy, as did Ziggy-Diamanté. The Sofas played along, giving the ambassador's music an odd heavy metal flavour. Tim stood wiping his eyes.

Glyn was throwing me extremely unsettled glances.

Terrible worry began to rise up from my gullet.

I looked again at the Romanian folk dancers, each man-handling a grinning and mostly naked British girl back and forth across the stage, and I scanned the crowd, many of whom were looking avowedly displeased at the awkward symbolism now headlining The Dig Street Festival. I spotted the bronze-armed market trader from the morning, standing amid a crowd of angry-looking men. They were mouthing something, and pointing at the stage.

What was it?

They're faking?

They're baking?

They're takin our fackin women!

THEY'RE TAKIN OUR FACKIN WOMEN!!

THEY'RE TAKIN OUR FACKIN WOMEN!!

I felt the atmosphere around us harden and tense. There was a surge from the crowd. A significant proportion of them were about to attack! Many looked very angry, and those who didn't look very angry looked very panicked. Everything was going wrong.

I thought of Captain Scott's diary:

We are very near the end, but have not and will not lose our good cheer. We have been to the pole and will die like gentlemen.

The stage shifted as the weight of the crowd pressed upon it. The ambassador fled to the edge and climbed down to the road, as did the Romanian Morris Dancers, the mostly naked girls, Tim and his Life Skills Group, and Marcus and Barney.

Gabby, Glyn and Ziggy Diamanté looked to me, terrified.

I do not regret this journey, which has shown that Englishmen can endure hardships, help one another, and meet death with as great a fortitude as ever in the past. For God's sake, look after our people!

63

BAND ON THE RUN

I pocketed the key to Bucharest, and told my fellows to RUN! They didn't need telling twice, apart from Gabby.

'My drum kit, man!' he yelled, legging it in his little black dress with zips. 'My new stereo!'

'Gab, you won't be able to use them if you're dead!' I shouted.

'Are you sure, man?'

We jumped off the stage and sprinted around the back of the Tube station to the disused car park, coming upon the blue tarpaulin lying undisturbed atop our worldly possessions. For a minute we hid behind a wall to see if we'd been followed. No one appeared – I figured everyone was either too drunk, too confused, too shell-shocked from the music, or suddenly too aware of being too naked, to have tracked us.

'Get under the tarp!' I shouted.

'What's a tarp, man?' asked Gabby.

'THAT ENORMOUS BIG BLUE THING!!' I yelled, and we ran across the broken tarmac, and inside.

'Tarp is a funny word, man!'

Everything within appeared more or less as we'd left it. I wondered what Karl Marx would have made of my People's Revolution.

'I told you it mattered,' said Glyn.

'What did?' I asked.

'It mattered that you tried to buy a revolution,' he said, presumably also recalling his nocturnal visitor.

'At least I had a go!' I snapped.

'You were amazing, dude!' said Ziggy-Diamanté.

Our conversation was broken by voices outside the tarpaulin. We froze.

'Come on, love, you know you want it!' said a man's voice.

'*Harry*!' laughed a woman's voice.

'Oh yes you do, you naughty lady!'

'Don't!' she giggled.

'You're going to get it, Samantha!' bellowed Harry. ''ere, 'ave of piece of this!'

'Ooh, innit big?' said Samantha.

Inside the tent we exchanged uncomfortable glances, hemmed in as we were by a drunken couple moving swiftly through the bases. Gabby looked perplexed. He had some catching up to do before his date with Douglas.

All of a sudden the thought of a nice boozy Friday evening in The Edgar Evans as slightly eccentric but boring old John Torrington, not *the* John Torrington, rock star and love revolutionary, began to appeal. Then I thought of Lois, her plummy voice, milk-white skin, bad-girl tattoos, and what she'd said to Roofie in the paint aisle. I shivered.

It was actually quite hard not to think of sex, partially because we are programmed that way, but mostly because at this moment Harry and Samantha were engaged in some energetic horizontal calisthenics about ten feet from where we four cowered. I noticed Diamanté taking shorthand notes. Glyn sat with his hands over his privates, showing his teeth like a hungry pony.

Five minutes later we were still being treated to a performance of increasing urgency. It appeared that Harry was either very fit, or just drunk enough, or both, and Samantha seemed to be enjoying her afternoon enormously, emitting gasps of pleasure, loud moans, or simply screaming at the top of her lungs for Harry to go *FASTER! FASTER!*

Gabby still looked confused. He kept edging over to me; presumably to ask what the hell was going on, only to decide against it.

I got sick of waiting. It seemed ironic I'd spent the last week trying to make the people of Leytonstow a little bit nicer to one another – had spectacularly failed – and here were Harry and Samantha engaged in a consensual bout of extreme *niceness* while I was pinned down in a tent with two idiots, one weirdo and a staggering collection of magazines of a certain genre.

While the loving couple still hammered away, I slowly rose, and crept over to the trolley containing Old Brian's worldly possessions, having hatched a plan.

I delved into the trolley and pulled out the contents. Out came the biography of Margaret Thatcher, the sticky photo albums, and his milkman's cap. I reached in further and drew forth what I sought – the four double-breasted suits from 1962, each of different hues: blue, green, grey and fawn. Next I pulled out the ruffle shirts, in black, yellow, turquoise and pink.

Glyn, Gabby and Diamanté watched me; well, Gabby watched the milkman's cap, with what I assumed was an urgent desire to try it on.

Harry and Samantha's carnal aerobics showed no signs of abating. I tiptoed back to the boys and gave each of them one of Old Brian's suits and a shirt.

Gabby shook his head vigorously, citing the little black dress with zips.

Glyn and Diamanté began to undress.

I shook the fawn double-breasted suit at Gabby, and mouthed *They only recognise you in that dress, and will kill you if they find you.*

Gabby refused point-blank to put on the suit.

Glyn and Diamanté were dressed – Glyn in the blue suit and yellow shirt, Diamanté in the green suit and black shirt. It was a shame Old Brian was so short – Glyn's blue trousers looked like linen Bermuda shorts, and his jacket looked like that of an organ grinder's monkey.

Finally, and to the distinct relief of at least three of us, Harry announced there was a package in the post. Samantha said he should deliver that package without further delay.

I nodded at Glyn and Diamanté, and we got to work. I gagged Gabby, and as he bucked in rhythm with the sprinting postman outside, Glyn and Diamanté removed the little black dress with zips, pulled on the fawn trousers, buttoned up the turquoise shirt, and helped Gabby on with the fawn jacket. Everything fitted him perfectly. He did look sweet.

This left the grey suit and pink ruffled shirt for me. I was loath to remove the white summer dress with the red flowers and green leaves. We'd covered some ground together. But there was no time for sentiment, so I took it off, bundled it into my box of papers, and just as Harry breathlessly rapped on a door, I squeezed into Old Brian's suit and shirt.

Samantha signed for the package with a piercing shriek.

We stood there in our double breasted suit and shirt combos.

I made a signal. Gabby lunged for the milkman's cap, placed it atop his head, smiled, and the four of us marched out of the tent past the recovering Harry and Samantha, who looked, it's fair to say, a bit shocked.

Unsurprisingly, the lovers were gone when several minutes later we returned to collect our belongings, Glyn and Gabby having been reduced to tears at the realisation of their losses. I'd argued that by returning we risked being arrested, but in the end it transpired that heavy metal and magazines of a certain genre transcended all.

In the event, our return went without hitch. Carefully, I

peered around a corner at the intersection between Dig Street and Market Street and, amazingly, normal business seemed to have resumed. The market was in full swing. Buses and cars shunted along the main thoroughfare. People consumed more fried chicken. The magic and madness of The Dig Street Festival had evaporated, and I thought back to poor Tim's heartfelt words about how easy it was for most people to ditch the hard but invisible rules of society, only to pick them up effortlessly when they'd had enough. I hoped his Life Skills Group were not too confused by what they had today witnessed. I wondered if Tim would have to go back to basics. I reflected that he would probably quite like that.

It was rather hard to be furtive in our half-masted 1962 suits and lurid frilly shirts, and even harder to be inconspicuous considering we pulled three friction-happy trollies containing Glyn and Gabby's offensive belongings plus my box of papers; nonetheless we attempted it, dragging our train down Dig Street in the direction of Erebus Road and Clements Markham House. We couldn't think where else to go.

I made an educated guess that much as Beardmore and I had become bosom-buddies, there was little chance Povey would ever let me touch a mop again. We were jobseekers once more, but I couldn't face the thought of another trip to Leytonstow Jobcentre.

We passed an electrical store. The TVs in the window were replaying images from the day. There I was swinging the microphone, there I was inspecting the *flood defences*, and there I was accepting the Romanian wine.

News updates scrolled across a banner at the bottom of the screens:

Breaking: Police trying to establish John Torrington's full identity – banks plan to freeze assets.

I took out the brick of bank cards pressed upon me by the esteemed financial institutions in question. It wouldn't take them long to link me to the lunatic they'd seen advertising Romania on TV. I figured this might have an adverse effect on my credit rating.

'We need to draw out as much money as we can,' I said to my colleagues.

'Cool, man!' enthused Gabby.

'It's not cool, Gab,' I said, 'it's a matter of life and death. We are penniless, unemployable, and probably stateless.'

'I'm currently a mixture of solid, liquid and gaseous states,' said Glyn. It was a weird time to tell a joke, and no one laughed.

We found a cashpoint. Nervously I inserted the Pubclays Bank card, tapped in the PIN, and prayed. Out came one thousand pounds. It seemed, for the moment, I was still in the pink.

A little way down the street, we found another. I tried the Bank of Strood card. Same result. I performed a quick scan of our surroundings, then tried all of my remaining cards in this same cashpoint. Amazingly all of them came up trumps. We did the same at two more cashpoints along the way, and by the time we got to Dark Secrets, our double breasted suit pockets were brimming with no less than thirty thousand pounds of hard cash, enough to live outside of society until something else newsworthy happened and The Dig Street Festival was erased from the nation's collective memory forever.

Aware that it was highly dangerous for Glyn to pass Dark Secrets with his pockets stuffed with cash, I told him that if he made a break for the place I'd set fire to the trolley containing the remnants of the magazines of a certain genre. But the place distorted poor Glyn like light passing a star, so that despite my threats Diamanté and I still had to restrain him physically from sprinting to its garish deep purple door.

Glyn tearfully gave up the struggle about a hundred yards further down the street.

'Where's Gabby?' I said.

Nowhere to be seen. I let out a sigh. More bottoms and sausages. Luckily I'd had the forethought to let him have only five hundred quid.

Diamanté and I sat on a bench, with Glyn between us still shooting desperate glances at Dark Secrets, as if we hadn't unearthed enough of them today all by ourselves. Then Diamanté told me that he was rather keen on paying a visit too.

There was nothing else for it. I gave up. *Fuck it*, I thought.

But I was damned if they were going to blow half our money on bottoms and sausages. So I mugged the pair of them right there. They were so surprised they let me. I gave them five hundred each, and bid them farewell.

'I need a thousand to – raaagh! – go downstairs!' cried Glyn, with such a pitiful look that I assented and gave him another five hundred, upon which the pair of them immediately ran for the entrance.

'Make sure Gabby gets to the pub tonight!' I shouted, then realised that by now The Sofas' instruments must have been stolen. Perhaps Gabby and the boys could use Brendan's gear.

Glyn and Diamanté disappeared inside Dark Secrets.

Alone again, naturally.

Nor was I going to tow their ridiculous belongings home. I removed my small box of papers, delivered each trolley a kick, and strolled off in the direction of the former Clements Markham House, the pockets of my 1962 grey double-breasted suit guarding twenty-eight thousand pounds sterling, and a giant key to the city of Bucharest.

64

AFTERNOON TEA IN THE FOREST

Whistling "Greensleeves", and dreamily allowing my eyes to wander the splendidly complex forms of London plane trees, I turned into Erebus Road and immediately recognised someone standing by the new contours of Clements Markham House.

I'd quite forgotten about my own *date*.

'It seems you have found me,' said Mr Kapoor, resting against the bonnet of his black Range Rover. There was no sign of Indeep, and this was good. 'I see you've been... how to put it... rather *busy*, Mr Torrington,' said Mr Kapoor, lazily inspecting a cuticle.

The suspicion that Mr Kapoor was about to blackmail me crossed my mind. As he humorously related how he'd followed this morning's news, I desperately tried to reverse-engineer the bank heist – would they, eventually, pin it on me, or him? Stateless outlaw and upholder of Romanian values, or respected pillar of the local community? I didn't stand a chance.

'I just need to make a phone call, Mr Torrington,' said Kapoor.

He wandered off and made the call. Who the hell was he talking to? I instructed myself to calm down. He was a businessman, and businessmen make calls. Presently, he returned.

'Where were we?' he smiled.

'I have... I have no more money, Mr Kapoor,' I said.

He found this funny, but in the manner of so many Bond villains, didn't immediately address my implication. Instead he took a great sniff of air, remarked what a fine, fine day it was, and opened the passenger door of his Range Rover, indicating with *faux* disinterest that it would be a good idea if I got in.

'Where are we going?' I asked.

'I want to show you something, Mr Torrington.'

What to do? We both had reasons to want to trust each other. I'd tumbled down enough rabbit holes in the past week to explore one more.

I clambered in, and soon we were winding our way northeast through thinning suburbia and remnants of the Epping Forest, thicker as we progressed. As he drove, Mr Kapoor delved into a pocket of his expensive-looking suit, pulled out a piece of paper, and placed it upon my lap.

'What's this?' I asked.

'Read, please,' smiled Mr Kapoor. 'This time, a little more carefully.'

It was from Leytonstow Council, Planning Department. I vaguely recognised it as the letter Mr Kapoor had shown me on the day we'd been frogmarched to the bank. I'd only scanned it quickly against the backdrop of Indeep's threats.

...Regarding Clements Markham House, which is in a pitiful state of repair. Leytonstow Council will have no option but to issue a compulsory demolition notice unless urgent modern development works commence, therefore immediate planning permission is granted for three extra floors, a penthouse and renovation of existing studios...

I was dumbfounded! Mr Kapoor evidently understood this, and chuckled.

'You see, Mr Torrington, in this life one must have an eye for detail!'

'So the Council were going to knock it down unless you redeveloped it?'

'Exactly, Mr Torrington,' said Mr Kapoor, as we parked up outside a café by a lake, in a clearing deep within the forest.

'Isn't it beautiful here?' stated Mr Kapoor as we strolled and found ourselves a table. 'Makes one wonder why on earth we choose to live in cities.'

I could only look at the lake and think of body bags and heavy stones. I peered nervously in each direction, fully expecting Indeep to jump out and finish me off. Mr Kapoor found my aspect rather amusing. 'You're ill at ease, Mr Torrington,' he smiled.

'Yes, a bit,' I said. 'I can think of at least one reason it would suit you for me to go away.'

At this Mr Kapoor lost his smile and looked rather offended.

'Mr Torrington!' he said, pulling out a red handkerchief and dabbing his nose. 'Have you ever heard of a murderous Hindu?'

I wasn't sure what to say. It stood to reason that *some* Hindus must be murderous. I decided not to mention it, and again glanced at the lake. Some ducks paddled past.

'Mr Torrington, here we are half an hour into our prearranged meeting, and you've already suggested by implication I might be a blackmailer, and now you're accusing me of being a potential murderer.'

'Sorry,' I said, then whispered, 'but what about the bank?'

'Business is business, Mr Torrington,' said Mr Kapoor. 'I am an opportunist like any businessman. Tell me, do you think that just because they have billions to spend on marketing, the large corporations, the household names, are whiter than white?'

'I guess not,' I said, though privately thought there was opportunism, and there was *opportunism*.

'I can reassure you, Mr Torrington, I am a good Hindu, as you shall see.'

Before I'd had time to think about what he meant, and why he kept referring to Hinduism, a jolly-looking woman emerged from the café, chatted briefly to us about what a lovely day it was, and took our order. After she'd headed back in, we sat in silence for several minutes watching squirrels run up and down trees, listening to birdsong, and consciously tasting clean air; a novelty for me.

'Mr Kapoor,' I said, 'I accept that you *had* to rebuild Clements Markham House.'

'You read the letter, Mr Torrington,' said Kapoor.

'But I wish you'd *restored* it, and not changed it utterly, destroyed its original character, as if erasing history itself.'

Mr Kapoor picked up a dry twig and snapped it in two.

'Mr Torrington,' said Kapoor, 'I am not… how shall I put it?… wedded to the architecture of Clements Markham House, as you appear to be. Plus, the young professionals moving into Leytonstow want *swish*, and will pay for it. Time moves on, and tastes change. They don't want *old*.' Then he smiled, and gestured to our surroundings. 'It would perhaps be different here.'

He studied me.

I felt myself blush.

Of course! Why would Mr Kapoor go out of his way to preserve British Edwardian architecture? I thought of Glyn's words regarding immigration, and the lone voice of the old man with the long orange beard who'd waved his walking stick and congratulated him. The Raj!

How could I have been so one-dimensional?

And Captain Scott! My God, the man had been inflexible to the core, utterly convinced of British omnipotence, our

401

Godliness, the need to protect the natives from themselves, and claim entire continents for King and Country.

The jolly woman brought out a teapot, two cups and saucers, and milk in a little jug.

Mr Kapoor did the honours, trickling the tea into my cup, all the time continuing to study me.

'This is a very English scene!' I said. I laughed.

'You're right, Mr Torrington! You see how accommodating I am being? But I haven't brought you here just to drink tea.'

'No?'

'No,' said Kapoor, presumably once again sensing my distrust. 'I've brought you here to make you a proposition. Two. One business, one pleasure.'

'Go on,' I said.

'Don't look so worried, Mr Torrington!' laughed Kapoor, 'I'm extremely sure they'll be quite acceptable to you!'

We sipped our tea.

'First, business,' said Mr Kapoor, 'and for this it would be better if we took a ride. Shall we?'

We drained our tea, and got back into the Range Rover. I had butterflies. I kept reminding myself that if he wasn't going to kill me, then he needed to keep me sweet. Or did he?

'Let's listen to some music, Mr Torrington,' he said, and inserted a CD. I don't know what I expected him to play, but was overjoyed as the first towering peals of Haydn's *London Symphony* emerged sonorously from his top-of-the-range stereo.

It occurred to me to wonder whether Haydn had ever visited Glyn.

This thought evaporated as we rounded a tree-lined bend, and came upon the most fabulous Georgian terrace I'd ever seen in my life. Mr Kapoor slowed, and parked before it. Was this our destination? Four storeys high, built of pale stone, with long colonnades of Ionic columns and cornices embellished with gorgeous decorative mouldings, it must have been a quarter of a mile long, and set in the most verdant forest. Despite my recent vow to leave history behind, my mouth watered at such neoclassical grandeur, and as the symphony got into its stride I fairly brimmed with ecstasy! What a showman Kapoor was.

Then, as if my senses weren't already overloaded, another car pulled up alongside us. It was a familiar SUV with blacked-out windows. No, surely not! But plain as day, the exact individual I had in mind clambered out, and lit up a cigar.

'What the hell's going on?' I said, as Haydn plucked one by one the giddy fruits of my dreams.

'All will become clear, Mr Torrington,' said Mr Kapoor. He cut the engine. 'Shall we?' he said.

Gingerly I got out. We walked towards the visitor.

'I trust you've met Mr Beardmore, my business associate?' said Kapoor.

'We've fackin met all right,' said Beardmore.

'What, you two?' I blustered.

They both fell about laughing.

'Oh yeah, we go way back,' said Beardmore.

'Why didn't you tell me?' I asked.

'Mr Torrington,' said Mr Kapoor, 'until last week, you were the most junior employee at Amundsen Enterprises.'

'Apart from that fackin puff what coughs before 'e says anything,' added Beardmore.

'Granted, Mr Beardmore, but nonetheless Mr Torrington here was extremely junior,' said Kapoor. 'Mr Torrington, given this fact, would you expect Mr Beardmore or myself to discuss *matters* with you?'

I had to admit it would have been a bit odd.

'I'm sure Mr Beardmore would agree that in the last week,' continued Kapoor, 'you have shown yourself to be a rather talented, and shall we say, *trusted*, individual.'

They both watched me carefully.

'I can be... trusted,' I said.

With what? The beautiful building towering over us?

Beardmore laughed.

'Good, Mr Torrington.'

I must have looked as if I wanted to ask something.

'Have you a question, Mr Torrington?' asked Kapoor.

'Yes,' I said. 'Are you both... you know?'

They both looked faintly alarmed.

'No! I don't mean that!' I spluttered. 'I mean, are you both... involved in Amundsen Enterprises? I mean, in it together?'

Mr Kapoor and Beardmore exchanged a glance.

'We're *all* in it, John,' said Beardmore, his narrow eyes twinkling.

I took a deep breath, and they laughed.

'Now to the proposal, Mr Torrington,' smiled Kapoor. 'We have both been impressed by your *ingenuity* of late, and your educated eye for all things historical and poetic.'

I blushed, and Beardmore chuckled. *I'm sorry, Philip Larkin*, I thought.

'Mr Beardmore and I,' continued Kapoor, 'have just acquired Cobham Terrace, the magnificent Georgian building you see before you. We need a good, *trusted* man to project manage its full renovation, with the aim of returning it to more or less the way it looked upon completion in 1826, with the obvious addition of modern utilities. And we think you, Mr Torrington, might be the man for the job.'

I thought I might explode. Being a criminal was turning out to be really rather wonderful.

'We also understand,' said Kapoor, 'that due to certain recent events, you might need to, shall we say, *lie low*, for a while.'

Beardmore laughed.

'So, what we're proposing, Mr Torrington,' said Kapoor, 'is that first of all, to prepare you for your new role, you should go on holiday for a few weeks, at our expense, to a destination of your choosing, with a companion of the same. Upon your return, you will move into a generously-sized apartment within Cobham Terrace, and thereafter manage the works through to completion, after which time you will receive certain shares in our interests, and we'll see where we go from there.'

I looked at Cobham Terrace, sitting there like a magical ocean liner fringed with a blue-green sea of sky and trees, and gulped.

As kind an offer as this was (if we suppose kindness was their motivation), I couldn't help but come to the obvious and immediate conclusion that I was absolutely and definitively unqualified.

I looked at each man in turn, and wondered whether I should say something. But then I remembered I had not applied for a normal job. I'd not applied at all. It wasn't like picking a job at the Jobcentre; having to run the gauntlet of the bored operative's stock questions, which, in my case, invariably concluded with the plain fact that I didn't possess the relevant *hands-on* experience to bag anything but the most menial of jobs – unable to add anything more than a purely physical presence to the British economy.

This job was different. What counted most was my ability to keep secrets.

'So, Mr Torrington?'

Now it was my turn to negotiate.

'I thank you for your kind offer, and I would like to accept your proposal,' I said, 'but only if certain minor conditions are met.'

Beardmore chuckled.

'List them, Mr Torrington,' said Kapoor.

I did:

1. That seeing as Gabriel Longfeather, Glyn Hopkins and Bobby Diamanté were also implicated in the debacle of The Dig Street Festival, and that this posed a risk that, if interviewed by the authorities, they might, perhaps under duress, inadvertently lead the police (and eventually the taxman) back to Amundsen Enterprises, and, in turn, Beardmore and Mr Kapoor, it stood to reason that they too needed to lie low, and therefore should also be housed at Cobham Terrace, Gabby in a specially sound-proofed apartment which could thereafter be purchased by a rock star (I also offered them Gabby's services as a quantity surveyor).

2. That Indeep should not, ever, upon any occasion, visit Cobham Terrace.

3. That the remainder of the former tenants of Clements Markham House be rehoused immediately in modest but sanitary lodgings – Mr Beardmore would be sure to locate all of these gentlemen at The Edgar Evans this evening.

4. That Mr Beardmore should seek medical assistance to stop smoking, and moreover enrol on a *Diversity* evening class at Leytonstow Community College – I could put Mr Beardmore in touch with just the man to facilitate this.

'Diversifackinwhat?' spluttered Beardmore.

'An excellent plan on that last count, Mr Torrington!' said Kapoor. 'Now, Mr Beardmore and I will just hold a quick conference.

They walked around the back of Beardmore's SUV, and held quite a hot discussion. After a couple of minutes the men returned to me, Mr Kapoor wearing a broad smile, Beardmore looking confused but nonetheless happy enough.

'Mr Torrington,' said Kapoor, 'Mr Beardmore and I have had a chance to debate your conditions, and I'm happy to say we are prepared to accept them in their present form!'

'Do we have we a deal?' I asked.

'We do!' said Kapoor, dabbing his nose with the red hand-kerchief. 'Indeed, in terms of your conditions, it is just that kind of ingenious thinking which has so impressed us in recent days! I think this is a moment we should celebrate.'

'Eric?' I asked.

Mr Kapoor plucked the cigar from Beardmore's lips and crushed it under his well-appointed shoe. I was beginning to perceive who owned the balance of power.

My benefactor went to his boot and produced a chilled bottle of champagne and three glasses. As he popped the cork, I thought of poor old Karl Marx again, and begged his forgiveness.

'I will propose a toast – to *trust*, and to Cobham Terrace!' said Mr Kapoor.

We up-ended our glasses. And then it was time to leave.

Mr Kapoor climbed into his car, and I shook hands with Beardmore.

I turned to join Mr Kapoor.

'Oh, John?' said Beardmore. Bugger, he'd done it again!

'Yes?' I said.

'You know this fackin place'll need about an 'undred marble fire surrounds, don't yer?'

65

MR KAPOOR'S SECOND PROPOSAL

I took one more look at the fabulous Cobham Terrace before we again rounded the bend and lost it to the green ocean of trees.

Mr Kapoor got right on with things. 'Now that we've successfully dispatched our business matters, Mr Torrington, we can move to matters of a more personal nature.'

It would not have surprised me one bit had I turned to Mr Kapoor to see him wearing a periwig. He was an Indian Samuel Pepys, with his fingers in as many pies.

'It is ironic, Mr Torrington,' continued Kapoor, 'that you have perceived me as a man who does not appreciate architecture.'

I started to apologise, but he waved it away.

'The truth is, Mr Torrington, I love architecture, but as I told you while we were enjoying our tea, not necessarily in the same tradition as yourself. Tell me, Mr Torrington, have you ever seen a Hindu temple?'

I told him I hadn't. Actually I started by saying I had, and described one, but Mr Kapoor had quickly pointed out that I was describing a mosque.

'Mr Torrington, I have been lucky enough to be involved in the building of a magnificent Hindu temple in the area of Chingford, a temple which took fifteen years to build, wrought by the finest Indian craftsmen. It is a beautiful structure, and most holy, constructed of choice Bulgarian limestone and over three thousand tons of finest Italian marble.'

Another mention of the Balkans threw me, but not as much as my suspicion that having been entrusted with Cobham Terrace I was about to be given a Hindu temple to boot.

But Mr Kapoor was to allay my fears.

'Hindus appreciate beauty in all its forms, like poetry, which I love. I have been exceedingly moved by yours, and so I would be very honoured if you would come to the temple to read your work for the pleasure and appreciation of my dear friends and brothers.'

I didn't know what to say. I stole a glance at my little box of scribblings on the back seat of Mr Kapoor's Range Rover and my insides sighed.

'Which poems in particular did you like?' I asked, fearing I already knew the answer.

'The poem you recited to me over the phone, Mr Torrington, about a home! It moved me to tears! What was it? *That vase*... Mr Torrington, it was exquisitely observed, a quite perfect window into the gloomy attic of melancholy.'

'What about the haiku?' I asked.

'Pardon, Mr Torrington?'

'The little poems I recited to you in my room.'

'One also likes to laugh, Mr Torrington!'

He was the second literary critic I'd met in as many days.

Should I come clean? *Actually, Mr Kapoor, the poem you liked was written by perhaps the most-quoted and best-loved post-war English poet.*

I looked at him as he drove, a fine middle-aged man at the apex of health, intellect and judgement, a man of culture, a man of power and mercy. I could not tell him that I'd fleeced him with an extraordinarily well-known poem; a poem that, had he really been as well-versed in the finer things in life as his deportment loudly claimed, he should surely have known immediately.

I was about to admit my plagiarism when another thought struck me; perhaps I could write some poems to order. I pictured Cobham Terrace, its glorious lines, almost as organic as the trees rubbing their branches upon its high windows. Yes, perhaps I could.

'I'm very flattered, Mr Kapoor,' I said. 'I would love to!'

'Then it's settled, Mr Torrington!' enthused Kapoor.

The poems were as good as written.

The purpose of our conversation expired, we drove on in the sort of silence our business deal entailed. Mr Kapoor clicked on the radio. The five o'clock news:

'...In other news, the Prime Minister has been criticised by the National Association of Farmers for cancelling a delivery of black pudding as a delivery lorry stood waiting to enter Downing Street. Eyewitnesses say the driver argued with police and unloaded the black puddings, leaving them on the Whitehall pavement. Animal rights groups have condemned both the Prime Minister and the black pudding...'

'Will you drop me off, please?' I asked. 'I fancy a walk.'

Mr Kapoor pulled into a lay-by, and I made to leave the car.

'Oh, by the way, Mr Torrington, you have post.'

Mr Kapoor reached into his jacket pocket and gave me a hand-delivered letter. I could be in no doubt about whom the writing on the envelope belonged to, and my heart turned somersaults.

'So long, Mr Torrington,' said Mr Kapoor. 'I will see you soon.'

His bulky Range Rover shrank into the distance.

Standing on the kerbside, I opened the letter.

410

Dear John

Thanks for your lovely letter. You are so perceptive. I want to tell you that I am going to end it with Rufus. To hell with what my parents think. Love is more important than meeting expectations. I saw you on the news. I'm worried about you, John. I hope I see you soon. I really miss you.

Love, Lois.

66

THE LAST WALTZ

I stood in my grey 1962 suit and pink ruffled shirt clutching my box of belongings and a letter from the woman I loved and now desperately wanted to see. I wondered how my friends had fared at Dark Secrets. For Gabby, I hoped they'd taken pity and set him up with a fizzy drink and a comic. For Glyn, I hoped his guiltless alter ego had not created a black hole of historical forgetfulness to swallow us all. As for Diamanté, I hoped he'd scored some stardust.

This was true suburbia – different in flavour from the slumping weed-ravaged confusion of entirely-consumed villages like Leytonstow – here there was not a house or structure built before 1930, save the odd out-of-place ancient cottage hard upon the kerb, which spoke of a time long lost when the road might have been a track, and the cottage a single dwelling in a forest clearing.

Musing upon my new career as petty criminal, poet, and guardian of Cobham Terrace, I set off in the direction of the white noise of London upon a treeless wide boulevard.

I passed a decrepit parade of shops, and met a group of grinning teenagers downing energy drinks and smoking cigarettes.

'Good day!' I smiled and gave them a thumbs up.

'Is iiiitttttt!' said one of them.

'Yes, it is,' I confirmed, and the smallest among them, a lad of perhaps thirteen, took three warlike steps in my direction and stood stiffly watching me pass, presumably ready to pounce should I emit any more pleasantries.

I gave this little lad another smile and walked on, after which he returned to his commander-in-chief for a debrief, a young man of about seventeen astride a silver BMX with bright red handlebars.

Approaching the inner postcodes was akin to time travel – light was fading, and now the Epping Forest's luxuriant greenery was replaced by air-gasping urban infrastructure; chicken joints, launderettes, taxi ranks, sex shops, corner shops, pawn shops, betting shops, bus terminals, flyovers, underpasses, churches proclaiming *He is risen*, unnecessary street furniture, pylons, pie shops and post offices. Street-lights were coming on, set to cast once more their sodium glow into space. Boy racers zoomed away from green lights. Dirty yellow bulbs lit workers finishing up dull desks. Police cars strobed lined faces with blue. A pink moon sat on the rooftops.

Night had fallen. I stood at the threshold of The Edgar Evans holding my box. Three shopping trollies were parked outside containing unmistakable cargos, along with a royal blue Rolls Royce and a familiar black SUV. I could feel the pub throbbing with Friday night glee.

I walked inside and the whole place shushed, before spontaneously erupting into rapturous applause. A crowd, among them Gabby, Glyn, Diamanté, Old Brian and the exotic literary critic, were running, or at least limping, towards me, arms outstretched.

But I had already locked eyes with Lois.

'John!' she said. 'You made it home.'

I noticed she wore a silver pendant. It was a little sphere.

ACKNOWLEDGEMENTS

I couldn't have placed this book in your hand without the help of some wonderful people. Firstly, I owe much gratitude to Louise Walters, who took a chance on what is a rather odd book. Thanks also to the great work of Louise's team; Helen Kitson, Leigh Forbes, and Jennie Rawlings. I am indebted also to Kit de Waal, who kindly brought me in from the cold after I happened to listen to her radio show about working class writing. Alex Beattie, Jeremy Bray, Tony Sumner, Suzanne Turner, and VB, all gave me encouragement during the long process of *Dig Street*'s birth. Lastly, I owe everything to my loving parents, Mary and Jim, and my sister Helen. Sorry I didn't become an accountant.

LWB INTERVIEWS CHRIS WALSH...

When did you decide to become a writer?
I think I was always a writer. I remember being young with my head stuffed full of impressions and ideas, and not having a clue how to go about putting them down – no vehicle, no ability to characterise, or plot, and no idea how to find out. I am a writer by nature, but learning *how to write* – I'm self-taught, by reading, and trying – was both the toughest and most rewarding pursuit of my life.

What kind of books do you enjoy reading?
I enjoy literary fiction, particularly Russian classics and twentieth century American. I also read a lot of non-fiction and biography because I've always been a drinker-in of information, whether from life or the page – the raw materials for thinking/writing.

Apart from writing, what are your passions?
I love art, photography, and music, as much as writing. I think walking is my favourite pursuit. It's my meditation, my place to think and put ideas together. It's said Erik Satie walked to think, daily, to Paris and back from his suburb. I do the same, but from my flat above a chemist to the town centre, via the industrial estate. Sometimes I get a sausage roll from Greggs.

How did you conceive *The Dig Street Festival*?
I conceived this book over a long period of time. I first had the idea of John as a lowly character who wants to upset the status quo, in about 2007. I finished the first draft of the book in November 2014 (in my mind, my life is divided into pre- and post-November 2014) and while writing it the book evolved and gained a life of its own. I learned to write on this book, weekends and evenings/early mornings, amid kids and full-time work. My early attempts were very gauche and I knew it. I frequently despaired.

Do you have a favourite among your characters?
Glyn is my favourite. I really enjoyed writing anything where Glyn appears. He makes me laugh, and he makes me sad. Glyn is a character I'd like to resurrect.

Who are your favourite writers, and why?
Sounds corny, but I love some of the biggies – Tolstoy is amazing; I completely lost myself in *War & Peace* and *Anna Karenina*, and learned a huge amount about how to present scenes and interactions. His lightness of touch is incredible. I also think he wrote one of the best short stories ever in "The Death of Ivan Ilyich". Another writer I very much admire is John Williams – *Stoner* and *Butcher's Crossing*. I've always liked Charles Bukowski, that git. And Philip Larkin has always knocked my socks off.

What are the highlights so far of being a published author?
The sense of achievement. I started with a head full of ideas, and no ability to set them down to my own satisfaction. And somehow, I did it, and here we are.

And what are the lows?
The realisation that the writing world is not a meritocracy. BUT – neither is any other part of life. So, looking back, I had unrealistic expectations, probably because writing starts when you are young, as a dream.

Do you have any advice for readers who are also writers?
My favourite piece of advice comes from Stephen King. He uses his memoir/how-to *On Writing* to basically say 'Just f****** do it'. Books are only written when authors apply trousers/skirts/floral dresses to seats – same goes for learning the craft. The other bit of advice is to not give up. But writing is a terrible addiction. It demands you sacrifice all sorts of other things in your life, which can lead to much regret.

Louise Walters Books is the home of intelligent
and beautifully written works of fiction.
We are proud of our impressive list of authors and titles.
We publish in most genres, but all our titles have one
aspect in common: they are brilliantly written.

Further information about all our books and
authors can be found on our website:

louisewaltersbooks.co.uk

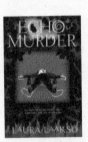

Louise Walters Books extends its gratitude to our Supporters. Supporter subscriptions are invaluable to a small publisher like us.

Please visit louisewaltersbooks/lwb-supporters
if you would like to receive a year's worth of books,
invitations to launch parties, exclusive newsletters,
early glimpses of forthcoming covers,
and many other nice bookish things.

Heartfelt thanks to:

Claire Allen
Edie Anderson
Karen Ankers
Francesca Bailey-Karel
Tricia Beckett
JEJ Bray
Melanie Brennan
Tom & Sue Carmichael
Liz Carr
Penny Carter-Francis
Pippa Chappell
Eric Clarke
Karen Cocking
Louise Cook
Deborah Cooper
Tina deBellegarde
Giselle Delsol
James Downs
Jill Doyle
Kathryn Eastman
Rowena Fishwick

Harriet Freeman
Diane Gardner
Ian Hagues
Andrea Harman
Stephanie Heimer
Debra Hills
Henrike Hirsch
Claire Hitch
Amanda Huggins
Cath Humphris
Christine Ince
Julie Irwin
Merith Jones
Seamus Keaveny
Moon Kestrel
Ania Kierczyńska
Anne Lindsay
Michael Lynes
Karen Mace
Anne Maguire
Marie-Anne Mancio

Karen May
Cheryl Mayo
Jennifer McNicol
MoMoBookDiary
Rosemary Morgan
Jackie Morrison
Louise Mumford
Trevor Newton
Aveline Perez de Vera
Mary Picken
Helen Poore
Helen Poyer
Clare Rhoden
Rebecca Shaw
Gillian Stern

John Taylor
Julie Teckman
Sarah Thomas
Sue Thomas
Mark Thornton
Penny Tofiluk
Mary Turner
Ian Walters
Steve Walters
Charles Waterhouse
Elizabeth Waugh
Alexis Wolfe
Finola Woodhouse
Louise Wykes